A Tale of a Tub

Plate 1

Jonathan Swift

A TALE OF A TUB
The Battle of the Books
The Mechanical Operation of the Spirit

Edited by
Frank H. Ellis

PETER LANG
Frankfurt am Main · Berlin · Bern · Bruxelles · New York · Oxford · Wien

**Bibliographic Information published by the Deutsche
Nationalbibliothek**
The Deutsche Nationalbibliothek lists this publication in the
Deutsche Nationalbibliografie; detailed bibliographic data is
available in the internet at <http://www.d-nb.de>.

Jacket illustrations.
Front: Throwing tubs overboard to divert
Hobbes's Leviathan from destroying the ship of state.
From Conrad Gesner, *Nomenclator aquatilium animantium*
(Zürich, 1560; see also plate 1 facing title-page).
Back: "The ironic element", taken from the *New York Times*,
16 July 1996".

ISBN-10: 3-631-54673-4
ISBN-13: 978-3-631-54673-4
US-ISBN 0-8204-9825-4

© Peter Lang GmbH
Europäischer Verlag der Wissenschaften
Frankfurt am Main 2006
All rights reserved.

Printed in Germany 1 2 3 4 5 6 7

www.peterlang.de

I saw a fellow pasting up the Title Pages of Books at the Corners of the streets, and there... I saw one called *The Tale of the Tub*

(King 1704, 51).

What is badly needed is a new critical edition of the *Tale of a Tub*

(Quintana 1965, 9).

The reference x.10 means line 10 on p. x. in the front matter which is paginated i–xxv in roman numerals. The reference 10.10 means line 10 on p. 10 of this volume.

Contents

Illustrations

Plates 6, 12-15, 17, 21 and 25 are Sir Andrew Fountaine's drawings (Swift 1958, xxv-vi) from which Bernard Lens or John Sturt, or students in their drawing school, engraved the illustrations for the 1710 edition of *A Tale of a Tub.*

Opposite:

To the Reader:

A Tale of a Tub above all is an amazing comic book. It is "designed for the
Pleasure and Delight of Mortal Man" (23.3–4). It is like the joke books and
chapbooks of Grub Street, which it pretends to be (Plate 2). Even one of
the prime targets of the satire, William Wotton B.D., acknowledges that Swift
"intended to make himself and his Readers sport" (Wotton 1705[1], 66). And
it is pleasant to imagine what fun Swift must have had in skewering Richard
Bentley D.D., the enemy of Swift's employer, Sir William Temple, and the
enemies of Swift's church, the rabid Protestant sects and the Catholic
Church in Rome, including John Dryden, the recent convert to Papism.

Samuel Johnson, who did not like Swift, retails Dryden's (apocryphal)
remark: "Cousin Swift, you will never be a poet... [which] was the motive of
Swift's perpetual malevolence to Dryden" (Johnson 1779-81, viii.112). But
Swift had a less petty and more ideological motive for his "malevolence":
half the lines in [Dryden's] The *Hind and the Panther* [1687] advocate
"repeal of the Test Act" (Gardiner 1998, x). The Test Act (1673), a self-
administered loyalty check, was designed to bar Dissenters from public
office, civil, military, or ecclesiastical. Swift regarded it as a bulwark of the
Established Church and defended it all his life. "Who can avoid smiling,"
Lord Orrery remarks, "when he finds [Dryden's] the *Hind and Panther*
mentioned [25.30–34] as *a compleat abstract of sixteen thousand* [Roman
Catholic] *schoolmen*" to which the chapbook, Tommy Potts, "supposed by
the same Hand" is a "*supplement*" (Boyle 2000, 300). Thus John Dryden, the
poet laureate, is exposed as a writer of chapbooks, that sold for a penny.

The *style* as well as the content of *A Tale of a Tub* is "designed for the
Pleasure and Delight of Mortal Man" (23.3–4). It is not the "*plain simple
Style*" (Swift 1939-68, xi.xxx) usually associated with Swift, but a highly
decorated style that is fun to read. It is particularly rich in

Alliteration:
Proceedings not only... unjust but... ungrateful, undutiful, and unnatural (23.21–
22)
There can hardly pop out a *Play*, a *Pamphlet*, or a *Poem*, without a Preface
(82.56).
Who, that sees a little paultry Mortal, droning, and dreaming, and drivelling to
a Multitude, can think it agreeable to common good Sense, that either Heaven
or Hell should be put to the Trouble of Influence or Inspection upon what he is
about (131.36–37).

Onomatopoeia:
There can hardly pop out a *Play* (23.22)
[Bentley's spear] after a dead Bang against the Enemy's Shield, fell blunted to the Ground (121.20–21).

Oxymoron:
Common places *equally* new and eloquent (17.41)
Labor is the Seed of Idleness (64.25)
blind Guides (89.14)

Comic Excess:
not that he is curious to observe the Colour and Complexion of the Ordure... much less to be padling in or tasting it (37.27–29)
a *Wild Ass* broke loose... trampling and kicking, and dunging in their Faces (119.33–35).

Irony:
How shrunk is every Thing, as it appears in the Glass of Nature? (77.24–25).
'Tis a great Ease to my Conscience that I have writ so elaborate and useful a Discourse without one grain of Satyr intermixt (16.3–4)

Swift could make fun even with a single word, both existing words, such as *atramentous* (inky), *fuliginous* (sooty), *tentiginous* (sexy), and his own coinages: *Fastidiosity* (fussiness), *Amorphy* (shapelessness), *Eructation* (improvised preaching).

The explicit target of the satire in *A Tale of a Tub* is "*the numerous and gross Corruptions in Religion and Learning*" (140.27): the Papists have run mad with "Pride, Projects, and Knavery" (48.28); the dissenters have run mad with "Spleen, and Spight, and Contradiction" (62.18). "The hasty Reader" might easily miss the point that only Swift's Church of England retains its sanity. The Narrator himself, the "*Tale-Teller*" as Wotton calls him (Wotton 1705[1], 524) is one "whose Imaginations are hard-mouth'd, and exceedingly disposed to run away with his *Reason*" (81.19–20). Indeed, if *A Tale of a Tub* were a mock diary instead of a mock chapbook, Swift could have called it *The Diary of a Madman*.

To deny the existence of the Narrator (Ehrenpreis 1963, 34–36) is to deny Swift credit for creating an authentic comic-pathetic character, with his cropped ears, ill-cured pox and suicidal impulses (93.2–3, 26.16, 81.21–22). He is an auto-didact, a compulsive reader, note-taker, commonplace-book compiler, indexer, and scribbler. He seems to have had no childhood at all and an "unfortunate Life", penniless and frequently hungry (26.9,

14.20,22), an amalgam of Edmund Hickeringill, John Dunton, and Swift himself perhaps. Hickeringill, an ordained Anglican priest, who was a closet dissenter, deserved his reputation as the "great scribbler of the nation" (*ODNB*, xxvii.3). Dunton was the publisher of *The Athenian Gazette* wherein "Jonathan Swift" first appeared in print and which Swift bitterly regretted. He descended to "abusive scribbling" and went mad (*ODNB*, xvii.366-67). The Narrator thinks of himself first as an apprentice Modern, then as a "true Modern", and finally as the most modern Modern (14.27–28, 54.9, 56.26), the perfect postmodern theorist. He is all compact of "Uncertainty and Confusion", the "defining characteristics of... the post-modern condition" (*TLS*, 27 September 1996, 26). He is the archetypal Sad Sack, a buck private in "the Army of Unalterable Muddle" (Forster 1927, 112). Much of what he says is contradicted by something else he says:

> *Criticks* and *Wits*... I profess to be of the former Sort (57.8)::we *Modern Wits* (66.4).

> my small Reading (125.34–35)::[my] great Reading (98.2).

He suffers from severe memory loss (22.3, 37.56, 39.8–10), including loss of the sense of chronology (Ramsey 1974, 107). He also suffers delusional disorders (125.10–11, 128.28–29), including the persecutory type (8.5). He does not relieve the text of its burden of meaning, but he does not conceal his admiration for dissenting preachers who have "spiritualized and refined ['the Writings of our *Modern Saints* in *Great Britain*'] from the Dross and Grossness of *Sense* and *Human Reason*" (22.19–21). Like the Sad Sack he ends up a loser. His letter to "*T.H. Esquire*", "*Concerning the Mechanical Operation of the Spirit*" (124.1–8) never appears in the pages of *Philosophical Transactions*, the house organ of the Royal Society at Gresham College, London, the epicycle of scientific research in Britain (Plate 9), of which he claimed to have been a member (125.9–11). He was in fact for "some Time" a patient (79.22, 31–32) at Bethlehem Hospital for the Insane (Plate 23). But if you read *A Tale of a Tub* as if spoken by this pathetic lunatic, and expecting to be entertained, you will be reading it as Swift intended.

In many ways, however, the Narrator is Swift's ironic other. He is childishly delighted with anything new: "New Empires... New Schemes in Philosophy... New Religions" (72.10–12). Swift abominates innovation (63.12–13, 74.12–25). The Narrator is tickled by the mere thought of "Orgyes" and "*Communities of Women*" (137.22, 137.34). *Ex officio* the vicar of Laracor is required to be horrified. The Narrator admires his "most ingenious Friend, Mr. *W-tt-n*" (75.33), whose banter Swift finds "*despisable*"

A
DELECTABLE
LITTLE
HISTORY
IN METTER.

Of a Lord and his three sons, containing his
Latter-will and Legacie to them upon his
Deathbed, & what befell them after his Death
especally the midmost and the youngest.

Revifed, Correcteb, and Amended, for
the ufe of Schools.

Omne tulit punctum qui mifcuit ut ille dulci.

He gotten hes all commendation, (one:
VVho profit hes with pleafure mixt in

G L A S G O W,

Printed in the Year 1695,

Plate 2

(148.4). The Narrator is proud to be a confidante of John Dryden, the poet laureate. For Swift Cousin Dryden is a Grub Street hack who writes chapbooks. No other narrative device could give *A Tale of a Tub* such astonishing complexity, could make it so challenging to read, and so funny.

Swift tells us that he *"personates the Style and Manner of other Writers, whom he has a mind to expose"* (142.23–24) and he offers Dryden and Sir Roger L'Estrange as examples. But he does not tell us that he quotes passages from Sir Thomas Browne (21.30–32) and Andrew Marvell (70.21–22), that he *"has a mind to expose"* as utter nonsense. Since he cannot have expected all his readers to register these *"exposures"*, they can be put down as private jokes, like "my good Master *Bates*" in *Gulliver's Travels* (Swift 1939–68, xi.4). The possibility of private jokes adds to the fun of reading the book. It introduces a detective-story element that leads the reader to expect the unexpected, as it does in the novels of Umberto Eco.

Being this funny, however, did not advance Swift's career in the Church. Francis Atterbury, who was Dean of Carlisle when he read *A Tale of a Tub* in 1704 said "Mr. Swift's book is very well written and will do good Service [to the Church]" (HMC Portland MSS.iv.155), but the bishops were not amused; they were afraid that the Narrator's observation that "the Learned, in our Illustrious Age… deal entirely with *Invention,* and strike all Things out of themselves, or at least by Collision, from each other" (59.11–13) is Swift's reflection on speculative theology in general and in particular on the disgraceful Trinitarian controversy (20.24–25) of 1690–96. So Swift never preached at Court or sat on the Bishops' Bench in the House of Lords. To this extent he was a martyr to satire.

As a result of its complexity *A Tale of a Tub* is frequently misunderstood. One eighteenth century reader claimed that it led "to the utter Confusion of all Religion" (Anony. 1715, 3). The Victorians claimed to be shocked by its "insufferable coarseness" (Forster 1876, i.164), but subversiveness and coarseness are of the nature of comedy, e.g. Aristophanes, Chaucer, Rabelais. Twentieth century readers are troubled by the difficulty of the work: it "defies analysis"(Burlingame 1920, 131). But it is not all that difficult. *A Tale of a Tub* proper is a mock chapbook on the story of the Reformation (Plate 2), a Grub Street production cobbled together from "antient Records" (67.20). *The Battle of the Books* is a mock-epic fragment. *The Mechanical Operation of the Spirit* handles such familiar catalysts as religious hysteria, alcohol, and hemp. Like many submissions to *Philosophical Transactions*, including the Narrator's letter to "T.H. *Esquire*" (124.7), it is a discourse in the form of a letter.

The story that is patched together in *A Tale of a Tub* proper is a version of folk motif D1052, Magical Garment (Thompson 1963, ii.131): a man with no estate leaves each of his three sons a magic coat that with good care will always fit and never wear out. The three sons, Peter, Martin, and Jack, represent Roman Catholicism, the Church of England, and Dissent. The magic coats are *"the Doctrine and Faith of Christianity"* (28 n[†]). So the plot of *A Tale of a Tub* is a mock-history of Christianity from the beginning to 7 November 1697 (Swift 1958, 204 n[†]). But the plot, which occupies less than half of the text, is padded out with large digressions that make "a very considerable Addition to the Bulk" (57.13–14) of the work.

The second work in *A Tale of a Tub, The Battle of the Books*, Ancient vs. Modern, is a mock-epic fragment. Venus's chariot is drawn by doves and her son is Cupid; the chariot of Criticism is drawn by tame geese and her son is William Wotton B.D. "whom an unknown Father of mortal race begot by stolen Embraces with this Goddess" (114.10–11).

The third work in *A Tale of a Tub* is *A Discourse concerning the Mechanical Operation of the Spirit*. This work ignores Peter and intensifies the attack on Jack. Swift was aware of this disparity, but without the benefit of hindsight the history of Christianity in England by the end of the 17th century looked like this to him:

> This Nation of ours hath for a Hundred Years past been infested by two Enemies, the Papists and Fanatics, who each, in their Turns, filled it with Blood and Slaughter, and for a Time destroyed both the Church and the Government... the *Puritans* and other Schismaticks... by an open Rebellion, destroyed that legal Reformation... murdered their King, and changed the Monarchy into a Republick (Swift 1939–68, ix.172, xii..290).

By 1697–98, when Swift was writing *A Discourse*, the "fanaticks" had, by the Act of Toleration (1689), been legalized into "dissenting Protestants"(*EHD* 1966, 402), the Dissenters had been politicized into Whigs, and seemed to Swift a more imminent danger than the Papists:

> We are thirteen Times and one Third more in Danger of being ruined by the [Dissenters] than the [Papists] (Swift 1939–68, iv.78).

A Discourse concerning the Mechanical Operation of the Spirit is much more of a *satura*, the etymological source of *satire*, a dish composed of a variety of ingredients, an olio, a Spanish stew (63.9–12). Without mentioning Jack, and without even a simulacrum of a plot, Swift keeps the focus on the religious practices of "our *Modern Saints* in *Great Britain*" (22.19–21). Deploying an astonishing variety of material he still manages to sustain a highly inflammatory level of satire to the last dozen words: *"Pray, burn this Letter as soon as it comes into your Hands"* (139.18–21).

It is remarkable that neither a Catholic apologist like John Dryden nor a Dissenter like Daniel Defoe undertook a reply to *A Tale of a Tub*. Perhaps they thought it was unanswerable. The papal hierarchy in Rome, however, did answer *A Tale of a Tub*. In 1734 they put it on the *Index Librorum Prohibitorum* (Haight 1955, 36).

Table of Dates:

> Dates are important.
> Czeslaw Milosz (*TLS*, 15 February 2002)

30 November 1667	Jonathan Swift born in county Dublin, the son of Abigail Erick, who was baptized 16 May 1630 in Wigston Magna, Leicester, the daughter of a butcher (Johnston 1959, 45); shipped off with a wet nurse to Whitehaven, Cumberland, while his mother decamps to Leicestershire.
1670	Brought back and taken into the house of polyphiloprogenitive uncle Godwin Swift, an attorney, of Hoey's Court, Dublin City, who already had two children and was to have 12 more. His second wife (of four), Katherine Webster, became Swift's foster-mother.
1673–81	Attended grammar school at Kilkenny, the best secondary school in Ireland, where William Congreve became his schoolmate.
14 April 1682	Matriculated at Trinity College Dublin, the Protestant college founded by Elizabeth I in 1591.
Easter Term 1685	Received *bene* in Greek and Latin, *male* in philosophy, and *negligenter* in theology.
February 1686	Graduated B.A. *speciali gratia* (by special dispensation); remained in residence studying for the M.A. degree.
1689	During 'the Troubles'(the invasion of Ireland by William III), retired to Leicester, where his mother suggested he seek work with Sir William Temple, a retired diplomat and belletrist, whose father, Sir John Temple (1600–77), Master of the Irish Parliament, 'had been a great Friend to the Family'(Swift 1939–68, v.193).
Spring 1689	Secretary to Sir William Temple, first at Sheen, and then at Moor Park, Surrey.
5 July 1692	Graduated M.A. from Hart Hall, Oxford, after less than a month of residence.
January 1695	Ordained a priest in the Church of England, appointed prebend of Kilroot (Cill-ruaidh), near

Structure and Date of Composition:

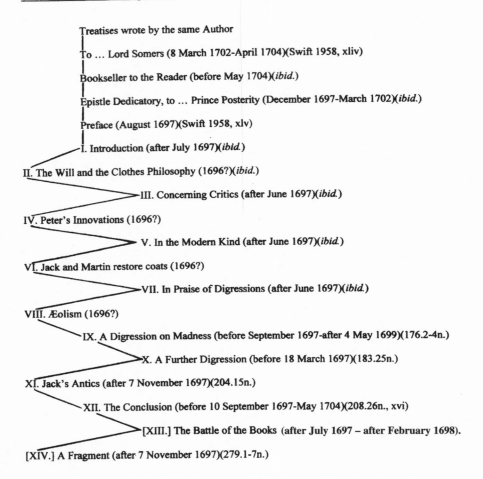

Treatises wrote by the same Author

To … Lord Somers (8 March 1702-April 1704)(Swift 1958, xliv)

Bookseller to the Reader (before May 1704)(*ibid.*)

Epistle Dedicatory, to … Prince Posterity (December 1697-March 1702)(*ibid.*)

Preface (August 1697)(Swift 1958, xlv)

I. Introduction (after July 1697)(*ibid.*)

II. The Will and the Clothes Philosophy (1696?)(*ibid.*)

III. Concerning Critics (after June 1697)(*ibid.*)

IV. Peter's Innovations (1696?)

V. In the Modern Kind (after June 1697)(*ibid.*)

VI. Jack and Martin restore coats (1696?)

VII. In Praise of Digressions (after June 1697)(*ibid.*)

VIII. Æolism (1696?)

IX. A Digression on Madness (before September 1697-after 4 May 1699)(176.2-4n.)

X. A Further Digression (before 18 March 1697)(183.25n.)

XI. Jack's Antics (after 7 November 1697)(204.15n.)

XII. The Conclusion (before 10 September 1697-May 1704)(208.26n., xvi)

[XIII.] The Battle of the Books (after July 1697 – after February 1698).

[XIV.] A Fragment (after 7 November 1697)(279.1-7n.)

This serpentine column has been called 'an astonishing baroque work of art'. (Quintana 1962, 143)

Plate 3

	Belfast, in the overwhelmingly Presbyterian county of Antrim.
May 1696–January 1699	Under a license of absence from his cure, returned to Moor Park, where he wrote most of *A Tale of a Tub* (Plate 3) and remained until the death of Sir William Temple in January 1699, which left him "unprovided".
January 1698	Resigned the prebend of Kilroot.
February 1700	Appointed vicar of Laracor, 30 miles north-west of Dublin, in the overwhelmingly Catholic county of Meath.
10 May 1704	With no advance publicity, Benjamin Tooke Jr. (Treadwell 1983, 9) published in London an anonymous octavo volume *A Tale of a Tub* (Arber 1903–06, iii.401).
23 April 1713	Promoted dean of St. Patrick's Cathedral, Dublin. "Dublin" said Stanislaus Joyce, "is an old, small, seaport Capital with a tradition. Yes, Dean Swift is the tradition" (Stanislaus Joyce 1962, 61).

Text of this Edition:

A Tale of a Tub was published on 10 May 1704 during Swift's visit to London from his parish at Laracor, co. Meath. That year must have been a hard year for turnips in Covent Garden, for the publisher told Swift that his book "would never *take*" unless "it should happen to be a hard Year for Turnips". The book did take: four editions within twelve months (Swift 1958, 206–07; Arber 1903–06, iii.401, 418, 454). A fifth, commercialized, edition, tarted up "With the Authors Apology and Explanatory Notes. By W. W–tt–n B.D. and others [i.e. Jonathan Swift]" and eight engraved illustrations after drawings by Sir Andrew Fountaine, followed shortly before or on 19 June 1710 when Edmund Curll published *A Complete Key to the Tale of a Tub* (Swift 1999–2003, i.283.n2) and at least fifteen more editions in English before Swift's death in October 1745, besides three editions in French, two in German, and one in Dutch. The five original editions were printed by Benjamin Tooke Jr. and published, i.e. distributed, by John Nutt (Treadwell 1983, 11–14), who had also published Swift's first book, *A Discourse of the Contests and Dissentions*, in October 1701.

A posthumous edition appeared in 1755 in volume one of a six volume set in quarto published by a consortium of the publishers who owned copyright to Swift's works published in London. It was edited by John Hawkesworth. Hawkesworth took as his copytext the last (and worst) of Tooke's five octavo editions, that of 1710. But he also had in hand Deane Swift's copy of the first and best of Tooke's editions: "I have... the Tale of the Tub corrected by [Jonathan Swift] himself," Deane Swift told John Nichols in 1799 (Nichols 1817–58, v.278). "His corrections will be found in this impression [i.e. edition]", Hawkesworth declared in his preface (Swift 1755, i.Alr). And the evidence of collation bears out Hawkesworth's claim. His conflated text includes corrections of Tooke's first printing. None of Hawkesworth's variants may seem to be beyond the scope of a publisher's proof reader, but 6–7 of them correct errors in the first printing and are incorporated (and recorded) in the present text.

Each of these six editions is set up from the preceding one, to form the following stemma:

$$1704^1$$
|
$$1704^2$$
|
$$1705^3$$
|
$$1705^4$$
|
$$1710^5$$
|
$$1755^H$$

While 1710^5 adds new material to the work, only 1704^1 and 1755^H are textually authorial. The "Apology" is relegated to an Appendix, but the "Explanatory Notes" of 1710^5 and eight of the illustrations are included in the present edition. A Yale copy of the first edition (Beinecke Library 1995.55) provides the copytext. Samuel Johnson reminds us that "they who had the [author's manuscript] before their eyes were more likely to read it right" than the compositors of later editions.

Editorial emendations and Hawkesworth's variants are recorded in the end notes, but obvious errors are corrected silently: "The Editors of Profane Authors do not use to trouble their Readers… by an useless List of every small slip by a lazy or ignorant Scribe" (Bentley 1713, i.67).

Side Notes, Footnotes, and End Notes:

As part of his parody of scholarly apparatus Swift had included in 1704[1] 57
largely useless side notes. Since only Swift could have written some of them
(50), it is assumed that he wrote all of them. Some are *totally* useless:
'*Lib——', 'Lib.' (70, 71). Others are incomplete: 'Vid. Homer' (166, 167),
'*Ctesiae fragm. apud Photium*' (103), '*Guagnini Hist. Sarmat.*' (175), but
fulfill '*one of the Authors Designs... to set curious men a hunting thro' Indexes, and
enquiring for Books out of the Common Road*' (125 n.*). Another part of the
parody of scholarly apparatus is the hiatuses that Swift introduces in
imitation of early texts in manuscript (Swift 1721, *84). Each hiatus has a
Latin note, some of which relate to the text: '*Hic multa desiderantur*', '*Ingens
hiatus hic in MS*', '*Here the whole Scheme of spiritual Mechanism was deduced and
explained, with an Appearance of great reading... but it was thought neither safe nor
Convenient to Print it*' (116, 158, 178).

In the 1710 edition Swift retained the 57 side notes and added 199
footnotes, of which 29 are advertised on the title-page as 'Explanatory
Notes. By W. W–tt–n, B.D.', verbatim quotations from Wotton's *Reflections
upon Ancient and Modern Learning... With Observations upon the Tale of a Tub*
(1705[1]). Again it is assumed that all the 'others', including 56 n.[†],
attributed to Dionysus Lambinus, are written by Swift.

To this total the present editor has added about 1200 end notes. He
would like to have taken "The Part of... Farnaby" (194.20–21) and kept the
notes short, infrequent, and "calculated for the Understanding of the
Text" (Bayle 1710, ii.1286). But he was defeated by Swift's method of composition. Swift knew exactly how *A Tale of a Tub* had to be annotated because he knew how he had put it together. We can imagine him at Moor
Park in 1696–97, in Sir William Temple's library painfully copying into his
commonplace book extracts from Pausanias, Herodotus, Ctesias, Diodorus, Lucretius, finding or enforcing outlandish parallels, laying out his
'*Memorandums... with a wonderful Facility of Application*' (171.37–38), and
then piecing together a mock genealogy of '*the true Critick*' (69–72).

Although the Narrator claimed he had '*not borrowed one single Hint from
any Writer in the World*' (193.4–5), it is closer to the truth to say that
everything is borrowed. *A Tale of a Tub* is 'patch'd up of a thousand
incoherent pieces' (162.1), like Richard Bentley's armour or a Spanish
olio. And the only reason that every hemistich is not annotated here is that
the source has not yet been found. Swift did not write *A Tale of a Tub* in the
usual sense of "write"; he put *A Tale of a Tub* together like a mosaic. Swift's
method of composition does not, of course, diminish the work. On the

contrary 'It exhibits a vehemence and rapidity of mind, a copiousness of images, and vivacity of diction, such as he afterwards never possessed' (Johnson 1779–81, viii. [1]84–85). The publishers therefore, but not the editor, apologize for the numerousness of the end notes.

Acknowledgements

It is a great pleasure to be able to name those who have helped me prepare this edition. My first obligation is to the editors of *The Oxford English Dictionary* from James A.H. Murray to R.W. Burchfield and the editors of the Clarendon edition of *A Tale of a Tub* of 1920 with a second edition of 1958 and further corrections in 1970, A.C. Guthkelch and D. Nichol Smith. These two works are cited here more times than I care to count.

My second obligation is to Harold D. Kelling and Cathy Lynn Preston, editors of *A KWIC Concordance to Jonathan Swift's A Tale of a Tub* (1984) that is cited here only twice but was constantly consulted.

Individuals who have helped in ways too various to mention are Howard Adelman, Michael O. Albertson, Elizabeth S. Alexander, Elizabeth A. Barone, John Bidwell, Barbara B. Blumenthal, Frank T. Boyle, Jessica Bumpous, Thomas Cleary, Brittany S. Columbia, Geoffrey Dawe, Oliver Ferguson, Andrew L. Ford, Randy O. Frost, Justina Gregory, Susan Halpert, David Hayton, Maja Horn, Steven C. Jones and his crew, Seth Kasten, Margit Kaye, Ann C. Kelly, James Kilvington, Bernard M.W. Knox, Karen V. Kukil, Thomas V. Lange, F.P. Locke, Patricia J. Lutz, Melissa Maday, Howard Nenner, Dirk F. Passmann, Clive Probyn, Jennie Rathbun, Claude Rawson, Hermann J. Real, J.C. Ross, Christina M. Ryan and her crew, Michael T. Ryan, Christa Sammons, Harold L. Skulsky, Malcolm B.E. Smith, Emily Walhout, Joan Sussler, Mary K.A. Trechock, Ciona van Dijk, David Woolley, *il miglior fabbro*.

Besides these individuals I want to thank the following institutions for allowing me to reproduce images in their possession: Yale University, Williams College, Smith College, the Pierpont Morgan Library, the Oxford University Press, the British Library, the Huntington Library, Art Collections and Botanic Gardens, Rijksmuseum Amsterdam, Christ Church (Oxford University), the Bodleian Library, Oxford University.

This satire on index-learning could not be complete without an index "by which the whole Book is governed" (64.8–9).

A TALE
OF A
TUB.

Written for the Univerſal Improve-ment of Mankind.

Diu multumque deſideratum.

To which is added,

An ACCOUNT of a
BATTEL
BETWEEN THE
Antient and Modern BOOKS
in St. James's Library.

Baſima eacabaſa eanaa irrauriſta, diarba da caeo-taba fobor camelanthi. *Iren. Lib.* 1. *C.* 18.

———— *Juvatque novos decerpere flores,*
Inſignemque meo capiti petere inde coronam,
Unde prius nulli velarunt tempora Muſæ. Lucret.

LONDON:
Printed for *John Nutt*, near *Stationers-Hall*.
MDCCIV.

Plate 4

Treatises writ by the same Author, most of them mentioned in the following Discourses; which will be speedily published.

A *Character of the present Set of* Wits *in this Island.*

A Panegyrical Essay upon the Number THREE.

A Dissertation upon the principal Productions of Grub-street.

Lectures upon a Dissection of Human Nature.

A Panegyrick upon the World.

An Analytical Discourse upon Zeal, Histori-theo-physi-logically *considered.*

A general History of Ears.

A modest Defence of the Proceedings of the Rabble *in all Ages.*

A Description of the Kingdom of Absurdities.

A Voyage into England, *by a Person of Quality in* Terra Australis incognita, *translated from the Original.*

A Critical Essay upon the Art of Canting, *Philosophically, Physically, and Musically considered.*

TO
The Right Honourable,
John
Lord SOMMERS.

My Lord,

T HO' the Author has written a large Dedication, yet That being address'd to a Prince, whom I am never likely to have the Honor of being known to; A Person, besides, as far as I can observe, not at all regarded, or thought on by any of our present Writers; And, being wholly free from that Slavery, which Booksellers usually lye under, to the Caprices of Authors; I think it a wise Piece of Presumption, to inscribe these Papers to your Lordship, and to implore your Lordship's Protection of them. God and your Lordship know their Faults, and their Merits; for as to my own Particular, I am altogether a Stranger to the Matter; And, though every Body else should be equally ignorant, I do not fear the Sale of the Book; at all the worse, upon that Score. Your Lordship's Name on the Front, in Capital Letters, will at any time get off one Edition: Neither would I desire any other Help, to grow an Alderman, than a Patent for the sole Priviledge of Dedicating to your Lordship.

I should now, in right of a Dedicator, give your Lordship a List of your own Virtues, and at the same time, be very unwilling to offend your Modesty; But, chiefly, I should celebrate your Liberality towards Men of great Parts and Small Fortunes, and give you broad Hints, that I mean my self. And, I was just going on in the usual Method, to peruse a hundred or two of Dedications, and transcribe an Abstract, to be applied to your Lordship; But, I was diverted by a certain Accident. For, upon the Covers of these Papers, I casually observed, written in large Letters, the two following Words, DETUR DIGNISSIMO; which, for ought I knew, might contain some important Meaning. But, it unluckily fell out, that none of the Authors I employ, understood *Latin* (tho' I have them often in pay, to translate out of that Language) I was therefore compelled to have recourse to the Curate of our Parish, who Englished it thus, *Let it be given to the Worthiest*; And his Comment was, that the Author meant, his Work should be dedicated to the sublimest Genius of the Age, for Wit, Learning, Judgment, Eloquence and Wisdom. I call'd at a Poet's Chamber (who works for my Shop) in an Alley hard by, shewed him the Translation, and desired his Opinion, who it was that the Author could mean; He told me, after some Consideration, that Vanity was a Thing he abhorr'd; but by the Description, he thought Himself to be the Person aimed at; And, at the same time, he very kindly offer'd his own Assistance *gratis*, towards penning a Dedication to Himself. I desired him, however, to give a second Guess; Why then, said he, It must be I, or my Lord *Sommers*. From thence I went to several other Wits of my Acquaintance, with no small Hazard and Weariness to my Person, from a prodigious Number of dark, winding Stairs; But found them all in the same Story, both of your Lordship and themselves. Now, your Lordship is to understand, that this Proceeding was not of my own Invention; For, I have somewhere heard, it is a Maxim, that those, to whom every Body allows the second Place; have an undoubted Title to the First.

THIS, infallibly, convinced me, that your Lordship was the Person intended by the Author. But, being very unacquainted in the Style and Form of Dedications, I employ'd those Wits aforesaid, to furnish me with Hints and Materials, towards a Panegyrick upon your Lordship's Virtues.

IN two Days, they brought me ten Sheets of Paper, fill'd up on every Side. They swore to me, that they had ransack'd whatever could be found in the Characters of *Socrates, Aristides, Epaminondas, Cato, Tully, Atticus*, and other hard Names, which I cannot now recollect. However, I have Reason to believe, they imposed upon my Ignorance, because, when I came to read over their Collections, there was not a Syllable there, but what I and every body else knew as well as themselves: Therefore, I grievously suspect a Cheat; and, that these Authors of mine, stole and transcribed every Word, from the universal Report of Mankind. So that I look upon my self, as fifty Shillings out of Pocket, to no manner of Purpose.

IF, by altering the Title, I could make the same Materials serve for another Dedication (as my Betters have done) it would help to make up my Loss: But, I have made several Persons, dip here and there in those Papers, and before they read three Lines, they have all assured me, plainly, that they cannot possibly be applied to any Person besides your Lordship.

I expected, indeed, to have heard of your Lordship's Bravery, at the Head of an Army; Of your undaunted Courage, in mounting a Breach, or scaling a Wall; Or, to have had your Pedigree trac'd in a Lineal Descent from the House of *Austria*; Or, of your wonderful Talent at Dress and Dancing; Or, your Profound Knowledge in *Algebra, Metaphysicks*, and the Oriental Tongues: But to ply the World with an old beaten Story of your Wit, and Eloquence, and Learning, and Wisdom, and Justice, and Politeness, and Candor, and Evenness of Temper in all Scenes of Life; Of that great Discernment in Discovering, and Readiness in Favouring deserving Men; with forty other common Topicks: I confess, I have neither Conscience, nor Countenance to do it. Because, there is no Virtue, either of a Publick or

Private Life, which some Circumstances of your own, have not often produced upon the Stage of the World; And those few, which for want of Occasions to exert them, might otherwise have pass'd unseen or unobserved by your *Friends*, your *Enemies* have at length brought to Light.

'TIS true, I should be very loth, the Bright Example of your Lordship's Virtues should be lost to after Ages, both for their sake and your own; but chiefly, because they will be so very necessary to adorn the History of a *late Reign*; And That is another Reason, why I would forbear to make a Recital of them here; Because, I have been told by Wise Men, that as Dedications have run for some Years past, a good Historian will not be apt to have Recourse thither, in search of Characters.

THERE is one Point, wherein I think we Dedicators would do well to change our Measures; I mean, instead of running on so far, upon the Praise of our Patrons' *Liberality*, to spend a Word or two, in admiring their *Patience*. I can put no greater Compliment on your Lordship's, than by giving you so ample an Occasion to exercise it at present. Tho', perhaps, I shall not be apt to reckon much Merit to your Lordship upon that Score, who having been formerly used to tedious Harangues, and sometimes to as little Purpose, will be the readier to pardon this, especially when it is offered by one, who is with all Respect and Veneration,

    My LORD,

      Your Lordship's most Obedient,

      and most Faithful Servant,

       The Bookseller

THE
BOOKSELLER
TO THE
READER.

IT *is now Six Years since these Papers came first to my Hands, which seems to have been about a Twelvemonth after they were writ : For, the Author tells us in his Preface to the first Treatise, that he hath calculated it for the Year 1697, and in several Passages of that Discourse, as well as the second, it appears, they were written about that Time.*

As to the Author, I can give no manner of Satisfaction; However, I am credibly informed that this Publication is without his Knowledge; for he concludes the Copy is lost, having lent it to a Person, since dead, and being never in Possession of it after: So that, whether the Work is received his last Hand, or, whether he intended to fill up the defective Places, is like to remain a Secret.

If I should go about to tell the Reader, by what Accident, I became Master of these Papers, it would, in this unbelieving Age, pass for little more than the Cant, or Jargon of the Trade. I, therefore, gladly spare both him and my self so unnecessary a Trouble. There yet remains a difficult Question, why I publish'd them no sooner. I forbore upon two Accounts: First, because I thought I had better Work upon my Hands: and Secondly, because, I was not without some Hope of hearing from the Author, and receiving his Directions. But, I have been lately alarm'd with Intelligence of a surreptitious Copy, which a certain great Wit had new polish'd and refin'd, or as our present Writers express themselves, fitted to the Humor of the Age; as they have already done, with great Felicity, to Don Quixot, Boccalini, la Bruyere *and other Authors. However, I thought it fairer Dealing, to offer the whole Work in its Naturals. If any Gentleman will please to furnish me with a Key, in order to explain the more difficult Parts, I shall very gratefully acknowledge the Favour, and print it by it self.*

THE
Epistle Dedicatory,
TO
His Royal Highness
PRINCE POSTERITY.

SIR,

I HERE present *Your Highness* with the Fruits of a very few leisure Hours, stollen from the short Intervals of a World of Business, and of an Employment quite alien from such Amusements* as this: The poor Production of that Refuse of Time which has lain heavy upon my Hands, during a long Prorogation of Parliament, a great Dearth of Forein News, and a tedious Fit of rainy Weather: For which, and other Reasons, it cannot chuse extreamly to deserve such a Patronage as that of *Your Highness,* whose numberless Virtues in so few Years, make the World look upon You as the future Example to all Princes: For altho' *Your Highness* is hardly got clear of Infancy, yet has the universal learned World already resolv'd upon appealing to Your future Dictates with the lowest and most resigned Submission; Fate having decreed You sole Arbiter of the Productions of human Wit, in this polite and most accomplish'd Age. Methinks, the Number of Appellants were enough to shock and startle any Judge of a Genius less unlimited than Yours: But in order to prevent such glorious Tryals, the *Person* (it seems) to whose Care the Education of *Your Highness* is committed, has resolved (as I am told) to keep You in almost an universal Ignorance of our Studies, which it is Your inherent Birth-right to inspect.

IT is amazing to me, that this *Person* should have Assurance in the face of the Sun, to go about persuading *Your Highness,* that our Age is almost wholly illiterate, and has hardly produc'd one Writer upon any Subject. I know very well, that when *Your Highness* shall come to riper Years, and have gone thro' the Learning of Antiquity, you will be too curious to neglect inquiring into the Authors of the very Age before you; And to think that this *Insolent,*

---

* *The Citation out of* Irenæus *in the* Title-Page, *which seems to be all* Gibberish, *is a Form of Initiation used antiently by the* Marcosian *Hereticks.* W. Wotton

It is the usual Style of decry'd Writers to appeal to Posterity, who is here represented as a Prince in his Nonage, and Time as his Governour, and the Author begins in a way very frequent with him, by personating other Writers, who sometimes offer such Reasons and Excuses for publishing their Works as they ought chiefly to conceal and be asham'd of.

in the Account he is preparing for Your View, designs to reduce them to a Number so insignificant as I am asham'd to mention; it moves my Zeal and my Spleen for the Honor and Interest of our vast flourishing Body, as well as of my self, for whom I know by long experience, he has profess'd, and still continues a peculiar Malice.

'TIS not unlikely, that when *Your Highness* will one day peruse what I am now writing, You may be ready to expostulate with your Governour upon the Credit of what I here affirm, and command Him to shew You some of our Productions. To which he will answer (for I am well informed of his Designs) by asking *Your Highness*, where they are? and what is become of them? and pretend it a Demonstration that there never were any, because they are not then to be found: Not to be found! Who has mislaid them? Are they sunk in the Abyss of Things? 'Tis certain, that in their own Nature they were *light* enough to swim upon the Surface for all Eternity: Therefore the Fault is in Him, who tied Weights so heavy to their Heels, as to depress them to the Center. Is their very Essence destroyed? Who has annihilated them? Were they drowned by *Purges* or martyred by *Pipes*? Who administered them to the Posteriors of ——? But that it may no longer be a Doubt with *Your Highness*, who is to be the Author of this universal Ruin; I beseech You to observe that large and terrible *Scythe* which your *Governour* affects to bear continually about him. Be pleased to remark the Length and Strength, the Sharpness and Hardness of his *Nails* and *Teeth*; Consider his baneful abominable *Breath*, Enemy to Life and Matter, infectious and corrupting: And then reflect whether it be possible for any mortal Ink and Paper of this Generation to make a suitable Resistance. Oh, that *Your Highness* would one day resolve to disarm this Usurping *Maire du Palais,* of his furious Engins, and bring Your Empire *hors de Page.*†

IT were endless to recount the several Methods of Tyranny and Destruction, which Your *Governour* is pleased to practise upon this Occasion. His inveterate Malice is such to the Writings of our Age, that of several Thousands produced yearly from this renowned City, before the next Revolution of the Sun, there is not one to be heard of: Unhappy Infants, many of them barbarously destroyed, before they have so much as learnt their *Mother-Tongue* to beg for Pity. Some he stifles in their Cradles, others he frights into Convulsions, whereof they suddenly die; Some he flays alive, others he tears Limb from Limb: Great Numbers are offered to *Moloch*, and the rest, tainted by his Breath, die of a languishing Consumption.

BUT the Concern I have most at Heart, is for our Corporation of *Poets,* from whom I am preparing a petition to *Your Highness*, to be subscribed

---

† Out of Guardianship.

with the Names of one hundred thirty-six of the first Rate, but whose immortal Productions are never likely to reach your Eyes, tho' each of them is now an humble and an earnest Appellant for the Laurel, and has large comely Volumes ready to shew for a Support to his Pretensions. The *never-dying* Works of these illustrious Persons, Your *Governour*, Sir, has devoted to unavoidable Death, and *Your Highness* is to be made believe, that our Age has never arrived at the Honor to produce one single Poet.

WE confess *Immortality* to be a great and powerful Goddess; but in vain we offer up to her our Devotions and our Sacrifices, if *Your Highness's Governour*, who has usurped the *Priesthood*, must by an unparallel'd Ambition and Avarice, wholly intercept and devour them.

TO affirm that our Age is altogether Unlearned, and devoid of Writers in any kind, seems to be an Assertion so bold and so false, that I have been sometime thinking, the contrary may almost be proved by uncontroulable Demonstration. 'Tis true indeed, that altho' their Numbers be vast, and their Productions numerous in proportion, yet are they hurryed so hastily off the Scene, that they escape our Memory, and delude our Sight. When I first thought of this Address, I had prepared a copious List of *Titles* to present *Your Highness* as an undisputed Argument for what I affirm. The Originals were posted fresh upon all Gates and Corners of Streets; but returning in a very few Hours to take a Review, they were all torn down, and fresh ones in their Places: I enquired after them among Readers and Booksellers, but I enquired in vain, the *Memorial of them was lost among Men, their Place was no more to be found;* and I was laughed to scorn, for a *Clown* and a *Pedant*, devoid of all Taste and Refinement, little versed in the Course of *present* Affairs, and that knew nothing of what had pass'd in the best Companies of Court and Town. So that I can only avow in general to *Your Highness*, that we *do* abound in Learning and Wit; but to fix upon Particulars, is a Task too slippery for my slender Abilities. If I should venture in a windy Day, to affirm to *Your Highness*, that there is a huge Cloud near the *Horizon* in the Form of a *Bear*, another in the *Zenith* with the Head of an *Ass*, a third to the Westward with Claws like a *Dragon*, and *Your Highness* should in a few Minutes think fit to examine the Truth; 'tis certain, they would all be changed in Figure and Position, new ones would arise, and all we could agree upon would be, that Clouds there were, but that I was grosly mistaken in the *Zoography* and *Topography* of them.

BUT Your *Governour*, perhaps, may still insist, and put the Question; What is then become of those immense Bales of Paper, which must needs have been employ'd in such Numbers of Books? Can these also be wholly annihilate, and so of a sudden as I pretend? What shall I say in return of so invidious an Objection? It ill befits the Distance between *Your Highness* and

Me, to send You for ocular Conviction to a *Jakes* or an *Oven*; to the Windows
of a *Bawdy-house*, or to a sordid *Lanthorn*. Books like Men their Authors,
have no more than one Way of coming into the World, but there are ten
Thousand to go out of it, and return no more.

I profess to *Your Highness* in the Integrity of my Heart, that what I am
going to say is literally true this Minute I am writing: What Revolutions may
happen before it shall be ready for your Perusal, I can by no means warrant;
However, I beg You to accept it as a Specimen of our Learning, our
Politeness and our Wit. I do therefore affirm upon the word of a sincere
Man, that there is now actually in being, a certain Poet called *John Dryden*,
whose Translation of *Virgil* was lately printed in a large Folio, well bound,
and if diligent search were made, for ought I know, is yet to be seen. There
is another call'd *Nahum Tate*, who is ready to make Oath that he has caused
many Rheams of Verse to be published, whereof both himself and his
Bookseller (if lawfully required) can still produce authentick Copies, and
therefore wonders why the World is pleased to make such a Secret of it.
There is a Third, known by the Name of *Tom Durfey*, a Poet of a vast
Comprehension, an universal Genius, and most profound Learning. There
are also one Mr. *Rymer*, and one Mr. *Dennis*, most profound Criticks. There
is a person styl'd Dr. *B—tl–y*, who has wrote near a thousand Pages of
immense Erudition, *giving a full and true Account* of a certain *Squable* of
wonderful Importance between himself and a Bookseller: He is a Writer of
infinite Wit and Humour; no Man raillyes with a better Grace, and in more
sprightly Turns. Further, I avow to *Your Highness*, that with these Eyes I have
beheld the Person of *William W-tt-n*, B. D. who has written a good sizeable
Volume against a *Friend of Your Governor* (from whom, alas! he must
therefore look for little Favour) in a most gentlemanly Stile, adorned with
utmost Politeness and Civility; replete with Discoveries equally valuable for
their Novelty and Use; and embellish'd with *Traits* of Wit so poignant and
so apposite, that he is a worthy Yokemate to his fore-mentioned *Friend*.

WHY should I go upon further Particulars, which might fill a Volume
with the just Elogies of my cotemporary Brethren? I shall bequeath this
Piece of Justice to a larger Work; wherein I intend to write a Character of
the present Set of *Wits* in our Nation: Their Persons I shall describe
particularly, and at Length, their Genius and Understandings in *Mignature*.

IN the mean time, I do here make bold to present *Your Highness* with a
faithful Abstract drawn from the universal Body of all Arts and Sciences,
intended wholly for Your Service and Instruction: Nor do I doubt in the
least, but *Your Highness* will peruse it as carefully, and make as considerable
Improvements, as *other* young *Princes* have already done by the many
Volumes of late Years written for a Help to their Studies.

THAT *Your Highness* may advance in Wisdom and Virtue, as well as Years, and at last out-shine all Your Royal Ancestors, shall be the daily Prayer of,

        S I R,

Decemb.
1697.   *Your Highness's*
          Most devoted, &c.

THE

PREFACE.

THE Wits of the present Age being so very numerous and penetrating, it seems, the Grandees of *Church* and *State* begin to fall under horrible Apprehensions, lest these Gentlemen, during the intervals of a long Peace, should find leisure to pick Holes in the weak sides of Religion and Government. To prevent which, there has been much Thought employ'd of late upon certain Projects for taking off the Force and Edge of those formidable Enquirers, from canvasing and reasoning upon such delicate Points. They have at length fixed upon one, which will require some Time as well as Cost, to perfect. Mean while, the Danger hourly increasing, by new Levies of Wits all appointed (as there is Reason to fear) with Pen, Ink, and Paper, which may at an hour's Warning be drawn out into Pamphlets, and other Offensive Weapons, ready for immediate Execution; It was judged of absolute necessity, that some present Expedient be thought on, till the main Design can be brought to Maturity. To this end, at a Grand Committee, some Days ago, this important Discovery was made by a certain curious and refined Observer; that Sea-men have a Custom when they meet a *Whale,* to fling him out an empty *Tub,* by way of Amusement, to divert him from laying violent Hands upon the Ship. This Parable was immediately mythologiz'd; The *Whale* was interpreted to be *Hob's Leviathan,* which tosses and plays with all other Schemes of Religion and Government, whereof a great many are hollow, and dry, and empty, and noisy, and wooden, and given to Rotation. This is the *Leviathan* from whence the terrible Wits of our Age are said to borrow their Weapons. The *Ship* in danger, is easily understood to be its old Antitype the *Commonwealth.* But, how to analyze the *Tub,* was a Matter of Difficulty; when after long Enquiry and Debate, the literal Meaning was preserved: And it was decreed, that in order to prevent these *Leviathans* from tossing and sporting with the *Commonwealth,* (which of it self is too apt to *fluctuate*) they should be diverted from their Game by a *Tale of a Tub.* And my Genius being conceived to lye not unhappily that way, I had the Honor done me to be engaged in the Performance.

THIS is the sole Design in publishing the following Treatise, which I hope will serve for an *Interim* of some Months to employ those unquiet Spirits, till the perfecting of that great Work, into the Secret of which, it is reasonable the courteous Reader should have some little Light.

IT is intended that a large Academy be erected, capable of containing nine thousand seven hundred forty and three Persons; which by modest

Computation is reckoned to be pretty near the current Number of *Wits* in this Island. These are to be disposed into the several Schools of this Academy, and there pursue those Studies to which their Genius most inclines them. The Undertaker himself will publish his Proposals with all convenient speed, to which I shall refer the curious Reader for a more particular Account, mentioning at present only a few of the Principal Schools. There is first, a large *Pederastick* School, with *French* and *Italian* Masters. There is also, the *Spelling* School, *a very spacious Building*: the School of *Looking-Glasses*: The School of *Swearing*: the School of *Criticks*: the School of *Salivation*: The School of *Hobby-Horses*: The School of *Poetry*: [1]The School of *Tops*: The School of *Spleen*: The School of *Gaming*; with many others too tedious to recount. No Person to be admitted Member into any of these Schools, without an Attestation under two sufficient Persons Hands, certifying him to be a *Wit*.

BUT, to return. I am sufficiently instructed in the Principal Duty of a Preface, if my Genius were capable of arriving at it. Thrice have I forced my Imagination to take the *Tour* of my Invention, and thrice it has returned empty; the latter having been wholly drained by the following Treatise. Not so, my more successful Brethren the *Moderns*, who will by no means let slip a Preface or Dedication, without some notable distinguishing Stroke, to surprize the Reader at the Entry, and kindle a Wonderful Expectation of what is to ensue. Such was that of a most ingenious Poet, who solliciting his Brain for something new, compared himself to the *Hangman*, and his Patron to the *Patient*: This was **Insigne, recens, indictum ore alio.* When I went thro' That necessary and noble [†]Course of Study, I had the happiness to observe many such egregious Touches, which I shall not injure the Authors by transplanting: Because I have remarked, that nothing is so very tender as a *Modern* Piece of Wit, and which is apt to suffer so much in the Carriage. Some things are extreamly witty *to day*, or *fasting*, or *in this Place*, or *at eight a Clock*, or *over a Bottle*, or spoken by Mr. Whatdicall'um, or *in a Summer's Morning*: Any of which, by the smallest Transposal or Misapplication, is utterly annihilate. Thus, *Wit* has its Walks and Purlieus, out of which it may not stray the breadth of a Hair, upon peril of being lost. The *Moderns* have artfully fixed this *Mercury*, and reduced it to the Circumstances of Time, Place, and Person. Such a Jest there is, that will not pass out of *Covent-Garden*; and such a one, that is no where intelligible but at *Hide-Park*

* *Hor.*

† *Reading Prefaces, &c.*

[1] *This I think the Author should have omitted, it being of the very same Nature with the* School of Hobby Horses, *if one may venture to censure one who is so severe a Censurer of others, perhaps with too little Distinction.*
* *Something extraordinary, new and never hit upon before.*

Corner. Now, tho' it sometimes tenderly affects me to consider, that all the towardly Passages I shall deliver in the following Treatise, will grow quite out of date and relish with the first shifting of the present Scene; yet I must need subscribe to the Justice of this Proceeding: because, I cannot imagine why we should be at Expence to furnish Wit for succeeding Ages, when the former have made no sort of Provision for ours; wherein I speak the Sentiment of the very newest, and consequently the most Orthodox Refiners, as well as my own. However, being extreamly sollicitous that every accomplished Person who has got into the Taste of Wit, calculated for this present Month of *August* 1697, should descend to the very *bottom* of all the *Sublime* throughout this Treatise; I hold it fit to lay down this general Maxim. Whatever Reader desires to have a thorow Comprehension of an Author's Thoughts, cannot take a better Method, than by putting himself into the Circumstances and Posture of Life, that the Writer was in, upon every important Passage as it flowed from his Pen; For this will introduce a Parity and strict Correspondence of Ideas between the Reader and the Author. Now, to assist the diligent Reader in so delicate an Affair, as far as brevity will permit, I have recollected, that the shrewdest Pieces of this Treatise, were conceived in Bed, in a Garrat: At other times (for a Reason best known to my self) I thought fit to sharpen my Invention with Hunger; and in general, the whole Work was begun, continued, and ended, under a long Course of Physick, and a great want of Money. Now, I do affirm, it will be absolutely impossible for the candid Peruser to go along with me in a great many bright Passages, unless upon the several Difficulties emergent, he will please to capacitate and prepare himself by these Directions. And this I lay down as my principal *Postulatum*.

BECAUSE I have profess'd to be a most devoted Servant of all *Modern* Forms; I apprehend some curious *Wit* may object against me, for proceeding thus far in a Preface, without declaiming, according to the Custom, against the Multitude of Writers whereof the whole Multitude of Writers most reasonably complains. I am just come from perusing some hundreds of Prefaces, wherein the Authors do at the very beginning address the gentle Reader concerning this enormous Grievance. Of these I have preserved a few Examples, and shall set them down as near as my Memory has been able to retain them.

One begins thus;

For a Man to set up for a Writer, when the Press swarms with, &c.

Another;

The Tax upon Paper does not lessen the Number of Scribblers, who daily pester, &c.

Another;

When every little Would-be-wit takes Pen in hand, 'tis in vain to enter the Lists, &c.

The Infallible MOUNTEBANK, or Quack DOCTOR.

SEE SIRS, see here
a Doctor rare,
who Travels much at home!
Here take my Bills,
I cure all Ills,
past, present, and to come;
The Cramp, the Stitch,
The Squirt, the Itch,
the Gout, the Stone the Pox;
The Mulligrubs,
The Bonny Scrubs,
and all Pandora's Box;
Thousands I've Dissected,
Thousands new erected,
and such Cures effected,
as none e're can tell,
Let the Palsie shake ye,
Let the Chollick rack ye,
Let the Crinkums break ye,
Let the Murrain take ye;
take this and you are well.
Come wits so keen,

Devour'd with Spleen;
come Beaus who sprain'd your Backs,
Great Belly'd Maids,
Old Founder'd Jades,
and Pepper'd Vizard Cracks.
I soon remove,
The Pains of Love,
and cure the Love-sick Maid;
The Hot, the Cold,
The Young, the Old,
the Living, and the Dead.
I Clear the Lass,
With Wainscot Face,
and from Pimginets free,
Plump Ladies Red,
Like Saracen's Head,
with Toaping Rattafia.
This with a Jirk,
will do your Work,
and Scour you e're and s're,
Read, Judge and Try,
And if you Die,
never believe me more.

Plate 5

Another;

To observe what Trash the Press swarms with, &c.

Another;

SIR. *It is meerly in Obedience to your Commands that I venture into the Publick; for who upon a less Consideration would be of a Party with such a Rabble of Scriblers,* &c.

NOW, I have two Words in my own Defence, against this Objection. First: I am far from granting the Number of Writers, a Nuisance to our Nation, having strenuously maintained the contrary in several Parts of the following Discourse. Secondly: I do not well understand the Justice of this Proceeding, because I observe many of these polite Prefaces, to be not only from the same Hand, but from those who are most voluminous in their several Productions: Upon which I shall tell the Reader a short Tale.

A Mountebank in Leicester-Fields (Plate 5) *had drawn a huge Assembly about him. Among the rest, a fat unweildy Fellow, half stifled in the Press, would be every fit crying out, Lord! what a filthy Crowd is here; Pray, good people, give way a little; Bless me! what a Devil has rak'd this Rabble together: Z———ds! what squeezing is this! Honest Friend, remove your Elbow. At last a Weaver that stood next him could hold no longer: A Plague confound you* (said he) *for an over-grown Sloven; and who (in the Devil's Name) I wonder, helps to make up the Crowd half so much as your self? Don't you consider (with a Pox,) that you take up more room with that Carcass than any five here? Is not the Place as free for us as for you? Bring your own Guts to a reasonable Compass (and be d———n'd) and then I'll engage we shall have room enough for us all.*

THERE are certain common Privileges of a Writer, the Benefit whereof, I hope there will be no Reason to doubt; particularly, that where I am not understood, it shall be concluded, that something very useful and profound is coutcht underneath: And again, that whatever Word or Sentence is Printed in a different Character, shall be judged to contain something extraordinary either of *Wit* or *Sublime.*

AS for the Liberty I have thought fit to take of praising my self, upon some Occasions or none; I am sure it will need no Excuse, if a Multitude of great Examples be allowed sufficient Authority: For; it is here to be noted, that *Praise* was originally a Pension paid by the World; but the *Moderns* finding the Trouble and Charge too great in collecting it, have lately bought out the *Fee-Simple;* since which time, the Right of Presentation is wholly in our selves. For this Reason it is, that when an Author makes his own Elogy, he uses a certain Form to declare and insist upon his Title, which is commonly in these or the like words, *I speak without Vanity;* which I think plainly shows it to be a Matter of Right and Justice. Now, I do here once for all declare, that in every Encounter of this Nature, thro' the following Treatise, the Form aforesaid is imply'd; which I mention, to save the Trouble of repeating it on so many Occasions.

'TIS a great Ease to my Conscience that I have writ so elaborate and useful a Discourse without one grain of Satyr intermixt; which is the sole point wherein I have taken leave to dissent from the famous Originals of our Age and Country. I have Observ'd some Satyrists to use the Publick much at the rate that Pedants do a naughty Boy ready hors'd for Discipline; First expostulate the Case, then plead the Necessity of the Rod, from great Provocations, and conclude every Period with a Lash. Now, if I know any thing of Mankind, these Gentlemen might very well spare their Reproof and Correction: For, there is not through all Nature another so callous and insensible a Member as *the World's Posteriors*, whether you apply to it the *Toe* or the *Birch*. Besides, most of our late Satyrists seem to lye under a sort of Mistake, that because *Nettles* have the Prerogative to Sting, therefore all *other Weeds* must do so too. I make not this Comparison out of the least Design to detract from these worthy Writers: For it is well known among *Mythologists*, that *Weeds* have the Preeminence over all other Vegetables; and therefore the first *Monarch* of this Island, whose Taste and Judgment were so acute and refined, did very wisely root out the *Roses* from the Collar of *the Order*, and plant the *Thistles* in their stead, as the nobler Flower of the two. For which Reason it is conjectured by profounder Antiquaries, that the Satyrical Itch, so prevalent in this part of our Island, was first brought among us from beyond the *Tweed*. Here may it long flourish and abound; May it survive and neglect the Scorn of the World, with as much Ease and Contempt, as the World is insensible to the Lashes of it. May their own Dullness, or that of their Party, be no Discouragement for the Authors to proceed; but let them remember, it is with *Wits* as with *Razors*, which are never so apt to *cut* those they are employ'd on, as when they have *lost their Edge*. Besides, those whose Teeth are too rotten to bite, are best of all others qualified to revenge that Defect with their Breath.

I am not like other Men, to envy or undervalue the Talents I cannot reach; for which Reason I must needs bear a true Honor to this large eminent Sect of our *British* Writers. And I hope, this little Panegyrick will not be offensive to their Ears, since it has the Advantage of being only designed for themselves. Indeed, Nature her self has taken Order, that Fame and Honor should be purchased at a better Penyworth by Satyr, than by any other Productions of the Brain; the World being soonest provoked to *Praise* by *Lashes*, as Men are to *Love*. There is a Problem in an ancient Author, why Dedications, and other Bundles of Flattery run all upon stale musty Topicks, without the smallest Tincture of any thing New; not only to the torment and nauseating of the *Christian* Reader, but (if not suddenly prevented) to the universal spreading of that pestilent Disease, the Lethargy, in this Island: Whereas, there is very little Satyr which has not something in it untouch'd before, The Defects of the former are usually imputed to the want of Invention among those who are Dealers in that kind: But, I think, with a great deal of Injustice; the Solution being easy and natural. For, the Materials of Panegyrick being very few in Number, have been long since exhausted: For, as Health is but one Thing, and has been always the same, whereas Diseases are by thousands, besides new and daily Additions: So, all the Virtues that have been ever in Mankind, are to be counted upon a few Fingers, but his Follies and Vices are innumerable, and Time adds hourly to the Heap. Now, the utmost a poor Poet can do, is to get by heart a List of the Cardinal Virtues, and deal them with his utmost Liberality to his Hero or his Patron: He may ring the Changes as far as it will go, and vary his Phrase till he has talk'd round; but the Reader quickly finds, it is all *Pork, with a little variety of Sawce: For there is   * *Plutarch* no inventing Terms of Art beyond our Ideas; and when Ideas are exhausted, Terms of Art must be so too.

BUT, tho' the Matter for Panegyrick were as fruitful as the Topicks of Satyr, yet would it not be hard to find out a sufficient Reason, why the latter will be alway better received than the first. For, this being bestowed only upon one or a few Persons at a time, is sure to raise Envy, and consequently ill Words from the rest, who have no share in the Blessing: But Satyr being levelled at all, is never resented for an Offence by any, since every in-dividual Person makes bold to understand it of others, and very wisely removes his particular Part of the Burthen upon the Shoulders of the World, which are broad enough, and able to bear it. To this purpose, I have sometimes reflected upon the Difference between *Athens*   * *Vid. Xenophon* and *England* with respect to the Point before us. In the *Attick* *Commonwealth, it was the Privilege and Birth-right of every Citizen and Poet, to rail aloud and in publick, or to expose upon the Stage by Name, any Person they pleased, tho' of the greatest Figure, whether a *Creon*, an *Hyperbolus*, an *Alcibiades*, or a *Demosthenes*: But on the other side, the least reflecting Word let fall against the *People* in general, was immediately caught up, and revenged upon the Authors, however considerable for their Quality or their Merits. Whereas, in *England* it is just the Reverse of all this. Here, you may securely display your utmost *Rhetorick* against Mankind, in the Face of the World; tell them, "*That all are gone astray; That there is none that doth good, no not one; That we live in the very Dregs of Time; That Knavery and Atheism "are Epidemick as the Pox; That Honesty is fled with Astræa*"; with any other Common Places *equally* new and eloquent, which are furnished

† *Hor.*   by the †*Splendida bilis.* And when you have done, the whole Audience, far from from being offended, shall return you Thanks, as a Deliverer of precious and useful Truths. Nay further; It is but to venture your Lungs, and you may Preach in *Covent-Garden* against Foppery and Fornication, and *something else.* Against Pride, and Dissimulation, and Bribery, at *White Hall:* You may expose Rapine and Injustice in the *Inns* of *Court* Chapel: And in a *City* Pulpit be as fierce as you please, against Avarice, Hypocrisy and Extortion. 'Tis but a *Ball* bandied to and fro, and every Man carries a *Racket* about Him to strike it from himself among the rest of the Company. But on the other side, whoever should mistake the Nature of things so far, as to drop but a single Hint in publick, How *such a one* starved half the Fleet, and half-poyson'd the rest: How *such a one*, from a true Principle of *Love* and *Honor*, pays no Debts but for *Wenches* and *Play:* How *such a one* has got a Clap, and runs out of his Estate: How *Paris* bribed by ¶*Juno* and *Venus*, loath to offend either Party, slept out the whole Cause on the Bench: Or, how *such an Orator* makes long Speeches in the Senate with much Thought, little Sense, and to no Purpose. Whoever, I say, should venture to be thus particular, must expect to be imprisoned for *Scandalum Magnatum;* to have *Challenges* sent him; to be sued for Defamation; and to be *brought before the Bar of the House.*

BUT, I forget that I am expatiating on a Subject, wherein I have no Concern, having neither a Talent nor an Inclination for Satyr; On the other side, I am so entirely satisfied with the whole present Procedure of human Things, that I have been for some Years preparing Materials towards *A Panegyrick upon the World;* to which I intended to add a Second Part, entitled, *A Modest Defence of the Proceedings of the Rabble in all Ages.* Both these I had Thoughts to publish by way of Appendix to the following Treatise; but finding my Common-Place-Book fill much slower than I had reason to expect, I have chosen to defer them to another Occasion. Besides, I have been unhappily prevented in that Design by a certain Domestick Misfortune, in the Particulars whereof, tho' it would be very seasonable, and much in the *Modern* way, to inform the *gentle Reader,* and would also be of great Assistance towards extending this Preface into the Size now in Vogue, which by Rule ought to be *large* in proportion as the subsequent Volume is *small;* Yet I shall now dismiss our impatient Reader from any further Attendance at the *Porch;* and having duly prepared his Mind by a preliminary Discourse, shall gladly introduce him to the sublime Mysteries that ensue.

† *Spleen*
¶ Juno *and* Venus *are Money and a Mistress, very powerful Bribes to a Judge, if Scandal says true. I remember such Reflexions were cast about that time, but I cannot fix the Person intended here.*

A
TALE
OF A
TUB, &c.

SECT. I

THE INTRODUCTION

WHOEVER hath an Ambition to be heard in a Crowd, must press, and squeeze, and thrust, and climb with indefatigable Pains, till he has exalted himself to a certain Degree of Altitude above them. Now, in all Assemblies, tho' you wedge them ever so close, we may observe this peculiar Property; that, over their Heads there is Room enough; but how to reach it, is the difficult Point; It being as hard to get quit of *Number* as of *Hell*;

* ———— *Evadere ad auras,*
Hoc opus, hic labor est.

TO this End, the Philosopher's Way in all Ages has been by erecting certain *Edifices in the Air;* But, whatever Practice and Reputation these kind of Structures have formerly possessed, or may still continue in; not excepting even that of *Socrates,* when he was suspended in a Basket to help Contemplation; I think, with due Submission, they seem to labor under two Inconveniencies. First, That the Foundations being laid too high, they have been often out of *Sight,* and ever out of *Hearing.* Secondly, that the Materials being very transitory, have suffered much from Inclemencies of Air, especially in these North-West Regions.

THEREFORE, towards the just Performance of this great Work, there remain but three Methods that I can think on; Whereof the Wisdom of our Ancestors being highly sensible, has, to encourage all aspiring Adventurers, thought fit to erect three wooden Machines; for the Use of those Orators who desire to talk much without Interruption. These are, the *Pulpit,* the *Ladder,* and the *Stage-Itinerant.* For, as to the *Bar,* tho' it be compounded of the same Matter, and designed for the same Use, it cannot however be well

---

* *But to return, and view the cheerful Skies; In this the Task and mighty Labour lies.*

allowed the Honor of a fourth, by reason of its level or inferior Situation, exposing it to perpetual Interruption from Collaterals. Neither can the *Bench* it self, tho' raised to a proper Eminency, put in a better Claim, whatever its Advocats insist on. For if they please to look into the original Design of its Erection, and the Circumstances or Adjuncts subservient to that Design, they will soon acknowledge the present Practice exactly correspondent to the Primitive Institution, and both to answer the Etymology of the Name, which in the *Phœnician* Tongue is a Word of great Signification, importing, if literally interpreted, *The Place of Sleep*; but in common Acceptation, *A Seat well bolster'd and cushion'd, for the Repose of old and gouty Limbs: Senes ut in otia tuta recedant.* Fortune being indebted to them this Part of Retaliation, that, as formerly, they have long *Talkt,* whilst others *Slept,* so now they may *Sleep* as long whilst others *Talk.*

BUT if no other Argument could occur to exclude the *Bench* and the *Bar* from the List of Oratorial Machines, it were sufficient, that the Admission of them would overthrow a Number which I was resolved to establish whatever Argument it might cost me; In imitation of that prudent Method observed by many other Philosophers and great Clerks, whose chief Art in Division has been, to grow fond of some proper mystical Number, which their Imaginations have rendered Sacred, to a Degree, that they force common Reason to find room for it in every part of Nature; reducing, including, and adjusting every *Genus* and *Species* within that Compass, by coupling some against their Wills, and banishing others at any Rate. Now, among all the rest, the profound Number *THREE* is that which hath most employ'd my sublimest Speculations, nor ever without wonderful Delight. There is now in the Press, (and will be publish'd next Term) a Panegyrical Essay of mine upon this Number, wherein I have by most convincing Proofs, not only reduced the *Senses* and the *Elements* under its Banner, but brought over several Deserters from its two great Rivals *SEVEN* and *NINE.*

NOW, the first of these Oratorial Machines in Place as well as Dignity, is the *Pulpit* (Plate 6). Of *Pulpits* there are in this Island several sorts; but I esteem only That made of Timber from the *Sylva Caledoniæ,* which agrees very well with our Climate. If it be upon its Decay, 'tis the better, both for Conveyance of Sound, and for other Reasons to be mentioned by and by. The Degree of Perfection in Shape and Size, I take to consist, in being extremely narrow, with little Ornament, and best of all without a Cover; (for by ancient Rule, it ought to be the only uncover'd *Vessel* in every Assembly where it is rightfully used) by which means, from its near Resemblance to a Pillory, it will ever have a mighty Influence on human Ears.

OF *Ladders* (Plate 8) I need say nothing: 'Tis observed by Foreiners themselves, to the Honor of our Country, that we excel all Nations in our

Plate 6

A True ACCOUNT of the

BEHAVIOUR, CONFESSION,

AND

Laſt Dying SPEECHES

Of the 15 Criminals that were Executed

On *Monday* the 22th of *December*, 1690.

The Ordinary viſited them every day after their Condemnation, and on the laſt Lord's Day a Sermon was preached to them, on this Text, *Deut* 32. 29. *O that they were wiſe, that they underſtood this, that they would conſider their latter end.*

Whence five things were obſervable, 1. The Benefit and Advantage of a Religious Conſideration in general. 2. The no leſs advantagious Benefit of conſidering our latter end in particular. 3. That to conſider our latter end, is an Argument of our Wiſdom and Underſtanding. 4. Some Seaſons and particular Occaſions were inſtanced wherein conſideration of our Latter End is more eſpecially neceſſary. 5. That Diſcourſe was concluded with ſome Motives for the putting in practice this important Duty, then a Charge given to the Condemned as follows.

O that you were wiſe, that you underſtood this, that you would conſider your latter end.

I know you do conſider it in one ſenſe, that is, your minds are in continual fearful Apprehenſion of it, but this is not that conſidering of your latter end, which the Text exhorts to, this is the minding in ſuch ſort their Deaths and Departures, as to prepare and make ready for them.

O that I may dye the death of the righteous, is the ardent Wiſh of every one; but O that I may live the Life of the Righteous of how very few. Sirs, deceive not your ſelves, there is no having your latter End like the Righteous Man, but only by having your precedent Life like his.

What? Will not you conſider your latter end, ſo as to prepare for it, who have it in ſo near a view, and Death ſtares you in the face, and is yet you unprovided againſt it?

O certainly it is your Wiſdom, it is your Underſtanding, to conſider the things belonging to your everlaſting Peace, before they be for ever hid from your Eyes. How utterly inexcuſable will you be, if you do not, to morrow, to morrow my Friends will be the latter end as to this Life. O that to morrow may be the beginning of an Eternity in Bleſſedneſs unto you.

Take care therefore that they be in a due Qualification for Heaven and Happineſs : take heed that they be meet to be partakers of the Inheritance of the Saints in Light and Glory.

This Life is the only State of Tryal and Probation, there is no amending in the other World what was left delicate in this Work of Converſation, at our departure out of this.

Therefore let us now give all Diligence to make our Calling and Election ſure, let us work out our Salvation with a cautious Fear and Trembling, leſt our Contrition be imperfect, and our Repentance unſincere.

O bleſſed God ! is this the buſineſs you are imployed about for an endleſs Eternity, and can you be too careful concerning it? Think not a few Tears, and Lord have Mercy on me, to be Repentance. This is not ſo cheap and eaſy a performance, eſpecially when there is a whole courſe of Life of wickedneſs to be repented of. Oh, no! it imports all the painful Throws and Pangs of of a ſecond Birth, of a life of Regeneration. It imports a broken and contrite Heart, an Hatred and Deteſtation of Sin, as well as a Sorrow for it. Sincere and ſtedfaſt Reſolution of new Obedience, yea, an actual ceaſing to do evil, and learning to do well. And, oh ! may your Repentance be ſuch ! may it be a repenting you

more that you have offended a good and gracious God by your Impieties, than that theſe have expoſed you to condign temporal Puniſhment.

O cauſe you new Joy in Heaven by your Repentance, as you have formerly grieved, quenched, and offered diſpight to Gods Holy Spirit by your obſtinately wicked and impenitent Lives. Think it not enough to ſay within your ſelves, We have an Advocate with the Father, Jeſus Chriſt the Righteous, for he is no Propitiation for your Sins, unleſs you truly repent and forſake them. The Redemption purchaſed by our Saviour, and the Promiſes of his Goſpel, belong not to you, if you have not the Qualifications of Redeemed ones, nor the performed Conditions of the Goſpel-promiſes, viz. Truth Faith, Repentance and Amendment: Without Holineſs there is no Happineſs without beholding Gods Face in Righteouſneſs here, there is no beholding that in Glory hereafter. And therefore ſee that you have a Divine and Holy Nature implanted in you in this Life, and then departing hence, meetly diſpoſed for eternal bleſſedneſs, when at the Reſurrection from the Dead you awake up, after Gods likeneſs, you ſhall be endleſly ſatisfied therewith.

I ſhall proceed to give an account of the condemned Criminals, as to their former courſe of Life, and in what frame of Heart they were for a bleſſed Eternity.

1. *John Bennet* alias *Freeman,* but more notoriouſly known by the name of the GOLDEN FARMER, condemned for the Murther of *Charles Teffer,* and ſeveral Robberies, to the value of ſome thouſand Pounds. I was with him ſeveral times in his Chamber, and exhorted him to disburthen his Conſcience, by a free Confeſſion of his Evil Courſes, yet after much Advice for his Souls Welfare, and many Prayers that God would work his Heart to Repentance, nothing more than what follows could be obtained: That he had been a great Sinner, and was guilty of moſt Sins. That he was not ſo much grieved for the Shame of this condign Puniſhment, as for offending God. And that he was not ſolicitous to lengthen out his Life upon Earth, but to get his Pardon ſealed in Heaven. He ſhed many Tears, yet ſaid, That he truſted only in Chriſt's Righteouſneſs for Pardon and Peace in Conſcience. He was exhorted chiefly to be deeply humbled for the Murther he had committed, and upon reading to him *David's* Penitential Prayer, in theſe Words, *Deliver me from Bloodguiltineſs O God, and my tongue ſhall ſing of thy righteouſneſs,* he gave ſome Signs of great Remorſe; yet I told him, That his Tears could not expiate his great Provocations of God, for they ſtood in need of cleanſing by the Merit and Efficacy of Chriſt's Blood ſhed. This he acknowledged. Then I endeavoured to make him more ſenſible, offering Violence to the Dictates of his own Conſcience, before he could ſo long proceed in the wicked Trade of Robbing, and putting many Perſons into affrightment of loſing their Lives: He did acknowledge this Crime, whereupon I exhorted him to make Reſtitution to the utmoſt, of what remained in his Hands, otherwiſe his Repentance could not be ſincere : He thought this to be ſtrange Doctrine, whereas, he ſaid, he dyed for robbing. I told him, that he paid his Life to the Juſtice of the Law, it made no Satisfaction nor Recompence to thoſe he had deſpoil'd of their Eſtates. And added farther, That he ſhould not content that his former Supplies of the Wants of the Poor was any

Practice and Understanding of this Machine. The ascending Orators do not only oblige their Audience in the agreeable Delivery, but the whole World in the *early* Publication of these Speeches; which I look upon as the choicest Treasury of our *British* Eloquence (Plate 7), and whereof I am informed, that worthy Citizen and Bookseller, Mr. *John Dunton,* hath made a faithful and a painful Collection, which he shortly designs to publish in Twelve Volumes in Folio, illustrated with Copper-Plates. A Work highly useful and curious, and altogether worthy of such a Hand.

THE last Engine of Orators, is the *Stage Itinerant (Plate 5), erected with much Sagacity, †*sub Jove pluvio, in triviis & quadriviis.* It is the great Seminary of the two former, and its Orators are sometimes preferred to the One, and sometimes to the Other, in proportion to their Deservings, there being a strict and perpetual Intercourse between all three.

FROM this accurate Deduction it is manifest that for obtaining Attention in Publick, there is of necessity required *a superior Position of Place.* But, altho' this Point be generally granted, yet the Cause is little agreed in; and it seems to me, that very few Philosophers have fallen into a true, natural Solution of this *Phænomenon.* The deepest Account, and the most fairly digested of any I have yet met with, is this, That Air being a heavy Body, and therefore (according to the System of *Epicurus) continually   * *Lucret.* descending, must needs be more so, when loaden and press'd   Lib.2, down by Words, which are also Bodies of much Weight and Gravity, as it is manifest from those deep *Impressions* they make and leave upon us; and therefore must be delivered from a due Altitude, or else they will neither carry a good Aim, nor fall down with a sufficient Force.

> * *Corpoream quoque enim vocem constare fatendum est,*
> *Et sonitum, quoniam possunt impellere Sensus.* Lucr. *Lib.* 4.

AND I am the readier to favour this Conjecture, from a common Observation; that in the several Assemblies of these Orators, Nature it self hath instructed the Hearers, to stand with their Mouths open, and erected parallel to the Horizon, so as they may be intersected by a perpendicular Line from the Zenith to the Center of the Earth. In which Position, if the Audience be well compact, every one carries home a Share, and little or nothing is lost.

I confess, there is something yet more refined in the Contrivance and Structure of our Modern Theatres. For, First; the Pit is sunk below the Stage

---

* *Is the* Mountebank's Stage, *whose Orators the Author determines either to the* Gallows *or a* Conventicle.

† *In the open Air, and in Streets where the greatest Resort is.*

* *'Tis certain then, that* Voice *that thus can wound*
  Is all Material; Body *every* Sound.

with due regard to the Institution above deduced; that whatever *weighty* Matter shall be delivered thence (whether it be *Lead* or *Gold*) may fall plum into the Jaws of certain *Criticks* (as I think they are called) which stand ready open to devour them. Then, the Boxes are built round, and raised to a Level with the Scene, in deference to the Ladies, because, That large Portion of Wit laid out in raising Pruriences and Protuberances, is observ'd to run much upon a Line, and ever in a Circle. The whining Passions and little starved Conceits, are gently wafted up by their own extreme Levity, to the middle Region, and there fix and are frozen by the frigid Under-standings of the Inhabitants. Bombast and Buffoonry, by Nature lofty and light, soar highest of all, and would be lost in the Roof, if the prudent Architect had not with much Foresight contrived for them a fourth Place, called *the Twelve-Peny Gallery*, and there planted a suitable Colony, who greedily intercept them in their Passage.

NOW this Physico-logical Scheme of Oratorial Receptacles or Machines, contains a great Mystery, being a Type, a Sign, an Emblem, a Shadow, a Symbol, bearing Analogy to the spatious Commonwealth of Writers, and to those Methods by which they must exalt themselves to a certain Eminency above the inferior World. By the *Pulpit* are adumbrated the Writings of our *Modern Saints* in *Great Britain*, as they have spiritualized and refined them from the Dross and Grossness of *Sense* and *Human Reason.* The Matter, as we have said, is of rotten Wood, and that upon two Considerations; Because it is the Quality of rotten Wood to give *Light* in the Dark: And secondly, Because its Cavities are full of Worms; which is a *Type with a Pair of Handles, having a Respect to the two principal Qualifications of the Orator, and the two different Fates attending upon his Works.

THE *Ladder* is an adequate Symbol of *Faction* and of *Poetry*, to both of which so noble a Number of Authors are indebted for their Fame. †Of *Faction*, because *   *   *   *   *   *   *   *   *   *

*   *   *   *   *   *   *   *   *   *

Hiatus in   *   *   *   *   *   *   *   *   *   *
     MS.   *   *   *   *   *   *   *   *   *   *

*   *   *   * Of *Poetry*, because its Orators do *perorare* with a Song; and because climbing up by slow Degrees, Fate is sure to turn them off before they can reach within many Steps of the Top: And because it is a

---

* *The Two Principal Qualifications of a Phanatick Preacher are, his Inward Light, and his Head full of Maggots, and the Two different Fates of his Writings are, to be burnt or Worm eaten.*

† *Here is pretended a Defect in the Manuscript, and this is very frequent with our Author, either when he thinks he cannot say any thing worth Reading, or when he has no mind to enter on the Subject, or when it is a Matter of little Moment, or perhaps to amuse his Reader (whereof he is frequently very fond) or lastly, with some Satyrical Intention.*

Plate 8

Gresham College.

Plate 9

Preferment attained by transferring of Propriety, and a confounding of *Meum* and *Tuum.*

UNDER the *Stage-itinerant* are couched those Productions designed for the Pleasure and Delight of Mortal Man; such as, *Six-peny-worth of Wit,* Westminster *Drolleries, Delightful Tales, Compleat Jesters,* and the like; by which the Writers of and for *GRUB-STREET,* have in these later Ages so nobly triumpht over *Time;* have clipt his Wings, pared his Nails, filed his Teeth, turn'd back his Hour-Glass, blunted his Scythe, and drawn the Hob-Nails out of his Shoes. It is under this Classis, I have presumed to list my present Treatise, being just come from having the Honor conferred upon me, to be adopted a Member of that Illustrious Fraternity.

NOW, I am not unaware, how the Productions of the *Grub-Street* Brotherhood, have of late Years fallen under many Prejudices; nor how it has been the perpetual Employment of two *Junior* start-up Societies, to ridicule them and their Authors, as unworthy their established Post in the Commonwealth of Wit and Learning. Their own Consciences will easily inform them, whom I mean; Nor has the World been so negligent a Looker on, as not to observe the continual Efforts made by the Societies of *Gresham* (Plate 9), and of ¶*Will's* to edify a Name and Reputation upon the Ruin of OURS. And this is yet a more feeling Grief to Us upon the Regards of Tenderness as well as of Justice, when we reflect on their Proceedings, not only as unjust, but as ungrateful, undutiful, and unnatural. For, how can it be forgot by the World or themselves, (to say nothing of our own Records, which are full and clear in the Point) that they both are Seminaries, not only of our *Planting,* but our W*atring* too? I am informed, Our two *Rivals* have lately made an Offer to enter into the Lists with united Forces, and challenge Us to a Comparison of Books, both as to *Weight* and *Number.* In Return to which, (with Licence from our *President*) I humbly offer two Answers: First, We say, the Proposal is like that which *Archimedes* made upon a *smaller Affair, including an Impossibility in the Practice; For, where can they find Scales of *Capacity* enough ** Viz. About moving the Earth.* for the first, or an Arithmetician of *Capacity* enough for the second. Secondly, We are ready to accept the Challenge, but with this Condition, that a third indifferent Person be assigned, to whose impartial Judgment it shall be left to decide, which Society each Book, Treatise or Pamphlet do most properly belong to. This point, God knows, is very far from being fixed at present; For, We, are ready to produce a Catalogue of some Thousands, which in all common Justice ought to be entitled to Our Fraternity, but by

¶ Will's Coffee-House, *was formerly the Place where the Poets usually met, which tho it be yet fresh in memory, yet in some Years may be forgot, and want this Explanation.*

the revolted and new-fangled Writers, most perfidiously ascribed to the others. Upon all which, we think it very unbecoming our Prudence, that the Determination should be remitted to the Authors themselves; when our Adversaries by Briguing and Caballing, have caused so universal a Defection from us, that the greatest Part of our Society hath already deserted to them, and our nearest Friends begin to stand aloof, as if they were half-ashamed to own Us.

THIS is the utmost I am authorized to say upon so ungrateful and melancholy a Subject; because We are extreme unwilling to inflame a Controversy, whose Continuance may be so fatal to the Interests of Us All, desiring much rather that Things be amicably composed, and We shall so far advance on our Side, as to be ready to receive the two *Prodigals* with open Arms, whenever they shall think fit to return from their *Husks* and their *Harlots*; which I think from the *present Course of their Studies they most properly may be said to be engaged in; and like an indulgent Parent, continue to them our Affection and our Blessing.

* Virtuoso Experiments, and Modern Comedies.

BUT the greatest Maim given to that general Reception, which the Writings of our Society have formerly received, next to the transitory State of all sublunary Things, hath been a superficial Vein among many Readers of the present Age, who will by no means be persuaded to inspect beyond the Surface and the Rind of Things; whereas, *Wisdom* is a *Fox*, who after long hunting, will at last cost you the Pains to dig out: 'Tis a *Cheese*, which by how much the richer, has the thicker, the homelier, and the courser Coat; and whereof to a judicious Palate, the *Maggots* are the best. 'Tis a *Sack-Posset*, wherein the deeper you go, you will find it the sweeter. *Wisdom* is a *Hen*, whose *Cackling* we must value and consider, because it is attended with an *Egg*; But then, lastly, 'tis a *Nut*, which unless you chuse with Judgment, may cost you a Tooth, and pay you with nothing but a *Worm*. In consequence of these momentous Truths, the *Grubæan* Sages have always chosen to convey their Precepts and their Arts, shut up within the Vehicles of Types and Fables, which having been perhaps more careful and curious in adorning, than was altogether necessary, it has fared with these Vehicles after the usual Fate of Coaches over-finely painted and gilt (Plate 10); that the transitory Gazers have so dazzled their Eyes, and fill'd their Imaginations with the outward Lustre, as neither to regard or consider, the Person or the Parts of the Owner within. A Misfortune we undergo with somewhat less Reluctancy, because it has been common to us with *Pythagoras, Æsop, Socrates*, and other of our Predecessors.

HOWEVER, that neither the World nor our selves may any longer suffer by such misunderstandings, I have been prevailed on, after much impor-

Plate 10

Plate 11

tunity from my Friends, to travel in a compleat and laborious Dissertation upon the prime Productions of our Society, which besides their beautiful Externals for the Gratification of superficial Readers, have darkly and deeply couched under them, the most finished and refined Systems of all Sciences and Arts; as I do not doubt to lay open by Untwisting or Unwinding, and either to draw up by Exantlation, or display by Incision.

THIS great work was entred upon some Years ago, by one of our most eminent Members: He began with the History of †*Reynard* the *Fox*, but neither lived to publish his Essay, nor to proceed further in so useful an Attempt, which is very much to be lamented, because the Discovery he made, and communicated with his Friends, is now universally received; Nor, do I think, any of the Learned will dispute, that famous Treatise to be a compleat Body of Civil Knowledge, and the *Revelation*, or rather, the *Apocalyps* of all State *Arcana*. But the Progress I have made is much greater, having already finished my Annotations upon several Dozens; From some of which, I shall impart a few Hints to the candid Reader, as far as will be necessary to the Conclusion at which I aim.

THE first Piece I have handled is that of *Tom Thumb*, whose Author was a *Pythagorean* Philosopher. This dark Treatise contains the whole Scheme of the *Metampsycosis*, deducing the Progress of the Soul thro' all her Stages.

THE next is Dr. *Faustus*, penn'd by *Artephius*, an Author *bonae notae*, and an *Adeptus*; He published it in the *nine hundred eighty-fourth Year of his Age; this Writer proceeds wholly by *Reincrudation*, or in the *via humida*: and the Marriage between *Faustus* and *Hellen*, does most conspicuously dilucidate the fermenting of the *Male* and *Female Dragon*.

* *He lived a thousand.*

WHITTINGTON *and his Cat*, is the Work of that Mysterious *Rabbi, Jehuda Hannasi*, containing a Defence of the *Guemara* of the *Jerusalem Misna*, and its just preference to that of *Babylon*, contrary to the vulgar Opinion.

THE *Hind and Panther*. This is the Master-piece of a famous Writer †now living, intended for a compleat Abstract of sixteen thousand Schoolmen from *Scotus* to *Bellarmin*.

† *Viz in the year 1697.*

TOMMY POTTS. Another Piece supposed by the same Hand, by way of Supplement to the former.

THE *Wise Men of* Gotham, *cum Appendice*. This is a Treatise of immense Erudition, being the great Original and Fountain of those Arguments, bandied about both in *France* and *England*, for a just Defence of the *Modern* Learning and Wit, against the Presumption, the Pride, and the Ignorance

---

† *The Author seems here to be mistaken, for I have seen a Latin Edition of* Reynard *the Fox* (Plate 11), *above an hundred Years old, which I take to be the Original; for the rest it has been thought by many People to contain some Satyrical Design in it.*

of the *Antients*. This unknown Author hath so exhausted the Subject, that a penetrating Reader will easily discover, whatever hath been written since upon that Dispute, to be little more than Repetition. *An Abstract of this Treatise hath been lately published by a *worthy Member* of our Society.

THESE Notices may serve to give the Learned Reader an Idea, as well as a Taste, of what the whole Work is likely to produce: wherein I have now altogether circumscribed my Thoughts and my Studies; and if I can bring it to a Perfection before I die, shall reckon I have well employ'd the †poor Remains of an unfortunate Life. This indeed is more than I can justly expect from a Quill worn to the Pith in the Service of the State, in *Pro's* and *Con's* upon *Popish Plots*, and ‖*Meal-Tubs*, and *Exclusion Bills*, and *Passive Obedience*, and *Addresses of Lives and Fortunes*; and *Prerogative*, and *Property*, and *Liberty of Conscience*, and *Letters to a Friend*: From an Understanding and a Conscience, thread-bare and ragged with perpetual turning; From a Head broken in a hundred places, by the Malignants of the opposite Factions, and from a Body spent with Poxes ill cured, by trusting to Bawds and Surgeons, who, (as it afterwards appeared) were profess'd Enemies to Me and the Government, and revenged their Party's Quarrel upon my Nose and Shins. Fourscore and eleven Pamphlets have I writ under three Reigns, and for the Service of six and thirty Factions. But finding the State has no farther Occasion for Me and my Ink, I retire willingly to draw it out into Speculations more becoming a Philosopher, having, to my unspeakable Comfort, passed a long Life, with a *Conscience void of Offence towards God and towards Man.*

BUT to return. I am assured from the Reader's Candor, that the brief Specimen I have given, will easily clear all the rest of our Society's Productions from an Aspersion grown, as it is manifest, out of Envy and Ignorance; That they are of little farther Use or Value to Mankind, beyond the common Entertainments of their Wit and their Style: For, these I am sure have never yet been disputed by our keenest Adversaries: In both which, as well as the more profound and mystical Part, I have throughout this Treatise closely followed the most applauded Originals. And to render all compleat, I have with much Thought and Application of Mind, so ordered, that the chief Title prefixed to it, (I mean, That under which I design it shall pass in the common Conversations of Court and Town) is modelled exactly after the Manner peculiar to *Our* Society.

---

* *This I suppose to be understood of Mr. W-tt-ns Discourse of Antient and Modern Learning.*

† *Here the Author seems to personate L'Estrange, Dryden, and some others, who after having past their Lives in Vices, Faction and Falshood, have the Impudence to talk of Merit and Innocence and Sufferings.*

‖ *In King* Charles *the* II. *Time, there was an Account of a* Presbyterian *Plot, found in a Tub, which then made much Noise.*

I confess to have been somewhat liberal in the Business of *Titles, having observed the Humor of multiplying them, to bear great Vogue among certain Writers, whom I exceedingly Reverence. And indeed, it seems not unreasonable, that

* The Title Page in the Original was so torn, that it was not possible to recover several Titles which the Author here speaks of.

Books, the Children of the Brain, should have the Honor to be Christned with variety of Names, as well as other Infants of Quality. Our famous *Dryden* has ventured to proceed a Point farther, endeavouring to introduce also a Multiplicity of *God-fathers*; which is an Improvement of much more Advantage, upon a very

* See Virgil *translated, &c.*

obvious Account. 'Tis a Pity this admirable Invention has not been better cultivated, so as to grow by this time into general Imitation, when such an Authority serves it for a Precedent. Nor have my Endeavours been wanting to second so useful an Example: But it seems, there is an unhappy Expence usually annexed to the Calling of a God-father, which was clearly out of my Head, as it is very reasonable to believe. Where the Pinch lay, I cannot certainly affirm; but having employ'd a World of Thoughts and Pains; to split my Treatise into forty Sections, and having entreated forty Lords of my Acquaintance, that they would do me the Honor to stand, they all made it a Matter of Conscience, and sent me their Excuses.

SECTION II.

ONCE upon a Time, there was a Man who had Three* Sons by one Wife, and all at a Birth, neither could the Mid-Wife tell certainly which was the Eldest. Their Father died while they were young, and upon his Death-Bed (Plate 12), calling the Lads to him, spoke thus,

SONS; *because I have purchased no Estate, nor was born to any, I have long considered of some good Legacies to bequeath You; And at last, with much Care as well as Expence, have provided each of you* (here they are) *a new † Coat. Now, you are to understand, that these Coats have two Virtues contained in them: One is, that with good wearing, they will last you fresh and sound as long as you live: The other is, that they will grow in the same Proportion with your Bodies, lengthning and widening of themselves, so as to be always fit. Here, let me see them on you before I die. So, very well, Pray Children, wear them clean, and brush them often. You will find in my* ¶ *Will* (here it is) *full Instructions in every particular concerning the Wearing and Management of your Coats; wherein you must be very exact, to avoid the Penalties I have appointed for every Transgression or Neglect, upon which your future Fortunes will entirely depend. I have also commanded in my Will, that you should live together in one House like Brethren and Friends, for then you will be sure to thrive, and not otherwise.*

HERE the Story says, this good Father died, and the three Sons went altogether to seek their Fortunes.

I shall not trouble you with recounting what Adventures they met for the first seven Years, any further than by taking notice, that they carefully observed their Father's Will, and kept their Coats in very good Order; That they travelled thro' several Countries, encountred a reasonable Quantity of Gyants, and slew certain Dragons.

BEING now arrived at the proper Age for producing themselves, they came up to Town, and fell in love with the Ladies, but especially three, who about that time were in chief Reputation: The ‖Dutchess *d'Argent, Madame de Grands Titres,* and the Countess *d'Orgueil.* On their first Appearance, our three Adventurers met with a very bad Reception; and soon with great

---

* *By these three sons,* Peter, Martyn *and* Jack; Popery, *the* Church *of* England, *and our Protestant* Dissenters *are designed.* W. Wotton.

† *By his Coats which he gave his Sons, the Garments of the* Israelites. W. Wotton.
An Error (with Submission) of the learned Commentator; for by the Coats are meant the Doctrine and Faith of Christianity, *by the Wisdom of the Divine Founder fitted to all Times, Places and Circumstances.* Lambin.

¶ *The New Testament.*

‖ *Their Mistresses are the* Dutchess d'Argent, Madamoiselle de Grands Titres, *and the* Countess d'Orgueil, *i.e.* Covetousness, Ambition, *and* Pride, *which were the three great Vices that the ancient Fathers inveighed against as the first Corruptions of Christianity.* W. Wotton.

Plate 12

Sagacity guessing out the Reason, they quickly began to improve in the good Qualities of the Town: They Writ, and Raillyed, and Rhymed, and Sung, and Said, and said Nothing: They Drank, and Fought, and Whor'd, and Slept, and Swore, and took Snuff: They went to new Plays on the first Night, haunted the *Chocolate*-Houses, beat the Watch, lay on Bulks, and got Claps: They bilkt Hackney-Coachmen, ran in Debt with Shop-keepers, and lay with their Wives: They kill'd Bayliffs, kick'd Fidlers down Stairs, eat at *Locket's*, loytered at *Will's*: They talk'd of the Drawing-Room and never came there, Dined with Lords they never saw; Whisper'd a Dutchess, and spoke never a Word; exposed the Scrawls of their Laundress for Billets-doux of Quality; came ever just from Court and were never seen in it; attended the Levee *sub dio*; Got a list of the Peers by heart in one Company, and with great Familiarity retailed them in another. Above all, they constantly attended those Committees of Senators who are silent in the *House*, and loud in the *Coffee-House*, where they nightly adjourn to chew the Cud of Politicks, and are encompass'd with a Ring of Disciples, who lye in wait to catch up their Droppings. The three Brothers had acquired fourty other Qualifications of the like Stamp, too tedious to recount, and by consequence, were justly reckoned the most accomplish'd Persons in Town: But all would not suffice, and the Ladies aforesaid continued still inflexible: To clear up which Difficulty, I must with the Reader's good Leave and Patience, have recourse to some Points of Weight, which the Authors of that Age have not sufficiently illustrated.

FOR, about this Time it happened, a Sect arose, whose Tenents obtained and spread very far, especially in the *Grand Monde*, and among every Body of good *Fashion. They worshipped a sort of ‖*Idol*, who, as their Doctrine delivered, did daily create Men, by a kind of Manufactury Operation. This Idol they placed in the highest Parts of the House, on an Altar erected about three Foot: He was shewn in the Posture of a *Persian* Emperor, sitting on a *Superficies*, with his Legs interwoven under him. This God had a *Goose* for his Ensign; whence it is, that some Learned Men pretend to deduce his Original from *Jupiter Capitolinus*. At his left Hand, beneath the Altar, *Hell* seemed to open, and catch at the Animals the *Idol* was creating; to prevent which, certain of his Priests hourly flung in Pieces of the uninformed Mass, or Substance, and sometimes whole Limbs already enlivened, which that horrid Gulph insatiably swallowed, terrible to behold. The *Goose* was also held a Subaltern Divinity, or *Deus minorum gentium*, before whose Shrine was sacrificed that Creature, whose hourly

---

* *This is an Occasional Satyr upon Dress and Fashion, in order to introduce what follows.*
‖ *By this* Idol *is meant a Taylor.*

Food is Human Gore, and who is in so great Renown abroad, for being the Delight and Favourite of the †*Ægyptian Cercopithecus*. Millions of these Animals were cruelly slaughtered every Day, to appease the Hunger of that consuming Deity. The chief *Idol* was also worshipped as the Inventor of the *Yard* and the *Needle*, whether as the God of Seamen, or on Account of certain other mystical Attributes, hath not been sufficiently cleared.

THE Worshippers of this Deity had also a System of their Belief, which seemed to turn upon the following Fundamental. They held the Universe to be a large *Suit of Cloaths*, which *invests* every Thing: That the Earth is *invested* by the Air; The Air is *invested* by the Stars; and the Stars are *invested* by the *Primum Mobile*. Look on this Globe of Earth, you will find it to be a very compleat and fashionable *Dress*. What is that which some call *Land*, but a fine Coat faced with Green? or the Sea, but a Wastcoat of Water-Tabby? Proceed to the particular Works of the Creation, you will find how curious a *Journey-man* Nature hath been, to trim up the *vegetable* Beaux: Observe how sparkish a Perewig adorns the Head of a *Beech*, and what a fine Doublet of white Satin is worn by the *Birch*. To conclude from all, what is Man himself but a *Micro-Coat, or rather a compleat Suit of Cloaths with all its Trimmings? As to his Body, there can be no Dispute; but examine even the Acquirements of his Mind, you will find them all contribute in their Order, towards furnishing out an exact Dress: To instance no more; Is not Religion a *Cloak*, Honesty a *Pair of Shoes*, worn out in the Dirt, Self love a *Surtout*, Vanity a *Shirt*, and Conscience a *Pair of Breeches*, which, tho' a Cover for Lewdness as well as Nastiness, is easily slipt down for the Service of both.

THESE P*ostulata* being admitted, it will follow in due course of Reasoning, that those Beings which the World calls improperly *Suits of Cloaths*, are in Reality the most refined Species of Animals, or to proceed higher, that they are Rational Creatures, or Men. For, is it not manifest, that They live, and move, and talk, and perform all other Offices of Human Life? Are not Beauty, and Wit, and Mien, and Breeding, their inseparable Proprieties? In short, we see nothing but them, hear nothing but them. Is it not they who walk the Streets, fill up *Parliament-, Coffee-, Play-, Bawdy-houses?* 'Tis true indeed, that these Animals, which are vulgarly called *Suits of Cloaths*, or *Dresses*, do according to certain Compositions receive different Appellations. If one of them be trimm'd up with a Gold Chain, and a red Gown, and a white Rod, and a great Horse, it is called a *Lord Mayor;* If certain Ermines and Furs be placed in a certain Position, we stile them a

---

† *The Ægyptians worship'd a Monkey, which Animal is very fond of eating Lice, styled here Creatures that feed on Human Gore.*
* *Alluding to the Word* Microcosm, *or a little World, as Man hath been called by Philosophers.*

Judge, and so, an apt Conjunction of Lawn and black Satin, we entitle a *Bishop*.

OTHERS of these Professors tho' agreeing in the main System, were yet more refined upon certain Branches of it; and held, that Man was an Animal compounded of two *Dresses*, the *Natural* and the *Celestial Suit*, which were the Body and the Soul: That the Soul was the outward, and the Body the inward Cloathing; that the latter was *ex traduce*, but the former of daily Creation and Circumfusion. This last they proved by *Scripture*, because, *in Them we Live, and Move, and have our Being*; As likewise by Philosophy, because they are *All in All, and All in every Part*. Besides, said they; Separate these two, and you will find the Body to be only a sensless unsavory Carcass. By all which it is manifest, that the outward Dress must needs be the Soul.

TO this System of Religion were tagged several subaltern Doctrines, which were entertained with great Vogue; as particularly, the Faculties of the Mind were deduced by the Learned among them in this manner: *Embroidery*, was *Sheer wit*; *Gold Fringe* was *agreeable Conversation*, *Gold Lace* was *Repartee*, a huge long *Perewig* was *Humor*, and a *Coat full of Powder* was very good *Raillery*: All which required abundance of *Finesse* and *Delicatesse* to manage with Advantage, as well as a strict Observance after Times and Fashions.

I have with much Pains and Reading, collected out of antient Authors, this short Summary of a Body of Philosophy and Divinity, which seems to have been composed by a Vein and Race of Thinking, very different from any other Systems, either *Antient* or *Modern*. And it was not meerly to entertain or satisfy the Reader's Curiosity, but rather to give him Light into several Circumstances of the following Story: that knowing the State of Dispositions and Opinions in an Age so remote, he may better comprehend those great Events which were the Issue of them. I advise therefore the courteous Reader, to peruse with a world of Application, again and again, whatever I have written upon this Matter. And so leaving these broken Ends, I carefully gather up the chief Thread of my Story, and proceed.

THESE Opinions therefore were so universal, as well as the Practices of them, among the refined Part of Court and Town, that our three Brother-Adventurers, as their Circumstances then stood, were strangely at a loss. For, on the one side, the three Ladies they address'd themselves to, (whom we have named already) were ever at the very Top of the Fashion, and abhorred all that were below it, but the breadth of a Hair. On the other side, their Father's Will was very precise, and it was the main Precept in it, with the greatest Penalties annexed, not to add to, or diminish from their Coats, one Thread, without a positive Command in the Will. Now, the Coats their Father had left them were, 'tis true, of very good Cloath, and besides, so neatly sown, you would swear they were all of a Piece, but at the same time, very plain, and with little or no Ornament; And it happened, that before they were a Month in Town, great *Shoulder-knots came up: Strait, all the World was *Shoulder-knots*; no approaching the Ladies *Ruelles* without the *Quota* of *Shoulder-knots: That Fellow*, cries one, *has no Soul; where is his Shoulder-knot?* Our three Brethren soon discovered their Want by sad Experience, meeting in their Walks, with forty Mortifications and Indignities. If they went to the *Play-house*, the Door-keeper shewed them into the Twelvepeny Gallery. If they called a Boat, says a Water-man, *I am first Sculler:* If they stept to the *Rose* to take a Bottle, the Drawer would cry, *Friend we sell no Ale.* If they went to visit a Lady, a Footman met them at the Door with, *Pray send up your Message.* In this unhappy Case, they went immediately to consult their Father's Will (Plate 13), read it over and over, but not a Word of the *Shoulder-knot.* What should they do? What Temper should they find? Obedience was absolutely necessary, and yet *Shoulder-knots* appeared extreamly requisite. After much Thought, one of the Brothers who happened to be more *Book-learned* than the other two, said he had found an Expedient. *'Tis true*, said he, *there is nothing here in this Will,* †totidem verbis, *making mention of* Shoulder-knots, *but I dare conjecture, we may find them* inclusivè, *or* totidem syllabis. This Distinction was immediately approved by all; and so they fell again to examine the Will. But their evil Star had so directed the Matter, that the first Syllable was not to be found in the whole Writing. Upon which Disappointment, he, who found the former Evasion, took heart, and said, *Brothers, there is yet Hopes; for tho' we cannot find them* totidem verbis, *nor* totidem syllabis, *I dare engage we shall make them out*, tertio modo, *or* totidem literis. This Discovery was also highly commended, upon which they fell

The first part of the Tale *is the History of* Peter; *thereby* Popery *is exposed, every Body knows the* Papists *have made great Additions to Christianity, that indeed is the great Exception which the* Church of England *makes against them, accordingly* Peter *begins his Pranks, with adding a* Shoulder-knot *to his Coat.* W. Wotton.

His Description of the Cloth of which the Coat was made, *has a farther meaning than the Words may seem to import,* "The Coats their Father had left them, were of very good Cloth, and besides so neatly Sown, you would swear it had been all of a Piece, but at the same time very plain with little or no Ornament. *This is the distinguishing Character of the Christian Religion.* Christiana Religio absoluta & simplex, *was* Ammianus Marcellinus's *Description of it, who was himself a Heathen.* W. Wotton.

* By this is understood the first introducing of Pageantry, and unnecessary Ornaments in the Church, *such as were neither for Convenience nor Edification, as a* Shoulder-knot, *in which there is neither Symmetry nor Use.*

† When the Papists cannot find any thing which they want in Scripture, they go to Oral Tradition: *Thus* Peter *is introduced dissatisfy'd with the Tedious way of looking for all the Letters of any Word, which he has occasion for in the* Will, *when neither the constituent Syllables, nor much less the whole Word, were there* in Terminis. W. Wotton.

Plate 13

once more to the Scrutiny, and soon pickt out S,H,O,U,L,D,E,R; when the same Planet, Enemy to their Repose, had wonderfully contrived, that a K was not to be found. Here was a weighty Difficulty! But the distinguishing Brother (for whom we shall hereafter find a Name) now his Hand was in, proved by a very good Argument, that *K* was a modern illegitimate Letter, unknown to the Learned Ages, nor any where to be found in ancient Manuscripts. 'Tis true, said he, the Word *Calendæ* hath in †Q.V.C. been sometimes writ with a *K,* but erroneously, for in the best Copies it is ever spelt with a *C.* And by consequence it was a gross Mistake in our Language to spell *Knot* with a *K,* but that from henceforward, he would take care it should be writ with a *C.* Upon this, all farther Difficulty vanished; *Shoulder-knots* were made clearly out, to be *Jure Paterno,* and our three Gentlemen swaggered with as large and as flanting ones as the best.

> † Quibusdam Veteribus Codicibus.

BUT, as human Happiness is of a very short Duration, so in those Days were human Fashions, upon which it entirely depends. *Shoulder-knots* had their Time, and we must now imagine them in their Decline; for a certain Lord came just from *Paris,* with fifty Yards of *Gold Lace* upon his Coat, exactly trimm'd after the Court Fashion of *that Month.* In two Days all Mankind appeared closed up in Bars of ¶*Gold Lace.* Whoever durst peep abroad without his Compliment of *Gold Lace,* was as scandalous as a —, and as ill received among the Women. What should our three Knights do in this momentous Affair; They had sufficiently strained a Point already, in the Affair of *Shoulder-knots:* Upon Recourse to the Will, nothing appeared there but *altum silentium.* That of the *Shoulder-knots* was a loose, flying, circumstantial Point; but this of *Gold Lace,* seemed too considerable an Alteration without better Warrant; it did *aliquo modo essentiæ adhærere,* and therefore required a positive Precept. But about this time it fell out, that the learned Brother aforesaid, had read *Aristotelis Dialectica,* and especially that wonderful Piece *de Interpretatione,* which has the Faculty of teaching its Readers to find out a Meaning in every Thing but itself; like Commentators on the *Revelations,* who proceed Prophets without understanding a Syllable of the Text. *Brothers,* said he, **You are to be informed, that of Wills* duo sunt genera, †*Nuncupatory and Scriptory; that in the Scriptory Will here before us, there is no Precept or Mention about Gold Lace,* conceditur: *But,* si idem affirmetur de nuncupatorio, negatur, *For Brothers, if you remember, we heard a Fellow say when*

¶ *I cannot tell whether the Author means any new Innovation by this Word, or whether it be only to introduce the new Methods of forcing and perverting Scripture.*

* *The next Subject of our Author's Wit, is the Glosses and Interpretations of Scripture, very many absurd ones of which are allow'd in the most Authentick Books of the* Church of Rome. W. Wotton.

† *By this is meant* Tradition, *allowed to have equal Authority with the Scripture, or rather greater.*

we were Boys, that he heard my Father's Man say, that he heard my Father say, that he would advise his Sons to get Gold Lace *on their Coats, as soon as ever they could procure Money to buy it. By G—, that is very true,* cries the other; *I remember it perfectly well,* said the third. And so without more ado they got the largest *Gold Lace* in the Parish, and walkt about as fine as Lords.

A while after, there came up *all in Fashion,* a pretty sort of [1] *flame- coloured Satin* for Linings, and the *Mercer* brought a Pattern of it immediately to our three Gentlemen. *An please your Worships,* (said he) [II] My Lord C ——, *and Sir* J. W. *had Linings out of this very Piece last Night; it takes wonderfully, and I shall not have a Remnant left, enough to make my Wife a Pin-cushion by to morrow Morning at ten a Clock.* Upon this, they fell again to romage the Will, because the present Case also required a positive Precept, the Lining being held by Orthodox Writers to be of the Essence of the Coat. After long search, they could fix upon nothing to the Matter in hand, except a short Advice of their Father's in the Will, [††] to take Care of *Fire,* and put out their *Candles* before they went to Sleep. This tho' a good deal for the Purpose, and helping very far towards Self-Conviction, yet not seeming wholly of Force to establish a Command; and being resolved to avoid farther Scruple, as well as future Occasion for Scandal, says He that was the Scholar; *I remember to have read in Wills, of a Codicil annexed, which is indeed a Part of the Will, and what it contains hath equal Authority with the rest. Now, I have been considering of this same Will here before us, and I cannot reckon it to be compleat for want of such a Codicil. I will therefore fasten one in its proper Place very dexterously; I have had it by me some Time, it was written by a ** Dog-keeper of my Grand-father's, and talks a great deal (as good Luck would have it) of this very flame-colour'd Sattin.* The Project was immediately approved by the other two; an old Parchment Scrowl was tagged on according to Art, in the Form of a *Codicil annexed,* and the *Sattin* bought and worn.

[1] *This is Purgatory, whereof he speaks more particularly hereafter, but here only to shew how Scripture was perverted to prove it, which was done by giving equal Authority with the* Canon *to* Apocrypha, *called here a* Codicil *annex'd. It is likely the Author, in every one of these Changes in the Brother's Dresses, refers to some particular Error in the* Church *of* Rome; *tho' it is not easy I think to apply them all, but by this of* Flame Colour'd Satin *is manifestly intended* Purgatory; *by* Gold Lace *may perhaps be understood, the lofty Ornaments and Plate in the Churches, The* Shoulder-Knots *and* Silver Fringe, *are not so obvious, at least to me; but the* Indian *Figures of Men, Women and Children plainly relate to the Pictures in the Romish Churches, of God like an old Man, of the Virgin* Mary *and our Saviour as a Child.*

[II] *This shews the Time the Author writ, it being about fourteen Years since those two Persons were reckoned the fine Gentlemen of the Town.*

[††] *That is, to take care of Hell, and, in order to do that, to subdue and extinguish their Lusts.*

[**] *I believe this refers to that part of the* Apocrypha *where mention is made of* Tobit *and his* Dog.

NEXT Winter, a *Player*, hired for the Purpose by the Corporation of
Fringe-makers, acted his Part in a new Comedy, all covered with †*Silver Fringe*,
and according to the laudable Custom gave Rise to that Fashion. Upon
which, the Brothers consulting their Father's Will, to their great Astonish-
ment found these Words: Item, *I charge and command my said three Sons, to
wear no sort of* Silver Fringe *upon or about their said Coats*, &c. with a Penalty in
case of Disobedience, too long here to insert. However, after some Pause
the Brother so often mentioned for his Erudition, who was well Skill'd in
Criticisms, had found in a certain Author, which he said should be nameless, that the same Word which in the Will is called *Fringe*, does also signify a
Broom-stick, and doubtless ought to have the same Interpretation in this
Paragraph. This, another of the Brothers disliked, because of that Epithet,
Silver, which could not, he humbly conceived, in Propriety of Speech be
reasonably applied to a *Broom-stick*: but it was replied upon him, that this
Epithet was understood in a *Mythological*, and *Allegorical Sense*. However, he
objected again, why their Father should forbid them to wear a *Broom-stick*
on their Coats, a Caution that seemed unnatural and impertinent; upon
which he was taken up short, as one that spoke irreverently of a *Mystery*,
which doubtless was very useful and significant, but ought not to be over-
curiously pryed into, or nicely reasoned upon. And in short, their Father's
Authority being now considerably sunk, this Expedient was allowed to serve
as a lawful Dispensation, for wearing their full Proportion of *Silver Fringe*.

A while after, was revived an old Fashion, long antiquated, of *Embroidery*
with *Indian Figures* of Men, Women, and Children. Here they had no
Occasion to examine the Will. They remembred but too well, how their
Father had always abhorred this Fashion; that he made several Paragraphs
on purpose, importing his utter Detestation of it, and bestowing his
everlasting Curse to his Sons, whenever they should wear it. For all this, in a
few Days, they appeared higher in the Fashion than any Body else in Town.
But they solved the Matter by saying, that these Figures were not at all the
same with those that were formerly worn, and were meant in the Will:
Besides, they did not wear them in that Sense, as forbidden by their Father,
but as they were a commendable Custom, and of great Use to the Publick.
That these rigorous Clauses in the Will did therefore require some
Allowance, and a favourable Interpretation, and ought to be understood
cum grano Salis.

---

† *This is certainly the farther introducing the Pomps of Habit and Ornament.*
* *The Images of Saints, the Blessed Virgin and our Saviour an Infant.*
 Ibid. *Images in the* Church of Rome *give him but too fair a Handle*, The Brothers remembred,
&c. The Allegory here is direct. W. Wotton.

BUT, Fashions perpetually altering in that Age, the Scholastick Brother grew weary of searching further Evasions, and solving everlasting Contradictions. Resolved therefore at all Hazards to comply with the Modes of the World, they concerted Matters together, and agreed unanimously to *lock up their Father's Will in a *Strong-Box*, brought out of *Greece* or *Italy*, (I have forgot which) and trouble themselves no further to examine it, but onely refer to its Authority whenever they thought fit. In consequence whereof, a while after it grew a general Mode to wear an infinite Number of *Points*, most of them *tagg'd with Silver*. Upon which the Scholar pronounced †*ex Cathedrâ*, that *Points* were absolutely *Jure Paterno*, as they might very well remember. 'Tis true indeed, the Fashion prescribed somewhat more than were directly named in the Will; However, that they, as Heirs general of their Father, had power to make and add certain Clauses for publick Emolument, though not deduceable, *totidem verbis* from the Letter of the Will, or else, *Multa absurda sequerentur*. This was understood for *Canonical*, and therefore on the following *Sunday* they came to Church all covered with *Points*.

THE Learned Brother so often mentioned, was reckon'd the best Scholar in all that, or the next Street to it; insomuch, as having run something behind-hand with the World, he obtained the Favour from a ¶*certain Lord*, to receive him into his House, and to teach his Children. A while after, the *Lord* died, and He by long Practice upon his Father's Will, found the Way of contriving a *Deed of Conveyance* of that House to Himself and his Heirs: Upon which he took Possession, turned the young Squires out, and received his Brothers in their stead.

---

* *The Papists formerly forbad the People the Use of Scripture in a Vulgar Tongue*, Peter *therefore* locks up his Father's Will in a Strong Box, brought out of *Greece* or *Italy. Those Countries are named because the* New Testament *is written in* Greek; *and the* Vulgar Latin, *which is the Authentick Edition of the* Bible *in the Church of* Rome, *is in the Language of old* Italy. W. Wotton.

† *The* Popes *in their Decretals and Bulls, have given their Sanction to very many gainful Doctrines which are now received in the* Church of Rome *that are not mention'd in Scriptures, and are unknown to the Primitive Church*, Peter *accordingly pronounces* ex Cathedra, *That* Points tagged with Silver were absolutely *Jure Paterno, and so they wore them in great Numbers*. W. Wotton.

¶ *This was* Constantine the Great, *from whom the* Popes *pretend a Donation of St. Peter's Patrimony, which they have been never able to produce.*

Ibid *The Bishops of* Rome *enjoyed their Priviledges in* Rome *at first by the favour of Emperors, whom at last they shut out of their own Capital City, and then forged a Donation from* Constantine the Great, *the better to justifie what they did. In Imitation of this*, Peter having run something behind hand in the World, obtained Leave of a certain Lord, &c. W. Wotton.

SECT. III.

A *Digression concerning* Criticks.

THO' I have been hitherto as cautious as I could, upon all Occasions, most nicely to follow the Rules and Methods of Writing, laid down by the Example of our illustrious *Moderns*; yet has the unhappy shortness of my Memory led me into an Error, from which I must immediately extricate my self, before I can decently pursue my principal Subject. I confess with Shame, it was an unpardonable Omission to proceed so far as I have already done, before I had performed the due Discourses, Expostulatory, Supplicatory, or Deprecatory with my *good Lords* the *Criticks*. Towards some Attonement for this grievous Neglect, I do here make humbly bold to present them with a short Account of Themselves and their *Art*, by looking into the Original and Pedigree of the Word, as it is generally understood among us, and very briefly considering the antient and present State thereof.

BY the Word, Critick, at this Day so frequent in all Conversations, there have sometime been distinguished three very different Species of Mortal Men, according as I have read in *Antient Books and Pamphlets*. For first, by this Term were understood, such Persons as invented or drew up Rules for Themselves and the World, by observing which, a careful Reader might be able to pronounce upon the productions of the *Learned*, form his Taste to a true Relish of the *Sublime* and the *Admirable*, and divide every Beauty of Matter or of Style from the Corruption that Apes it: In their common perusal of Books, singling out the Errors and Defects, the Nauseous, the Fulsom, the Dull, and the Impertinent, with the Caution of a Man that walks thro' *Edenborough* Streets in a Morning, who is indeed as careful as he can, to watch diligently, and spy out the Filth in his Way, not that he is curious to observe the Colour and Complexion of the Ordure, or take its Dimensions, much less to be paddling in, or tasting it: but only with a Design to come out as cleanly as he may. These men seem, tho' very erroneously, to have understood the Appellation of, *Critick* in a literal Sense; That, one principal Part of his Office was, to Praise and Acquit; and, that a Critick who sets up to Read, only for an Occasion of Censure and Reproof, is a Creature as barbarous, as a *Judge*, who should take up a Resolution to *hang* all Men that came before Him upon a Tryal.

AGAIN; by the Word, *Critick*, have been meant, the Restorers of Antient Learning from the Worms, and Graves, and Dust of Manuscripts.

NOW, the Races of these two have been for some Ages utterly extinct; and besides, to discourse any further of them would not be at all to my Purpose.

THE Third, and Noblest Sort, is that of the *TRUE CRITICK*, whose Original is the most Antient of all. Every *True Critick* is a Hero born, descending in a direct Line from a Celestial Stem, by *Momus* and *Hybris*, who begat *Zoilus*, who begat *Tigellius*, who begat *Etcætera* the Elder; who begat *B—tl–y*, and *Rym–r*, and *W–tt–n*, and *Perrault*, and *Dennis*, who begat *Etcætera* the Younger.

AND these are the *Criticks* from whom the Commonwealth of Learning has in all Ages received such immense Benefits, that the Gratitude of their Admirers placed their Origine in Heaven, among those of *Hercules, Theseus, Perseus*, and other great Deservers of Mankind. But Heroick Virtue it self hath not been exempt from the Obloquy of Evil Tongues. For it hath been objected, that those Ancient Heroes, famous for their Combating so many Giants, and Dragons, and Robbers, were in their own Persons a greater Nuisance to Mankind, than any of those Monsters they subdued; and therefore, to render their Obligations more Compleat, when all *other* Vermin were destroy'd, should in Conscience have concluded with the same Justice upon themselves: as *Hercules* most generously did, and hath upon that Score, procured to himself more Temples and Votaries than the best of his Fellows. For these Reasons, I suppose it is why some have conceived, it would be very expedient for the Publick Good of Learning, that every *True Critick*, as soon as he had finished his Task assigned, should immediately deliver himself up to Ratsbane, or Hemp, or from some convenient *Altitude*, and that no Man's Pretensions to so illustrious a Character, should by any means be received, before That Operation were performed.

NOW, from this Heavenly Descent of *Criticism*, and the close Analogy it bears to *Heroick Virtue*, 'tis easy to assign the proper Employment of a *True, Antient, Genuin Critick*; Which is, to travel thro' this vast World of Writings: to pursue and hunt those Monstrous Faults bred within them: to drag out the lurking Errors like *Cacus* from his Den; to multiply them like *Hydra's* Heads; and rake them together like *Augeas*'s Dung. Or else to drive away a sort of *Dangerous Fowl*, who have a perverse Inclination to plunder the best Branches of the *Tree of Knowledge*, like those *Stymphalian* Birds that eat up the Fruit.

THESE Reasonings will furnish us with an adequate Definition of a *True Critick;* that, He is *a Discoverer and Collector of Writers Faults*. Which may be farther put beyond Dispute by the following Demonstration: That whoever will examine the Writings in all kinds, wherewith this ancient Sect has honoured the World, shall immediately find from the whole Thread and Tenor of them, that the Idea's of the Authors have been altogether conversant, and taken up with the Faults and Blemishes, and Oversights, and

Mistakes of other Writers; and let the Subject treated on be whatever it will, their Imaginations are so entirely possess'd and replete with the Defects of other Pens, that the very Quintessence of what is bad, does of necessity distil into their own: by which means the whole appears to be nothing else but an *Abstract* of the *Criticisms* themselves have made.

HAVING thus briefly considered the Original and Office of a *Critick*, as the Word is understood in its most noble and universal Acceptation, I proceed to refute the Objections of those who argue from the Silence and Pretermission of Authors; by which they pretend to prove, that the very Art of *Criticism*, as now exercised, and by me explained, is wholly *Modern*; and consequently, that the *Criticks* of *Great Britain* and *France*, have no Title to an Original so Antient and Illustrious as I have deduced. Now, if I can clearly make out on the contrary, that the most antient Writers have particularly described, both the Person and the Office of a *True Critick*, agreeable to the Definition laid down by me; their grand Objection from the Silence of Authors will fall to the Ground.

I confess to have for a long time born a part in this general Error; From which I should never have acquitted my self, but thro' the Assistance of our Noble *Moderns*, whose most edifying Volumes I turn indefatigably over Night and Day, for the Improvement of my Mind, and the good of my Country: These have with unwearied Pains made many useful Searches into the weak sides of the *Antients*, and given us a comprehensive List of them. *Besides, they have proved beyond Contradiction, that the very finest Things delivered of old, have been long since invented, and brought to Light by much later Pens, and that the noblest Discoveries those *Antients* ever made of Art or of Nature, have all been produced by the transcending Genius of the present Age. Which clearly shews, how little Merit those *Ancients* can justly pretend to; and takes off that blind Admiration paid them by Men in a Corner, who have the Unhappiness of conversing too little with *present Things*. Reflecting maturely upon all this, and taking in the whole Compass of Human Nature, I easily concluded, that these *Antients*, highly sensible of their many Imperfections, must needs have endeavoured from some Passages in their Works, to obviate, soften, or divert the Censorious Reader, by *Satyr*, or *Panegyrick* upon the *True Criticks*, in Imitation of their *Masters* the *Moderns*. Now, in the *Common-Places* of *both these, I was plentifully instructed, by a long Course of useful Study in *Prefaces* and *Prologues*; and therefore immediately resolved to try what I could discover of either, by a diligent Perusal of the most Antient Writers, and especially those who treated of the earliest Times. Here I found to my great

* See Wotton *of Ancient and Modern Learning*

* Satyr, and Panegyrick upon Criticks

Surprise, that although they all entred, upon Occasion, into particular Descriptions of the *True Critick*, according as they were governed by their Fears or their Hopes: yet whatever they toucht of that kind, was with abundance of Caution, adventuring no farther than *Mythology* and *Hieroglyphick*. This, I suppose, gave ground to superficial Readers, for urging the Silence of Authors, against the Antiquity of the *True Critick*; tho' the *Types* are so apposite, and the Applications so necessary and natural, that it is not easy to conceive, how any Reader of a *Modern Eye* and *Taste* could over-look them. I shall venture from a great Number to produce a few, which I am very confident, will put this Question beyond Dispute.

IT well deserves considering, that these *Antient Writers* in treating Enigmatically upon this Subject, have generally fixed upon the very *same Hieroglyph*, varying only the Story according to their Affections or their Wit. For first; *Pausanias* is of Opinion, that the Perfection of Writing correct, was entirely owing to the Institution of *Criticks*; and, that he can possibly mean no other than the *True Critick*, is, I think, manifest enough from the following Description. He says, *They were a Race of Men, who delighted to nibble at the Superfluities, and Excrescencies of Books; which the Learned at length observing, took Warning of their own Accord, to lop the Luxuriant, the Rotten, the Dead, the Sapless, and the Overgrown Branches from their Works*. But now, all
* *Lib* — this he cunningly shades under the following Allegory; That the *Nauplians *in* Argos, *learned the Art of pruning their Vines, by observing, that when an* ASS *had browsed upon one of them, it thrived the better,*
* *Lib. 4* *and bore fairer Fruit*. But *Herodotus holding the very same Hieroglyph, speaks much plainer, and almost *in terminis*. He hath been so bold as to tax the *True Criticks*, of Ignorance and Malice; telling us openly, for I think nothing can be plainer, that *in the Western Part of* Libya, *there were* ASSES *with* HORNS: Upon which Re-
* Vide *excerpta ex eo apud* Photium lation *Ctesias yet refines, mentioning the very same Animal about *India*, adding, *That whereas all other* ASSES *wanted a* Gall, *these horned ones were so redundant in that Part, that their Flesh was not to be eaten because of its extream* Bitterness.

NOW, the Reason why those Antient Writers treated this Subject only by Types and Figures, was, because they durst not make open Attacks against a Party so Potent and so Terrible, as the *Criticks* of those Ages were: whose very Voice was so Dreadful, that a Legion of Authors would tremble, and
* *Lib. 4* drop their Pens at the Sound; For so *Herodotus tells us expressly in another Place, how *a vast Army of* Scythians *was put to flight in a Panick Terror, by the Braying of an* ASS. From hence it is conjectured by certain profound Philologers, that the great Awe and Reverence paid to a *True Critick*, by the Writers of *Britain*, have been derived

to Us, from those our *Scythian* Ancestors. In short, this Dread was so universal, that in process of Time, those Authors who had a mind to publish their Sentiments more freely, in describing the *True Criticks* of their several Ages, were forced to leave off the use of the former *Hieroglyph*, as too nearly approaching the *Prototype*, and invented other Terms instead thereof, that were more cautious and mystical; so †*Diodorus* speaking to the same purpose, ventures no farther than to say, That *in the Mountains of* Helicon *there grows a certain* Weed, *which bears a Flower of so damned a Scent, as to poison those who offer to smell it.* Lucretius gives exactly the Same Relation,

† *Lib.*

> ‖*Est etiam in magnis Heliconis montibus arbos,*
> *Floris odore hominem taetro consueta necare. Lucretius* Lib. 6

BUT *Ctesias*, whom we lately quoted, hath been a great deal bolder; He had been used with much severity by the *True Criticks* of his own Age, and therefore could not forbear to leave behind him, at least one deep Mark of his Vengeance, against the whole Tribe. His Meaning is so near the Surface, that I wonder how it possibly came to be overlookt by those who deny the Antiquity of the *True Criticks.* For pretending to make a Description of many strange Animals about *India*, he hath set down these remarkable Words. *Among the rest,* says he, *there is a* Serpent *that wants* Teeth, *and consequently cannot bite, but if its* Vomit (*to which it is much addicted*) *happens to fall upon any Thing, a certain Rottennness or Corruption ensues: These* Serpents *are generally found among the Mountains where* Jewels *grow, and they frequently emit a* poisonous Juice *whereof, whoever drinks, that Person's* Brains *flie out of his Nostrils.*

THERE was also among the *Antients* a sort of *Critick*, not distinguished in *specie* from the Former, but in Growth or Degree, who seem to have been only the *Tyro's* or *junior* Scholars; yet, because of their differing Employments, they are frequently mentioned as a Sect by themselves. The usual exercise of these younger Students, was to attend constantly at Theatres, and learn to Spy out the *worst Parts* of the Play, whereof they were obliged carefully to take Note, and render a rational Account, to their Tutors. Flesht at these smaller Sports, like young Wolves, they grew up in Time, to be nimble and strong enough for hunting down large Game. For it hath been observed both among Antients and Moderns, that a *True Critick* hath one Quality in common with a *Whore* and an *Alderman*, never to change his Title or his Nature; that a *Grey Critick* has been certainly a *green* one, the Perfections and Acquirements of his Age being only the improved Talents of his Youth; like *Hemp*, which some Naturalists inform us, is bad for

---

‖ *Near* Helicon, *and round the Learned Hill, Grow Trees, whose Blossoms with their Odour kill.*

Suffocations, tho' taken but in the Seed. I esteem the Invention, or at least the Refinement of *Prologues*, to have been owing to these younger Proficients, of whom *Terence* makes frequent and honourable mention, under the Name of *Malevoli*.

NOW, 'tis certain, the Institution of the *True Criticks*, was of absolute Necessity to the Commonwealth of Learning. For all Human Actions seem to be divided like *Themistocles* and his Company; One Man can *Fiddle*, and another can make *a small Town a great City*; and he that cannot do either one or the other, deserves to be kick'd out of the Creation. The avoiding of which Penalty, has doubtless given the first Birth to the Nation of *Criticks* and withal, an Occasion for their secret Detractors to report; that a *True Critick* is a sort of Mechanick, set up with a Stock and Tools for his Trade, at as little Expence as a *Taylor*; and that there is much Analogy between the Utensils and Abilities of both: That the *Taylor's Hell* is the Type of a Critick's *Common-place-Book*, and his Wit and Learning held forth by the *Goose*: That it requires at least as many of these, to the making up of one Scholar, as of the others to the Composition of a Man: That the Valor of both is equal, and their *Weapons* near of a Size. Much may be said in answer to these invidious Reflections; and I can positively affirm the first to be a Falshood: For, on the contrary, nothing is more certain, than that it requires greater Layings out, to be free of the *Critick's* Company, than of any other you can name. For, as to be a *true Beggar*, it will cost the richest Candidate every Groat he is worth; so, before one can commence a *True Critick*, it will cost a man all the good Qualities of his Mind; which, perhaps, for a less Purchase, would be thought but an indifferent Bargain.

HAVING thus amply proved the Antiquity of *Criticism*, and described the Primitive State of it; I shall now examine the present Condition of this Empire, and shew how well it agrees with its antient self. *A certain Author, whose Works have many Ages since been entirely lost, does in his fifth Book and eighth Chapter, say of *Criticks*, that *their Writings are the Mirrors of Learning*. This I understand in a literal Sense, and suppose our Author must mean, that whoever designs to be a perfect Writer, must inspect into the Books of *Criticks*, and correct his Invention there as in a Mirror. Now, whoever considers, that the *Mirrors* of the Antients were made of *Brass*, and *sine Mercurio*, may presently apply the two Principal Qualifications of a *True Modern Critick*, and consequently, must needs conclude, that these have always been, and must be for ever the same. For, *Brass* is an Emblem of Duration, and when it is skilfully burnished, will cast *Reflections* from its own *Superficies*, without any Assistance of *Mercury* from behind. All the other Talents of a *Critick* will not require a particular

* A quotation after the manner of a great Author. Vide Bently's Dissertation, &c.

Mention, being included, or easily deduceable to these. However, I shall conclude with three Maxims, which may serve both as Characteristicks to distinguish a *True Modern Critick* from a Pretender, and will be also of admirable Use to those worthy Spirits, who engage in so useful and honorable an Art.

THE first is, That *Criticism,* contrary to all other Faculties of the Intellect, is ever held the truest and best, when it is the very *first* Result of the *Critick's* Mind: As Fowlers reckon the first Aim for the surest, and seldom fail of missing the Mark, if they stay for a Second.

SECONDLY; The *True Criticks* are known by their Talent of swarming about the noblest Writers, to which they are carried meerly by Instinct, as a Rat to the best Cheese, or a Wasp to the fairest Fruit. So, when the *King* is a Horse-back, he is sure to be the *dirtiest* Person of the Company, and they that make their Court best, are such as *bespatter* him most.

LASTLY; A *True Critick,* in the Perusal of a Book, is like a *Dog* at a Feast, whose Thoughts and Stomach are wholly set upon what the Guests *fling away,* and consequently, is apt to *Snarl* most, when there are the fewest *Bones.*

THUS much, I think, is sufficient to serve by way of Address to my Patrons, the *True Modern Criticks,* and may very well atone for my past Silence, as well as That which I am like to observe for the future. I hope I have deserved so well of their whole *Body,* as to meet with generous and tender Usage at their *Hands.* Supported by which Expectation, I go on boldly to pursue those Adventures already so happily begun.

SECT. IV.

A TALE of a TUB.

I HAVE now with much Pains and Study, conducted the Reader to a Period, where he must expect to hear of great Revolutions. For no sooner had Our *Learned Brother*, so often mentioned, got a warm House of his own over his Head, than he began to look big, and to take mightily upon him; insomuch, that unless the Gentle Reader out of his great Candor, will please a little to exalt his Idea, I am afraid he will henceforth hardly know the *Hero* of the Play, when he happens to meet Him; his Part, his Dress, and his Mien being so much altered.

HE told his Brothers, he would have them to know, that he was their Elder, and consequently his Father's sole Heir; Nay, a while after, he would not allow them to call Him, Brother, but Mr. *PETER*; And then he must be styled, *Father PETER*; and sometimes, *My Lord PETER*. To support this Grandeur, which he soon began to consider, could not be maintained without a Better *Fonde* than what he was born to; After much Thought, he cast about at last, to turn *Projector* and *Virtuoso;* wherein he so well succeeded, that many famous Discoveries, Projects and Machines, which bear great Vogue and Practice at present in the World, are owing entirely to *Lord Peter's* Invention. I will deduce the best Account I have been able to collect of the Chief amongst them, without considering much the Order they came out in; because, I think, Authors are not well agreed as to that Point.

I hope, when this Treatise of mine shall be translated into Forein Languages, (as I may without Vanity affirm, That the Labour of collecting, the Faithfulness in recounting, and the great Usefulness of the Matter to the Publick, will amply deserve that Justice) that the worthy Members of the several *Academies* abroad, especially those of *France* and *Italy*, will favourably accept these humble Offers, for the Advancement of Universal Knowledge. I do also advertise the most Reverend Fathers, the *Eastern* Missionaries, that I have purely for their sakes, made use of such Words and Phrases, as will best admit an easy Turn into any of the *Oriental* Languages, especially the *Chinese*. And so I proceed with great Content of Mind, upon reflecting, how much Emolument this whole Globe of Earth is like to reap by my Labors.

THE first Undertaking of Lord *Peter*, was to purchase a *Large Continent, lately said to have been discovered in *Terra Australis incognita*. This Tract of Land he bought at a very great Penny-worth from the Discoverers themselves, (tho' some pretended to doubt whether they had ever been

---

* *That is Purgatory.*

there) and then retailed it into several Cantons to certain Dealers, who carried over Colonies, but were all Shipwreckt in the Voyage. Upon which, *Lord Peter* sold the said Continent to other Customers *again*, and *again*, and *again*, and *again*, with the same Success.

THE second Project I shall mention, was his *Sovereign Remedy of the *Worms*, especially those in the *Spleen*. †The Patient was to eat nothing after Supper for three Nights: As soon as he went to Bed, he was carefully to lye on one Side, and when he grew weary, to turn upon the other: He must also duly confine his two Eyes to the same Object; and by no means break Wind at both Ends together, without manifest Occasion. These Prescriptions diligently observed, the *Worms* would void insensibly by Perspiration, ascending thro' the *Brain*.

A third Invention, was the erecting of a ¶*Whispering-Office*, for the Publick Good and Ease of all such as were Hypochondriacal, or troubled with the Cholick; as likewise of all Eves-droppers, Physicians, Midwives, small Politicians, Friends fallen out, Repeating Poets, Lovers Happy or in Despair, Bawds, Privy-Counsellours, Pages, Parasites and Buffoons: In short, of all such as are in Danger of bursting with too much *Wind*. An *Ass*'s Head was placed so conveniently, that the Party affected might easily with his Mouth accost either of the Animal's Ears; which he was to apply close for a certain Space, and by a fugitive Faculty, peculiar to the Ears of that Animal, receive immediate Benefit, either by Eructation, or Expiration, or Evomition.

ANOTHER very beneficial Project of *Lord Peter's* was an ‖*Office of Ensurance*, for Tobacco-Pipes, Martyrs of the Modern Zeal; Volumes of Poetry, Shadows, — — — — ?, and Rivers: That these, nor any of these shall receive Damage by *Fire*. From whence our *Friendly Societies* may plainly find themselves, to be only Transcribers from this Original; tho' the one and the other have been of *great* Benefit to the Undertakers, as well as of *equal* to the Publick.

LORD *Peter* was also held the Original Author of *****Puppets* and *Raree-Shows*; the great Usefulness whereof being so generally known, I shall not enlarge further upon this Particular.

---

* Penance *and* Absolution *are plaid upon under the Notion of a* Sovereign Remedy *for the* Worms, *especially in the* Spleen, *which by observing* Peters *Prescription would void sensibly by Perspiration ascending thro' the Brain,* &c. W. Wotton.

† *Here the Author ridicules the Penances of the Church of* Rome, *which may be made as easy to the Sinner as he pleases, provided he will pay for them accordingly.*

¶ *By his* Whispering-Office, *for the Relief of Eves-droppers, Physitians, Bawds, and Privy-counsellours, he ridicules Auricular Confession, and the Priest who takes it, is described by the Asses Head.* W.Wotton.

‖ *This I take to be the Office of* Indulgences, *the gross Abuses whereof first gave Occasion for the Reformation.*

** *I believe are the Monkeries and ridiculous Processions,* &c. *among the Papists.*

BUT, another Discovery for which he was much renowned, was his famous Universal ††*Pickle*. For having remarkt how your [11]common *Pickle* in use among Huswives, was of no further Benefit than to preserve dead Flesh, and certain kinds of Vegetables; *Peter*, with great Cost as well as Art, had contrived a *Pickle* proper for Houses, Gardens, Towns, Men, Women, Children, and Cattle; wherein he could preserve them as Sound as Insects in Amber. Now, this *Pickle* to the Taste, the Smell, and the Sight, appeared exactly the same, with what is in common Service for Beef, and Butter, and Herrings, (and has been often that way applied with great Success) but for its many Sovereign Virtues was quite a different Thing. For *Peter* would put in a certain Quantity of his *Powder Pimperlim-pimp*, after which it never failed of Success. The Operation was performed by *Spargefaction* in a proper Time of the Moon. The Patient who was to be *pickled*, if it were a House, would infallibly be preserved from all Spiders, Rats and Weazels; If the Party affected were a Dog he should be exempt from Mange, and Madness, and Hunger. It also infallibly took away all Scabs and Lice, and scall'd Heads from Children, never hindring the Patient from any Duty, either at Bed or Board.

BUT of all *Peter's* Rarities, he most valued a certain Set of †*Bulls*, whose Race was by great Fortune preserved in a lineal Descent from those that guarded the *Golden Fleece*. Tho' some who pretended to observe them curiously, doubted the Breed had not been kept entirely chast; because they had degenerated from their Ancestors in some Qualities and had acquired others very extraordinary, but a Forein Mixture. The *Bulls* of *Colchos* are recorded to have *brazen Feet*; But whether it happen'd by ill Pasture and Running, by an Allay from intervention of other Parents, from stolen Intrigues; Whether a Weakness in their Progenitors had impaired the seminal Virtue; Or by a Decline necessary thro' a long Course of Time, the Originals of Nature being depraved in these latter sinful Ages of the World; Whatever was the Cause, 'tis certain that *Lord Peter's Bulls* were extremely vitiated by the Rust of Time in the Metal of their Feet, which was now sunk into common *Lead*. However the terrible *roaring* peculiar to their Lineage, was preserved; as likewise that Faculty of breathing out *Fire* from

---

†† *Holy Water, he calls an* Universal Pickle *to preserve Houses, Gardens, Towns, Men, Women, Children and Cattle, wherein he could preserve them as sound as Insects in Amber.* W. Wotton.

[11] *This is easily understood to be Holy Water, composed of the same Ingredients with many other Pickles.*

* *And because Holy Water differs only in Consecration from common Water, therefore he tells us that his Pickle by the Powder of* Pimperlimpimp *receives new Virtues though it differs not in Sight nor Smell from the common Pickles, which preserves Beef, and Butter, and Herrings.* W. Wotton.

† *The Papal* Bulls *are ridicul'd by Name, So that here we are at no loss for the Authors Meaning.* W. Wotton.

Ibid. *Here the Author has kept the Name, and means the* Popes Bulls, *or rather his Fulminations and Excommunications, of Heretical Princes, all sign'd with Lead and the Seal of the Fisherman.*

their Nostrils; which notwithstanding, many of their Detractors took to be a Feat of Art, and to be nothing so terrible as it appeared; proceeding only from their usual Course of Dyet, which was of **¶** *Squibs* and *Crackers*. However, they had two peculiar Marks which extreamly distinguished them from the *Bulls of Jason*, and which I have not met together in the Description of any other Monster, beside that in *Horace*.

> *Varias inducere plumas,*
> and
> *Atrum desinit in piscem.*

For these had *Fishes Tails*, yet upon Occasion, could *out-fly* any Bird in the Air. *Peter* put these *Bulls* upon several Employs. Sometimes he would set them a *roaring* to fright *Naughty Boys*, and make them quiet. Sometimes he would send them out upon Errands of great Importance; where it is wonderful to recount, and perhaps the cautious Reader may think much to believe it; An *Appetitus sensibilis*, deriving itself thro' the whole Family, from their Noble Ancestors, Guardians of the *Golden-Fleece;* they continued so extremely fond of *Gold*, that if *Peter* sent them abroad, though it were only upon a Compliment, they would *Roar*, and *Spit*, and *Belch*, and *Piss*, and *Fart*, and *Snivel* out *Fire*, and keep a perpetual Coyl, till you flung them a Bit of *Gold*; but then, *Pulveris exigui jactu*, they would grow calm and quiet as Lambs. In short, whether by secret Connivance, or Encouragement from their Master, or out of their own Liquorish Affection to Gold, or both; it is certain they were no better than a sort of sturdy, swaggering Beggars; and where they could not prevail to get an Alms, would make Women miscarry, and Children fall into Fits; who, to this very Day, usually call Sprites and Hobgoblins by the Name of *Bull-Beggars*. They grew at last so very troublesome to the Neighbourhood, that some Gentlemen of the *North-West*, got a Parcel of right *English Bull-Dogs*, and baited them so terribly, that they felt it ever after.

I must needs mention one more of *Lord Peter's* Projects, which was very extraordinary, and discovered him to be Master of a high Reach, and profound Invention. Whenever it happened that any Rogue of *Newgate* was condemned to be hang'd, *Peter* would offer him a Pardon for a certain Sum of Money, which when the poor Caitiff had made all Shifts to scrape up and send; *His Lordship* would return a †Piece of Paper in this form.

¶ *These are the Fulminations of the Pope threatening Hell and Damnation to those Princes who offend him.*

* *That is Kings who incurr his Displeasure*

† *This is a Copy of a General Pardons sign'd* Servus Servorum

Ibid. *Absolution in* Articulo Mortis, *and the Tax* Cameræ Apostolicæ *are jested upon in Emperor* Peter's *Letter.* W.Wotton..

TO all Mayors, Sheriffs, Jaylors, Constables, Bayliffs, Hangmen, &c. Whereas we are informed that A. B. *remains in the Hands of you, or any of you, under the Sentence of Death. We will and command you upon Sight hereof, to let the said Prisoner depart to his own Habitation, whether he stands condemned for Murder, Sodomy, Rape, Sacrilege, Incest, Treason, Blasphemy, &c. for which this shall be your sufficient Warrant: And if you fail hereof, G-d d-mn You and Yours to all Eternity. And so we bid you heartily Farewel.*

Your most Humble

Man's Man,

Emperor Peter.

THE Wretches trusting to this, lost their Lives and Money too.

I desire of those whom the *Learned* among Posterity will appoint for Commentators upon this elaborate Treatise; that they will proceed with great Caution upon certain dark Points, wherein all who are not *Verè adepti,* may be in Danger to form rash and hasty Conclusions, especially in some mysterious Paragraphs, where certain *Arcana* are joyned for Brevity sake, which in the Operation must be divided. And, I am certain, that future Sons of Art, will return large Thanks to my Memory, for so grateful, so useful an *Innuendo.*

IT will be no difficult Part to persuade the Reader, that so many worthy Discoveries met with great Success in the World; tho' I may justly assure him, that I have related much the smallest Number; My Design having been only to single out such, as will be of most Benefit for Publick Imitation, or which best served to give some Idea of the Reach and Wit of the Inventor. And therefore it need not be wondred, if by this Time, *Lord Peter* was become exceeding Rich. But alas, he had kept his Brain so long, and so violently upon the Rack, that at last it *shook* it self, and began to *turn round* for a little Ease. In short, what with Pride, Projects, and Knavery, poor *Peter* was grown distracted, and conceived the strangest Imaginations in the World. In the Height of his Fits (as it is usual with those who run mad out of Pride) He would call Himself *God Almighty,* and sometimes *Monarch of the Universe.* I have seen him, (says my Author) take three old †*high-crown'd Hats,* and clap them all on his Head, three Story high, with a huge Bunch of ||*Keys* at his Girdle, and an *Angling Rod* in his Hand. In which Guise, whoever went to take him by the Hand in the way of Salutation, *Peter* with much

---

* *The Pope is not only allow'd to be the Vicar of* Christ, *but by several Divines is call'd* God upon Earth, *and other blasphemous Titles.*

† *The Triple Crown.*

|| *The Keys of the Church.*

Ibid. *The Pope's Universal Monarchy, and his Triple Crown, and Fisher's Ring.* W. Wotton

Plate 14

Grace like a well educated Spaniel, would present them with his ¶*Foot*, and if they refused his Civility, then he would raise it as high as their Chops, and give them a damn'd Kick on the Mouth, which hath ever since been called a *Salute*. Whoever walkt by, without paying him their Compliments, having a wonderful strong Breath, he would blow their Hats off (Plate 14) into the Dirt. Mean time, his Affairs at home went upside down; and his two Brothers had a wretched Time; Where his first *******Boutade* was, to kick both their ††Wives one Morning out of Doors, and his own too, and in their stead, gave Orders to pick up the first three Strolers could be met with in the Streets. A while after, he nail'd up the Cellar Door, and would not allow his Brothers a ¶¶Drop of *Drink* to their Victuals. Dining one Day at an Alderman's in the City, *Peter* observed him expatiating after the Manner of his Brethren, in the Praises of his Surloyn of Beef. *Beef*, said the Sage Magistrate, *is the King of Meat; Beef comprehends in it the Quintessence of Partridge, and Quail, and Venison, and Pheasant, and Plum-pudding and Custard.* When *Peter* came home, he would needs take the Fancy of cooking up this Doctrine into use, and apply the Precept in default of a Sirloyn, to his brown Loaf: *Bread*, says he, *Dear Brothers, is the Staff of Life; in which Bread is contained,* inclusivè, *the Quintessence of Beef, Mutton, Veal, Venison, Partridge, Plum-pudding, and Custard: And to render all compleat, there is intermingled a due Quantity of Water, whose Crudities are also corrected by Yeast or Barm, thro' which means it becomes a wholsome fermented Liquor, diffused thro' the Mass of the Bread.* Upon the Strength of these Conclusions, next Day at Dinner was the brown Loaf served up in all the Formality of a City Feast. *Come brothers*, said *Peter, fall to, and spare not; here is excellent good* **Mutton; or hold, now my Hand is in, I'll help you.* At which word, in much Ceremony, with Fork and Knife, he carves out two good Slices of the Loaf, and presents each on a Plate to his Brothers. The Elder of the two not suddenly entring into *Lord Peter's* Conceit, began with very civil Language to examine the Mystery. *My lord*, said he, *I doubt, with great Submission, there may be some Mistake. What*, says *Peter, you are pleasant; Come then, let us hear this Jest, your Head is so big with. None in the World, my Lord; but unless I am very much deceived, your Lordship was pleased a while ago, to let fall a Word about Mutton, and I would be glad to see it with all my*

¶ *Neither does his arrogant way of requiring men to kiss his Slipper, escape Reflexion.* Wotton.
** *This Word properly signifies a sudden Jerk, or Lash of an Horse, when you do not expect it.*
†† *The* Celibacy of the *Romish* Clergy *is struck at in* Peter's *beating his own and Brothers Wives out of Doors.* W. Wotton.
¶¶ *The* Pope's *refusing the Cup to the Laity, persuading them that the Blood is contain'd in the Bread, and that the Bread is the real and entire Body of* Christ.
* Transubstantiation. Peter *turns his Bread into Mutton, and according to the Popish Doctrine of Concomitants, his Wine too, which in his way he calls,* Pauming his damn'd Crusts upon the Brothers for Mutton. *W. Wotton.*

Heart. How, said *Peter*, appearing in great Surprize, *I do not comprehend this at all–*. Upon which, the younger interposing, to set the Business right; *My Lord*, said he, *My Brother, I suppose, is hungry, and longs for the Mutton, your Lordship hath promised us to Dinner. Pray*, said Peter, *take me along with you; either you are both mad, or disposed to be merrier than I approve of; If* You *there, do not like your Piece, I will carve you another, tho' I should take that to be the choice Bit of the whole Shoulder. What then, my Lord*, replied the first, *it seems this is a shoulder of Mutton all this while. Pray, Sir*, says *Peter, eat your Vittels and leave off your Impertinence, if you please, for I am not disposed to relish it at present:* But the other could not forbear, being over provoked at the affected Seriousness of *Peter's* Countenance. *By G—, My Lord*, said he, *I can only say, that to my Eyes, and Fingers, and Teeth, and Nose, it seems to be nothing but a Crust of Bread.* Upon which, the second put in his Word; *I never saw a Piece of Mutton in my Life, so nearly resembling a Slice from a Twelve-peny Loaf. Look ye, Gentlemen*, cries *Peter* in a Rage, *to convince you, what a couple of blind, positive, ignorant, wilful Puppies you are, I will use but this plain Argument; by G—, it is true, good, natural Mutton as any in* Leaden-Hall *Market; and G— confound you both eternally, if you offer to believe otherwise.* Such a thundring Proof as this, left no further Room for Objection: The two Unbelievers began to gather and pocket up their Mistake as hastily as they could. *Why, truly*, said the first, *upon more mature Consideration — Ay*, says the other, interrupting him, *now I have thought better on the Thing, your Lordship seems to have a great deal of Reason. Very well*, said Peter. *Here Boy, fill me a Beer-Glass of Claret. Here's to you both with all my Heart.* The two Brethren much delighted to see him so readily appeas'd returned their most humble Thanks, and said, they would be glad to pledge His Lordship. *That you shall*, said Peter, *I am not a Person to refuse you any Thing that is reasonable; Wine moderately taken, is a Cordial; Here is a Glass a piece for you; 'Tis true natural Juice from the Grape, none of your damn'd* Vintner's *Brewings.* Having spoke thus, he presented to each of them another large dry Crust, bidding them drink it off (Plate 15), and not be bashful, for it would do them no Hurt. The two Brothers, after having performed the usual Office in such delicate Conjunctures, of staring a sufficient Period at *Lord Peter,* and each other; and finding how Matters were like to go, resolved not to enter on a new Dispute, but let him carry the Point as he pleased; for he was now got into one of his mad Fits, and to Argue or Expostulate further, would only serve to render him a hundred times more untractable.

I have chosen to relate this worthy Matter in all its Circumstances, because it gave a principal Occasion to that great and famous **Rupture,* which happened about the same time among these Brethren, and was

---

* *By this* Rupture *is meant the* Reformation.

Plate 15

Plate 16

never afterwards made up. But of That, I shall treat at large in another Section.

HOWEVER, it is certain, that *Lord Peter*, even in his lucid Intervals, was very lewdly given in his common Conversation, extream wilful and positive, and would at any time rather argue to the Death, than allow himself to be once in an Error. Besides, he had an abominable Faculty of telling huge palpable *Lies* upon all Occasions; and not only swearing to the Truth, but cursing the whole Company to Hell, if they pretended to make the least Scruple of believing Him. One time, he swore he had a †*Cow* at home, which gave as much Milk at a Meal, as would fill three thousand Churches; and what was yet more extraordinary, would never turn Sower. Another time, he was telling of an old ¶*Sign-Post* that belonged to his *Father*, with Nails and Timber enough on it, to build sixteen large Men of War. Talking one Day of *Chinese* Waggons (Plate 16), which were made so light as to sail over Mountains: *Z—nds*, said *Peter, where's the Wonder of that? By G—, I saw a ***Large House of Lime and Stone travel over Sea and Land (granting that it stopt sometimes to bait) above two thousand* German *Leagues.* And that which was the good of it, he would swear desperately all the while, that he never told a Lye in his Life; And at every Word; *By G—, Gentlemen, I tell you nothing but the Truth; and the D—l broil them eternally that will not believe me.*

IN short, *Peter* grew so scandalous that all the Neighbourhood began in plain Words to say, he was no better than a Knave. And his two Brothers long weary of his ill Usage, resolved at last to leave him; but first, they humbly desired a Copy of their Father's *Will*, which had now lain by neglected, time out of Mind. Instead of granting this Request, he called them *damn'd Sons of Whores, Rogues, Traytors*, and the rest of the vile Names he could muster up. However, while he was abroad one Day upon his Projects, the two Youngsters watcht their Opportunity, made a Shift to come at the *Will*,* and took a *Copia vera*, by which they presently saw how grosly they had been abused: Their Father having left them equal Heirs, and strictly commanded, that whatever they got, should lye in common among them all. Pursuant to which, their next Enterprise was to break

---

† *The ridiculous Multiplying of the Virgin* Mary's Milk *among the Papists, under the Allegory of a* Cow, *which gave as much Milk at a Meal, as would fill three thousand Churches.* W. Wotton.
¶ *By this* Sign-Post *is meant the* Cross *of our Blessed Saviour.*
** *The Chappel of* Loretto. *He falls here only upon the ridiculous Inventions of Popery; The Church of* Rome *intended by these Things, to gull silly, superstitious People, and rook them of their Money; that the World had been too long in Slavery, our Ancestors gloriously redeem'd us from that Yoke. The Church of* Rome *therefore ought to be expos'd, and he deserves well of Mankind that does expose it.* W.Wotton.
Ibid. *The Chappel of* Loretto, *which travell'd from the* Holy Land *to* Italy.
* *Translated the Scriptures into the vulgar Tongues.*

open the Cellar-Door, and get a little good ¶*Drink* to spirit and comfort their Hearts. In copying the *Will*, they had met another Precept against Whoring, Divorce, and separate Maintenance; Upon which, their next †Work was to discard their Concubines, and send for their Wives. Whilst all this was in agitation, there enters a Sollicitor from *Newgate*, desiring *Lord Peter* would please to procure a *Pardon* for a *Thief* that was to be *hanged* to morrow. But the two Brothers told him, he was a Coxcomb to seek Pardons from a Fellow, who deserv'd to be hang'd much better than his Client; and discovered all the Method of that Imposture, in the same Form I delivered it a while ago, advising the Sollicitor to put his Friend upon obtaining ‖*a Pardon from the King*. In the midst of all this Clutter and Revolution, in comes *Peter* with a File of **Dragoons at his Heels, and gathering from all Hands what was in the Wind, He and his Gang, after several Millions of Scurrilities and Curses, not very important here to repeat, by main Force, very fairly ††kicks them both out of Doors (Plate 17), and would never let them come under his Roof from that Day to this.

¶ *Administred the Cup to the Laity at the Communion.*
† *Allowed the Marriages of Priests.*
‖ *Directed Penitents not to trust to Pardons and Absolutions procur'd for Money, but sent them to implore the Mercy of God, from whence alone Remission is to be obtain'd.*
** *By* Peter's *Dragoons, is meant the Civil Power which those Princes, who were bigotted to the Romish Superstition, employ'd against the Reformers.*
†† *The Pope shuts all who dissent from him out of the Church.*

Plate 17

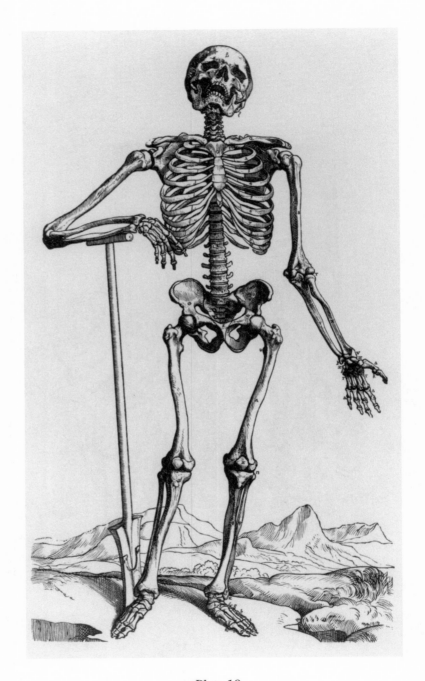

Plate 18

SECT. V.

A Digression in the Modern Kind.

WE whom the World is pleased to honor with the Title of *Modern Authors*, should never have been able to compass our great Design of an everlasting Remembrance, and never dying Fame, if our Endeavours had not been so highly serviceable to the general Good of Mankind. This, *O Universe*, is the Adventurous Attempt of me thy Secretary;

——— *Quemvis perferre laborem*
Suadet, & induct noctes vigilare serenas.

TO this End, I have some Time since, with a World of Pains and Art, dissected the Carcass of *Human Nature*, and read many useful Lectures upon the several Parts, both *Containing* and *Contained*; till at last it *smelt* so strong, I could preserve it no longer. Upon which, I have been at a great Expense to fit up all the Bones with exact Contexture, and in due Symmetry; so that I am ready to shew a very compleat Anatomy (Plate 18) thereof to all curious *Gentlemen* and *Others*. But not to Digress further in the midst of a Digression, as I have known some Authors inclose Digressions in one another, like a Nest of Boxes; I do affirm, that having carefully cut up *Human Nature*, I have found a very strange, new, and important Discovery; That the Publick Good of Mankind is performed by two Ways, *Instruction*, and *Diversion*. And I have further proved in my said several Readings, (which, perhaps, the World may one day see, if I can prevail on any Friend to steal a Copy, or on certain Gentlemen of my Admirers, to be very Importunate) that, as Mankind is now disposed, he receives much greater Advantage by being *Diverted* than *Instructed*; His Epidemical Diseases being *Fastidiosity, Amorphy,* and *Oscitation*; whereas in the present universal Empire of Wit and Learning, there seems but little Matter left for *Instruction*. However, in Compliance with a Lesson of great Age and Authority, I have attempted carrying the Point in all its Heights; and accordingly throughout this Divine Treatise, have skilfully kneaded up both together with a *Layer* of *Utile* and a *Layer* of *Dulce*.

WHEN I consider how exceedingly our Illustrious *Moderns* have eclipsed the weak glimmering Lights of the *Antients*, and turned them out of the Road of all fashionable Commerce, to a degree, that our choice *Town Wits

---

* *The Learned Person here meant by our Author, hath been endeavouring to annihilate so many Antient Writers, that until he is pleas'd to stop his hand it will be dangerous to affirm, whether there have been any Antients in the World.*

of most refined Accomplishments, are in grave Dispute, whether there have
been ever any *Antients* or no: In which Point we are like to receive wonderful Satisfaction from the most useful Labours and Lucubrations of that
Worthy *Modern*, Dr. B——l–y. I say, when I consider all this, I cannot but be-
wail, that no famous *Modern* hath ever yet attempted an universal System in
a small portable Volume, of all Things that are to be Known, or Believed, or
Imagined, or Practised in Life. I am, however, forced to acknowledge, that
such an Enterprise was thought on some Time ago by a great Philosopher of
*O. Brazile (Plate 19). The Method he proposed, was by a certain curious
Receipt, a *Nostrum*, which after his untimely Death, I found among his Papers;
and do here out of my great Affection to the *Modern Learned*, present them
with it, not doubting, it may one Day encourage some worthy Undertaker.

YOU *take fair correct Copies, well bound in Calf's Skin, and Lettered at the Back,
of all Modern Bodies of Arts and Sciences whatsoever, and in what Language you
please. These you distil in* balneo Mariæ, *infusing* Quintessence of Poppy Q.S.
together with three Pints of Lethe, *to be had from the Apothecaries. You cleanse away
carefully the* Sordes *and* Caput mortuum, *letting all that is volatile evaporate.
You preserve onely the first Running, which is again to be distilled seventeen times,
till what remains will amount to about two Drams. This you keep in a Glass Viol*
Hermetically *sealed, for one and twenty Days. Then you begin your Catholick
Treatise, taking every Morning fasting, (first shaking the Viol), three Drops of this*
Elixir, *snuffing it strongly up your Nose. It will dilate it self about the Brain (where
there is any) in fourteen Minutes, and you immediately perceive in your Head an
infinite Number of* Abstracts, Summaries, Compendiums, Extracts, Collections,
Medulla's, Excerpta quædam's, Florilegia's *and the like, all disposed into great
Order, and reduceable upon Paper.*

I must needs own, it was by the Assistance of this *Arcanum*, that I, tho'
otherwise *impar*, have adventured upon so daring an Attempt; never
atchieved or undertaken before, but by a certain Author called *Homer*, in
whom, tho' otherwise a Person not without some Abilities, and *for an
Ancient*, of a tolerable Genius; I have discovered many
gross Errors, which are not to be forgiven his very Ashes,
if by chance any of them are left. For whereas, we are
assured, he design'd his Work for a †compleat Body of all
Knowledge, Human, Divine, Political, and Mechanick; it
is manifest, he hath wholly neglected some, and been
very imperfect in the rest. For, first of all, as eminent a Cabalist as his
Disciples would represent Him, his Account of the *Opus magnum* is

† *Homerus omnes res
humanas Poematis
complexus est.*
Xenophon. In
conviv.

---

* *This is an imaginary Island, of Kin to that which is call'd the* Painters Wives Island, *placed in
some unknown part of the Ocean, merely at the Fancy of the Map-maker.*

Plate 19

Any Card matches or Saveaffs
Aux Allumettes et Binets
Lesca e Solfanelli da vendere

Mauron delin.

F. Tempest ex
Cum Privilegi:

Plate 20

extreamly poor and deficient; he seems to have read but very superficially, either *Sendivogius, Behmen,* or ¶*Anthroposophia Theomagica.* He is also quite mistaken about the *Sphæra Pyroplastica,* a neglect not to be atoned for; and (if the Reader will admit so severe a Censure) *Vix crederem Autorem hunc, unquam audivisse ignis vocem.* His Failings are not less prominent in several Parts of the *Mechanicks.* For, having read his Writings with the utmost Application usual among *Modern Wits,* I could never yet discover the least Direction about the Structure of that useful Instrument a *Save-all* (Plate 20). For want of which, if the *Moderns* had not lent their Assistance, we might yet have wandred *in the Dark.* But I have still behind, a Fault far more notorious to tax this Author with; I mean, his gross Ignorance in the *Common Laws of this Realm,* and in the Doctrine as well as Discipline of the Church of *England.* A Defect indeed, for which both he and all the Antients stand most justly censured by my worthy and ingenious Friend *Mr. *W–tt–on,* Batchelor of Divinity, in his incomparable Treatise of *Ancient and Modern Learning;* A Book never to be sufficiently valued, whether we consider the happy Turns and Flowings of the Author's Wit, the great Usefulness of his sublime Discoveries upon the Subject of *Flies* and *Spittle,* or the laborious Eloquence of his Stile. And I cannot forbear doing that Author the Justice of my publick Acknowledgments, for the great *Helps* and *Liftings* I had out of his incomparable Piece, while I was penning this Treatise.

BUT, besides these Omissions in *Homer* already mentioned, the curious Reader will also observe several Defects in that Author's Writings, for which he is not altogether so accountable. For whereas every Branch of Knowledge has received such wonderful Acquirements since his Age, especially within these last three Years, or thereabouts; it is almost impossible, he could be so very perfect in Modern Discoveries, as his Advocates pretend. We freely acknowledge Him to be the Inventor of the *Compass,* of *Gun-powder,* and the *Circulation of the Blood*: But, I challenge any of his Admirers to shew me in all his Writings, a compleat Account of the *Spleen*; Does he not also leave us wholly to seek in the Art of *Political Wagering*? What can be more defective and unsatisfactory than his long Dissertation upon *Tea*? And as to his Method of *Salivation without Mercury,* so much celebrated of late, it is to my own Knowledge and Experience, a Thing very little to be relied on.

¶ *A Treatise written about fifty Years ago, by a* Welsh *Gentleman of* Cambridge, *his Name, as I remember, was* Vaughan, *as appears by the Answer to it, writ by the Learned Dr.* Henry Moor, *it is a Piece of the most unintelligible Fustian, that, perhaps, was ever publish'd in any Language.*

* *Mr.* W–tt–n (*to whom our Author never gives any Quarter*) *in his Comparison of Antient and Modern Learning, Numbers Divinity, Law,* &c. *among those Parts of Knowledge wherein we excel the Antients.*

IT was to supply such momentous Defects, that I have been prevailed on after long Sollicitation, to take Pen in Hand; and I dare venture to Promise, the Judicious Reader shall find nothing neglected here, that can be of Use upon any Emergency of Life. I am confident to have included and exhausted all that Human Imagination can *Rise* or *Fall* to. Particularly, I recommend to the Perusal of the Learned, certain Discoveries that are wholly untoucht by others; whereof I shall only mention among a great many more; *My New Help of Smatterers,* or the *Art of being Deep learned, and Shallow read. A curious Invention about Mouse-Traps. An Universal Rule of Reason, or Every Man his own Carver;* Together with a most useful Engine for *catching of Owls.* All which the judicious Reader will find largely treated on, in the several Parts of this Discourse.

I hold my self obliged to give as much Light as is possible, into the Beauties and Excellencies of what I am writing, because it is become the Fashion and Humor most applauded among the first Authors of this Polite and Learned Age, when they would correct the ill Nature of Critical, or inform the Ignorance of Courteous Readers. Besides, there have been several famous Pieces lately published both in Verse and Prose; wherein, if the Writers had not been pleased, out of their great Humanity and Affection to the Publick, to give us a nice Detail of the *Sublime,* and the *Admirable* they contain; it is a thousand to one, whether We should ever have discovered one Grain of either. For my own particular, I cannot deny, that whatever I have said upon this Occasion, had been more proper in a Preface, and more agreeable to the Mode, which usually directs it there. But I here think fit to lay hold on that great and honorable Privilege of being the *Last Writer;* I claim an absolute Authority in Right, as the *freshest Modern,* which gives me a Despotick Power over all Authors before me. In the Strength of which Title, I do utterly disapprove and declare against that pernicious Custom, of making the Preface a Bill of Fare to the Book. For I have always lookt upon it as a high Point of Indiscretion in *Monster-mongers* and other *Retailers of strange Sights;* to hang out a fair large Picture over the Door, drawn after the Life, with a most eloquent Description underneath: This hath saved me many a Threepence, for my Curiosity was fully satisfied, and I never offered to go in, tho' often invited by the urging and attending Orator, with his last *moving* and *standing* Piece of Rhetorick; *Sir, Upon my Word, we are just going to begin.* Such is exactly the Fate, at this Time, of *Prefaces, Epistles, Advertisements, Introductions, Prolegomena's, Apparatus's, To-the- Readers's.* This Expedient was admirable at first; Our Great *Dryden* has long carried it as far as it would go, and with incredible Success. He has often said to me in Confidence, that the World would have never suspected him to be so great a Poet, if he had not assured them so frequently in his

Prefaces, that it was impossible they could either doubt or forget it. Perhaps it may be so; However, I much fear, his Instructions have edify'd out of their Place, and taught Men to grow Wiser in certain Points, where he never intended they should: For it is lamentable to behold, with what a lazy Scorn, many of the yawning Readers in our Age, do now a-days twirl over forty or fifty Pages of *Preface* and *Dedication,* (which is the usual *Modern* Stint) as if it were so much *Latin.* Tho' it must be also allowed on the other Hand that a very considerable Number is known to proceed *Criticks* and *Wits,* by reading nothing else. Into which two Factions, I think, all present Readers may justly be divided. Now, for my self, I profess to be of the former Sort; and therefore having the *Modern* Inclination to expatiate upon the Beauty of my own Productions, and display the bright Parts of my Discourse; I thought best to do it in the Body of the Work, where, as it now lies, it makes a very considerable Addition to the Bulk of the Volume, *a Circumstance by no means to be neglected by a skilful Writer.*

HAVING thus paid my due Deference and Acknowledgment to an establish'd Custom of our newest Authors, by *a long Digression unsought for,* and *an universal Censure unprovoked;* By forcing into the Light, with much Pains and Dexterity, my own Excellencies and other Mens Defaults, with great Justice to my self and Candor to them; I now happily resume my Subject, to the infinite Satisfaction both of the Reader and the Author.

SECT. VI.

A TALE of a TUB

WE left *Lord Peter* in open Rupture with his two Brethren; both for ever discarded from his House, and resigned to the wide World, with little or nothing to trust to. Which are Circumstances that render them proper Subjects for the Charity of a Writer's Pen to work on; Scenes of Misery ever affording the fairest Harvest for great Adventures. And in this, the World may perceive the Difference between the Integrity of a generous Author, and that of a common Friend. The latter is observed to adhere close in Prosperity, but on the Decline of Fortune, to drop suddenly off. Whereas, the generous Author, just on the contrary, finds his Hero on the Dunghil, from thence by gradual Steps, raises Him to a Throne, and then immediately withdraws, expecting not so much as Thanks for his Pains: In imitation of which Example, I have placed *Lord Peter* in a Noble House, given Him a Title to wear, and Money to spend. There I shall leave Him for some Time; returning where common Charity directs me, to the Assistance of his Brothers, at their lowest Ebb. However, I shall by no means forget my Character of an Historian, to follow the Truth, step by step, whatever happens, or wherever it may lead me.

THE two Exiles so nearly united in Fortune and Interest, took a Lodging together; Where, at their first Leisure, they began to reflect on the numberless Misfortunes and Vexations of their Life past, and could not tell, of the sudden, to what Failure in their Conduct they ought to impute them; When, after some Recollection, they called to Mind the Copy of their Father's *Will*, which they had so happily recovered. This was immediately produced, and a firm Resolution taken between them, to alter whatever was already amiss, and reduce all their future Measures to the strictest Obedience prescribed therein. The main Body of the *Will* (as the Reader cannot easily have forgot) consisted in certain admirable Rules about the wearing of their Coats; in the Perusal whereof, the two Brothers at every Period duely comparing the Doctrine with the Practice, there was never seen a wider Difference between two Things; horrible down-right Transgressions of every Point. Upon which, they both resolved without further Delay, to fall immediately upon reducing the Whole, exactly after their Father's Model.

BUT, here it is good to stop the hasty Reader, ever impatient to see the End of an Adventure, before We Writers can duly prepare him for it. I am to record, that these two Brothers began to be distinguished at this Time, by certain Names. One of them desired to be called *MARTIN, and the other

* *Martin Luther*

took the Appellation of †*JACK.* These two had lived in much Friendship and Agreement under the Tyranny of their Brother *Peter,* as it is the Talent of Fellow-Sufferers to do; Men in Misfortune, being like Men in the Dark, to whom all Colours are the same: But when they came forward into the World, and began to display themselves to each other, and to the Light, their Complexions appear'd extremely different; which the present Posture of their Affairs gave them sudden Opportunity to discover.

BUT, here the severe Reader may justly tax me as a Writer of short Memory, a Deficiency to which a true *Modern* cannot but of Necessity be a little subject: Because, *Memory* being an Employment of the Mind upon things past, is a Faculty, for which the Learned, in our illustrious Age, have no manner of Occasion, who deal entirely with *Invention,* and strike all Things out of themselves, or at least, by Collision, from each other: Upon which Account, we think it highly reasonable to produce our great Forget-fulness, as an Argument unanswerable for our great Wit. I ought in Method, to have informed the Reader about fifty Pages ago, of a Fancy *Lord Peter* took, and infused into his Brothers, to wear on their Coats whatever Trimmings came up in Fashion; never pulling off any, as they went out of the Mode, but keeping on all together; which amounted in time to a Medley, the most Antick you can possibly conceive; and this to a Degree, that upon the Time of their Falling out there was hardly a Thread of the Original Coat to be seen, but an infinite Quantity of *Lace,* and *Ribbands,* and *Fringe,* and *Embroidery,* and *Points*; (I mean, only those *tagg'd with Silver,* for the rest fell off.) Now, this material Circumstance, having been forgot in due Place; as good Fortune hath ordered, comes in very properly here, when the two Brothers are just going to reform their Vestures into the Primitive State, prescribed by their Father's *Will.*

THEY both unanimously entred upon this great Work, looking sometimes on their Coats, and sometimes on the *Will. Martin* laid the first Hand; at one twitch brought off a large Handful of *Points,* and with a second pull, stript away ten dozen Yards of *Fringe.* But when He had gone thus far, he demurred a while: He knew very well, there yet remained a great deal more to be done; however, the first Heat being over, his Violence began to cool, and he resolved to proceed more moderately in the rest of the Work; having already very narrowly scaped a swinging Rent in pulling of the *Points,* which being *tagged with Silver* (as we have observed before) the judicious Workman had with much Sagacity, double sown, to preserve them from *falling.* Resolving therefore to rid his Coat of a huge Quantity of *Gold*

---

† *John Calvin.*

* *Points tagg'd with Silver, are those Doctrines that promote the Greatness and Wealth of the Church, which have been therefore woven deepest in the Body of Popery.*

Lace; he pickt up the Stitches with much Caution, and diligently gleaned out all the loose Threads as he went, which proved to be a Work of Time. Then he fell about the embroidered *Indian* Figures of Men, Women, and Children; against which, as you have heard in its due Place, their Father's Testament was extreamly exact and severe: These, with much Dexterity and Application, were after a while, quite eradicated, or utterly defaced. For the rest, where he observed the Embroidery to be workt so close, as not to be got away without damaging the Cloth, or where it served to hide or strengthen any Flaw in the Body of the Coat, contracted by the perpetual tampering of Workmen upon it; he concluded the wisest Course was to let it remain, resolving in no Case whatsoever, that the Substance of the Stuff should suffer Injury; which he thought the best Method for serving the true Intent and Meaning of his Father's *Will.* And this is the nearest Account I have been able to collect, of *Martin's* Proceedings upon this great Revolution.

BUT, his Brother *Jack,* whose Adventures will be so extraordinary, as to furnish a great Part in the Remainder of this Discourse; entred upon the Matter with other Thoughts, and a quite different Spirit. For, the Memory of *Lord Peter's* Injuries, produced a Degree of Hatred and Spight, which had a much greater Share of inciting Him, than any Regards after his Father's Commands, since these appeared at best, only Secondary and Subservient to the other. However, for this Meddly of Humor, he made a Shift to find a very plausible Name, honoring it with the Title of *Zeal;* which is, perhaps, the most significant Word that hath been ever yet produced in any Language; As, I think, I have fully proved in my excellent *Analytical* Discourse upon that Subject; wherein I have deduced a *Histori-theo-physi-logical* Account of *Zeal,* shewing how it first proceeded from a *Notion* into a *Word,* and from thence in a hot Summer, ripened into a *tangible Substance.* This Work containing three large Volumes in Folio, I design very shortly to publish by the *Modern* way of *Subscription,* not doubting but the Nobility and Gentry of the Land will give me all possible Encouragement, having already had such a Taste of what I am able to perform.

I record therefore, that Brother *Jack,* brim-full of this miraculous Compound, reflecting with Indignation upon *PETER's* Tyranny, and further provoked by the Despondency of *Martin;* prefaced his Resolutions to this purpose. *What?,* said he; *A Rogue that lockt up his Drink, turned away our Wives, cheated us of our Fortunes; paumed his damned Crusts upon us for Mutton; and at last kickt us out of Doors; must we be in His Fashions with a Pox? a Rascal, besides, that all the Street cries out against.* Having thus kindled and enflamed himself as high as possible, and by Consequence, in a delicate Temper for beginning a Reformation, he set about the Work immediately (Plate 21), and in three

Plate 21

Minutes, made more Dispatch than *Martin* had done in as many Hours. For, (Courteous Reader) you are given to understand, that *Zeal* is never so highly obliged, as when you set it a *Tearing;* and *Jack,* who doated on that Quality in himself, allowed it at this Time its full Swinge. Thus it happened, that stripping down a Parcel of *Gold Lace,* a little too hastily, he rent the *main Body* of his *Coat* from Top to Bottom; and whereas his Talent was not of the happiest in *taking up a Stitch,* he knew no better way, than to dern it again with *Packthread* and a *Scewer.* But the Matter was yet infinitely worse (I record it with Tears) when he proceeded to the *Embroidery:* For, being Clumsy by Nature, and of Temper, Impatient; withal, beholding Millions of Stitches, that required the nicest Hand, and sedatest Constitution, to extricate; in a great Rage, he tore off the whole Piece, Cloth and all, and flung it into the Kennel, and furiously thus continuing his Career; *Ah, Good Brother* Martin, said he, *do as I do, for the love of God; Strip, Tear, Pull, Rent, Flay off all, that we may appear as unlike that Rogue* Peter, *as it is possible: I would not for a hundred Pounds carry the least Mark about me, that might give Occasion to the Neighbours, of suspecting I was related to such a Rascal.* But *Martin,* who at this Time happened to be extremely flegmatick and sedate, *begged his Brother of all Love, not to damage his Coat by any Means; for he never would get such another.* Desired him *to consider, that it was not their Business to form their Actions by any Reflection upon* Peter's, *but by observing the Rules prescribed in their Father's* Will. That *he should remember,* Peter *was still their Brother, whatever Faults or Injuries he had committed; and therefore they should by all means avoid such a Thought, as that of taking Measures for Good and Evil, from no other Rule, than of Opposition to him.* That *it was true, the Testament of their good Father was very exact in what related to the wearing of their* Coats; *yet was it no less penal and strict in prescribing Agreement, and Friendship, and Affection between them. And therefore, if straining a Point were at all dispensable, it would certainly be so, rather to the Advance of Unity, than Increase of Contradiction.*

MARTIN had still proceeded as gravely as he began; and doubtless, would have delivered an admirable Lecture of Morality, which might have exceedingly contributed to my Reader's *Repose, both of Body and Mind:* (the true ultimate End of *Ethicks;*) But *Jack* was already gone a Flight-shot beyond his Patience. And as in Scholastick Disputes, nothing serves to rouze the Spleen of him that *Opposes,* so much as a kind of Pedantick affected Calmness in the *Respondent;* Disputants being for the most part like unequal Scales, where the *Gravity* of one Side advances the *Lightness* of the Other, and causes it to fly up and kick the Beam; So it happened here, that the *Weight* of *Martin's* Arguments exalted *Jack's Levity,* and made him fly out and spurn against his Brother's Moderation. In short, *Martin's Patience* put *Jack* in a *Rage;* but that which most afflicted him was, to observe his

Brother's Coat so well reduced into the State of Innocence; while his own was either wholly rent to his Shirt; or those Places which had scaped his cruel Clutches, were still in *Peter's* Livery. So that he looked like a drunken *Beau*, half rifled by *Bullies*; Or like a fresh Tenant of *Newgate*, when he has refused the Payment of *Garnish*; Or like a discovered *Shoplifter*, left to the Mercy of *Exchange-Women*; Or like a *Bawd* in her old Velvet-Petticoat, resigned into the secular Hands of the *Mobile*. Like any, or like all of these, a Meddley of *Rags*, and *Lace*, and *Rents*, and *Fringes*, unfortunate *Jack* did now appear: He would have been extreamly glad to see his Coat in the Condition of *Martin's*, but infinitely gladder to find that of *Martin's* in the same Predicament with his. However, since neither of these was likely to come to pass, he thought fit to lend the whole Business another Turn, and to dress up Necessity into a Virtue. Therefore, after as many of the *Fox's* Arguments, as he could muster up, for bringing *Martin* to *Reason*, as he called it; or, as he meant it, into his own ragged, bobtail'd Condition; and observing he said all to little purpose; what, alas, was left for the forlorn *Jack* to do, but after a Million of Scurrilities against his Brother, to run mad with Spleen, and Spight, and Contradiction. To be short, here began a mortal Breach between these two. *Jack* went immediately to *New Lodgings*, and in a few Days it was for certain reported, that he had run out of his Wits. In a short time after, he appeared abroad, and confirmed the Report, by falling into the oddest Whimsies that ever a sick Brain conceived.

AND now the little Boys in the Streets began to salute him with several Names. Sometimes they would call Him, **Jack the Bald*; sometimes, †*Jack with a Lanthorn;* sometimes, ‖*Dutch Jack*; sometimes, **French Hugh*; sometimes, †*Tom the Beggar;* and sometimes, ¶*Knocking Jack of the North*. And it was under one or some, or all of these Appellations (which I leave the Learned Reader to determine) that he hath given Rise to the most Illustrious and Epidemick Sect of *Æolists*; who with honourable Commemoration, do still acknowledge the Renowned *JACK* for their Author and Founder. Of whose Originals, as well as Principles, I am now advancing to gratify the World with a very particular Account.

—— *Mellæo contingens cuncta Lepore.*

---

* *That is* Calvin, *from* Calvus, *Bald.*
† *All those who pretend to Inward Light.*
‖ Jack *of* Leyden, *who gave Rise to the* Anabaptists.
* *The* Hugonots.
† *The* Gueuses, *by which Name some Protestants in* Flanders *were call'd.*
¶ John Knox, *the Reformer of* Scotland.

SECT. VII.

A Digression in Praise of Digressions.

I HAVE sometimes *heard* of an *Iliad* in a *Nut-shell*; but it hath been my Fortune to have much oftner *seen* a *Nut-shell* in an *Iliad*. There is no doubt, that Human Life has received most wonderful Advantages from both; but to which of the two the World is chiefly indebted, I shall leave among the Curious, as a Problem worthy of their utmost Enquiry. For the Invention of the latter, I think the Commonwealth of Learning is chiefly obliged to the great *Modern* Improvement of *Digressions*: The late Refinements in Knowledge, running parallel to those of Dyet in our Nation, which among Men of a judicious Taste, are drest up in various Compounds, consisting in *Soupes* and *Ollioes, Fricassées,* and *Ragousts.*

'TIS true, there is a sort of morose, detracting, ill-bred People, who pretend utterly to disrelish these polite Innovations: And as to the Similitude from Dyet, they allow the Parallel, but are so bold to pronounce the Example it self, a Corruption and Degeneracy of Taste. They tell us, that the Fashion of jumbling fifty Things together in a Dish, was at first introduced in Compliance to a depraved and *debauched Appetite*, as well as to a *crazy Constitution;* And to see a Man hunting thro' an *Ollio*, after the *Head* and *Brains* of a *Goose,* a *Wigeon,* or a *Woodcock,* is a Sign, he wants a Stomach and Digestion for more substantial Victuals. Further, they affirm, that *Digressions* in a Book, are like *Forein Troops* in a *State*, which argue the Nation to want a *Heart* and *Hands* of its own, and often, either *subdue* the *Natives,* or drive them into the most *unfruitful Corners.*

BUT, after all that can be objected by these supercilious Censors; 'tis manifest, the Society of Writers would quickly be reduced to a very inconsiderable Number, if Men were put upon making Books, with the fatal Confinement of delivering nothing beyond what is to the Purpose. 'Tis acknowledged, that were the Case the same among Us, as with the *Greeks* and *Romans,* when Learning was in its *Cradle,* to be reared and fed, and cloathed by *Invention;* it would be an easy Task to fill up Volumes upon particular Occasions, without further exspatiating from the Subject, than by moderate Excursions, helping to advance or clear the main Design. But with *Knowledge,* it has fared as with a numerous Army, encamped in a fruitful Country; which for a few Days maintains it self by the Product of the Soyl it is on; Till Provisions being spent, they send to forrage many a Mile, among Friends or Enemies it matters not. Mean while, the neighbouring Fields trampled and beaten down, become barren and dry, affording no Sustenance but Clouds of Dust.

THE whole Course of Things being thus entirely changed between *Us* and the *Antients*; and the *Moderns* wisely sensible of it, we of this Age have discovered a shorter, and more prudent Method, to become *Scholars* and *Wits*, without the Fatigue of *Reading* or of *Thinking*. The most accomplisht Way of using Books at present, is twofold: Either first, to serve them as some Men do *Lords*, learn their *Titles* exactly, and then brag of their Acquaintance. Or Secondly, which is indeed the choicer, the profounder, and politer Method, to get a thorough Insight into the *Index*, by which the whole Book is governed and turned, like *Fishes* by the *Tail*. For, to enter the Palace of Learning at the *great Gate*, requires an Expence of Time and Forms; therefore Men of much Haste and little Ceremony, are content to get in by the *Back-Door*. For, the Arts are all in a *flying* March, and therefore more easily subdued by attacking them in the *Rear*. Thus Physicians discover the State of the whole Body, by consulting only what comes from *Behind*. Thus Men catch Knowledge by throwing their Wit on the *Posteriors* of a Book, as Boys do Sparrows with flinging *Salt* upon their *Tails*. Thus Human Life is best understood by the wise man's Rule of *Regarding the End*. Thus are the Sciences found like *Hercules*'s Oxen, by *tracing them backwards*. Thus are *old Sciences* unravelled like *old Stockins*, by beginning at the *Foot*.

BESIDES all this, the Army of the Sciences hath been of late with a world of Martial Discipline, drawn into its *close Order*, so that a View, or a Muster may be taken of it with abundance of Expedition. For this great Blessing we are wholly indebted to *Systems* and *Abstracts*, in which the *Modern* Fathers of Learning, like prudent Usurers, spent their Sweat for the Ease of Us their Children. For *Labor* is the Seed of *Idleness*, and it is the peculiar Happiness of our Noble Age to gather the *Fruit*.

NOW the Method of growing Wise, Learned, and *Sublime*, having become so regular an Affair, and so established in all its Forms; the Number of Writers must needs have encreased accordingly, and to a Pitch that has made it of absolute Necessity for them to interfere continually with each other. Besides, it is reckoned, that there is not at this present, a sufficient Quantity of new Matter left in Nature, to furnish and adorn any one particular Subject to the Extent of a Volume. This I am told by a very skillful *Computer*, who hath given a full Demonstration of it from Rules of *Arithmetick*.

THIS, perhaps, may be objected against, by those, who maintain the Infinity of Matter, and therefore, will not allow that any *Species* of it can be exhausted. For Answer to which, let us examine the noblest Branch of *Modern* Wit or Invention, planted and cultivated by the present Age, and, which of all others, hath born the most, and the fairest Fruit. For tho' some Remains of it were left us by the *Antients*, yet have not any of those, as I

remember, been translated or compiled into Systems for *Modern* Use.
Therefore We may affirm, to our own Honor, that it has in some sort, been
both invented, and brought to a Perfection by the same Hands. What I
mean, is that highly celebrated Talent among the *Modern* Wits, of deducing
Similitudes, Allusions, and Applications, very Surprizing, Agreeable, and
Apposite, from the Genitals of either Sex, together with *their proper Uses.*
And truly, having observed how little Invention bears any Vogue, besides
what is derived into these *Channels*, I have sometimes had a Thought, That
the happy Genius of our Age and Country, was pro-
phetically held forth by that antient *typical Description of   * *Ctesiæ fragm.*
the *Indian* Pygmies; *whose Stature did not exceed above two Foot;*   *apud Photium*
S*ed quorum pudenda crassa, & ad talos usque pertingentia.* Now, I have been
very curious to inspect the late Productions, wherein the Beauties of this
kind have most prominently appeared. And altho' this *Vein* hath bled so
freely, and all Endeavours have been used in the Power of Human Breath,
to dilate, extend, and keep it open: Like the Scythians, †*who*
had a Custom, and an Instrument, to blow up the Privities of their   † *Herodot. L. 4.*
Mares, that they might yield the more Milk; Yet I am under an Apprehension, it
is near growing dry, and past all Recovery; And that either some new *Fonde*
of Wit should, if possible, be provided, or else that we must e'en be content
with Repetition here, as well as upon all other Occasions.

THIS will stand as an uncontestable Argument, that our *Modern* Wits are
not to reckon upon the Infinity of Matter, for a constant Supply. What
remains therefore, but that our last Recourse must be had to large *Indexes*,
and little *Compendiums*; *Quotations* must be plentifully gathered, and bookt
in Alphabet; To this End, tho' Authors need be little consulted, yet *Criticks*,
and *Commentators*, and *Lexicons* carefully must. But above all, those judicious
Collectors of *bright Parts*, and *Flowers*, and *Observanda's*, are to be nicely
dwelt on; by some called the *Sieves* and *Boulters* of Learning; tho' it is left
undetermined, whether they dealt in *Pearls* or *Meal*; and consequently,
whether we are more to value that which *passed thro'*, or what *staid behind.*

BY these Methods, in a few Weeks, there starts up many a Writer, capable
of managing the profoundest, and most universal Subjects. For, what tho'
his *Head* be empty, provided his *Common-place-Book* be full; And if you will
bate him but the Circumstances of *Method*, and *Style*, and *Grammar*, and
Invention; allow him but the common Privileges of transcribing from others,
and digressing from himself, as often as he shall see Occasion; He will
desire no more Ingredients towards fitting up a Treatise, that shall make a
very comely Figure on a Bookseller's Shelf, there to be preserved neat and
clean, for a long Eternity, adorn'd with the Heraldry of its Title, fairly
inscribed on a Label; never to be thumb'd or greas'd by Students, nor

bound to everlasting Chains of Darkness in a Library (Plate 22): But when the Fulness of Time is come, shall haply undergo the Tryal of Purgatory, in order *to ascend the Sky.*

WITHOUT these Allowances, how is it possible, we *Modern* Wits should ever have an Opportunity to introduce our Collections, listed under so many thousand Heads of a different Nature? for want of which, the Learned World would be deprived of infinite Delight, as well as Instruction, and we our selves buried beyond Redress in an inglorious and undistinguisht Oblivion.

FROM such Elements as these, I am alive to behold the Day, wherein the Corporation of Authors can out-vie all its Brethren in the Yield. A Happiness derived to us with a great many others, from our *Scythian* Ancestors; among whom, the Number of *Pens* was so infinite, that the * *Grecian* Eloquence had no other way of expressing it, than by saying, *That in the Regions, far to the* North, *it was hardly possible for a Man to travel, the very Air was so replete with* Feathers.

* *Herodot.* L. 4.

THE Necessity of this Digression, will easily excuse the Length; and I have chosen for it as proper a Place as I could readily find. If the judicious Reader can assign a fitter, I do here empower him to remove it into any other Corner he please. And so I return with great Alacrity to pursue a more important Concern.

Plate 22

SECT. VIII.

A TALE of a TUB.

THE Learned *Æolists, maintain the Original Cause of all Things to be *Wind*, from which Principle this whole Universe was at first produced, and into which it must at last be resolved; that the same Breath which had kindled, and blew *up* the Flame of Nature, should one Day blow it *out*.

Quod procul à nobis flectat Fortuna gubernans.

THIS is what the *Adepti* understand by their *Anima Mundi*; that is to say, the *Spirit*, or *Breath*, or *Wind* of the World: Or Examine the whole System by the Particulars of Nature, and you will find it not to be disputed. For, whether you please to call the *Forma informans* of Man, by the Name of *Spiritus, Animus, Afflatus, or Anima*; what are all these but several Appellations for *Wind*? which is the ruling *Element* in every Compound, and into which they all resolve upon their Corruption. Further, what is Life it self, but as it is commonly called, the *Breath* of our Nostrils? Whence it is very justly observed by Naturalists, that *Wind* still continues of great Emolument in *certain Mysteries* not to be named, giving Occasion for those happy Epithets of *Turgidus*, and *Inflatus*, apply'd either to the *Emittent*, or *Recipient* Organs.

BY what I have gathered out of antient Records, I find, the *Compass* of their Doctrine took in two and thirty Points, wherein it would be tedious to be very particular. However, a few of their most important Precepts, deduceable from it, are by no means to be omitted; among which, the following Maxim was of much Weight; That since *Wind* had the Master Share, as well as Operation in every Compound, by Consequence, those Beings must be of chief Excellence, wherein that *Primordium* appears most prominently to abound; and therefore, *Man* is in highest Perfection of all created Things, as having by the great Bounty of Philosophers, been endued with three distinct *Anima's* or *Winds*, to which the Sage *Æolists*, with much Liberality, have added a fourth, of equal Necessity, as well as Ornament with the other three; by this *quartum Principium*, taking in the four Corners of the World. Which gave Occasion to that Renowned *Cabalist*, †*Bumbastus*, of placing the Body of a Man, in due Position to the four *Cardinal* Points.

---

* *All Pretenders to Inspiration whatsoever.*
† *This is one of the Names of* Paracelsus; *He was call'd* Christophorus, Theophrastus, Paracelsus, Bumbastus.

IN Consequence of this, their next Principle was, that *Man* brings with Him into the World a peculiar Portion, or Grain of *Wind*, which may be called a *Quinta essentia*, extracted from the other four. This *Quintessence* is of Catholick Use upon all Emergencies of Life, is improveable into all Arts and Sciences, and may be wonderful refined, as well as enlarged by certain Methods in Education. This, when *blown* up to its Perfection, ought not to be covetously hoarded up, stifled, or hid under a Bushel, but freely communicated to Mankind. Upon these Reasons, and others of equal Weight, the Wise *Æolists*, affirm the Gift of *BELCHING*, to be the noblest Act of a Rational Creature. To cultivate which Art, and render it more serviceable to Mankind, they made Use of several Methods. At certain Seasons of the Year, you might behold the Priests amongst them in vast Numbers, with their *Mouths gaping wide against a Storm.* At other times were to be seen several Hundreds link'd together in a circular Chain, with every Man a Pair of Bellows applied to his Neighbour's Breech, by which they blew up each other to the Shape and Size of a *Tun*; and for that Reason, with great Propriety of Speech, did usually call their Bodies, their *Vessels*. When, by these and the like Performances, they were grown sufficiently replete, they would immediately depart, and disembogue for the Publick Good a plentiful Share of their Acquirements into their Disciples Chaps. For we must here observe, that all Learning was esteemed among them to be compounded from the same Principle. Because, First, it is generally affirm'd, or confess'd, that Learning *puffeth Men up*. And Secondly, they proved it by the following Syllogism; *Words are but Wind; and Learning is nothing but Words*; Ergo, *Learning is nothing but Wind.* For this Reason, the Philosophers among them, did in their Schools, deliver to their Pupils, all their Doctrines and Opinions, by *Eructation*, wherein they had acquired a wonderful Eloquence, and of incredible Variety. But the great Characteristick, by which their chief Sages were best distinguished, was a certain Position of Countenance, which gave undoubted Intelligence to what Degree or Proportion, the Spirit agitated the inward Mass. For, after certain Gripings, the *Wind* and Vapors issuing forth; having first by their Turbulence and Convulsions within, caused an Earthquake in Man's little World; distorted the Mouth, bloated the Cheeks, and gave the Eyes a terrible kind of *Relievo*. At which Junctures, all their *Belches* were received for Sacred, the Sourer the better, and swallowed with infinite Consolation by their meager Devotes. And to render these yet more compleat, because the Breath of Man's Life is in his Nostrils, therefore, the choicest, most edifying, and most enlivening *Belches*, were very wisely conveyed thro' that Vehicle, to give them a Tincture as they passed.

* *This is meant of those Seditious Preachers, who blow up the Seeds of Rebellion, &c.*

THEIR Gods were the four *Winds*, whom they worshipped, as the Spirits that pervade and enliven the Universe, and as those from whom alone all *Inspiration* can properly be said to proceed. However, the Chief of these, to whom they performed the Adoration of *Latria*, was the *Almighty North*, an ancient Deity, whom the Inhabitants of *Megalopolis* in *Greece*, had likewise in highest Reverence. †*Omnium Deorum Boream maxime cele-*
brant. This God, tho' endued with Ubiquity, was yet sup-   † *Pausan.* L.8.
posed by the profounder *Æolists*, to possess one peculiar Habitation, or (to speak in Form) a *Cœlum Empyrœum*, wherein he was more intimately present. This was situated in a certain Region, well known to the Antient *Greeks*, by them called, Σκοτία, or the *Land of Darkness*. And altho' many Controversies have arisen upon that Matter; yet so much is undisputed, that from a Region of the *like Denomination*, the most refined *Æolists* have borrowed their Original, from whence, in every Age, the zealous among their Priesthood, have brought over their choicest *Inspiration*, fetching it with their own Hands, from the Fountain Head, in certain *Bladders*, and disploding it among the Sectaries in all Nations, who did, and do, and ever will, daily Gasp and Pant after it.

NOW, their Mysteries and Rites were performed in this Manner. 'Tis well known among the Learned, that the Virtuoso's of former Ages, had a Contrivance for carrying and preserving *Winds* in Casks or Barrels, which was of great Assistance upon long Sea Voyages; and the Loss of so useful an Art at present, is very much to be lamented, tho' I know not how, with great Negligence omitted by *Pancirollus*. It was an Invention ascribed to *Æolus* himself, from whom this Sect is denominated, and who in Honor of their Founder's Memory, have to this Day preserved great Numbers of those *Barrels*, whereof they fix one in each of their Temples, first beating out the Top. Into this *Barrel* (Plate 6), upon Solemn Days, the Priest enters; where, having before duly prepared himself by the methods already described, a secret Funnel is also convey'd from his Posteriors, to the Bottom of the Barrel, which admits new Supplies of Inspiration from a *Northern* Chink or Crany. Whereupon, you behold him swell immediately to the Shape and Size of his *Vessel*. In this Posture he disembogues whole Tempests upon his Auditory, as the Spirit from beneath gives him Utterance; which, issuing *ex adytis*, and *penetralibus*, is not performed without much Pain and Gripings. And the *Wind* in breaking forth, †deals with his Face, as it does with that of the Sea; first *blackning*, then *wrinkling*, and at last, *bursting it into a Foam*. It is in this Guise, the Sacred *Æolist* delivers his oracular *Belches* to his panting

---

* *An Author who writ* De Artibus Perditis, &c. *of Arts lost, and of Arts invented.*
† *This is an exact Description of the Changes made in the Face by Enthusiastick Preachers.*

Disciples; Of whom, some are greedily gaping after the sanctified Breath; others are all the while hymning out the Praises of the *Winds*; and gently wafted to and fro by their own Humming, do thus represent the soft Breezes of their Deities appeased.

IT is from this Custom of the Priests, that some Authors maintain these *Æolists*, to have been very antient in the World. Because, the Delivery of their Mysteries, which I have just now mentioned, appears exactly the same with that of other ancient Oracles; whose Inspirations were owing to certain subteraneous *Effluviums* of *Wind*, delivered with the *same* Pain to the Priest, and much about the *same* Influence on the People. It is true indeed, that these were frequently managed and directed by *Female* Officers, whose Organs were understood to be better disposed for the Admission of those Oracular *Gusts*, as entring, and passing up thro' a Receptacle of greater Capacity, and causing also a Pruriency by the Way, such as with due Management, hath been refined from a Carnal, into a Spiritual Extasie. And to strengthen this profound Conjecture, it is further insisted, that this Custom of [1]*Female* Priests is kept up still in certain refined Colleges of our *Modern Æolists*, who are agreed to receive their Inspiration, derived thro' the Receptacle aforesaid, like their Ancestors, the *Sybils*.

AND, whereas the Mind of Man, when he gives the Spur and Bridle to his Thoughts, doth never stop, but naturally sallies out into both Extreams of High and Low, of Good and Evil; His first Flight of Fancy, commonly transports Him to Idea's of what is most Perfect, finished, and exalted; till having soared out of his own Reach and Sight, not well perceiving how near the Frontiers of Height and Depth, border upon each other; With the same Course and Wing, he falls down plum into the lowest Bottom of Things; like one who travels the *East* into the *West;* or like a strait Line drawn by its own Length into a Circle. Whether a Tincture of Malice in our Natures, makes us fond of furnishing every bright Idea with its Reverse; Or, whether Reason reflecting upon the Sum of Things, can, like the Sun, serve only to en-lighten one half of the Globe, leaving the other half, by Necessity, under Shade and Darkness, Or, whether Fancy, flying up to the Imagination of what is Highest and Best, becomes over-shot, and Spent, and weary, and suddenly falls like a dead Bird of Paradise, to the Ground. Or, whether after all these *Metaphysical* Conjectures, I have not entirely missed the true Reason; The Proposition, however, which hath stood me in so much Cir-cumstance, is altogether true; That, as the most unciviliz'd Parts of Man-kind, have some way or other, climbed up into the Conception of a *God*, or Supream Power, so they have seldom forgot to provide their Fears with

---

[1] *Quakers who suffer their Women to preach and pray.*

certain gastly Notions, which instead of better, have served them pretty tolerably for a *Devil.* And this Proceeding seems to be natural enough; For it is with Men, whose Imaginations are lifted up very high, after the same Rate, as with those, whose Bodies are so; that, as they are delighted with the Advantage of a nearer Contemplation upwards, so they are equally terrified with the dismal Prospect of the Precipice below. Thus, in the Choice of a *Devil,* it hath been the usual Method of Mankind, to single out some Being, either in Act, or in Vision, which was in most Antipathy to the God they had framed. Thus, also, the Sect of *Æolists,* possessed themselves with a Dread, and Horror, and Hatred of two Malignant Natures, betwixt whom, and the Deities they adored, perpetual Enmity was established. The first of these, was the **Camelion,* sworn Foe to *Inspiration,* who in Scorn, devoured large Influences of their God; without refunding the smallest Blast by *Eruction.* The other was a huge terrible Monster, called *Moulinavent,* who with four strong Arms, waged eternal Battel with all their Divinities, dextrously turning to avoid their Blows, and repay them with Interest.

THUS furnisht, and set out with *Gods,* as well as *Devils,* was the renowned Sect of *Æolists;* which makes at this Day so illustrious a Figure in the World, and whereof, that Polite Nation of *Laplanders,* are beyond all Doubt, a most Authentick Branch; Of whom, I therefore cannot, without Injustice, here omit to make honourable Mention; since they appear to be so closely allied in Point of Interest, as well as Inclinations, with their Brother *Æolists* among Us, as not only to buy their *Winds* by wholesale from the *same* Merchants, but also to retail them after the *same* Rate and Method, and to Customers much alike.

NOW, whether the System here delivered, was wholly compiled by *Jack,* or, as some Writers believe, rather copied from the Original at *Delphos,* with certain Additions and Emendations suited to Times and Circumstances, I shall not absolutely determine. This I may affirm, that *Jack* gave it at least a new Turn, and formed it into the same Dress and Model, as it lies deduced by me.

I have long sought after this Opportunity, of doing Justice to a Society of Men, for whom I have a peculiar Honor, and whose Opinions, as well as Practices, have been extremely misrepresented, and traduced by the Malice or Ignorance of their Adversaries. For, I think it one of the greatest and best of human Actions, to remove Prejudices, and place Things in their truest and fairest Light; which I therefore boldly undertake without any Regards of my own, beside the Conscience, the Honor, and the Thanks.

---

* *I do not well understand what the Author aims at here, any more than by the terrible Monster, mention'd in the following Lines, called* Moulinavent, *which is the* French *Word for a Windmill.*

SECT. IX.

A Digression concerning the Original, the Use, and Improvement of Madness in a Commonwealth.

NOR shall it any ways detract from the just Reputation of this famous Sect, that its Rise and Institution are owing to such an Author as I have described *Jack* to be; A Person whose Intellectuals were overturned, and his Brain shaken out of its Natural Position; which we commonly suppose to be a Distemper, and call by the Name of *Madness* or *Phrenzy*. For, if we take a Survey of the greatest Actions that have been performed in the World, under the Influence of Single Men; which are, *The Establishment of New Empires by Conquest; The Advance and Progress of New Schemes in Philosophy; and the contriving, as well as the propagating of New Religions.* We shall find the Authors of them all, to have been Persons, whose natural Reason hath admitted great Revolutions from their Dyet, their Education, the Prevalency of some certain Temper, together with the particular Influence of Air and Climate. Besides, there is something Individual in human Minds, that easily kindles at the accidental Approach and Collision of certain Circumstances, which tho' of paltry and mean Appearance, do often flame out into the greatest Emergencies of Life. For, great Turns are not always given by strong Hands, but by lucky Adaption, and at proper Seasons; and it is of no import, where the Fire was kindled, if the Vapor has once got up into the Brain. For the *upper Region* of Man, is furnished like the *middle Region* of the Air; The Materials are formed from Causes of the widest Difference, yet produce at last the same Substance and Effect. Mists arise from the Earth, Steams from Dunghils, Exhalations from the Sea, and Smoak from Fire; yet all Clouds are the same in Composition, as well as Consequences: and the Fumes issuing from a Jakes, will furnish as comely and useful a Vapor, as Incense from an Altar. Thus far, I suppose, will easily be granted me: And then it will follow, that as the Face of Nature never produces Rain, but when it is overcast and disturbed; so Human Understanding, seated in the Brain, must be troubled and over-spread by Vapors, ascending from the lower Faculties, to water the Invention, and render it fruitful. Now, altho' these Vapors (as it hath been already said) are of as various Original, as those of the Skies, yet the Crop they produce, differs both in Kind and Degree, meerly according to the Soil. I will produce two Instances to prove and Explain what I am now advancing.

 *A certain Great Prince raised a mighty Army, filled his Coffers with infinite Treasures, provided an invincible Fleet, and all this, without giving

* *This was* Harry *the Great of France.*

the least Part of his Design to his greatest Ministers, or his nearest Favourites. Immediately the whole World was alarmed; the neighbouring Crowns, in trembling Expectation, towards what Point the Storm would burst; the small Politicians, every where forming profound Conjectures. Some believed he had laid a Scheme for Universal Monarchy: Others, after much Insight, determined the Matter to be a Project for pulling down the *Pope*, and setting up the *Reformed* Religion, which had once been his own. Some, again, of a deeper Sagacity, sent him into *Asia* to subdue the *Turk*, and recover *Palestine*. In the midst of all these Projects and Preparations; a certain *State-Surgeon, gathering the Nature of the Disease by these Symptoms, attempted the Cure, at one Blow performed the Operation, broke the Bag, and out flew the *Vapor*, nor did any thing want to render it a compleat Remedy, only, that the Prince unfortunately happened to Die in the Performance. Now, is the Reader exceeding curious to learn, from whence this Vapor took its Rise, which had so long set the Nations at a Gaze? What secret Wheel, what hidden Spring could put into Motion so wonderful an Engine? It was afterwards discovered, that the Movement of this whole Machine had been directed by an absent *Female*, whose Eyes had raised a Protuberancy, and before Emission, she was removed into an Enemy's Country. What should an unhappy Prince do in such ticklish Circumstances as these? He tried in vain the Poet's never-failing Receipt of *Corpora quæque*, For,

> *Idque petit corpus mens unde est saucia amore;*
> *Unde feritur, eo tendit gestiq; coire.* Lucr.

HAVING to no purpose used all peaceable Endeavors, the collected part of the *Semen*, raised and enflamed, became adust, converted to Choler, turned head upon the spinal Duct, and ascended to the Brain. The very same Principle that influences a *Bully* to break the Windows of a Whore, who has jilted him, naturally stirs up a Great Prince to raise Mighty Armies, and dream of nothing but Sieges, Battles, and Victories.

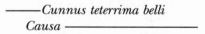

> ———*Cunnus teterrima belli*
> *Causa* ————

THE other ¶Instance is, what I have read somewhere, in a very antient Author, of a Mighty King, who for the space of above thirty Years, amused himself to take and lose Towns; beat Armies, and be beaten; drive Princes out of their Dominions; fright Children from their Bread and Butter; burn,

---

* Ravillac, *who stabb'd* Henry *the Great in his Coach.*
¶ *This is meant of the Present* French *King.*

lay waste, plunder, dragoon, massacre, Subject and Stranger, Friend and Foe, Male and Female. 'Tis recorded, that the Philosophers of each Country were in grave Dispute, upon Causes Natural, Moral, and Political, to find out where they should assign an original Solution of this *Phœnomenon*. At last the *Vapor* or *Spirit*, which animated the Hero's Brain, being in perpetual Circulation, seised upon that Region of the Human Body, so renown'd for furnishing the †*Zibeta Occidentalis*, and gathering there into a Tumor, left the rest of the World for that Time in Peace. Of such mighty Consequence it is, where those Exhalations fix; and of so little, from whence they proceed. The same Spirits which in their superior Progress would conquer a Kingdom, descending upon the *Anus*, conclude in a *Fistula*.

LET us next examine the great Introducers of new Schemes in Philosophy, and search till we can find, from what Faculty of the Soul, the Disposition arises in mortal Man, of taking it into his Head, to advance new Systems with such an eager Zeal, in things agreed on all hands impossible to be known: From what Seeds this Disposition springs, and to what Quality of human Nature these Grand Innovators have been indebted for their Number of Disciples. Because, it is plain, that several of the Chief among them, both *Antient* and *Modern*, were usually mistaken by their Adversaries, and indeed, by all except their own Followers, to have been Persons crazed, or out of their Wits, having generally proceeded in the common Course of their Words and Actions, by a Method very different from the vulgar Dictates of *unrefined* Reason: agreeing for the most Part in their several Models, with their present undoubted Successors in the *Academy* of *Modern Bedlam* (Plate 23) (whose Merits and Principles I shall further examine in due Place.) Of this Kind were *Epicurus, Diogenes, Apollonius, Lucretius, Paracelsus, Des Cartes*, and others; who, if they were now in the World, tied fast, and separate from their Followers, would in this our undistinguishing Age, incur manifest Danger of *Phlebotomy*, and *Whips*, and *Chains*, and *dark Chambers*, and *Straw*. For, what Man in the natural State, or Course of Thinking, did ever conceive it in his Power, to reduce the Notions of all Mankind, exactly to the same Length, and Breadth, and Heighth of his own? Yet this is the first humble and civil Design of all Innovators in the Empire of Reason. *Epicurus,* modestly hoped, that one Time or other, certain Fortuitous Concourse of all Mens Opinions, after perpetual Justlings, the Sharp with the Smooth, the Light and the Heavy, the Round and the Square, would by certain *Clinamina*, unite in the Notions of *Atoms* and *Void*, as these did in the

---

† Paracelsus, *who was so famous for Chymistry, try'd an Experiment upon human Excrement, to make a Perfume of it, which when he had brought to Perfection, he called* Zibeta Occidentalis, *or* Western-Civet, *the back Parts of Man (according to his Division mention'd by the Author,* page 67) *being the* West.

Bethlehem Hospital

Plate 23

Originals of all Things. *Cartesius* reckoned to see before he died, the Sentiments of all Philosophers, like so many lesser Stars in his *Romantick* System, rapt and drawn within his own *Vortex*. Now, I would gladly be informed, how it is possible to account for such Imaginations as these in particular Men, without Recourse to my *Phænomenon* of *Vapors*, ascending from the lower Faculties to over-shadow the Brain, and thence distilling into Conceptions, for which the Narrowness of our Mother-Tongue has not yet assigned any other Name, beside that of *Madness* or *Phrenzy*. Let us therefore now conjecture how it comes to pass, that none of these great Prescribers, do ever fail providing themselves and their Notions, with a Number of implicite Disciples. And, I think, the Reason is easie to be assigned: For, there is a peculiar *String* in the Harmony of Human Understanding, which in several individuals is exactly of the same Tuning. This, if you can dexterously screw up to its right Key, and then strike gently upon it, Whenever you have the Good Fortune to light among those of the same Pitch, they will by a secret necessary Sympathy, strike exactly at the same Time. And in this one Circumstance, lyes all the Skill or Luck of the Matter; for if you chance to jar the String among those who are either above or below your own Height, instead of subscribing to your Doctrine, they will tie you fast, call you Mad, and feed you with Bread and Water. It is therefore a Point of the nicest Conduct to distinguish and adapt this noble Talent, with respect to the Differences of Persons and of Times. *Cicero* understood this very well, when writing to a Friend in *England,* with a Caution, among other Matters, to beware of being cheated by our *Hackney-Coachmen* (who, it seems, in those days, were as arrant Rascals as they are now) has these remarkable Words: **Est quod gaudeas te in ista loca venisse, ubi aliquid sapere viderere.* For, to speak a bold Truth, it ** Epist. Ad Fam. Trebatio* is a fatal Miscarriage, so ill to order Affairs, as to pass for a *Fool* in one Company, when in another you might be treated as a *Philosopher*. Which I desire *some certain Gentlemen of my Acquaintance,* to lay up in their Hearts, as a very seasonable Innuendo.

THIS, indeed, was the Fatal Mistake of that worthy Gentleman, my most ingenious Friend, Mr. W–tt–n: A Person, in appearance, ordain'd for great Designs, as well as Performances; whether you will consider his *Notions* or his *Looks* (Plate 28). Surely, no Man ever advanced into the Publick, with fitter Qualifications of Body and Mind, for the Propagation of a new Religion. Oh, had those happy Talents misapplied to vain Philosophy, been turned into their proper Channels of *Dreams* and *Visions,* where *Distortion* of Mind and Countenance, are of such Sovereign Use; the base detracting World would not then have dared to report, that something is amiss, that his Brain hath undergone an unlucky Shake; which even his Brother *Modernists* themselves, like Ungrates, do whisper so loud, that it reaches up to the very *Garrat* I am writing in.

LASTLY, Whosoever pleases to look into the Fountains of *Enthusiasm*, from whence, in all Ages, have eternally proceeded such fatning Streams, will find the Spring Head to have been as *troubled* and *muddy* as the Current; Of such great Emolument, is a Tincture of this *Vapor*, which the World calls *Madness*, that without its Help, the World would not only be deprived of those two great Blessings, *Conquests* and *Systems*, but even all Mankind would unhappily be reduced to the same Belief in Things Invisible. Now, the former *Postulatum* being held, that it is of no Import from what Originals this *Vapor* proceeds, but either in what *Angles* it strikes and spreads over the Understanding, or upon what *Species* of Brain it ascends; It will be a very delicate Point, to cut the Feather, and divide the several Reasons to a Nice and Curious Reader, how this numerical Difference in the Brain, can produce Effects of so vast a Difference from the same *Vapor*, as to be the sole Point of Individuation between *Alexander the Great, Jack of Leyden,* and Monsieur *Des Cartes.* The present Argument, is the most abstracted that ever I engaged in, it strains my Faculties to their highest Stretch; and I desire the Reader to attend with utmost Perpensity; For, I now proceed to unravel this knotty Point.

THERE is in Mankind a certain * * * * * *
* * * * * * * * * * *

Hic multa   * * * * * * * * * *
desiderantur   * * * * * * * * * *

* * * * * * * * * *

* * *   AND this I take to be a clear Solution of the Matter.

HAVING therefore so narrowly past thro' this intricate Difficulty, the Reader will, I am sure, agree with me in the Conclusion; that if the *Moderns* mean by *Madness*, only a Disturbance or Transposition of the Brain, by Force of certain Vapors issuing up from the lower Faculties; Then has this *Madness* been the Parent of all those mighty Revolutions, that have happened in *Empire*, in *Philosophy*, and in *Religion.* For, the Brain in its natural Position and State of Serenity, disposeth its Owner to pass his Life in the common Forms, without any Thought of subduing Multitudes to his own *Power*, his *Reasons*, or his *Visions*; And the more he shapes his Understanding by the Pattern of Human Learning, the less he is inclined to form Parties after his particular Notions; Because that instructs him in his private Infirmities, as well as in the stubborn Ignorance of the People. But when a Man's Fancy gets *astride* on his Reason, when Imagination is at Cuffs with the Senses, and common Understanding, as well as common Sense, is

Kickt out of Doors; the first Proselyte he makes, is Himself, and when that is once compass'd, the Difficulty is not so great in bringing over others; A strong Delusion always operating from *without*, as vigorously as from *within*. For, Cant and Vision are to the Ear and the Eye, the same that Tickling is to the Touch. Those Entertainments and Pleasures we most value in Life, are such as *Dupe* and play the Wag with the Senses. For, if we take an Examination of what is generally understood by *Happiness*, as it has Respect, either to the Understanding or the Senses, we shall find all its Properties and Adjuncts, will herd under this short Definition; *That, it is a perpetual Possession of being well Deceived.* And first, with Relation to the Mind or Understanding; 'tis manifest, what mighty Advantages Fiction has over Truth; and the Reason is just at our Elbow; because Imagination can build nobler Scenes, and produce more wonderful Revolutions than Fortune or Nature will be at Expense to furnish. Nor is Mankind so much to blame in his Choice, thus determining him, if we consider that the Debate meerly lies between *Things past*, and *Things conceived*; and so the Question is only this; Whether Things that have Place in the *Imagination*, may not as properly be said to *Exist*, as those that are seated in the *Memory*; which may be justly held in the Affirmative, and very much to the Advantage of the former, since This is acknowledged to be the *Womb* of Things, and the Other allowed to be no more than the *Grave*. Again, if we take this Definition of Happiness, and examine it with Reference to the Senses, it will be acknowledged wonderfully adapt. How fade and insipid do all Objects accost us, that are not convey'd in the Vehicle of *Delusion*? How shrunk is every Thing, as it appears in the Glass of Nature? so, that if it were not for the Assistance of Artificial *Mediums*, false Lights, refracted Angles, Vernish, and Tinsel; there would be a mighty Level in the Felicity and Enjoyments of Mortal Men. If this were seriously considered by the World, as I have a certain Reason to suspect it hardly will; Men would no longer reckon among their high Points of Wisdom, the Art of exposing weak Sides, and publishing Infirmities; an Employment in my Opinion, neither better nor worse than that of *Unmasking*, which, I think, has never been allowed fair Usage, either in the *World* or the *Play-House*.

IN the Proportion that Credulity is a more peaceful Possession of the Mind, than Curiosity, so far preferable is that Wisdom, which converses about the Surface, to that pretended Philosophy which enters into the Depth of Things, and then comes gravely back with Informations and Discoveries, that in the Inside they are good for nothing. The two Senses, to which all Objects first Address themselves, are the Sight and the Touch; These never examine further than the Color, the Shape, the Size, and whatever other Qualities dwell, or are drawn by Art upon the Outward of

Bodies; and then comes Reason officiously, with Tools for cutting, and opening, and mangling, and piercing, offering to demonstrate, that they are not of the same consistence quite thro'. Now, I take all this to be the last Degree of perverting Nature; one of whose Eternal Laws it is, to put her best Furniture forward. And therefore, in order to save the Charges of all such expensive Anatomy for the Time to come; I do here think fit to inform the Reader, that in such Conclusions as these, Reason is certainly in the Wrong; And that in most Corporeal Beings, which have fallen under my Cognizance, the *Outside* hath been infinitely preferable to the *In*; Whereof I have been further convinced from some late Experiments. Last Week I saw a Woman *flay'd*, and you will hardly believe, how much it altered her Person for the worse. Yesterday I ordered the Carcass of a *Beau* to be stript in my Presence; when we were all amazed to find so many unsuspected Faults under one Suit of Cloaths: Then I laid open his *Brain*, his *Heart*, and his *Spleen*; But I plainly perceived at every Operation, that the farther we proceeded, we found the Defects encrease upon us in Number and Bulk: From all which, I justly formed this Conclusion to my self; That whatever Philosopher or Projector can find out an Art to sodder and patch up the Flaws and Imperfections of Nature, will deserve much better of Mankind, and teach us a more useful Science, than that so much in present Esteem, of widening and exposing them (like him who held *Anatomy* to be the ultimate End of *Physick*.) And he, whose Fortunes and Dispositions have placed him in a convenient Station to enjoy the Fruits of this noble Art; He that can with *Epicurus*, content his Idea's with the *Films* and *Images* that fly off upon his Senses from the *Superficies* of Things; Such a Man truly wise, creams off Nature, leaving the Sower and the Dregs, for Philosophy and Reason to lap up. This is the sublime and refined Point of Felicity, called, *the Possession of being well deceived*; The Serene Peaceful State of being a Fool among Knaves.

BUT to return to *Madness*. It is certain, that according to the System I have above deduced; every *Species* thereof proceeds from a Redundancy of *Vapor;* therefore, as some Kinds of *Phrenzy* give double Strength to the Sinews, so there are of other *Species*, which add Vigor, and Life, and Spirit to the Brain: Now, it usually happens, that these active Spirits, getting Possession of the Brain, resemble those that haunt other Waste and Empty Dwellings, which for want of Business, either vanish, and carry away a Piece of the House, or else stay at home and fling it all out of the Windows. By which are mystically display'd the two principal Branches of *Madness*, and which some Philosophers not considering so well as I, have mistook to be different in their Causes, over-hastily assigning the first to Deficiency, and the other to Redundance.

I think it therefore manifest, from what I have here advanced, that the main Point of Skill and Address, is to furnish Employment for this Redundancy of *Vapor*, and prudently to adjust the Seasons of it; by which Means, it may certainly become of cardinal and catholick Emolument in a Commonwealth. Thus one Man chusing a proper Juncture, leaps into a Gulph, from thence proceeds a Hero, and is called the Saver of his Country; Another atchieves the same Enterprise, but unluckily timing it, has left the Brand of *Madness*, fixt as a Reproach upon his Memory; Upon so nice a Distinction are we taught to repeat the Name of *Curtius* with Reverence and Love; that of *Empedocles*, with Hatred and Contempt. Thus, also it is usually conceived, that the Elder *Brutus* only personated the *Fool* and *Madman*, for the Good of the Publick: but this was nothing else, than a Redundancy of the same *Vapor*, long misapplied, called by the *Latins*, *_Ingenium par negotiis_: Or, (to translate it as nearly as I can) a sort   * *Tacit.* of *Phrenzy*, never in its right Element, till you take it up in Business of the State.

UPON all which, and many other Reasons of equal Weight, though not equally curious; I do here gladly embrace an Opportunity I have long sought for, of Recommending it as a very noble Undertaking to Sir *E——d S——r*, Sir *C————r M——ve*, Sir *J—n B—les*, *J—n H-we*, Esq., and other Patriots concerned, that they would move for Leave to bring in a Bill, for appointing Commissioners to Inspect into *Bedlam*, and the Parts adjacent; who shall be empowered to *send for Persons, Papers, and Records:* to examine into the Merits and Qualifications of every Student and Professor; to observe with utmost Exactness their several Dispositions and Behaviour; by which means, duly distinguishing and adapting their Talents, they might produce admirable Instruments for the several Offices in a State, ———, *Civil* and *Military*, proceeding in such Methods, as I shall here humbly propose. And, I hope, the Gentle Reader will give some Allowance to my great Solicitudes in this important Affair, upon Account of that high Esteem I have ever born that honourable Society, whereof I had some Time the Happiness to be an unworthy Member.

IS any Student tearing his Straw in piece-meal, Swearing and Blaspheming, biting his Grate, foaming at the Mouth, and emptying his Pispot in the Spectator's Faces? Let the Right Worshipful, the *Commissioners of Inspection*, give him a Regiment of Dragoons, and send him into *Flanders* among the *rest*. Is another eternally talking, sputtering, gaping, bawling, in a Sound without Period or Article? What wonderful Talents are here mislaid! Let him be furnished immediately with a green Bag   * *A Lawyer's* and Papers, and * *three Pence* in his Pocket, and away with Him to   *Coach-hire.* *Westminster-Hall.* You will find a Third, gravely taking the Dimensions of his Kennel; A Person of Foresight and Insight, tho' kept quite in the Dark; for why, like *Moses, Ecce* †*cornuta erat ejus facies.* He walks duly in one Pace, intreats your Penny with due Gravity and Ceremony; talks much of hard Times, and Taxes, and the *Whore of Babylon;* Bars up the woodden Window of his Cell constantly at eight a Clock: Dreams of *Fire,* and *Shop-lifters,* and *Court-Customers,* and *Priviledg'd Places.* Now, what a Figure would all these Acquirements amount to, if the Owner were sent into the *City* among his Brethren! Behold a Fourth, in much and deep Conversation with himself, biting his Thumbs at proper Junctures; His Countenance chequered with Business and Design; sometimes walking very fast, with his Eyes nailed to a Paper that he holds in his Hands: A great Saver of Time, somewhat thick of Hearing, very short of Sight, but more of Memory. A Man ever in Haste, a great Hatcher and Breeder of Business, and excellent at the Famous Art of *whispering Nothing.* A huge Idolater of Monosyllables and Procrastination; so ready to *Give* his Word to every Body, that he never *keeps* it. One that has forgot the common *Meaning* of Words, but an admirable Retainer of the *Sound.* Extreamly subject to the *Looseness,* for his *Occasions* are perpetually *calling him away.* If you approach his Grate in his familiar Intervals; *Sir,* says he, *Give me a Penny, and I'll sing you a Song: But give me the Penny first.* (Hence comes the common Saying, and commoner Practice of parting with Money for a *Song.*) What a compleat System of *Court-Skill* is here described in every Branch of it, and all utterly lost with wrong Application? Accost the Hole of another Kennel, first stopping your Nose, you will behold a surley, gloomy, nasty, slovenly Mortal, raking in his own Dung, and dabling in his Urine. The best Part of his Diet, is the Reversion of his own Ordure, which exspiring into Steams, whirls per-petually about, and at last reinfunds. His Complexion is of a dirty Yellow, with a thin scattered Beard, exactly agreeable to that of his Dyet upon its first Declination: like other Insects, who having their Birth and Education in an Excrement, from thence borrow their Colour and their Smell. The Student of this Apartment is very sparing of his Words, but somewhat over-liberal of his Breath; He holds his Hand out ready to receive your Penny, and immediately upon Receipt, withdraws to his former Occupations. Now, is it not amazing to think, the Society of *Warwick-Lane,* should have no more Concern, for the Recovery of so useful a Member, who, if one may judge from these Appearances, would become the greatest Ornament to that Illustrious Body? Another Student struts up fiercely to your Teeth, puffing with his Lips, half squeezing out his Eyes, and very graciously holds you out

---

† Cornutus, *is either Horned or Shining, and by this Term,* Moses *is described in the vulgar* Latin *of the Bible.*

his Hand to kiss. The *Keeper* desires you not to be afraid of this Professor, for he will do you no Hurt: To him alone is allowed the Liberty of the Anti-Chamber, and the *Orator* of the Place gives you to understand, that this solemn Person is a *Taylor* run mad with Pride. This considerable Student is adorned with many other Qualities, upon which, at present, I shall not farther enlarge – – – – –* *Heark in your Ear* – – – – – – I am strangely mistaken, if all his Address, his Motions, and his Airs, would not then be very natural, and in their proper Element.

I shall not descend so minutely, as to insist upon the vast Number of *Beaux*, *Fidlers*, *Poets*, and *Politicians*, that the World might recover by such a Reformation; But what is more material, beside the clear Gain redounding to the Commonwealth, by so large an Acquisition of Persons to employ, whose Talents and Acquirements, if I may be so bold as to affirm it, are now buried, or at least misapplied: It would be a mighty Advantage accruing to the Publick from this Enquiry, that all these would very much excel, and arrive at great Perfection in their several Kinds; which, I think, is manifest from what I have already shewn; and shall inforce by this one plain Instance; That even, I my self, the Author of these momentous Truths, am a Person, whose Imaginations are hard-mouth'd, and exceedingly disposed to run away with his *Reason*, which I have observed from long Experience, to be a very light Rider, and easily shook off; upon which Account, my Friends will never trust me alone, without a solemn Promise, to vent my Speculations in this, or the like manner, for the universal Benefit of Human kind; which, perhaps, the gentle, courteous, and candid Reader, brimful of that *Modern* Charity and Tenderness, usually annexed to his *Office*, will be very hardly persuaded to believe.

---

* *I cannot conjecture what the Author means here, or how this Chasm could be fill'd, tho' it is capable of more than one Interpretation.*

SECT. X.

A TALE of a TUB

IT is an unanswerable Argument of a very refined Age, the wonderful Civilities that have passed of late Years, between the Nation of *Authors*, and that of *Readers*. There can hardly * pop out a *Play*, a *Pamphlet*, or a *Poem*, without a Preface full of Acknowledgments to the World, for the general Reception and Applause they have given it, which the Lord knows where, or when, or how, or from whom it received. In due Deference to so laudable a Custom, I do here return my humble Thanks to *His Majesty*, and both Houses of *Parliament*; To the *Lords* of the King's most honourable Privy-Council, to the Reverend the *Judges:* To the *Clergy*, and *Gentry*, and *Yeomantry* of this Land: But in a more especial manner, to my worthy Brethren and Friends at *Will's Coffee-House*, and *Gresham-College*, and *Warwick-Lane*, and *Moor-Fields*, and *Scotland-Yard*, and *Westminster-Hall*, and *Guild-Hall*; In short, to all Inhabitants and Retainers whatsoever, either in Court, or Church, or Camp, or City, or Country; for their generous and universal Acceptance of this Divine Treatise. I accept their Approbation and good Opinion with extream Gratitude, and to the utmost of my poor Capacity, shall take hold of all Opportunities to return the Obligation.

I am also happy, that Fate has flung me into so blessed an Age for the mutual Felicity of *Booksellers* and *Authors*, whom I may safely affirm to be at this Day the two only satisfied Parties in *England*. Ask an *Author* how his last Piece hath succeeded; *Why, truly he thanks his Stars, the World has been very favourable, and he has not the least Reason to complain: And yet, by G—, He writ it in a Week at Bits and Starts, when he could steal an Hour from his urgent Affairs;* as it is a hundred to one, you may see further in the Preface, to which he refers you, and for the rest, to the Bookseller. There you go as a Customer, and make the same Question: *He blesses his God, the* Thing *takes wonderful, he is just printing a Second Edition, and has but three left in his Shop. You beat down the* Price: *Sir, we shall not differ;* and in hopes of your Custom another Time, lets you have it as reasonable as you please; *And, pray send as many of your Acquaintance as you will, I shall upon your Account furnish them all at the same Rate.*

NOW, it is not well enough consider'd, to what Accidents and Occasions the World is indebted for the greatest Part of those noble Writings, which hourly start up to entertain it. If it were not for a *rainy Day, a drunken Vigil, a Fit of the Spleen, a Course of Physick, a sleepy Sunday, an ill Run at Dice, a long*

---

* *This is litterally true, as we may observe in the Prefaces to most Plays, Poems, &c.*

Taylor's Bill, a Beggar's Purse, a factious Head, a hot Sun, costive Dyet, Want of Books, and a just Contempt of Learning, but for these Events, I say, and some Others too long to recite, (especially a *prudent Neglect of taking Brimstone inwardly,*) I doubt, the Number of *Authors,* and of *Writings* would dwindle away to a Degree most woful to behold. To confirm this Opinion, hear the Words of the famous *Troglodyte* Philosopher: '*Tis certain* (said he) *some Grains of Folly are of course annexed, as Part in the Composition of Human Nature, only the Choice is left us, whether we please to wear them* Inlaid *or* Embossed; *And we need not go very far to seek how That is usually determined, when we remember, it is with Human Faculties as with Liquors, the lightest will be ever at the Top.*

THERE is in this famous Island of *Britain* a certain paultry *Scribbler,* very voluminous, whose Character the Reader cannot wholly be a Stranger to. He deals in a pernicious Kind of Writings, called *Second Parts,* and usually passes under the Name of *The Author of the First.* I easily foresee, that as soon as I lay down my Pen, this nimble *Operator* will have stole it, and treat me as inhumanly as he hath already done Dr. *Bl——re, L———ge,* and many others who shall here be nameless. I therefore fly for Justice and Relief, into the Hands of that great *Rectifier of Saddles,* and *Lover of Mankind,* Dr. *B——tl—y,* begging he will take this enormous Grievance into his most *Modern* Consideration: And if it should so happen, that the *Furniture of an Ass,* in the Shape of a *Second Part,* must for my Sins, be clapt by a Mistake, upon my Back, that he will immediately please, in the Presence of the World, to lighten me of the Burthen, and take it home to *his own House,* till the *true Beast* thinks fit to call for it.

IN the mean time I do here give this publick Notice, that my Resolutions are, to circumscribe within this Discourse the whole Stock of Matter I have been so many Years providing. Since my *Vein* is once opened, I am content to exhaust it all at a Running, for the peculiar Advantage of my dear Country, and for the universal Benefit of Mankind. Therefore, hospitably considering the Number of my Guests, they shall have my whole Entertainment at a Meal; And I scorn to set up the *Leavings* in the Cupboard. What the *Guests* cannot eat may be given to the *Poor,* and the **Dogs* under the Table may gnaw the *Bones;* This I understand for a more generous Proceeding, than to turn the Company's Stomachs, by inviting them again to morrow to a scurvy Meal of *Scraps.*

IF the Reader fairly considers the Strength of what I have advanced in the foregoing Section, I am convinced it will produce a wonderful Revolution in his Notions and Opinions; And he will be abundantly better

---

* *By Dogs, the Author means common injudicious Criticks, as he explains it himself before in his* Digression upon Criticks *(Page 38.)* [p. 43 of this edition]

prepared to receive and to relish the concluding Part of this miraculous Treatise. Readers may be divided into three Classes, the *Superficial*, the *Ignorant*, and the *Learned*: And I have with much Felicity fitted my Pen to the Genius and Advantage of each. The *Superficial* Reader will be strangely provoked to *Laughter*, which clears the Breast and the Lungs, is Soverain against the *Spleen*, and the most innocent of all *Diureticks*. The *Ignorant* Reader (between whom and the former, the Distinction is extreamly nice) will find himself disposed to *Stare*, which is an admirable Remedy for ill Eyes, serves to raise and enliven the Spirits, and wonderfully helps *Perspiration*. But the Reader truly *Learned*, chiefly for whose Benefit, I wake, when others sleep, and sleep when others wake, will here find sufficient Matter to employ his Speculations for the rest of his Life. It were much to be wisht, and I do here humbly propose for an Experiment, that every Prince in *Christendom* will take seven of the *deepest Scholars* in his Dominions, and shut them up close for *seven* Years, in *seven* Chambers, with a Command to write *seven* ample Commentaries on this comprehensive Discourse. I shall venture to affirm, that whatever Difference may be found in their several Conjectures, they will be all without the least Distortion, manifestly deduceable from the Text. Mean time, it is my earnest Request, that so useful an Undertaking may be entered upon (if their Majesties please) with all convenient speed; because I have a strong Inclination, before I leave the World, to taste a Blessing, which we *mysterious* Writers can seldom reach, till we have got into our Graves. Whether it is, that *Fame* being a Fruit grafted on the Body, can hardly grow, and much less ripen, till the Stock is in the Earth: Or, whether she be a Bird of Prey, and is lured among the rest, to pursue after the Scent of a *Carcass*: Or, whether she conceives her Trumpet sounds best and farthest, when she stands on a *Tomb*, by the Advantage of a rising Ground, and the Echo of a hollow Vault.

'TIS true, indeed, the Republick of *dark* Authors, after they once found out this excellent Expedient of *Dying*, have been peculiarly happy in the Variety, as well as Extent of their Reputation. For, *Night* being the universal Mother of Things, wise Philosophers hold all Writings to be *fruitful* in the Proportion they are *dark*; And therefore, the **true Illuminated* (that is to say, the *Darkest* of all) have met with such numberless Commentators, whose *Scholiastick* Midwifry hath deliver'd them of Meanings, that the Authors themselves, perhaps, never conceived, and yet may very justly be allowed the Lawful Parents of them: †The Words of such Writers being like Seed, which, however scattered at random, when

* *A Name of the Rosycrucians.*

† *Nothing is more frequent than for Commentators to force Interpretations, which the Author never meant.*

they light upon a fruitful Ground, will multiply far beyond either the Hopes or Imagination of the Sower.

AND therefore in order to promote so useful a Work, I will here take Leave to glance a few *Innuendo*'s, that may be of great Assistance to those sublime Spirits, who shall be appointed to labor in a universal Comment upon this wonderful Discourse. And First, **¶**I have couched a very profound Mystery in the Number of O's, multiply'd by *Seven*, and divided by *Nine*. Also, if a devout Brother of the *Rosy-Cross* will pray fervently for sixty three Mornings, with a lively Faith, and then transpose certain Letters and Syllables according to Prescription, in the second and fifth Section; they will certainly reveal into a full Receit of the *Opus Magnum*. Lastly, Whoever will be at the Pains to calculate the whole Number of each Letter in this Treatise, and sum up the Difference exactly between the several Numbers, assigning the true natural Cause for every such Difference; the Discoveries in the Product, will plentifully reward his Labor. But then he must beware of ‖*Bythus* and *Sigè*, and be sure not to forget the Qualities of *Acamoth; A cujus lacrymis humecta prodit Substantia, à risu lucida, à tristitiâ solida, & à timore mobilis*, wherein * *Eugenius Philalethes* hath committed an unpardonable Mistake.

* *Vid. Anima magica abscondita.*

¶ *This is what the* Cabbalists *among the* Jews *have done with the* Bible, *and pretend to find wonderful Mysteries by it.*

‖ *I was told by an Eminent Divine, whom I consulted on this Point, that these two Barbarous Words, with that of* Acamoth *and its Qualities, as here set down, are quoted from* Irenæus. *This he discover'd by searching that Antient Writer for another Quotation of our Author, which he has placed in the Title Page, and refers to the Book and Chapter; the Curious were very Inquisitive, whether those Barbarous Words,* Basima Eacabasa, &c. *are really in* Irenæus, *and upon enquiry 'twas found they were a sort of Cant or Jargon of certain Hereticks, and therefore very properly prefix'd to such a Book as this of our Author.*

* *To the abovementioned Treatise, called* Anthroposophia Theomagica, *there is another annexed, called* Anima Magica Abscondita, *written by the same Author* Vaughan, *under the Name of* Eugenius Philalethes, *but in neither of those Treatises is there any mention of* Acamoth *or its Qualities, so that this is nothing but Amusement, and a Ridicule of dark, unintelligible Writers; only the Words,* A cujus lacrymis, &c. *are as we have said, transcribed from* Irenæus, *tho' I know not from what part. I believe one of the Authors Designs was to set curious Men a hunting thro' Indexes, and enquiring for Books out of the common Road.*

SECT. XI.

A TALE of a TUB

AFTER so wide a Compass as I have wandred, I do now gladly overtake, and close in with my Subject, and shall henceforth hold on with it an even Pace to the End of my Journey, except some beautiful Prospect appears within sight of my Way; whereof, tho' at present I have neither Warning nor Expectation, yet upon such an Accident, come when it will, I shall beg my Readers Favour and Company, allowing me to conduct him thro' it along with my self. For in *Writing*, it is as in *Travelling*: If a Man is in haste to be at home, (which I acknowledge to be none of my Case, having never so little Business, as when I am there) if his *Horse* be tired with long Riding, and ill Ways, or be naturally a Jade, I advise him clearly to make the straitest and the commonest Road, be it ever so dirty; But, then surely, we must own such a Man to be a scurvy Companion at best; He *spatters* himself and his Fellow-Travellors at every Step: All their Thoughts, and Wishes, and Conversation, turn entirely upon the Subject of their Journey's End; and at every Splash, and Plunge, and Stumble, they heartily wish one another at the Devil.

ON the other side, when a Traveller and his *Horse* are in Heart and Plight, when his Purse is full, and the Day before him; he takes the Road only where it is clean or convenient; entertains his Company there as agreeably as he can; but upon the first Occasion, carries them along with him to every delightful Scene in View, whether of Art, of Nature, or of both; and if they chance to refuse out of Stupidity or Weariness; let them jog on by themselves, and be d—n'd; He'll overtake them at the next Town; at which arriving, he Rides furiously thro', the Men, Women, and Children run out to gaze, a hundred *noisy Curs run barking after him, of which, if he honors the boldest with a *Lash of his Whip*, it is rather out of Sport than Revenge: But should some *sourer Mungrel* dare too near an Approach, he receives a *Salute* on the Chaps by an accidental Stroak from the Courser's Heels, (nor is any Ground lost by the Blow) which sends him yelping and limping home.

I now proceed to sum up the singular Adventures of my renowned *Jack*; the State of whose Dispositions and Fortunes, the careful Reader does, no doubt, most exactly remember, as I last parted with them in the Conclusion of a former Section. Therefore, his next Care must be from two of the foregoing, to extract a Scheme of Notions, that may best fit his Understanding for a true Relish of what is to ensue.

---

* *By these are meant what the Author calls, The* True Criticks, *Page 38.* [p. 43 of this edition]

JACK had not only calculated the first Revolutions of his Brain so prudently, as to give Rise to that Epidemick Sect of *Æolists*, but succeeding also into a new and strange Variety of Conceptions, the Fruitfulness of his Imagination led him into certain Notions, which, altho' in Appearance very unaccountable, were not without their Mysteries and their Meanings, nor wanted Followers to countenance and improve them. I shall therefore be extremely careful and exact in recounting such material Passages of this Nature, as I have been able to collect, either from undoubted Tradition, or indefatigable Reading; and shall describe them as graphically as it is possible, and as far as Notions of that Height and Latitude can be brought within the Compass of a Pen. Nor do I at all question, but they will furnish Plenty of noble Matter for such, whose converting Imaginations dispose them to reduce all Things into *Types*; who can make *Shadows*, no thanks to the Sun; and then mould them into Substances, no thanks to Philosophy; whose peculiar Talent lies in fixing Tropes and Allegories to the *Letter*, and refining what is Literal into Figure and Mystery.

JACK had provided a fair Copy of his Father's *Will*, engrossed in Form upon a large Skin of Parchment; and resolving to act the Part of a most dutiful Son, he became the fondest Creature of it imaginable. For, altho', as I have often told the Reader, it consisted wholly in certain plain, easy Directions about the management and wearing of their Coats, with Legacies and Penalties, in case of Obedience or Neglect; yet He began to entertain a Fancy, that the Matter was *deeper* and *darker*, and therefore must needs have a great deal more of Mystery at the Bottom. *Gentlemen,* said he, *I will prove this very Skin of Parchment to be Meat, Drink, and Cloth, to be the Philosopher's Stone, and the Universal Medicine.* *In consequence of which Raptures, he resolved to make use of it in the most necessary, as well as the most paltry Occasions of Life. He had a Way of working it into any Shape he pleased; so that it served him for a Night-cap when he went to Bed, and for an Umbrello in rainy Weather. He would lap a Piece of it about a sore Toe, or when he had Fitts, burn two Inches under his Nose; or if any Thing lay heavy on his Stomach, scrape off, and swallow as much of the Powder as would lye on a silver Penny; they were all infallible Remedies. With Analogy to these Refinements, his common Talk and Conversation, †ran wholly in the Phrase of his Will, and he circumscribed the utmost of his Eloquence within that Compass, not daring to let slip a Syllable without Authority from

---

* *The Author here lashes those Pretenders to Purity, who place so much Merit in using Scripture Phrase on all Occasions.*

† *The* Protestant Dissenters *use* Scripture Phrases *in their Serious Discourses, and Composures more than the* Church of England-Men, *accordingly* Jack *is introduced making his common Talk and Conversation to run wholly in the Phrase of his WILL.* W.Wotton.

thence. Once at a strange House, he was suddenly taken short, upon an urgent Juncture, whereon it may not be allowed too particularly to dilate; and being not able to call to mind, with that Suddenness, the Occasion required, an Authentick Phrase for demanding the Way to the Backside; he chose rather as the more prudent Course, to incur the Penalty in such Cases usually annexed. Neither was it possible for the united Rhetorick of Mankind to prevail with him to make himself clean again: Because having consulted the Will upon this Emergency, he met with a ¶Passage near the Bottom (whether foisted in by the Transcriber, is not known) which seemed to forbid it.

HE made it a Part of his Religion, never to say ‖Grace to his Meat, nor could all the World persuade him, as the common Phrase is, to *eat his Victuals *like a Christian*.

HE bore a strange kind of Appetite to †*Snap-Dragon*, and to the livid Snuffs of a burning Candle, which he would catch and swallow with an Agility, wonderful to conceive; and by this Procedure, maintained a perpetual Flame in his Belly, which issuing in a glowing Steam from both his Eyes, as well as his Nostrils, and his Mouth; made his Head appear in a dark Night, like the Scull of an Ass, wherein a roguish Boy had conveyed a Farthing Candle, *to the Terror of His Majesty's Liege Subjects*. Therefore, he made use of no other Expedient to light himself home, but was wont to say, That *a Wise Man was his own Lanthorn*.

HE would shut his Eyes as he walked along the Streets, and if he happened to bounce his Head against a Post, or fall into the Kennel (as he seldom missed either to do one or both) he would tell the gibing Prentices, who looked on, that *he submitted with entire Resignation, as to a Trip, or a Blow of Fate, with whom he found, by long Experience, how vain it was either to wrestle or to cuff; and whoever durst undertake to do either, would be sure to come off with a swinging Fall, or a bloody Nose. It was ordained*, said he, *some few Days before the Creation, that my Nose and this very Post should have a Rencounter; and therefore, Providence thought fit to send us both into the World in the same Age, and to make us Country-men and Fellow-Citizens. Now, had my Eyes been open, it is very likely, the Business might have been a great deal worse; For, how many a confounded Slip is daily got by Man, with all his Foresight about him? Besides, the Eyes of the*

¶ *I cannot guess the Author's meaning here, which I would be very glad to know, because it seems to be of Importance.*

‖ *The slovenly way of Receiving the Sacrament among the Fanaticks.*

* *This is a common Phrase to express Eating cleanlily, and is meant for an Invective against that undecent Manner among some People in Receiving the Sacrament, so in the Lines before, which is to be understood of the Dissenters refusing to kneel at the Sacrament.*

† *I cannot well find the Author's meaning here, unless it be the hot, untimely, blind Zeal of Enthusiasts.*

Understanding see best, when those of the Senses are out of the way; and therefore, blind Men are observed to tread their Steps with much more Caution, and Conduct, and Judgment, than those who rely with too much Confidence, upon the Virtue of the visual Nerve, which every little Accident shakes out of Order, and a Drop, or a Film, can wholly disconcert; like a Lanthorn among a Pack of roaring Bullies, when they scower the Streets; exposing its Owner, and it self, to outward Kicks and Buffets, which both might have escaped, if the Vanity of Appearing would have suffered them to walk in the Dark. But, further; if we examine the Conduct *of these boasted Lights, it will prove yet a great deal worse than their* Fortune: *'Tis true, I have broke my Nose against this Post, because Providence either forgot, or did not think it convenient to twitch me by the Elbow, and give me notice to avoid it. But, let not this encourage either the present Age or Posterity, to trust their* Noses *into the keeping of their* Eyes, *which may prove the fairest Way of losing them for good and all. For, O ye Eyes, Ye blind Guides; miserable Guardians are Ye of our frail Noses; Ye, I say, who fasten upon the first Precipice in view, and then tow our wretched willing Bodies after You, to the very Brink of Destruction: But, alas, that Brink is rotten, our Feet slip, and we tumble down prone into a Gulph, without one hospitable Shrub in the Way to break the Fall; a Fall, to which not any Nose of mortal Make is equal,*   * *Vide* Don *except that of the Giant* *Laurcalco, *who was Lord of the Silver*   Quixot. *Bridge. Most properly, therefore, O Eyes, and with great Justice, may You be compared to those foolish Lights, which conduct Men thro' Dirt and Darkness, till they fall into a deep Pit, or a noisom Bog.*

THIS I have produced, as a Scantling of *Jack's* great Eloquence, and the Force of his Reasoning upon such abstruse Matters.

HE was besides, a Person of great Design and Improvement in Affairs of *Devotion,* having introduced a new Deity, who hath since met with a vast Number of Worshippers; by some called *Babel,* by others, *Chaos;* who had an ancient Temple of *Gothick* Structure upon *Salisbury* Plain; famous for its Shrine, and celebration by Pilgrims.

**WHEN he had some Roguish Trick to play, he would down with his Knees, up with his Eyes, and fall to Prayers, tho' in the midst of the Kennel. Then it was that those who understood his Pranks, would be sure to get far enough out of his Way; And whenever Curiosity attracted Strangers to Laugh, or to Listen; he would of a sudden, with one Hand out with his *Gear,* and piss full in their Eyes, and with the other, all to-bespatter them with Mud.

†IN Winter he went always loose and unbuttoned, and clad as thin as possible, to let *in* the ambient Heat; and in Summer, lapt himself close and thick to keep it *out.*

** *The Villanies and Cruelties committed by Enthusiasts and Phanaticks among us, were all performed under the Disguise of Religion and long Prayers.*
† *They affect Differences in Habit and Behaviour.*

¶IN all Revolutions of Government, he would make his Court for the Office of *Hangman* General; and in the Exercise of that Dignity, wherein he was very dextrous, would make use of ‖no other Vizard than a long Prayer.

HE had a Tongue so Musculous and Subtil, that he could twist it up into his Nose, and deliver a strange Kind of Speech from thence. He was also the first in these Kingdoms, who began to improve the *Spanish* Accomplishment of *Braying*; and having large Ears, perpetually exposed and arrect, he carried his Art to such a Perfection, that it was a Point of great Difficulty to distinguish either by the View or the Sound, between the *Original* and the *Copy*.

HE was troubled with a Disease, reverse to that called the Stinging of the *Tarantula*; and would ††run Dog-mad, at the Noise of *Musick*, especially a Pair of *Bag-Pipes*. But he would cure himself again, by taking two or three Turns in *Westminster-Hall*, or *Billingsgate*, or in a *Boarding-School*, or the *Royal-Exchange*, or a *State Coffee-House*.

HE was a Person that ¶¶*feared* no *Colours*, but mortally *hated* all, and upon that Account, bore a cruel Aversion to *Painters*; insomuch, that in his Paroxisms, as he walked the Streets, he would have his Pockets loaden with Stones, to pelt at the *Signs*.

HAVING from this manner of Living, frequent Occasions to *wash* himself, he would often leap over Head and Ears into the Water, tho' it were in the midst of the Winter, but was always observed to come out again much *dirtier*, if possible, than he went in.

HE was the first that ever found out the Secret of contriving a *Soporiferous* Medicine to be convey'd in at the Ears; It was a Compound of *Sulphur* and *Balm of Gilead*, with a little *Pilgrim's Salve*.

HE wore a large Plaister of artificial *Causticks* on his Stomach, with the Fervor of which, he could set himself a *groaning*, like the famous *Board* upon Application of a red-hot Iron.

†HE would stand in the Turning of a Street, and calling to those who passed by, would cry to One; *Worthy Sir, do me the Honor of a good Slap in the Chaps*: To another, *Honest Friend, pray, favour me with a handsom Kick on the*

¶　*They are severe Persecutors, and all in a Form of Cant and Devotion.*
‖　*Cromwell and his Confederates went, as they called it,* to seek God, *when they resolved to murther the King.*
††　*This is to expose our Dissenters Aversion to Instrumental Musick in Churches.* W.Wotton.
¶¶　*They quarrel at the most Innocent Decency and Ornament, and defaced the Statues and Paintings on all the Churches in* England.
*　*Fanatick Preaching, composed either of Hell and Damnation, or a fulsome Description of the Joys of Heaven, both in such a dirty, nauseous Style, as to be well resembled to Pilgrims Salve.*
†　*The Fanaticks have always had a way of affecting to run into Persecution, and count vast Merit upon every little Hardship they suffer.*

Arse: Madam, shall I entreat a small Box on the Ear, from your Ladyship's fair Hands? Noble Captain, Lend a reasonable Thwack, for the Love of God, with that Cane of yours, over these poor Shoulders. And when he had by such earnest Sollicitations, made a shift to procure a Basting sufficient to swell up his Fancy and his Sides, He would return home extremely comforted, and full of terrible Accounts of what he had undergone for the *Publick Good. Observe this Stroak,* (said he, shewing his bare Shoulders) *a plaguy* Janisary *gave it me this very Morning at seven a Clock, as, with much ado, I was driving off the* great Turk. *Neighbours mine, this broken Head deserves a Plaister; had poor* Jack *been tender of his Noddle, you would have seen the* Pope, *and the* French *King, long before this time of Day, among your Wives and your Ware-houses. Dear* Christians, *the* Great Mogul *was come as far as* White-Chappel, *and you may thank these poor Sides that he hath not (God bless us) already swallowed up Man, Woman, and Child.*

¶IT was highly worth observing, the singular Effects of that Aversion, or Antipathy, which *Jack* and his Brother *Peter* seemed, even to an Affectation, to bear towards each other. *Peter* had lately done *some Rogueries*, that forced him to abscond; and he seldom ventured to stir out before Night, for fear of Bayliffs. Their Lodgings were at the two most distant Parts of the Town, from each other; and whenever their Occasions, or Humors called them abroad, they would make Choice of the oddest unlikely Times, and most uncouth Rounds they could invent; that they might be sure to avoid one another: Yet after all this, it was their perpetual Fortune to meet. The Reason of which, is easy enough to apprehend: For, the Phrenzy and the Spleen of both, having the same Foundation, we may look upon them as two Pair of Compasses, equally extended, and the fixed Foot of each, remaining in the same Center; which, tho' moving contrary Ways at first, will be sure to encounter somewhere or other in the Circumference. Besides, it was among the great Misfortunes of *Jack*, to bear a huge Personal Resemblance with his Brother *Peter*. Their Humors and Dispositions were not only the same, but there was a close Analogy in their Shape, their Size, and their Mien. Insomuch, as nothing was more frequent than for a Bayliff to seize *Jack* by the Shoulders, and cry; *Mr.* Peter, *You are the King's Prisoner.* Or, at other Times, for one of *Peter's* nearest Friends, to accost *Jack* with open Arms, *Dear* Peter, *I am glad to see thee, pray send me one of your best*

---

1 *The Papists and Fanaticks, tho' they appear the most Averse to each other, yet bear a near Resemblance in many things, as has been observed by Learned Men.*
Ibid. *The Agreement of our Dissenters and the Papists in that which Bishop* Stillingfleet *called,* The Fanaticism of the Church of *Rome, is ludicrously described for several Pages together by* Jack's *Likeness to* Peter, *and their being often mistaken for each other, and their frequent Meeting, when they least intended it.* W.Wotton.

Medicines for the Worms. This we may suppose, was a mortifying Return of those Pains and Proceedings, *Jack* had labored in so long: And finding, how directly opposite all his Endeavours had answered to the sole End and Intention, which he had proposed to himself; How could it avoid having terrible Effects upon a Head and Heart so furnished as his? However, the poor Remainders of his *Coat* bore all the Punishment; The orient Sun never entred upon his diurnal Progress, without missing a Piece of it. He hired a Taylor to stitch up the Collar so close, that it was ready to choak him, and squeezed out his Eyes at such a Rate, as one could see nothing but the White. What little was left of the main Substance of the Coat, he rubbed every Day for two hours, against a rough-cast Wall, in order to grind away the Remnants of *Lace* and *Embroidery;* but at the same time went on with so much Violence, that he proceeded a *Heathen Philosopher.* Yet after all he could do of this kind, the Success continued still to disappoint his Expectation. For, as it is the Nature of Rags, to bear a kind of mock Resemblance to Finery; there being a sort of fluttering Appearance in both, which is not to be distinguished at a Distance, in the Dark, or by short-sighted Eyes: So, in those Junctures, it fared with *Jack* and his Tatters, that they offered to the first View a ridiculous Flanting, which assisting the Resemblance in Person and Air, thwarted all his Projects of Separation, and left so near a Similitude between them, as frequently deceived the very Disciples and Followers of both. *   *   *   *   *   *   *   *   *   *   *   *
*   *   *   *   *   *   *   *   *   *   *   *   *
          *   *   *   *   *   *   *   *   *   *   *
Desunt non-   *   *   *   *   *   *   *   *   *   *   *
nulla.
          *   *   *   *   *   *   *   *   *   *   *
*   *   *   *   *   *   *   *   *   *   *   *   *

THE old *Sclavonian* Proverb said well, That *it is with* Men, *as with* Asses; *whoever would keep them fast, must find a very good Hold at their Ears.* Yet, I think, we may affirm, and it hath been verified by repeated Experience, that,

Effugiet tamen hæc sceleratus vincula Proteus.

IT is good therefore, to read the Maxims of our Ancestors, with great Allowances to Times and Persons: For, if we look into Primitive Records, we shall find, that no Revolutions have been so great, or so frequent, as those of human *Ears.* In former Days, there was a curious Invention to catch and keep them; which, I think, we may justly reckon among the *Artes perditæ:* And how can it be otherwise, when in these latter Centuries, the very Species is not only diminished to a very lamentable Degree, but the poor Remainder is also degenerated so far, as to mock our skilfullest *Tenure?* For, if the only slitting of one *Ear* in a Stag, hath been found sufficient to propagate the Defect thro' a whole Forest; Why should we wonder at the greatest Consequences, from so many Loppings and Mutilations, to which the *Ears* of our Fathers and our own, have been of late so much exposed? 'Tis true, indeed, that while this *Island* of ours, was under the *Dominion of Grace,* many Endeavours were made to improve the Growth of *Ears* once more among us. The Proportion of Largeness, was not only lookt upon as an Ornament of the *Outward* Man, but as a Type of Grace in the *Inward.* Besides, it is held by Naturalists, that if there be a Protuberancy of Parts in the *Superiour* Region of the Body, as in the *Ears* and *Nose,* there must be a Parity also in the Inferior; And therefore in that truly pious Age, the *Males* in every Assembly, according as they were gifted, appeared very forward in exposing their *Ears* to view, and the Regions about them; because **Hippocrates* tells us, that *when the Vein behind the Ear happens to be cut, a Man becomes a Eunuch:* And the *Females* were nothing backwarder in beholding and edifying by them: Whereof those who had already *used the Means,* lookt about them with great Concern, in hopes of conceiving a suitable Offspring by such a Prospect: Others, who stood Candidates for *Benevolence,* found there a plentiful Choice, and were sure to fix upon such as discovered the largest *Ears,* that the Breed might not dwindle between them. Lastly, the devouter Sisters, who lookt upon all extraordinary Dilatations of that Member as Protrusions of Zeal, or spiritual Excrescencies, were sure to honor every Head they sat upon, as if they had been cloven Tongues; but, especially, that of the Preacher, whose *Ears* were usually of the prime Magnitude; which upon that Account, he was very frequent and exact in exposing with all Advantages to the People: in his Rhetorical *Paroxysms,* turning sometimes to *hold forth* the one, and sometimes to *hold forth* the other: From which Custom, the whole Operation of Preaching is to this very Day among their Professors, styled by the Phrase of *Holding forth.*

* Lib. de aere locis & aquis.

SUCH was the Progress of the *Saints,* for advancing the Size of that Member; And it is thought, the Success would have been every way answerable, if in Process of time, a *cruel King had not arose, who raised a bloody Persecution against all *Ears,* above a certain Standard: Upon which, some were glad to hide their flourishing Sprouts in a black Border, others crept wholly under a Perewig: some were slit, others cropt, and a great Number sliced off to the Stumps. But of this, more hereafter, in my *general History of Ears;* which I design very speedily to bestow upon the Publick.

FROM this brief Survey of the falling State of *Ears,* in the last Age, and the small Care had to advance their antient Growth in the present, it is

---

* *This was King* Charles *the Second, who at his Restauration, turned out all the Dissenting Teachers that would not conform.*

manifest, how little Reason we can have to rely upon a Hold so short, so weak, and so slippery; and that, whoever desires to catch Mankind fast, must have Recourse to some other Methods. Now, he that will examine Human Nature with Circumspection enough, may discover several *Handles,* whereof the ‖*Six* Senses afford one apiece, beside a great Number that are screwed to the Passions, and some few riveted to the Intellect. Among these last, *Curiosity* is one, and of all others, affords the firmest Grasp: *Curiosity,* that Spur in the side, that Bridle in the Mouth, that Ring in the Nose, of a lazy, and impatient, and a grunting Reader. By this *Handle* it is, that an Author should seize upon his Readers; which as soon as he has once compast, all Resistance and struggling are in vain; and they become his Prisoners as close as he pleases, till Weariness or Dullness force him to let go his Gripe.

‖ *Including Scaliger's.*

AND therefore, I the Author of this miraculous Treatise, having hitherto, beyond Expectation, maintained by the aforesaid *Handle,* a firm Hold upon my gentle Readers; It is with great Reluctance, that I am at length compelled to remit my Grasp; leaving them in the Perusal of what remains, to that natural *Oscitancy* inherent in the Tribe. I can only assure thee, Courteous Reader, for both our Comforts, that my Concern is altogether equal to thine, for my Unhappiness in losing, or mislaying among my Papers the remaining Part of these Memoirs; which consisted of Accidents, Turns, and Adventures, both New, Agreeable, and Surprizing; and therefore, calculated in all due Points, to the delicate Taste of this our noble Age. But, alas, with my utmost Endeavours, I have been able only to retain a few of the Heads. Under which, there was a full Account, how *Peter* got a *Protection* out of the *King's-Bench*; And of a Reconcilement between *Jack* and Him, upon a Design they had in a certain *rainy Night,* to trepan Brother *Martin* into a *Spunging-house,* and there strip him to the Skin. How *Martin,* with much ado, shew'd them both a fair pair of Heels. How a *new Warrant* came out against *Peter*; upon which, how *Jack* left him in the lurch, *stole his Protection, and made use of it himself.* How *Jack's* Tatters came into Fashion in *Court* and *City*; How he †*got upon a great Horse, and eat* ¶*Custard.* But the

---

* *In the Reign of King* James *the Second, the Presbyterians by the King's Invitation, joined with the* Papists, *against the Church of* England, *and Addrest him for Repeal of the Penal-Laws and Test. The King by his Dispensing Power, gave Liberty of Conscience, which both Papists and Presbyterians made use of, but upon the Revolution, the Papists being down of Course, the Presbyterians freely continued their Assemblies, by Virtue of King* James's *Indulgence, before they had a Toleration by Law; this I believe the Author means by* Jack's *stealing* Peter's *Protection, and making use of it himself.*

† *Sir* Humphry Edwyn, *a Presbyterian, was some Years ago Lord-Mayor of* London, *and had the Insolence to go in his Formalities to a Conventicle, with the Ensigns of his Office.*

¶ *Custard is a famous Dish at a Lord-Mayors Feast.*

Particulars of all these, with several others, which have now slid out of my Memory, are lost beyond all Hopes of Recovery. For which Misfortune, leaving my Readers to condole with each other, as far as they shall find it to agree with their several Constitutions; but conjuring them by all the Friendship that hath passed between Us, from the Title-Page to this, not to proceed so far as to injure their Healths, for an Accident past Remedy; I now go on to the Ceremonial Part of an accomplish'd Writer, and therefore, by a Courtly *Modern*, least of all others to be omitted.

THE
CONCLUSION.

G OING *too long* is a Cause of Abortion as effectual, tho' not so frequent, as *Going too short*; and holds true especially in the *Labors* of the Brain.

Well fare the Heart of that Noble **Jesuit*, who first adventur'd to confess in Print, that Books must be suited to their several Seasons, like Dress, and Dyet, and Diversions: And better fare our noble Nation, for refining upon this, among other *French* Modes. I am living fast, to see the Time, when a *Book* that misses its Tide, shall be neglected, as the *Moon* by Day, or like *Mackarel* a Week after the Season. No Man hath more nicely observed our Climat, than the Bookseller who bought the Copy of this Work; He knows to a Tittle what Subjects will best go off in a *dry Year*, and which it is proper to expose foremost, when the Weather-glass is fallen to *much Rain*. When he had seen this Treatise, and consulted his *Almanack* upon it; he gave me to understand, that he had maturely considered the two Principal Things, which were the *Bulk* and the *Subject*; and found it, would never *take*, but after a long Vacation, and then only, in case it should happen to be a hard Year for Turnips. Upon which I desired to know, *considering my urgent Necessities*, what he thought might be acceptable this Month. He lookt *Westward*, and said, *I doubt we shall have a Fit of bad Weather; However, if you could prepare some pretty little* Banter (but not in Verse) *or a small Treatise upon the* —— *it would run like Wild-Fire. But*, if it hold up, *I have already hired an Author to write something against* Dr. B——tl—y, *which, I am sure, will turn to Account.*

AT length we agreed upon this Expedient; That when a Customer comes for one of these, and desires in Confidence to know the Author; he will tell him very privately, as a Friend, naming which ever of the Wits shall happen to be that Week in the Vogue; and if *Durfy's* last Play should be in Course, I had as lieve he may be the Person as *Congreve*. This I mention, because I am wonderfully well acquainted with the present Relish of Courteous Readers; and have often observed, with singular Pleasure, that a *Fly* driven from a *Honey-pot*, will immediately, with very good Appetite alight, and finish his Meal on an *Excrement*.

I have one Word to say upon the Subject of *Profound Writers*, who are grown very numerous of late; And, I know very well, the judicious World is resolved to list me in that Number. I conceive therefore, as to the Business of being *Profound*, that it is with *Writers*, as with *Wells*; A Person with good Eyes may see to the Bottom of the deepest, provided any *Water* be there; and, that often, when there is nothing in the World at the Bottom, besides

Dryness and *Dirt*, tho' it be but a Yard and half under Ground, it shall pass, however, for wondrous *Deep*, upon no wiser a Reason than because it is wondrous *Dark.*

I am now trying an Experiment very frequent among Modern Authors; which is, to *write upon Nothing;* When the Subject is utterly exhausted, to let the Pen still move on; by some called, the Ghost of Wit, delighting to walk after the Death of its Body. And to say the Truth, there seems to be no Part of Knowledge in fewer Hands, than That of Discerning *when to have Done.* By the Time that an Author has writ out a Book, he and his Readers are become old Acquaintance, and grow very loath to part: So that I have sometimes known it to be in Writing, as in Visiting, where the Ceremony of taking Leave, has employ'd more Time than the whole Conversation before. The Conclusion of a Treatise, resembles the Conclusion of Human Life, which hath sometimes been compared to the End of a Feast; where few are satisfied to depart, *ut plenus vitæ conviva*: For Men will sit down after the fullest Meal, tho' it be only to *doze*, or to *sleep* out the rest of the Day. But, in this latter, I differ extreamly from other Writers; and shall be too proud, if by all my Labors, I can have any ways contributed to the *Repose* of Mankind, in †Times so turbulent and unquiet as these. Neither, do I think such an Employment so very alien from the Office of a *Wit*, as some would suppose. For among a very Polite Nation in   ** Trezenii* **Greece*, there were the *same* Temples built and consecrated to   *Pausan. 2.* *Sleep* and the *Muses*, between which two Deities, they believed the strictest Friendship was established.

I have one concluding Favour, to request of my Reader; that he will not expect to be equally diverted and informed by every Line, or every Page of this Discourse; but give some Allowance to the Author's Spleen, and short Fits or Intervals of Dullness, as well as his own; And lay it seriously to his Conscience, whether, if he were walking the Streets, in dirty Weather, or a rainy Day; he would allow it fair Dealing in Folks at their Ease from a Window, to Critick his Gate, and ridicule his Dress at such a Juncture.

IN my Disposure of Employments of the Brain, I have thought fit to make *Invention* the *Master,* and to give *Method* and *Reason,* the Office of its *Lacquays.* The Cause of this Distribution was, from observing it my peculiar Case, to be often under a Temptation of being *Witty,* upon Occasions, where I could be neither *Wise* nor *Sound,* nor any thing to the Matter in hand. And, I am too much a Servant of the *Modern* Way, to neglect any such Opportunities, whatever Pains or Improprieties I may be at, to introduce them. For, I have observed, that from a laborious Collection of Seven

---

† *This was writ before the Peace of* Riswick.

Hundred Thirty Eight *Flowers*, and *shining Hints* of the best *Modern* Authors, digested with great Reading, into my Book of *Common-places*; I have not been able after five Years to draw, hook, or force, into common Conversation, any more than a Dozen. Of which Dozen, the one Moiety failed of Success, by being dropt among unsuitable Company; and the other cost me so many Strains, and Traps, and *Ambages* to introduce, that I at length resolved to give it over. Now, this Disappointment, (to discover a Secret) I must own, gave me the first Hint of setting up for an *Author*; and, I have since found among some particular Friends, that it is become a very general Complaint, and has produced the same Effects upon many others. For, I have remarked many a *towardly Word*, to be wholly neglected or despised in *Discourse*, which hath passed very smoothly, with some Consideration and Esteem, after its Preferment and Sanction in *Print*. But now, since by the Liberty and Encouragement of the Press, I am grown absolute Master of the Occasions and Opportunities, to expose the Talents I have acquired; I already discover, that the *Issues* of my *Observanda* begin to grow too large for the *Receipts*. Therefore, I shall here pause awhile, till I find, by feeling the World's Pulse, and my own, that it will be of absolute Necessity for us both, to resume my Pen.

FINIS.

A
Full and True Account
OF THE
BATTEL
Fought last *FRIDAY*,

Between the

Antient and the *Modern*

BOOKS
IN
St. *JAMES's*
LIBRARY

LONDON:

Printed in the Year, MDCCIV.

Plate 24

Plate 25

THE
BOOKSELLER
TO THE
READER

THE following Discourse, as it is unquestionably of the same Author, so it seems to have been written about the same Time with the former, I mean, the Year 1697, when the famous Dispute was on Foot, about *Antient and Modern Learning*. The Controversy took its Rise from an Essay of Sir *William Temple*'s, upon that Subject; which was answer'd by W. *Wotton*, B.D. with an Appendix by Dr. *Bently*, endeavouring to destroy the credit of *Æsop* and Phalaris, for Authors, whom Sir *William Temple* had in the Essay before mentioned, highly commended. In that Appendix, the Doctor falls hard upon a new Edition of *Phalaris*, put out by the Honorable *Charles Boyle* (Plate 24) (now *Earl* of *Orrery*) to which, Mr. *Boyle* replyed at large, with great Learning and Wit; and the Doctor, voluminously, rejoyned. In this Dispute, the Town highly resented to see a Person of Sir *William Temple*'s Character and Merits, roughly used by the two reverend Gentlemen aforesaid, and without any manner of Provocation. At length, there appearing no End of the Quarrel, our Author tells us, that the BOOKS in St. *James*'s Library, looking upon themselves as Parties principally concerned, took up the Controversy, and came to a decisive Battel; But, the Manuscript, by the Injury of Fortune, or Weather, being in several Places imperfect, we cannot learn to which side the Victory fell.

I must warn the Reader, to beware of applying to Persons what is here meant, only of Books in the most literal Sense. So, when *Virgil* is mentioned, we are not to understand the Person of a famous Poet, call'd by that Name, but only certain Sheets of Paper, bound up in Leather (Plate 25), containing in Print, the Works of the said Poet, and so of the rest.

The
Preface
of the
Author.

*S*ATYR *is a sort of Glass, wherein Beholders do generally discover every body's Face but their Own; which is the chief Reason for that kind of Reception it meets in the World, and that so very few are offended with it. But if it should happen otherwise, the Danger is not great; and, I have learned from long Experience, never to apprehend Mischief from those Understandings, I have been able to provoke; For, Anger and Fury, though they add Strength to the* Sinews *of the* Body, *yet are found to relax those of the* Mind, *and to render all its Efforts feeble and impotent.*

THERE is a Brain *that will endure but one* Scumming: *Let the Owner gather it with Discretion, and manage his little Stock with Husbandry; but of all things, let him beware of bringing it under the* Lash *of this* Betters; *because, That will make it all bubble up into Impertinence, and he will find no new Supply: Wit, without knowledge, being a sort of* Cream, *which gathers in a Night to the Top, and by a skilful Hand, may be soon whipt into* Froth; *but once scumm'd away, what appears underneath will be fit for nothing, but to be thrown to the Hogs.*

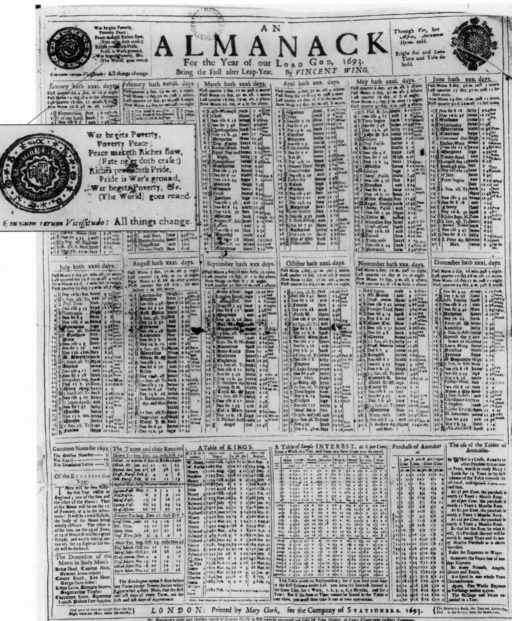

Plate 26

A Full and True
Account
of the
Battel
Fought last FRIDAY, &c.

WHOEVER examins with due Circumspection into the **Annual Records of Time* (Plate 26), will find it remarked, that *War is the Child of Pride*, and *Pride the Daughter of Riches;* The former of which Assertions may be soon granted; but one cannot so easily subscribe to the latter: For *Pride* is nearly related to Beggary and *Want*, either by Father or Mother, and sometimes by both; And, to speak naturally, it very seldom happens among Men to fall out, when all have enough: Invasions usually travelling from *North* to *South*, that is to say, from Poverty upon Plenty. The most antient and natural Grounds of Quarrels, are *Lust* and *Avarice;* which, tho' we may allow to be Brethren or collateral Branches of *Pride,* are certainly the issues of *Want.* For, to speak in the Phrase of Writers upon the Politicks, we may observe in the Republick of *Dogs,* (which in its Original seems to be an Institution of the *Many*) that the whole State is ever in the profoundest Peace, after a full Meal; and, that Civil Broils arise among them, when it happens for one great *Bone* to be seized on by some *leading Dog,* who either divides it among the *Few,* and then it falls to an *Oligarchy,* or keeps it to Himself, and then it runs up to a *Tyranny.* The same Reasoning also, holds Place among them, in those Dissensions we behold upon a Turgescency in any of their Females. For, the Right of Possession lying in common (it being impossible to establish a Property in so delicate a Case) Jealousies and Suspicions do so abound, that the whole Commonwealth of that Street, is reduced to a manifest *State of War,* of every *Citizen* against every *Citizen;* till some One of more Courage, Conduct, or Fortune than the rest, seizes and enjoys the Prize: Upon which, naturally arises Plenty of Heartburning, and Envy, and Snarling against the *Happy Dog.* Again, if we look upon any of these Republicks engaged in a Forein War, either of Invasion or Defence, we shall find, the same Reasoning will serve,

> * *Riches produceth Pride; Pride is War's Ground, &c.* Vid. Ephem. de *Mary Clarke;* opt. Edit.

as to the Grounds and Occasions of each; and, that *Poverty,* or *Want,* in some Degree or other, (whether Real, or in Opinion, which makes no Alteration in the Case) has a great Share, as well as *Pride,* on the Part of the Aggressor.

NOW, whoever will please to take this Scheme, and either reduce or adapt it to an intellectual State, or Commonwealth of Learning, will soon discover the first Ground or Disagreement between the two great Parties at this Time in Arms; and may form just Conclusions upon the Merits of either Cause. But the Issue or Events of this War are not so easy to conjecture at: For, the present Quarrel is so enflamed by the warm Heads of either Faction, and the Pretensions *somewhere or other* so exorbitant, as not to admit the least Overtures of Accommodation: This Quarrel first began (as I have heard it affirmed by an old Dweller in the Neighbourhood) about a small Spot of Ground, *lying* and *being* upon one of the two Tops of the Hill *Parnassus;* the highest and largest of which, had it seems, been time out of Mind, in quiet Possession of certain Tenants, call'd the *Antients;* And the other was held by the *Moderns.* But, these disliking their present Station, sent certain Ambassadors to the *Antients,* complaining of a great Nuissance, how, the Height of that Part of *Parnassus,* quite spoiled the Prospect of theirs, especially towards the East; and therefore, to avoid a War, offered them the Choice of this Alternative; either that the *Antients* would please to remove themselves and their Effects down to the lower Summity, which the *Moderns* would graciously surrender to them, and advance in their Place; or else, that the said *Antients* will give leave to the *Moderns* to come with Shovels and Mattocks, and level the said Hill, as low as they shall think it convenient. To which, the *Antients* made Answer; How little they expected such a Message as this, from a Colony, whom they had admitted out of their own Free Grace, to so near a Neighbourhood. That, as to their own Seat, they were Aborigines of it, and therefore, to talk with Them of a Removal or Surrender, was a Language they did not understand. That, if the Height of the Hill, on their side, shortned the Prospect of the *Moderns,* it was a Disadvantage they could not help, but desired them to consider, whether that Injury (if it be any) were not largely recompenced by the *Shade* and *Shelter* it afforded them. That, as to levelling or digging down, it was either Folly or Ignorance to propose it, if they did, or did not know, how that side of the Hill was an entire Rock, which would break their Tools and Hearts; without any Damage to it self. That they would therefore advise the *Moderns,* rather to raise their own side of the Hill, than dream of pulling down that of the *Antients,* to the former of which, they would not only give Licence, but also largely contribute. All this was rejected by the *Moderns,* with much Indignation, who still insisted upon one of the two Expedients; And so this Difference broke out into a long and obstinate War, maintained on the one

Part, by Resolution, and by the Courage of certain Leaders and Allies; but, on the other, by the greatness of their Number, upon all Defeats, affording continual Recruits. In this Quarrel, whole Rivulets of *Ink* have been exhausted, and the Virulence of both Parties enormously augmented. Now, it must here be understood, that *Ink* is the great missive Weapon, in all Battels of the *Learned,* which, convey'd thro' a sort of Engine, call'd a *Quill,* infinite Numbers of these are darted at the Enemy, by the Valiant on each side, with equal Skill and Violence, as if it were an Engagement of *Porcupines.* This malignant Liquor was compounded by the Engineer, who invented it, of two Ingredients, which are *Gall* and *Copperas,* by its Bitterness and Venom, to *Suit* in some Degree, as well as to *Foment* the Genius of the Combatants. And as the *Grecians,* after an Engagement, when they could not *agree* about the Victory, were wont to set up Trophies on both sides, the beaten Party being content to be at the same Expence, to keep it self in Countenance (A laudable and antient Custom, happily revived of late, in the Art of War) so the *Learned,* after a sharp and bloody Dispute, do on both sides hang out their Trophies too, which ever comes by the worst. These Trophies have largely inscribed on them the Merits of the Cause; a full impartial Account of such a Battel, and how the Victory fell clearly to the Party that set them up. They are known to the World under several Names; As, *Disputes, Arguments, Rejoynders, Brief Considerations, Answers, Replies, Remarks, Reflexions, Objections, Confutations.* For a very few Days they are fixed up in all Publick Places, either by themselves or their * *Their Title-Pages.* *Representatives, for Passengers to gaze at: From whence the chiefest and largest are removed to certain Magazines, they call, *Libraries,* there to remain in a Quarter purposely assign'd them, and from thenceforth, begin to be called, *Books of Controversy.*

IN these Books, is wonderfully instilled and preserved, the Spirit of each Warrier, while he is alive; and after his Death, his Soul transmigrates there, to inform them. This, at least, is the more common Opinion; But, I believe, it is with Libraries, as with other Cemetaries, where some Philosophers affirm, that a certain Spirit, which they call *Brutum hominis,* hovers over the Monument, till the Body is corrupted, and turns to *Dust,* or to *Worms;* but then vanishes or dissolves: So, we may say, a restless Spirit haunts over every *Book,* till *Dust* or *Worms* have seized upon it; which to some, may happen in a few Days, but to others, later; And therefore, *Books* of Controversy, being of all others, haunted by the most disorderly Spirits, have always been confined in a separate Lodge from the rest; and for fear of mutual violence against each other, it was thought Prudent by our Ancestors, to bind them to the Peace with strong Iron Chains (Plate 22). Of which Invention, the original occasion was this: When the Works of *Scotus* first came out, they were carried to a certain great Library, and had Lodgings appointed them; But this Author was no sooner settled, than he went to visit his Master *Aristotle*, and there both concerted together to seize *Plato* by main Force, and turn him out from his antient Station among the *Divines*, where he had peaceably dwelt near Eight Hundred Years. The Attempt succeeded, and the two Usurpers have reigned ever since in his stead: But to maintain Quiet for the future, it was decreed, that all *Polemicks* of the larger Size, should be held fast with a Chain.

BY this Expedient, the publick Peace of Libraries might certainly have been preserved, if a new Species of controversial Books had not arose of late years, instinct with a most malignant Spirit, from the War above-mentioned, between the *Learned*, about the higher Summit of *Parnassus*.

WHEN these Books were first admitted into the publick Libraries, I remember to have said upon Occasion, to several Persons concerned, how I was sure, they would create Broyls where-ever they came, unless a World of Care were taken; And therefore, I advised, that the Champions of each side should be coupled together, or otherwise mixt, that like the blending of contrary Poysons, their Malignity might be employ'd among themselves. And it seems, I was neither an ill Prophet, nor an ill Counsellor; for it was nothing else but the Neglect of this Caution, which gave Occasion to the terrible Fight that happened on *Friday* last between the *Antient* and *Modern Books* in the *King's Library*. Now, because the Talk of this Battel is so fresh in every body's Mouth, and the Expectation of the Town so great to be informed in the Particulars; I, being possessed of all Qualifications requisite in an *Historian*, and retained by neither Party; have resolved to comply with the urgent *Importunity of my Friends*, by writing down a full impartial Account thereof.

THE *Guardian* of the *Regal Library*, a Person of great Valor (Plate 27), but chiefly renowned for his *Humanity, had been a fierce Champion for the *Moderns*, and in an Engagement upon *Parnassus*, had vowed, with his own Hands, to knock down two of the *Antient* Chiefs, who guarded a small Pass on the superior Rock; but endeavouring to climb up, was cruelly obstructed by his own unhappy Weight, and tendency towards his Center; a Quality, to which, those of the *Modern* Party, are extreme subject; For, being light-headed, they have in Speculation, a wonderful Agility, and conceive nothing too high for them to mount; but in reducing to Practice, discover a mighty Pressure about their Posteriors and their Heels. Having thus failed in his Design, the disappointed Champion bore a cruel Rancour to the *Antients*,

---

* *The Honourable Mr.* Boyle, *in the Preface to his Edition of* Phalaris, *says, he was refus'd a Manuscript by the Library-Keeper,* pro solita Humanitate suâ.

which he resolved to gratify, by shewing all Marks of his Favor to the *Books* of their Adversaries, and lodging them in the fairest Apartments; when at the same time, whatever *Book* had the Boldness to own it self for an Advocate of the *Antients,* was buried alive in some obscure Corner, and threatned upon the least Displeasure, to be turned out of Doors. Besides, it so happened, that about this time, there was a strange Confusion of Place among all the *Books* in the Library; for which several Reasons were assigned. Some imputed it to a great heap of *learned Dust,* which a perverse Wind blew off from a Shelf of *Moderns* into the *Keeper's* Eyes. Others affirmed, He had a Humor to pick the *Worms* out of the *Schoolmen,* and swallow them fresh and fasting; whereof some fell upon his *Spleen,* and some climbed up into his Head, to the great Perturbation of both. And lastly, others maintained, that by walking much in the dark about the Library, he had quite lost the Situation of it out of this Head; And therefore, in replacing his *Books,* he was apt to mistake, and clap *Des-Cartes* next to *Aristotle; Poor Plato* had got between *Hobbes* and the *Seven Wise Masters,* and *Virgil* was hemm'd in with *Dryden* on one side, and *Withers* (*recte* Wither) on the other.

MEAN while, those *Books* that were Advocates for the *Moderns,* chose out one from among them, to make a Progress thro' the whole Library, examine the Number and Strength of their Party, and concert their Affairs. This Messenger performed all things very industriously, and brought back with him a List of their Forces, in all Fifty Thousand, consisting chiefly of *light Horse, heavy-armed Foot,* and *Mercenaries;* Whereof the *Foot* were in general but sorrily armed, and worse clad; Their *Horses* large, but extreamly out of Case and Heart; However, some few by trading among the *Antients,* had furnisht themselves tolerably enough.

WHILE Things were in this Ferment; *Discord* grew extreamly high, hot Words passed on both sides, and ill Blood was plentifully bred. Here a solitary *Antient,* squeez'd up among a whole Shelf of *Moderns,* offered fairly to dispute the Case, and to prove by manifest Reasons, that the Priority was due to them, from long Possession, and in regard of their Prudence, Antiquity, and above all, their great Merits towards the *Moderns.* But these denied the Premises, and seemed very much to wonder, how the *Antients* could pretend to insist upon their Antiquity; when it was so plain (if they went to that) that the *Moderns* were much the more **Antient* of the two. As for any Obligations they owed to the *Antients,* they renounced them all. 'Tis true, said they,

* *According to the Modern Paradox.*

we are informed, some few of our Party have been so mean to borrow their Subsistence from You; But the rest, infinitely the greater Number (and especially, we French *and* English) *were so far from stooping to so base an Example, that there never passed, till this very hour, six Words between us. For, our* Horses *are of our own breeding, our*

Arms *of our own forging, and our* Cloaths *of our own cutting out and sowing.* *Plato* was by chance upon the next Shelf, and observing those that spoke to be in the ragged Plight, mentioned a while ago; their *Jades* lean and foundred, their *Weapons* of rotten Wood, their *Armour* rusty, and nothing but Raggs underneath; he laughed loud, and in his pleasant way, swore, *by God* —, *he believed them.*

NOW, the *Moderns* had not proceeded in their late Negotiation, with Secrecy enough to escape the Notice of the Enemy. For, those Advocates, who had begun the Quarrel, by setting first on Foot the Dispute of Precedency, talkt so loud of coming to a Battel, that *Temple* happened to over-hear them, and gave immediate Intelligence to the *Antients;* who thereupon drew up their scattered Troops together, resolving to act upon the defensive; Upon which, several of the *Moderns* fled over to their Party, and among the rest, *Temple* himself. This *Temple* having been educated and long conversed among the *Antients,* was, of all the *Moderns,* their greatest Favorite, and became their greatest Champion.

THINGS were at this Crisis, when a material Accident fell out. For, upon the highest Corner of a large Window, there dwelt a certain *Spider,* swollen up to the first Magnitude, by the Destruction of infinite Numbers of *Flies,* whose Spoils lay scattered before the Gates of his Palace, like human Bones before the Cave of some Giant. The Avenues to his Castle were guarded with Turn-pikes, and Palissadoes, all after the *Modern* way of Fortification. After you had passed several Courts, you came to the Center, wherein you might behold the *Constable* himself in his own Lodgings, which had Windows fronting to each Avenue, and Ports to sally out upon all Occasions of Prey or Defence. In this Mansion, he had for some Time dwelt in Peace and Plenty, without Danger to his *Person* by *Swallows* from above, or to his *Palace* by *Brooms* from below: When it was the Pleasure of Fortune to conduct thither a wandring *Bee,* to whose Curiosity a broken Pane in the Glass had discovered itself; and in he went, where expatiating a while, he at last happened to alight upon one of the outward Walls of the *Spider's* Cittadel; which yielding to the unequal Weight, sunk down to the very Foundation. Thrice he endeavoured to force his Passage, and Thrice the Center shook. The *Spider* within, feeling the terrible Convulsion, supposed at first, that *Nature* was approaching to her final Dissolution; or else, that *Beelzebub* with all his Legions, was come to revenge the Death of many thousand of his Subjects, whom this Enemy had slain and devoured. However, he at length valiantly resolved to issue forth, and meet his Fate. Mean while, the *Bee* had acquitted himself of his Toils, and posted securely at some Distance, was employed in cleansing his Wings, and Disengaging them from the ragged Remnants of the Cobweb. By this Time the *Spider* was adventured out, when beholding the Chasms, and Ruins, and Dilapidations of his Fortress, he was very near at his Wit's end, he stormed and swore like a Mad-man, and swelled till he was ready to burst. At length, casting his Eye upon the *Bee,* and wisely gathering Causes from Events, (for they knew each other by Sight) *A Plague split you,* said he, *for a giddy Son of a Whore; Is it you, with a Vengeance, that have made this Litter here? Could you not look before you, and be d——n'd? Do you think I have nothing else to do (in the Devil's Name) but to Mend and Repair after your Arse? Good Words, Friend,* said the *Bee,* (having now pruned himself, and being disposed to drole) *I'll give you my Hand and Word to come near your Kennel no more; I was never in such a confounded Pickle since I was born. Sirrah,* replyed the *Spider, if it were not for breaking an old Custom in our Family, never to stir abroad against an Enemy, I should come and teach you better Manners. I pray, have Patience,* said the *Bee, or you will spend your Substance, and for ought I see, you may stand in need of it all, towards the Repair of your House. Rogue, Rogue,* replyed the *Spider, yet, methinks, you should have more Respect to a Person, whom all the World allows to be so much your Betters. By my Troth,* said the *Bee, the Comparison will amount to a very good Jest, and you will do me a Favor, to let me know the Reasons, that all the World is pleased to use in so hopeful a Dispute.* At this, the *Spider* having swelled himself into the Size and Posture of a Disputant, began his Argument in the true Spirit of Controversy, with a Resolution to be heartily scurrilous and angry, to urge *on* his own Reasons, without the least Regard to the Answers or Objections of his Opposite; and fully predetermined in his Mind against all Conviction.

NOT to disparage my self, said he, *by the Comparison with such a Rascal;* What *art thou, but a Vagabond without House or Home, without Stock or Inheritance? Born to no Possession of your own, but a Pair of Wings, and a Drone-Pipe. Your Livelihood is an universal Plunder upon Nature; a Freebooter over Fields and Gardens; and for the sake of Stealing, will rob a Nettle as readily as a Violet. Whereas I am a domestick Animal, furnisht with a Native Stock within my self. This large Castle (to shew my Improvements in the Mathematicks) is all built with my own Hands, and the Materials extracted altogether out of my own Person.*

I am glad, answered the *Bee, to hear you grant at least, that I am come honestly by my Wings and my Voice, for then, it seems, I am obliged to Heaven alone for my Flights and my Musick; and Providence would never have bestowed me two such Gifts, without designing them for the noblest Ends. I visit, indeed, all the Flowers and Blossoms of the Field and the Garden, but whatever I collect from thence, enriches my self, without the least Injury to their Beauty, their Smell, or their Taste, Now, for you, and your Skill in Architecture, and other Mathematicks, I have little to say: In that Building of yours, there might, for ought I know, have been Labor and Method enough, but by woful Experience for us both, 'tis too plain, the Materials are nought, and I hope, you will henceforth take Warning, and consider Duration and Matter, as well as Method and Art. You, boast, indeed, of being obliged to no other Creature, but of drawing, and spinning out all from your self; That is to say, if we may judge of the Liquor in the Vessel by what issues out, You possess a good plentiful Store of Dirt and Poison in your Breast; And, tho' I would by no means, lessen or disparage your genuine Stock of either, yet, I doubt, you are somewhat obliged for an Encrease of both, to a little forein Assistance. Your inherent Portion of Dirt, does not fail of Acquisitions, by Sweepings exhaled from below: and one Insect furnishes you with a share of Poison to destroy another. So that in short, the Question comes all to this; Whether is the nobler Being of the two, That which by lazy Contemplation of four Inches round; by an over-weening Pride, which feeding and engendering on it self, turns all into Excrement and Venom; produces nothing at last but Fly-bane and a Cobweb: Or That, which, by an universal Range, with long search, much Study, true Judgment, and Distinction of Things, brings home Honey and Wax:*

THIS dispute was managed with such Eagerness, Clamor, and Warmth, that the two Parties of *Books* in Arms below, stood Silent a while, waiting in Suspense what would be the Issue; which was not long undetermined: For the *Bee* grown impatient at so much loss of Time, fled strait away to a bed of Roses, without looking for a Reply; and left the *Spider* like an Orator, *collected* in himself, and just prepared to burst out.

IT happened upon this Emergency, that *Æsop* broke silence first. He had been of late most barbarously treated by a strange Effect of the *Regent's Humanity*, who had tore off his Title-page, sorely defaced one half of his Leaves, and chained him fast among a Shelf of *Moderns*. Where soon discovering how high the Quarrel was like to proceed, He tried all his Arts, and turned himself to a thousand Forms: At length in the borrowed Shape of an *Ass*, the *Regent* mistook Him for a *Modern*; by which means, he had Time and Opportunity to escape to the *Antients*, just when the *Spider* and the *Bee* were entring into their Contest; to which He gave His Attention with a World of Pleasure; and when it was ended, swore in the loudest Key, that in all his Life, he had never known two Cases so parallel and adapt to each other, as That in the Window, and this upon the Shelves. The *Disputants, said he, have admirably managed the Dispute between them, have taken in the full Strength of all that is to be said on both sides, and exhausted the Substance of every Argument* pro *and* con. *It is but to adjust the Reasonings of both to the present Quarrel, then to compare and apply the Labors and Fruits of each, as the* Bee *has learnedly deduced them; and we shall find the Conclusions fall plain and close upon the* Moderns *and Us. For, pray Gentlemen, was ever any thing so* Modern *as the* Spider *in his Air, his Turns, and his Paradoxes? He argues in the Behalf of You his Brethren, and Himself, with many Boastings of his native Stock, and great Genius; that he Spins and Spits wholly from himself, and scorns to own any Obligation or Assistance from without. Then he displays to you his great Skill in Architecture, and*

Improvement in the Mathematicks. To all this, the Bee, *as an Advocate, retained by us the* Antients, *thinks fit to Answer; That if one may judge of the great Genius or Inventions of the* Moderns, *by what they have produced, you will hardly have Countenance to bear you out in boasting of either. Erect your Schemes with as much Method and Skill as you please; yet, if the Materials be nothing but Dirt, spun out of your own Entrails (the guts of* Modern *Brains) the Edifice will conclude at last in a* Cobweb: *The Duration of which, like that of other* Spiders *Webs, may be imputed to their being forgotten, or neglected, or hid in a Corner. For any Thing else of Genuine, that the* Moderns *may pretend to, I cannot recollect; unless it be a large Vein of Wrangling and Satyr, much of a Nature and Substance with the* Spider's *Poison; which, however, they pretend to spit wholly out of themselves, is improved by the same Arts, by feeding upon the* Insects *and* Vermin *of the Age. As for* Us, *the* Antients, *We are content with the* Bee, *to pretend to Nothing of our own, beyond our* Wings *and our* Voice: *that is to say, our* Flights *and our* Language; *For the rest, whatever we have got, has been by infinite Labor, and search, and ranging thro' every Corner of* Nature: *The Difference is, that instead of* Dirt *and* Poison, *we have rather chose to fill our Hives with* Honey *and* Wax, *thus furnishing* Mankind *with the two Noblest of Things, which are* Sweetness *and* Light.

'TIS wonderful to conceive the Tumult arisen among the Books, upon the Close of this long Descant of *Æsop;* Both Parties took the Hint, and heightened their Animosities so on a sudden, that they resolved it should come to a Battel. Immediately, the two main Bodies withdrew under their several Ensigns, to the further Parts of the Library, and there entred into Cabals, and consults upon the present Emergency. The *Moderns* were in very warm Debates upon the Choice of their *Leaders,* and nothing less than the Fear impending from their Enemies, could have kept them from Mutinies upon this Occasion. The Difference was greatest among the *Horse,* where every private *Trooper* pretended to the chief Command, from *Tasso* and *Milton,* to *Dryden* and *Withers.* The *Light-Horse* were Commanded by *Cowly,* and *Despreaux.* There, came the *Bowmen* under their valiant Leaders, *Des-Cartes, Gassendi,* and *Hobbes,* whose Strength was such, that they could shoot their Arrows beyond the *Atmosphere,* never to fall down again, but turn like that of *Evander,* into *Meteors,* or like the *Canonball* into *Stars. Paracelsus* brought a *Squadron* of *Stink-Pot-Flingers* from the snowy Mountains of *Rhætia.* There, came a vast Body of *Dragoons,* of different Nations, under the leading of *Harvey,* their great *Aga:* Part armed with *Scythes,* the Weapons of Death; Part with *Launces* and long *knives,* all steept in *Poison;* Part shot *Bullets* of most malignant Nature, and used *white Powder* which infallibly killed without *Report.* There, came several Bodies of *heavy-armed Foot,* all *Mercenaries,* under the Ensigns of *Guicciardine, Davila, Polydore Virgil, Buchanan, Mariana, Cambden,* and others. The *Engineers* were commanded by *Regiomontanus* and *Wilkins*. The rest were a confused Multitude, led by *Scotus, Aquinas,* and *Bellarmine,* of mighty Bulk and Stature, but without either Arms, Courage, or Discipline. In the last Place, came infinite Swarms of *Calones, a disorderly Rout led by *Lestrange;* Rogues and Raggamuffins, that follow the Camp for nothing but the Plunder; All without *Coats* to cover them.

THE Army of the *Antients* was much fewer in Number; *Homer* led the *Horse,* and *Pindar* the *Light-Horse; Euclid* was chief *Engineer: Plato* and *Aristotle* commanded the *Bow-men, Herodotus* and *Livy* the *Foot, Hippocrates* the *Dragoons.* The *Allies,* led by *Vossius* and *Temple,* brought up the Rear.

ALL things violently tending to a decisive Battel; *Fame,* who much frequented, and had a large Apartment formerly assigned her in the *Regal Library,* fled up strait to *Jupiter,* to whom she delivered a faithful Account of all that passed between the two Parties below. (For among the Gods, she always tells Truth.) *Jove* in great Concern, convokes a Council in the *Milky-Way.* The Senate assembled, he declares the Occasion of convening them; a bloody Battel just impendent between two mighty Armies of *Antient* and *Modern* Creatures, call'd *Books,* wherein the Celestial Interest was but too deeply concerned. *Momus,* the Patron of the *Moderns,* made an excellent Speech in their Favor, which was answered by *Pallas* the Protectress of the *Antients.* The Assembly was divided in their Affections; when *Jupiter* commanded the Book of Fate to be laid before Him. Immediately were brought by *Mercury,* three large Volumes in Folio, containing Memoirs of all Things past, present, and to come. The Clasps were of Silver, double gilt; the Covers, of Celestial Turky-leather, and the Paper such as here on Earth might almost pass for Vellum. *Jupiter* having silently read the Decree, would communicate the *Import* to none, but presently shut up the Book.

WITHOUT the Doors of this Assembly, there attended a vast Number of light, nimble Gods, menial Servants to *Jupiter:* These are his ministring Instruments in all Affairs below. They travel in a Caravan, more or less together, and are fastened to each other like a Link of Gally-slaves, by a light Chain, which passes from them to *Jupiter's* great Toe: And yet in receiving or delivering a Message, they may never approach above the lowest Step of his Throne, where he and they whisper to each other thro' a long hollow Trunk. These Deities are call'd by mortal Men, *Accidents,* or *Events;* but the Gods call them, *Second Causes. Jupiter* having delivered his Message to a certain Number of these Divinities, they flew immediately down to the Pinnacle of the Regal Library, and consulting a few Minutes, entered unseen, and disposed the Parties according to their Orders.

---

* *These are Pamphlets, which are not bound or cover'd.*

MEAN while, *Momus* fearing the worst, and calling to mind an antient Prophecy, which bore no very good Face to his Children the *Moderns;* bent his Flight to the Region of a malignant Deity, call'd *Criticism.* She dwelt on the Top of a snowy Mountain in *Nova Zembla;* there *Momus* found her extended in her Den, upon the Spoils of numberless Volumes half devoured. At her right Hand sat *Ignorance,* her Father and Husband, blind with Age; at her left; *Pride* her Mother, dressing her up in the Scraps of Paper herself had torn. There, was *Opinion* her Sister, light of Foot, hoodwinkt, and headstrong, yet giddy and perpetually turning. About her play'd her Children, *Noise* and *Impudence, Dullness* and *Vanity, Positiveness, Pedantry,* and *Ill-Manners.* The Goddess herself had Claws like a Cat; Her Head, and Ears, and Voice, resembled those of an *Ass;* Her Teeth fallen out before; Her eyes turned inward, as if she lookt only upon herself: Her Diet was the overflowing of her own *Gall:* Her *Spleen* was so large, as to stand prominent like a Dug of the first Rate, nor wanted Excrescencies in form of Teats, at which a Crew of ugly Monsters were greedily sucking; and, what is wonderful to conceive, the Bulk of Spleen increased faster than the Sucking could diminish it. *Goddess,* said *Momus, can you sit idly here, while our devout Worshippers, the* Moderns, *are this Minute entring into a cruel Battel, and, perhaps, now lying under the Swords of their Enemies; Who then hereafter, will ever sacrifice, or build Altars to our Divinities? Haste therefore to the* British Isle, *and, if possible, prevent their Destruction, while I make Factions among the Gods, and gain them over to our Party.*

MOMUS having thus delivered himself, staid not for an answer, but left the Goddess to her own Resentments; Up she rose in a Rage, and as it is the Form upon such Occasions, began a Soliloquy. *'Tis I* (said she) *who give Wisdom to Infants and Idiots; By me, Children grow wiser than their Parents. By Me, Beaus become Politicians; and* School-Boys, *Judges of Philosophy. By Me, Sophisters debate, and conclude upon the Depths of Knowledge; and Coffee-house Wits instinct by Me, can correct an Author's Style, and display his minutest Errors, without understanding a Syllable of his Matter or his Language. By Me, Striplings spend their Judgment, as they do their Estate, before it comes into their Hands. 'Tis I, who have deposed Wit and Knowledge from their Empire over* Poetry, *and advanced my self in their stead. And shall a few* upstart Antients *dare to oppose me?* —— *But, come, my aged Parents, and you, my Children dear, and thou my beauteous Sister; let us ascend my Chariot, and haste to assist our devout* Moderns, *who are now sacrificing to us a* Hecatomb, *as I perceive by that grateful Smell, which from thence reaches my Nostrils.*

THE Goddess and her Train having Mounted the Chariot, which was drawn by *tame Geese,* flew over infinite Regions, shedding her Influence in due Places, till at length, she arrived at her beloved Island of *Britain;* But in hovering over its *Metropolis,* what Blessings did she not let fall upon her Seminaries of *Gresham* and *Covent-Garden?* And now she reacht the fatal Plain of St. *James*'s Library, at what time the two Armies were upon the Point to engage; where entring with all her Caravan, unseen, and landing upon a Case of Shelves, now desart, but once inhabited by a Colony of *Virtuoso's,* she staid a while to observe the Posture of both Armies.

BUT here, the tender Cares of a Mother began to fill her Thoughts, and move in her Breast. For, at the Head of a Troop of *Modern Bow-men,* she cast her Eyes upon her Son *W–tt–n;* to whom the Fates had assigned a very short Thread. *W–tt–n,* a young Hero, whom an unknown Father of mortal Race, begot by stollen Embraces with this Goddess. He was the Darling of his Mother, above all her Children, and she resolved to go and comfort Him. But first, according to the good old Custom of Deities, she cast about to change her Shape; for fear the Divinity of her Countenance might dazzle his mortal Sight, and over-charge the rest of this Senses. She therefore gathered up her Person into an *Octavo* Compass: Her Body grew white and arid, and split in Pieces with Driness; the thick turned into Pastboard, and the thin into Paper, upon which, her Parents and Children, artfully strowed a Black Juice, or Decoction of Gall and Soot, in Form of Letters; her Head, and Voice, and Spleen, kept their primitive Form, and that which before, was a Cover of Skin, did still continue so. In which Guise, she march'd on towards the *Moderns,* undistinguishable in Shape and Dress from the *Divine B–ntl–y* (Plate 27), *W–tt–n's* dearest Friend. *Brave W–tt–n, said* the Goddess, *Why do our Troops stand idle here, to spend their present Vigor and Opportunity of the Day? Away, let us haste to the Generals, and advise to give the Onset immediately.* Having spoke thus, she took the ugliest of her Monsters, full glutted from her Spleen, and flung it invisibly into his Mouth; which flying strait up into his Head, squeez'd out his Eye-balls, gave him a distorted Look, and half overturned his Brain. Then she privately ordered two of her beloved Children, *Dullness* and *Ill-Manners,* closely to attend his Person in all Encounters. Having thus accoutred him, she vanished in a Mist, and the *Hero* perceived it was the Goddess, his Mother.

THE destined Hour of Fate, being now arrived, the Fight began; whereof, before I dare adventure to make a particular Description, I must, after the Example of other Authors, petition for a hundred Tongues, and Mouths, and Hands, and Pens; which would all be too little to perform so immense a Work. Say, Goddess, that presidest over History; who was it that first advanced in the Field of Battel. *Paracelsus,* at the head of his *Dragoons,* observing *Galen* in the adverse Wing, darted his Javelin with a mighty force, which the brave *Antient* received upon his Shield, the Point breaking in the second fold.   *   *   *   *   *   *   *   *   *   *

<table>
<tr><td>*</td><td>*</td><td>*</td><td>*</td><td>*</td><td>*</td><td>*</td><td>*</td><td>*</td><td>*Hic pauca*</td></tr>
<tr><td>*</td><td>*</td><td>*</td><td>*</td><td>*</td><td>*</td><td>*</td><td>*</td><td>*</td><td>*desunt.*</td></tr>
</table>

They bore the wounded *Aga,* on their Shields to his Chariot   *   *

<table>
<tr><td>*</td><td>*</td><td>*</td><td>*</td><td>*</td><td>*</td><td>*</td><td>*</td><td>*</td><td></td></tr>
<tr><td>*</td><td>*</td><td>*</td><td>*</td><td>*</td><td>*</td><td>*</td><td>*</td><td>*</td><td>*Desunt*</td></tr>
<tr><td>*</td><td>*</td><td>*</td><td>*</td><td>*</td><td>*</td><td>*</td><td>*</td><td>*</td><td>*nonnulla*</td></tr>
<tr><td>*</td><td>*</td><td>*</td><td>*</td><td>*</td><td>*</td><td>*</td><td>*</td><td>*</td><td>*</td></tr>
</table>

THEN *Aristotle* observing *Bacon* advance with a furious Mien, drew his Bow to the Head, and let fly his Arrow, which miss'd the valiant *Modern,* and went hizzing over his Head; but *Des-Cartes* it hit; The Steel Point quickly found a *Defect* in his *Head-piece;* it pierced the Leather and the Pastboard, and went in at his right Eye. The Torture of the Pain, whirled the valiant *Bow-man* round, till Death, like a Star of superior Influence, drew him into his own *Vortex.*   *   *   *   *   *   *   *   *

<table>
<tr><td>*</td><td>*</td><td>*</td><td>*</td><td>*</td><td>*</td><td>*</td><td>*</td><td>*</td><td></td></tr>
<tr><td>*</td><td>*</td><td>*</td><td>*</td><td>*</td><td>*</td><td>*</td><td>*</td><td>*</td><td>*Ingens hiatus*</td></tr>
<tr><td>*</td><td>*</td><td>*</td><td>*</td><td>*</td><td>*</td><td>*</td><td>*</td><td>*</td><td>*hic in MS.*</td></tr>
<tr><td>*</td><td>*</td><td>*</td><td>*</td><td>*</td><td>*</td><td>*</td><td>*</td><td>*</td><td></td></tr>
</table>

when *Homer* appeared at the Head of the Cavalry, mounted on a furious Horse, with Difficulty managed by the Rider himself, but which no other Mortal durst approach; He rode among the Enemies Ranks, and bore down all before him. Say, Goddess, whom he slew first, and whom he slew last. First, *Gondibert* advanced against Him, clad in heavy Armor, and mounted on a staid sober Gelding, not so famed for his Speed as his Docility in kneeling, whenever his Rider would mount or alight. He had made a Vow to *Pallas,* that he would never leave the Field, till he had spoiled *Homer* of his Armor; Madman, who had never once *seen* the Wearer, nor understood his Strength. Him *Homer* overthrew, Horse and Man to the Ground, there to be trampled and choak'd in the Dirt. Then, with a long Spear, he slew *Denham,* a stout *Modern,* who from his †Father's side, derived his Lineage from *Apollo,* but his Mother was of Mortal Race. He fell, and bit the Earth. The Celestial Part *Apollo* took, and made it a Star, but the Terrestrial lay wallowing upon the Ground. Then *Homer* slew *W—sl—y* with a kick of his Horse's heel; He took *Perrault* by mighty Force out of his Saddle, then hurl'd him at *Fontenelle,* with the same Blow dashing out both their Brains.

ON the left Wing of the Horse, *Virgil* appeared in shining Armor, compleatly fitted to his Body; He was mounted on a dapple grey Steed, the slowness of whose Pace, was an Effect of the highest Mettle and Vigor. He cast his Eye on the adverse Wing, with a desire to find an Object worthy of

---

† *Sir* John Denham's *Poems are very Unequal, extremely Good, and very Indifferent, so that his Detractors said, he was not the real Author of* Cooper's Hill.

his valour, when behold, upon a sorrel Gelding of a monstrous Size, appeared a Foe, issuing from among the thickest of the Enemy's Squadrons; But his Speed was less than his Noise; for his Horse, old and lean, spent the Dregs of his Strength in a high Trot, which tho' it made slow advances, yet caused a loud Clashing of his Armor, terrible to hear. The two Cavaliers had now approach'd within the Throw of a Lance, when the Stranger desir'd a Parley, and lifting up the Vizard of his Helmet, a Face hardly appeared from within, which after a pause, was known for that of the renowned *Dryden.* The brave *Antient* suddenly started, as one possess'd with Surprize and Disappointment together: For, the Helmet was nine times too large for the Head, which appeared Situate far in the hinder Part, even like the Lady in a Lobster, or like a Mouse under a Canopy of State, or like a shrivled Beau from within the Pent-house of a Modern Perewig: And the voice was suited to the Visage, sounding weak and remote. *Dryden* in a long Harangue soothed up the good *Antient,* called him *Father,* and by a large deduction of Genealogies, made it plainly appear, that they were nearly related. Then he humbly proposed an Exchange of Armor, as a lasting Mark of Hospitality between them. *Virgil* consented (for the Goddess *Diffidence* came unseen, and cast a Mist before his Eyes) tho' his was of Gold, and cost a hundred Beeves, the other but of rusty Iron. However, this glittering Armor became the *Modern* yet worse than his Own. Then, they agreed to exchange Horses; but when it came to the Tryal *Dryden* was afraid, and utterly unable to mount.　　*　　*　　*　　*　　*　　*　　*　　*　　*

Alter hiatus　*　　*　　*　　*　　*　　*　　*　　*　　*
in MS.　　　*　　*　　*　　*　　*　　*　　*　　*　　*

*　　*　　*　　*　　*　　*　　*　　*Lucan* appeared upon a fiery Horse, of admirable Shape, but head-strong, bearing the Rider where he list, over the Field; he made a mighty Slaughter among the Enemy's Horse; which Destruction to stop, *Bl–ckm–re,* a famous *Modern* (but one of the *Mercenaries)* strenuously opposed himself; and darted a Javelin, with a strong Hand, which falling short of its Mark, struck deep in the Earth. Then *Lucan* threw a Lance, but *Æsculapius* came unseen, and turn'd off the Point. *Brave* Modern, *said* Lucan, *I perceive some God protects you, for never did my Arm so deceive me before; But, what Mortal can contend with a God? Therefore, let us Fight no longer, but present Gifts to each other.* Lucan then bestowed the *Modern a Pair of Spurs,* and *Bl–ckm–re* gave *Lucan* a Bridle.　　*　　　　*　　　　*

Pauca desunt.　　*　　*　　*　　*　　*　　*　　*　　*
　　　　　　*　　*　　*　　*　　*　　*　　*　　*　　*

Creech; But, the Goddess *Dulness* took a Cloud, formed into the Shape of *Horace,* armed and mounted, and placed it in a flying Posture before Him. Glad was the Cavalier, to begin a Combat with a flying Foe, and pursued the

RICHARDUS BENTLEIUS
ÆT : XLVIII. MDCCX.

Plate 27

Image, threatning loud; till at last it led him to the peaceful Bower of his Father *Ogleby*, by whom he was disarmed, and assigned to his Repose.

THEN *Pindar* slew ——, and ——, and *Oldham*, and ——, and *Afra* the *Amazon* light of foot; Never advancing in a direct Line, but wheeling with incredible Agility and Force, he made a terrible Slaughter among the Enemy's *Light-Horse*. Him, when *Cowley* observed, his generous Heart burnt within him, and he advanced against the fierce *Antient*, imitating his Address, and Pace, and Career, as well as the Vigor of his Horse, and his own Skill would allow. When the two Cavaliers had approach'd within the length of three Javelins; first *Cowley* threw a Lance, which miss'd *Pindar*, and passing into the Enemy's Ranks, fell ineffectual to the Ground. Then *Pindar* darted a Javelin, so large and weighty, that scarce a dozen *Cavaliers*, as *Cavaliers* are in our degenerate Days, could raise it from the Ground: yet he threw it with Ease, and it went by an unerring Hand, singing through the Air; Nor could the *Modern* have avoided present Death, if he had not luckily opposed the Shield that had been given Him by *Venus*. And now both Hero's drew their Swords, but the *Modern* was so agast and disordered, that he knew not where he was; His Shield dropt from his Hands; thrice he fled, and thrice he could not escape; at last he turned and lifting up his Hands, in the Posture of a Suppliant, *God-like* Pindar, said he, *spare my Life, and possess my Horse with these Arms; beside the Ransom which my Friends will give, when they hear I am alive, and your Prisoner. Dog*, said Pindar, *Let your Ransom stay with your Friends; But your Carcass shall be left for the* Fowls of the Air, *and the* Beasts of the Field. With that, he raised his Sword, and with a mighty Stroak, cleft the wretched *Modern* in twain, the Sword, pursuing the Blow; and one half lay panting on the Ground, to be trod in pieces by the Horses Feet, the other half was born by the frighted Steed thro' the Field. This *Venus took, and wash'd it seven times in *Ambrosia*, then struck it thrice with a Sprig of *Amarant;* upon which, the Leather grew round and soft, the Leaves turned into Feathers, and being gilded before, continued gilded still; so it became a *Dove*, and She harness'd it to her Chariot. *   *

*   *   *   *   *   *   *   *   *Hiatus valdè*
*   *   *   *   *   *   *   *   *deflendus in MS.*
*   *   *   *   *   *   *   *   *   *   *

DAY being far spent, and the numerous Forces of the *Moderns*, half inclining to a Retreat, there issued forth from a Squadron of their *heavy armed Foot*, a Captain, whose Name was *B–ntl–y*   *The Episode* (Plate 27); the most deformed of all the *Moderns;* Tall, but   *of B–ntl–y and* without Shape or Comeliness; Large, but without Strength   *W–tt–n.*

---

* *I do not approve the Author's Judgement in this, for I think* Cowley's *Pindaricks are much preferable to his* Mistress.

or Proportion. His Armour was patch'd up of a thousand incoherent Pieces; and the Sound of it, as he march'd was loud and dry, like that made by the Fall of a Sheet of Lead, which an *Etesian* Wind blows suddenly down from the Roof of some Steeple. His Helmet was of old rusty Iron, but the Vizard was Brass, which tainted by his Breath, corrupted into Copperas, nor wanted Gall, from the same Fountain; so, that whenever provoked by Anger or Labor, an atramentous Quality, of most malignant Nature, was seen to distil from his Lips. In his **1**right Hand he grasp'd a Flail, and (that he might never be unprovided of an *offensive* Weapon) a Vessel full of *Ordure* in his left: Thus, compleatly arm'd, he advanc'd with a slow and heavy Pace, where the *Modern* Chiefs were holding a Consult upon the Sum of Things; who, as he came onwards, laugh'd to behold his crooked Leg, and hump Shoulder, which his Boot and Armor vainly endeavoring to hide were forced to comply with, and expose. The Generals made use of him for his Talent of Railing; which kept within Government, proved frequently of great Service to their Cause, but at other times did more Mischief than Good; For at the least Touch of Offence, and often without any at all, he would, like a wounded Elephant, convert it against his Leaders. Such, at this Juncture, was the Disposition of *B—ntl—y*, grieved to see the Enemy prevail, and dissatisfied with every Body's Conduct, but his own. He humbly gave the *Modern* Generals to understand, that he conceived, with great Submission, they were all a Pack of *Rogues*, and *Fools*, and *Son's of Whores*, and *d—mn'd Cowards*, and *confounded Loggerheads*, and *illiterate Whelps*, and *nonsensical Scoundrels;* That if himself had been constituted General, those *presumptuous Dogs*, the *Antients*, would long before this,

Vid. Homer de Thersite.

have been beaten out of the Field. *You*, said he, *sit here idle, but, when I, or any other valiant* Modern, *kill an Enemy, you are sure to seize the Spoil. But, I will not march one Foot against the Foe, till you all Swear to me, that, whomever I take or Kill, his Arms I shall quietly possess.* B—ntl—y having spoke thus, *Scaliger* bestowing him a sower Look; *Miscreant* Prater, said he, *Eloquent only in thine own Eyes, Thou railest without Wit, or Truth, or Discretion. The Malignity of thy Temper perverteth Nature, Thy* Learning *makes thee more* Barbarous, *thy Study of* Humanity, *more* Inhuman; *Thy* Converse *amongst Poets* more groveling, miry, *and* dull. *All Arts of* civilizing *others, render thee* rude *and* untractable; *Courts have taught thee* ill Manners, *and* polite Con-versation *has finish'd thee a* Pedant. *Besides, a greater Coward burtheneth not the Army. But never despond, I pass my Word, whatever Spoil thou takest, shall certainly be thy own; tho' I hope, that vile Carcass will first become a prey to Kites and Worms.*

---

1 *The Person here spoken of, is famous for letting fly at every Body without Distinction, and using mean and foul Scurrilities.*

his beloved *W–tt–n*: No likeness of Wotton is to be found.

Plate 28

Πρῶτος ἐπεὶ τ̄ Ταῦρον ἐκαίνισεν, ὃς τ̄ ὄλεθρον
Εὗρε, τὸν ἐν χαλκῷ ὴ πυρὶ γνόρμινον. Callim. fragm.

Plate 29

B–NTL–Y durst not reply; but half choaked with Spleen and Rage, withdrew, in full Resolution of performing some great Achievment. With him, for his Aid and Companion, he took his beloved *W–tt–n* (Plate 28); resolving by Policy or Surprize to attempt some neglected Quarter of the *Antients* Army. They began their March over Carcasses of their slaughtered Friends; then to the Right of their own Forces: then wheeled Northward, till they came to *Aldrovandus's* Tomb, which they pass'd on the side of the declining Sun. And now they arrived with Fear, towards the Enemy's Outguards; looking about, if haply, they might spy the Quarters of the Wounded, or some straggling Sleepers, unarm'd and remote from the rest. As when two *Mungrel-Curs*, whom *native Greediness*, and *domestick Want*, provoke, and joyn in Partnership, though fearful, nightly to invade the Folds of some rich Grazier; They, with Tails depress'd, and lolling Tongues, creep soft and slow; mean while, the conscious *Moon*, now in her *Zenith*, on their guilty Heads, darts perpendicular Rays; Nor dare they bark, though much provok'd at her refulgent Visage, whether seen in Puddle by Reflexion, or in Sphear direct; but one surveys the Region round, while t'other scouts the Plain, if haply, to discover at distance from the Flock, some *Carcass* half devoured, the Refuse of gorg'd Wolves, or ominous Ravens. So march'd this lovely, loving Pair of Friends, nor with less Fear and Circumspection; when, at distance, they might perceive two shining Suits of Armor, hanging upon an Oak, and the Owners not far off, in a profound Sleep. The two Friends drew Lots, and the pursuing of this Adventure, fell to *B–ntl–y;* On he went, and in his Van *Confusion* and *Amaze;* while *Horror* and *Affright* brought up the Rear. As he came near; Behold two Hero's of the *Antients* Army, *Phalaris* and *Æsop.* lay fast asleep: *B–ntl–y* would fain have dispach'd them both, and stealing close, aimed his Flail at *Phalaris's* Breast. But, then, the Goddess *Affright* interposing, caught the *Modern* in her icy Arms, and dragg'd him from the Danger she forsaw; For both the dormant Hero's happened to turn at the same Instant, tho' soundly Sleeping, and busy in a Dream. *For *Phalaris* was just that Minute dreaming, how a most vile *Poetaster* had lampoon'd him, and how he had got him roaring in his *Bull* (Plate 29). And *Æsop* dream'd, that as he and the *Antient Chiefs* were lying on the Ground, a *Wild Ass* broke loose, ran about trampling and kicking, and dunging in their Faces. *B–ntl–y* leaving the two Hero's asleep, seized on both their Armors, and withdrew in quest of his Darling *W–tt–n.*

HE, in the mean time, had wandred long in search of some Enterprise, till at length, he arrived at a small *Rivulet*, that issued from a Fountain hard by, call'd in the Language of mortal Men, *Helicon.* Here he stopt, and, parch'd

---

* *This is according to* Homer, *who tells the Dreams of those who were kill'd in their Sleep.*

with thirst, resolved to allay it in this limpid Stream. Thrice, with profane Hands, he essay'd to raise the Water to his Lips, and thrice it slipt all thro' his Fingers. Then he stoop'd prone on his Breast, but e'er his Mouth had kiss'd the liquid Crystal, *Apollo* came, and, in the Channel, held his *Shield* betwixt the *Modern* and the Fountain, so that he drew up nothing but *Mud*. For, altho' no Fountain on Earth can compare with the Clearness of *Helicon*, yet there lyes at Bottom, a thick sediment of *Slime* and *Mud;* For, so *Apollo* begged of *Jupiter,* as a Punishment to those who durst attempt to taste it with unhallowed Lips, and for a Lesson to all, not to *draw too deep,* or *far from the Spring.*

AT the Fountain Head, *W–tt–n* discerned two Hero's; The one he could not distinguish, but the other was soon known for *Temple,* General of the *Allies* to the *Antients*. His Back was turned, and he was employ'd in Drinking large Draughts in his Helmet, from the Fountain, where he had withdrawn himself to rest from the Toils of the War. *W–tt–n,* observing him, with quaking Knees, and trembling Hands, spoke thus to Himself: *Oh, that I could kill this Destroyer of our Army, what Renown should I purchase among the Chiefs! But to issue out against Him, Man for Man, Shield against* Vid. Homer. *Shield, and Launce against Launce; what* Modern *of us dare? For, he fights like a God, and* Pallas *or* Apollo *are ever at his Elbow. But, Oh,* Mother! *if what Fame reports, be true, that I am the Son of so great a Goddess, grant me to Hit* Temple *with this Launce, that the Stroak may send Him to Hell, and that I may return in Safety and Triumph, laden with his Spoils.* The first Part of his Prayer, the Gods granted, at the Intercession of His *Mother* and of *Momus;* but the rest, by a perverse Wind sent from *Fate,* was scattered in the Air. Then *W–tt–n* grasp'd his Launce, and brandishing it thrice over his head, darted it with all his Might, the *Goddess,* his *Mother,* at the same time, adding Strength to his Arm. Away the Launce went hizzing, and reach'd even to the Belt of the averted *Antient,* upon which lightly grazing, it fell to the Ground. *Temple* neither felt the Weapon touch him, nor heard it fall; And *W–tt–n,* might have escaped to his Army, with the Honor of having remitted his Launce against so great a Leader, unrevenged; But, *Apollo* enraged, that a Javelin, flung by the Assistance of so foul a *Goddess,* should pollute his Fountain, put on the Shape of ———, and softly came to young *Boyle,* who then accompanied *Temple:* He pointed first to the Launce, then to the distant *Modern* that flung it, and commanded the young Hero to take immediate Revenge. *Boyle,* clad in a suit of Armor which had been *given him by all the Gods,* immediately advanced against the trembling Foe, who now fled before him. As a young Lion, in the *Lybian Plains,* or *Araby Desart,* sent by his aged Sire to hunt for Prey, or Health, or Exercise; He scours along wishing to meet some Tiger from the Mountains, or a furious Boar; If Chance, a *Wild Ass,* with Brayings importune, affronts his Ear, the generous Beast, though loathing to distain his Claws with Blood so vile, yet much provok'd at the offensive Noise; which *Echo*, Foolish Nymph, like her *ill-judging Sex*, repeats much louder, and with more Delight than *Philomela's* Song: he vindicates the Honor of the Forest, and hunts the noisy, long-ear'd Animal. So *W–tt–n* fled, so *Boyle* pursued. But *W–tt–n* heavy-arm'd, and slow of foot, began to slack his Course; when his Lover *B–ntl–y* appeared, returning laden with the Spoils of the two sleeping *Antients*. *Boyle* observed him well, and soon discovering the Helmet and Shield of *Phalaris*, his Friend, both which he had lately with his own Hands, new polish'd and gilded; Rage sparkled in His Eyes, and leaving his Pursuit after *W–tt–n*, he furiously rush'd on against this new Approacher. Fain would he be revenged on both; but both now fled different Ways: *And as a Woman in a little House, that   *Vid. Homer.* gets a painful Livelihood by Spinning; if chance her Geese be scattered o'er the Common, she courses round the Plain from side to side, compelling here and there, the Stragglers to the Flock; They cackle loud, and flutter o'er the Champian. So *Boyle* pursued, so fled this Pair of Friends: finding at length, their Flight was vain, they bravely joyn'd, and drew themselves in *Phalanx*. First, *B–ntl–y* threw a Spear with all his Force, hoping to pierce the Enemy's Breast; But *Pallas* came unseen, and in the Air took off the Point, and clap'd on one of *Lead*, which after a dead Bang against the Enemy's Shield, fell blunted to the Ground. Then *Boyle*, observing well his Time, took a Launce of wondrous Length and sharpness; and as this Pair of Friends compacted stood close Side to Side, he wheel'd him to the right, and with unusual Force, darted the Weapon. *B–ntl–y* saw his Fate approach, and flanking down his Arms, close to his Ribs, hoping to save his Body; in went the Point, passing through Arm and Side, nor stopt, or spent its Force, till it had also pierc'd the valiant *W–tt–n*, who going to sustain his dying Friend, shared his Fate. As, when a skilful Cook has truss'd a Brace of *Woodcocks*, He, with Iron Scewer, pierces the tender Sides of both, their Legs and Wings close pinion'd to their Ribs; So was this pair of Friends transfix'd, till down they fell, joyn'd in their Lives, joyn'd in their Deaths; so closely joyn'd, that *Charon* will mistake them both for one, and waft them over *Styx* for half his Fare. Farewel, beloved, loving Pair; Few Equals have you left behind: And happy and immortal shall you be, if all my Wit and Eloquence can make you.

　　AND, now　　*　　*　　*　　*　　*　　*　　*　　*
*　　*　　*　　*　　*　　*　　*　　*　　*　　*　　*
*　　*　　*　　*　　*　　　　*Desunt cætera.*

FINIS

* *This is also, after the manner of* Homer*; the Woman's getting a painful Livelihood by Spinning, has nothing to do with the Similitude, nor would be excusable without such an Authority.*

THE
BOOKSELLER's
Advertisement.

T HE *following Discourse came into my Hands perfect and entire. But there being several Things in it, which the present Age would not very well bear, I kept it by me some Years resolving it should never see the Light. At length, by the Advice and Assistance of a judicious Friend, I retrench'd those Parts that might give most Offence, and have now ventured to publish the Remainder; Concerning the Author, I am wholly ignorant; neither can I conjecture, whether it be the same with That of the two foregoing Pieces, the Original having been sent me at a different Time, and in a different Hand. The learned Reader will better determine; to whose Judgment I entirely submit it.*

A

DISCOURSE

Concerning the

Mechanical Operation

OF THE

SPIRIT.

IN A

LETTER

To a FRIEND

A

FRAGMENT.

LONDON:
Printed in the Year, MDCCX.

A
DISCOURSE
Concerning the
Mechanical Operation
OF THE
SPIRIT, &c.

For T.H. Esquire, at His Chambers in the Academy of the Beaux Esprits in New England.

SIR,

It is now a good while, since I have had in my Head, something, not only very material, but absolutely necessary to my Health, that the World should be informed in. For, to tell you a Secret, I am able to *contain* it no longer. *However, I have been perplexed for some time, to resolve what would be the most proper Form to send it abroad in. To which End, I have three Days been coursing thro' *Westminster-Hall,* and St. *Paul's Church yard,* and *Fleet-street,* to peruse *Titles;* and, I do not find any which holds so general a Vogue, as that of *A Letter to a Friend:* Nothing is more common, than to meet with long Epistles addressed to Persons and Places, where, at first thinking, one would be apt to imagine it, not altogether so Necessary or Convenient; Such as, *a Neighbour at next Door, a mortal Enemy, a perfect Stranger,* or *a Person of Quality in the Clouds;* and these upon Subjects, in appearance, the least proper for Conveyance by the Post; as, *long Schemes in Philosophy; dark and wonderful Mysteries of State; Laborious Dissertations in Criticism and Philosophy, Advice to Parliaments,* and the like.

NOW, Sir, to proceed after the Method in present Wear. (For, let me say what I will to the contrary, I am afraid you will publish this *Letter,* as soon as ever it comes to your Hands;) I desire you will be my Witness to the World,

---

* *This Discourse is not altogether equal to the two Former, the best Parts of it being omitted; whether the Bookseller's Account be true, that he durst not print the rest, I know not, nor indeed is it easie to determine whether he may be rely'd on, in any thing he says of this, or the former Treatises, only as to the Time they were writ in, which, however, appears more from the Discourses themselves than his Relation.*

how careless and sudden a Scribble it has been; That it was but Yesterday, when You and I began accidentally to fall into Discourse on this Matter: That I was not very well, when we parted; That the Post is in such haste, I have had no manner of Time to digest it into Order, or correct the Style; And if any other Modern Excuses, for Haste and Negligence, shall occur to you in Reading, I beg you to insert them, faithfully promising they shall be thankfully acknowledged.

PRAY, Sir, in your next Letter to the *Iroquois Virtuosi,* do me the Favor to present my humble Service to that illustrious Body, and assure them, I shall send an Account of those *Phænomena,* as soon as we can determine them at *Gresham.*

I have not had a Line from the *Litterati* of *Tobinambou,* these three last Ordinaries.

AND now, Sir, having dispatch'd what I had to say of Forms, or of Business, let me intreat, you will suffer me to proceed upon my Subject; and to pardon me, if I make no farther Use of the Epistolary Stile, till I come to conclude.

SECTION I.

'TIS recorded of *Mahomet,* that upon a Visit he was going to pay in *Paradise,* he had an Offer of several Vehicles to conduct him upwards; as fiery Chariots, wing'd Horses, and celestial Sedans; but he refused them all, and would be born to Heaven upon nothing but his *Ass.* Now, this Inclination of *Mahomet,* as singular as it seems, hath been since taken up by a great Number of devout *Christians;* and doubtless, with very good Reason. For, since That *Arabian* is known to have borrowed a Moiety of his Religious System from the *Christian* Faith; it is but just he should pay Reprisals to such as would Challenge them; wherein the good People of *England,* to do them all Right, have not been backward. For, tho' there is not any other Nation in the World, so plentifully provided with Carriages for that Journey, either as to Safety or Ease; yet there are abundance of us, who will not be satisfied with any other Machine, beside this of *Mahomet.*

FOR my own part, I must confess to bear a very singular Respect to this Animal, by whom I take human Nature to be most admirably held forth in all its Qualities as well as Operations: And therefore, whatever in my small Reading, occurs, concerning this our Fellow Creature, I do never fail to set it down, by way of Common-place; and when I have occasion to write upon Human Reason, Politicks, Eloquence, or Knowledge; I lay my *Memorandums* before me, and insert them with a wonderful Facility of Application.

However, among all the Qualifications ascribed to this distinguish'd Brute, by Antient or Modern Authors; I cannot remember this Talent, of bearing his Rider to Heaven, has been recorded for a Part of his Character, except in the two Examples mentioned already; Therefore, I conceive the Methods of this Art, to be a Point of useful Knowledge in very few Hands, and which the Learned World would gladly be better informed in. This is what I have undertaken to perform in the following Discourse. For, towards the Operation already mentioned, many peculiar Properties are required, both in the *Rider* and the *Ass;* which I shall endeavour to set in as clear a Light as I can.

BUT, because I am resolved, by all means, to avoid giving Offence to any Party whatever; I will leave off discoursing so closely to the *Letter* as I have hitherto done, and go on for the future by way of Allegory, though in such a manner, that the judicious Reader, may without much straining, make his Applications as often as he shall think fit. Therefore, if you please from hence forward, instead of the Term, *Ass,* we shall make use of *Gifted,* or *enlightened Teacher;* And the Word *Rider,* we will exchange for that of *Fanatick Auditory,* or any other Denomination of the like Import. Having settled this weighty Point; the great Subject of Enquiry before us, is to examine, by what Methods this *Teacher* arrives at his *Gifts* or *Spirit,* or *Light;* and by what Intercourse between him and his Assembly, it is cultivated and supported.

IN all my Writings, I have had constant Regard to this great End, not to suit and apply them to particular Occasions and Circumstances of Time, of Place, or of Person; but to calculate them for universal Nature, and Mankind in general. And of such Catholick use, I esteem this present Disquisition: For I do not remember any other Temper of Body, or Quality of Mind, wherein all Nations and Ages of the World have so unanimously agreed, as That of a *Fanatick* Strain, or Tincture of *Enthusiasm;* which improved by certain Persons or Societies of Men, and by them practised upon the rest, has been able to produce Revolutions of the greatest Figure in History; as will soon appear to those who know any thing of *Arabia, Persia, India,* or *China,* of *Morocco* and *Peru:* Farther, it has possessed as great a Power in the Kingdom of Knowledge, where it is hard to assign one Art or Science, which has not annexed to it some *Fanatick* Branch: Such are the *Philosopher's Stone; * The Grand Elixir; The Planetary Worlds; The Squaring of the Circle; The Summum bonum;* Utopian *Commonwealths;* with some others of less or subordinate Note: Which all serve for nothing else, but to employ or amuse this Grain of *Enthusiasm,* dealt into every Composition.

* Some Writers hold them for the same, others, not.

BUT, if this Plant has found a Root in the Fields of *Empire,* and of *Knowledge,* it has fixt deeper, and spread yet further upon *Holy Ground.*

Wherein, though it hath pass'd under the general Name of *Enthusiasm,* and perhaps, arisen from the same Original, yet hath it produced certain Branches of a very different Nature, however often mistaken for each other. The Word in its universal Acceptation, may be defined, *A lifting up of the Soul or its Faculties above Matter.* This Description will hold good in general; but I am only to understand it, as applied to *Religion;* wherein there are three general Ways of ejaculating the Soul, or transporting it beyond the Sphere of Matter. The first, is the immediate Act of God, and is called, *Prophecy* or *Inspiration.* The second, is the immediate Act of the Devil, and is termed *Possession.* The third, is the Product of natural Causes, the effect of strong Imagination, Spleen, violent Anger, Fear, Grief, Pain, and the like. These three have been abundantly treated on by Authors, and therefore shall not employ my Enquiry. But, the fourth Method of *Religious Enthusiasm,* or launching out the Soul, as it is purely an Effect of Artifice and *Mechanick Operation,* has been sparingly handled, or not at all, by any Writer; because though it is an Art of great Antiquity, yet having been confined to few Persons, it long wanted those Advancements and Refinements, which it afterwards met with, since it has grown so Epidemick, and fallen into so many cultivating Hands.

IT is therefore upon this *mechanical Operation of the Spirit,* that I mean to treat, as it is at present performed by our *British Workmen.* I shall deliver to the Reader the Result of many judicious Observations upon the Matter; tracing, as near as I can, the whole Course and Method of this *Trade,* producing parallel Instances, and relating certain Discoveries that have luckily fallen in my way.

I have said, that there is one Branch of *Religious Enthusiasm,* which is purely an Effect of Nature; whereas, the Part I mean to handle, is wholly an Effect of Art, which, however, is inclined to work upon certain Natures and Constitutions, more than others. Besides, there is many an Operation, which in its Original, was purely an Artifice, but through a long Succession of Ages, hath grown to be natural. *Hippocrates,* tells us, that among our Ancestors, the *Scythians,* there was a nation call'd, *Long- heads, which at first began by a Custom among Midwives   * *Macrocephali.* and Nurses, of molding, and squeezing, and bracing up the Heads of Infants; by which means, Nature, shut out at one Passage, was forc'd to seek another, and finding room above, shot upwards, in the Form of a Sugar-Loaf; and being diverted that way, for some Generations, at last , found it out of her self, needing no Assistance from the Nurse's Hand. This was the Original of the *Scythian Long-heads,* and thus did Custom, from being a second Nature proceed to be a First. To all which, there is something very analogous, among Us, of this Nation, who are the undoubted Posterity of that refined People. For, in the Age of our Fathers, there arose a Generation of Men in this Island, call'd *Round-heads,* whose Race is now spread over three Kingdoms, yet in its Beginning, was meerly an Operation of Art, produced by a pair of Cizars, a Squeeze of the Face, and a black Cap. These Heads, thus formed into a perfect Sphear in all Assemblies, were most exposed to the view of the Female Sort, which did influence their Conceptions so effectually, that Nature, at last, took the Hint, and did it of her self; so that a *Round-head* has been ever since as familiar a Sight among Us, as a *Long-head* among the *Scythians.*

UPON these Examples, and others easy to produce, I desire the curious Reader to distinguish, First, between an Effect grown from *Art* into *Nature,* and one that is natural from its Beginning; Secondly, between an Effect wholly natural, and one which has only a natural Foundation, but where the Superstructure is entirely Artificial. For, the first and the last of these, I understand to come within the Districts of my Subject. And having obtained these Allowances, they will serve to remove any Objections that may be raised hereafter against what I shall advance.

THE Practitioners of this famous Art, proceed in general upon the following Fundamental; That, *the Corruption of the Senses is the Generation of the Spirit:* Because the *Senses* in Men are so many Avenues to the Fort of *Reason,* which in this Operation is wholly block'd up. All Endeavours must be therefore used, either to divert, bind up, stupify, fluster, and amuse the *Senses,* or else to justle them out of their Stations; and while they are either absent, or otherwise employ'd or engaged in a civil War against each other, the *Spirit* enters and *Performs its* Part.

NOW, the usual Methods of managing the Senses upon such Conjunctures, are what I shall be very particular in delivering, as far as it is lawful for me to do: But having had the Honor to be initiated into the Mysteries of every Society, I desire to be excused from divulging any Rites, wherein the *Profane* must have no Part.

BUT here, before I can proceed further, a very dangerous Objection must, if possible, be removed: For, it is positively denied by certain Criticks, that the *Spirit* can by any means be introduced into an Assembly of Modern Saints, the Disparity being so great in many material Circumstances, between the Primitive Way of Inspiration, and that which is practised in the present Age. This they pretend to prove from the second Chapter of the *Acts,* where comparing both, it appears; First, that *the Apostles were gathered together with one accord in one place;* by which is meant, an universal Agreement in Opinion, and Form of Worship; a Harmony (say they) so far from being found between any two Conventicles among Us, that it is in vain to expect it between any two Heads in the same. Secondly; the *Spirit*

The Quakers Meeting.

Plate 30

instructed the Apostles in the Gift of speaking several Languages; a Knowledge so remote from our Dealers in this Art, that they neither understand Propriety of Words, or Phrases in their own. Lastly, (say these Objectors) The Modern Artists do utterly exclude all Approaches of the *Spirit,* and bar up its antient Way of entring, by covering themselves so close, and so industriously a top. For, they will needs have it as a Point clearly gained, that the *Cloven Tongues* never sat upon the Apostles Heads, while their Hats were on (Plate 30).

NOW, the Force of these Objections, seems to consist in the different Acceptation of the Word, *Spirit:* which if it be understood for a supernatural Assistance, approaching from without, the Objectors have Reason, and their Assertions may be allowed; But the *Spirit* we treat of here, proceeding entirely from within, the Argument of these Adversaries is wholly eluded. And upon the same Account, our Modern Artificers, find it an Expedient of Absolute Necessity, to cover their Heads as close as they can, in order to prevent Perspiration, than which nothing is observed to be a greater Spender of Mechanick Light, as we may, perhaps, further shew in convenient Place.

TO proceed therefore upon the *Phænomenon* of *Spiritual Mechanism,* It is here to be noted, that in forming and working up the *Spirit,* the Assembly has a considerable Share, as well as the Preacher; The Method of this *Arcanum,* is as follows. They violently strain their Eye-balls inward, half closing the Lids; Then, as they sit, they are in perpetual Motion of *See-saw,* making long Hums at proper Periods, and continuing the Sound at equal Height, chusing their Time in those Intermissions, while the Preacher is at Ebb. Neither is this Practice, in any Part of it, so singular or improbable, as not to be traced in distant Regions, from Reading and Observation. For, first, the **Jauguis,* or enlightned Saints of *India,* see all their Visions, by Help of an acquired straining and pressure of the Eyes. Secondly, the Art of *See-saw* on a Beam, and swinging by Session upon a Cord, in order to raise artificial Extasies, hath been derived to Us, from our †*Scythian* Ancestors, where it is practised at this Day, among the Women. Lastly, the whole Proceeding, as I have here related it, is performed by the Natives of *Ireland,* with a considerable Improvement; And it is granted, that this noble Nation, hath of all others, admitted fewer Corruptions, and degenerated least from the Purity of the *Old Tartars.* Now it is usual for a Knot of *Irish,* Men and Women, to abstract themselves from Matter, bind up all their Senses, grow visionary and spiritual, by Influence of a short Pipe of Tobacco, handed round the Company; each preserving the Smoak in his Mouth, till it comes again to his Turn to take in fresh: At

** Bernier,
Mem. de Mogol.*

*† Guagnini
Hist. Sarmat.*

the same Time, there is a Consort of a continued gentle Hum, repeated and renewed by Instinct, as Occasion requires, and they move their Bodies up and down, to a Degree, that sometimes their Heads and Points lye parallel to the Horizon. Mean while, you may observe their Eyes turn'd up in the Posture of one, who endeavours to keep himself awake; by which, and many other Symptoms among them, it manifestly appears, that the Reasoning Faculties are all suspended and superseded, that Imagination hath usurped the Seat, scattering a thousand Deliriums over the Brain. Returning from this Digression, I shall describe the Methods, by which the *Spirit* approaches. The Eyes being disposed according to Art, at first, you can see nothing, but after a short Pause, a small glimmering Light begins to appear, and dance before you. Then, by frequently moving your Body up and down, you perceive the Vapors to ascend very fast, till you are perfectly dosed and flustred like one who drinks too much in a Morning. Mean while, the Preacher is also at work; He begins a loud Hum, which pierces you quite thro'; This is immediately returned by the Audience, and you find your self prompted to imitate them, by a meer spontaneous Impulse, without knowing what you do. The *Interstitia* are duly filled up by the Preacher, to prevent too long a Pause, under which the *Spirit* would soon faint and grow languid.

THIS is all I am allowed to discover about the Progress of the *Spirit,* with relation to that Part, which is born by the *Assembly;* But in the Methods of the Preacher, to which I now proceed, I shall be more large and particular.

SECTION II.

YOU will read it very gravely remarked in the Books of those illustrious and right eloquent Pen-men, the Modern Travellers; that the fundamental Difference in Point of Religion, between the wild *Indians* and Us, lyes in this; that We worship *God,* and they worship the *Devil.* But, there are certain Criticks, who will by no means admit of this Distinction; rather believing, that all Nations whatsoever, adore the *true God,* because, they seem to intend their Devotions to some invisible Power, of greatest *Goodness* and *Ability* to help them, which perhaps, will take in the brightest Attributes ascribed to the Divinity. Others, again, inform us, that those Idolaters adore two *Principles;* the *Principle* of *Good,* and That of *Evil:* Which indeed, I am apt to look upon as the most universal Notion, that Mankind, by the meer Light of Nature, ever entertained of Things Invisible. How this Idea hath been managed by the *Indians* and Us, and with what Advantage to the Understandings of either, may well deserve to be examined. To me, the difference appears little more than this, That They are put oftner upon their Knees by their *Fears,* and we by our *Desires*; That the former set them a *Praying,* and Us a *Cursing.* What I applaud them for, is their Discretion, in limiting their Devotions and their Deities to their several Districts, nor ever suffering the Liturgy of the *white* God, to cross or interfere with that of the *Black.* Not so with us; who pretending by the Lines and Measures of our Reason, to extend the Dominion of one invisible Power, and contract that of the other, have discovered a gross Ignorance in the Natures of Good and Evil, and most horribly confounded the Frontiers of both. After Men have lifted up the Throne of their Divinity to the *Cœlum Empyræum,* adorned him with all such Qualities and Accomplishments, as themselves seem most to value and possess: After they have sunk their *Principle* of *Evil* to the lowest Center, bound him with Chains, loaded him with Curses, furnished him with viler Dispositions than any *Rake-hell* of the Town, accoutred him with Tail, and Horns, and huge Claws, and Sawcer Eyes; I laugh aloud, to see these Reasoners, at the same Time, engaged in wise Dispute, about certain Walks and Purliews, whether they are in the Verge of God or the Devil, seriously debating, whether such and such Influences come into Mens Minds, from above or below, or whether certain Passions and Affections are guided by the Evil Spirit or the Good.

Dum fas atque nefas exiguo sine libidinum
Discernunt avidi ——

Thus do Men establish a Fellowship of *Christ* with *Belial,* and such is the Analogy between *cloven Tongues,* and *cloven Feet.* Of the like Nature, is the Disquisition before us: It hath continued these hundred Years an even Debate, whether the Deportment and the Cant of our *English* Enthusiastick Preachers, were *Possession,* or *Inspiration,* and a World of Argument has been drained on either Side, perhaps, to little purpose. For, I think, it is in *Life* as in *Tragedy,* where, it is held, a Conviction of great Defect, both in Order and Invention, to interpose the Assistance of preternatural Power, without an absolute and last Necessity. However, it is a Sketch of Human Vanity, for every Individual, to imagine the whole Universe is interess'd in his meanest Concern. If he hath got cleanly over a Kennel, some Angel, unseen, descended on purpose to help him by the Hand; if he hath knockt his Head against a Post, it was the Devil, for his Sins, let loose from Hell, on purpose to *buffet* him. Who, that sees a little paultry Mortal, droning, and dreaming, and driveling to a Multitude, can think it agreeable to common good Sense, that either Heaven or Hell should be put to the Trouble of Influence or Inspection upon what he is about? Therefore, I am resolved immediately, to weed this Error out of Mankind, by making it clear, that this

Mystery, of venting spiritual Gifts is nothing but a *Trade,* acquired by as much Instruction, and mastered by equal Practice and Application, as others are. This will best appear, by describing and deducing the whole Process of the Operation, as variously as it hath fallen under my Knowledge or Experience.

* * * * * * * * * * *

Here the whole Scheme * * * * * * * *
of Spiritual Mechanism was * * * * * * * *
deduced and explained, with * * * * * * * *
an Appearance of great * * * * * * * *
Reading and Observation; * * * * * * * *
but it was thought neither * * * * * * * *
Safe nor Convenient to Print * * * * * * * *
it. * * * * * * * *

* * * * * * * * * * *

HERE it may not be amiss, to add a few Words upon the laudable Practice of wearing *quilted Caps;* which is not a Matter of meer Custom, Humor, or Fashion, as some would pretend, but an Institution of great Sagacity and Use; these, when moistned with Sweat, stop all Perspiration, and by reverberating the Heat, prevent the Spirit from evaporating any way, but at the Mouth; even as a skilful Housewife, that covers her Still with a wet Clout, for the same Reason, and finds the same Effect. For, it is the Opinion of Choice *Virtuosi,* that the Brain is only a Crowd of little Animals, but with Teeth and Claws extremely sharp, and therefore, cling together in the Contexture we behold, like the Picture of *Hobbes's Leviathan* (Plate 31), or like Bees in perpendicular swarm upon a Tree, or like a Carrion corrupted into Vermin, still preserving the Shape and Figure of the Mother Animal; That all Invention is formed by the Morsure of two or more of these Animals, upon certain capillary Nerves, which proceed from thence, whereof three Branches spread into the Tongue, and two into the right Hand. They hold also, that these Animals are of a Constitution extremely cold; that their Food is the Air we attract, their Excrement Phlegm; and that what we vulgarly call Rheums, and Colds, and Distillations, is nothing else but an Epidemical Looseness, to which that little Commonwealth is very subject, from the Climate it lyes under. Further, that nothing less than a violent Heat, can disentangle these Creatures from their hamated Station of Life, or give them Vigor and Humor, to imprint the Marks of their little Teeth. That if the Morsure be Hexagonal, it produces Poetry; the Circular give Eloquence; If the Bite hath been Conical, the Person, whose Nerve is so affected, shall be disposed to write upon the Politicks; and so of the rest.

I shall now Discourse briefly, by what kind of Practices the Voice is best governed, towards the Composition and Improvement of the *Spirit;* for,

Plate 31

without a competent Skill in tuning and toning each Word, and Syllable, and Letter, to their due Cadence, the whole Operation is incompleat, misses entirely of its effect on the Hearers, and puts the Workman himself to continual Pains for new Supplies, without Success. For, it is to be understood, that in the Language of the Spirit, *Cant* and *Droning* supply the Place of *Sense* and *Reason,* in the Language of Men: Because, in Spiritual Harangues, the Disposition of the Words according to the Art of Grammar, hath not the least Use, but the Skill and Influence wholly lye in the Choice and Cadence of the Syllables; Even as a discreet *Composer,* who in setting a Song, changes the Words and Order so often, that he is forced to make it *Nonsense,* before he can make it *Musick.* For this Reason, it hath been held by some, that the Art of Canting is ever in greatest Perfection, when managed by *Ignorance:* Which is thought to be enigmatically meant by *Plutarch,* when he tells us, that the best Musical Instruments were made from the Bones of an *Ass.* And the profounder Criticks upon that Passage, are of Opinion, the Word in its genuine Signification, means no other than a *Jaw-bone:* tho' some rather think it to have been the *Os sacrum;* but in so nice a Case, I shall not take upon me to decide: The Curious are at Liberty, to *pick* from it whatever they please.

The first Ingredient, towards the Art of Canting, is a competent Share of *Inward Light:* that is to say, a large Memory, plentifully fraught with Theological Polysyllables and mysterious Texts from Holy Writ, applied and digested by those Methods, and Mechanical Operations already related: The Bearers of this *Light,* resembling *Lanthorns,* compact of Leaves from old *Geneva* Bibles; Which Invention, Sir *H–mphry Edw–n,* during his Mayoralty, of happy Memory, highly approved and advanced; affirming, the Scripture to be now fulfilled, where it says, *Thy Word is a Lanthorn to my Feet, and a Light to my Paths.*

NOW, the Art of *Canting* consists in skilfully adapting the Voice, to whatever Words the Spirit Delivers, that each may strike the Ears of the Audience, with its most significant Cadence. The Force, or Energy of this Eloquence, is not to be found, as among antient Orators, in the Disposition of Words to a Sentence, or the turning of long Periods; but agreeable to the Modern Refinements in Musick, is taken up wholly in dwelling, and dilating upon Syllables and Letters. Thus it is frequent for a single *Vowel* to draw Sighs from a Multitude; and for a whole Assembly of Saints to sob to the Musick of one solitary *Liquid.* But these are Trifles; when even Sounds inarticulate are observed to produce as forcible Effects. A Master Workman shall *blow his Nose so powerfully,* as to pierce the Hearts of his People, who are disposed to receive the *Excrements* of his Brain with the same Reverence, as the *Issue* of it. Hawking, Spitting, and Belching, the Defects of other Mens Rhetorick, are the Flowers, and Figures, and Ornaments of his. For, the *Spirit* being the same in all, it is of no Import through what Vehicle it is convey'd.

IT is a Point of too much Difficulty, to draw the Principles of this famous Art, within the Compass of certain adequate Rules. However, perhaps, I may one day, oblige the World with my Critical Essay upon the Art of *Canting, Philosophically, Physically, and Musically considered.*

BUT, among all Improvements of the *Spirit,* wherein the Voice hath born a Part, there is none to be compared with That of *conveying the Sound thro' the Nose,* which under the Denomination of *Snuffling, hath passed with so great Applause in the World. The Originals of this Institution are very dark; but having been initiated into the Mystery of it, and Leave being given me to publish it to the World, I shall deliver as direct a Relation as I can.

THIS Art, like many other famous Inventions, owed its Birth, or at least, Improvement and Perfection, to an Effect of Chance, but was established upon solid Reasons, and hath flourished in this Island ever since, with great Lustre. All agree, that it first appeared upon the Decay and Discouragement of *Bag-pipes,* which having long suffered under the Mortal Hatred of the *Brethren,* tottered for a Time, and at last fell with *Monarchy.* The Story is thus related.

AS yet, *Snuffling* was not; when the following Adventure happened to a *Banbury Saint.* Upon a certain Day, while he was far engaged among the Tabernacles of the *Wicked,* he felt the Outward Man put into odd Commotions, and strangely prick'd forward by the Inward: An Effect very usual among the Modern Inspired. For, some think, that the *Spirit* is apt to feed on the *Flesh,* like hungry Wines upon raw Beef. Others rather believe, there is a perpetual Game at *Leap-Frog* between both; and, sometimes, the *Flesh* is uppermost, and sometimes the *Spirit;* adding, that the former, while it is in the State of a *Rider,* wears huge *Rippon* Spurs, and when it comes to the Turn of being *Bearer,* is wonderfully head-strong, and hard-mouth'd. However it came about, the *Saint* felt his *Vessel* full *extended* in every Part (a very natural Effect of strong *Inspiration;*) and the Place and Time falling out so unluckily, that he could not have the Convenience of Evacuating upwards, by Repetition, Prayer, or Lecture; he was forced to open an inferior Vent. In short, he wrestled with the Flesh so long, that he at length subdued it, coming off with honourable Wounds, all *before.* The Surgeon had now cured the Parts, primarily affected ; but the Disease driven from its

---

* *The* Snuffling *of Men, who have lost their Noses by lewd Courses, is said to have given Rise to that Tone, which our Dissenters did too much Affect.* W. Wotton.

Scarmoes vlamd, met zyn dieve-en tover-
    nacht-lantaren,
Op Colombins boutiekje, om wind-breuk-zalf
    te gaaren.

E

Pag: 15.

Plate 32

Post, flew up into his Head; And, as a skilful General, valiantly attack'd in his Trenches, and beaten from the Field, by flying Marches withdraws to the Capital City, breaking down the Bridges to prevent Pursuit; So the Disease repell'd from its first Station, fled before the *Rod* of *Hermes,* to the upper Region, there fortifying it self; but, finding the Foe making Attacks at the *Nose,* broke down the *Bridge,* and retired to the *Head* Quarters. Now, the Naturalists observe, that there is in human Noses, an *Idiosyncrasy,* by Virtue of which, the more the Passage is obstructed, the more our Speech delights to go through, as the Musick of a Flagelate is made by the *Stops.* By this Method, the Twang of the Nose, becomes perfectly to resemble the *Snuffle* of a Bag-pipe, and is found to be equally attractive of *British* Ears; whereof the Saint had sudden Experience, by practicing his new Faculty with wonderful Success in the Operation of the *Spirit;* For, in a short Time, no Doctrine pass'd for Sound and Orthodox, unless it were delivered thro' the Nose. Strait, every Pastor copy'd after this Original; and those, who could not otherwise arrive to a Perfection, spirited by a noble Zeal, made use of the same Experiment to acquire it. So that, I think, it may be truly affirmed, the *Saints* owe their Empire to the *Snuffling* of one *Animal,* as *Darius* did his, to the *Neighing* of another; and both Stratagems were performed by the same Art; for we read, how the **Persian Beast* acquired his Faculty, by *covering a Mare* the Day before.

* *Herodot.*

I should now have done, if I were not convinced, that whatever I have yet advanced upon this Subject, is liable to great Exception. For, allowing all I have said to be true, it may still be justly objected, that there is in the Commonwealth of *artificial Enthusiasm,* some real Foundation for Art to work upon in the Temper and Complexion of Individuals, which other Mortals seem to want. Observe, but the Gesture, the Motion, and the Countenance, of some choice Professors, tho' in their most familiar Actions you will find them of a different Race from the rest of human Creatures. Remark your commonest Pretender to a Light *within,* how dark, and dirty, and gloomy he is *without;* As Lanthorns (Plate 32), which the more Light they bear in their Bodies, cast out so much the more Soot, and Smoak, and fuliginous Matter to adhere to the Sides. Listen, but to their ordinary Talk, and look on the Mouth that delivers it; you will imagine you are hearing some antient Oracle, and your Understanding will be *equally* informed. Upon these, and the like Reasons, certain Objectors pretend to put it beyond all Doubt, that there must be a sort of preternatural *Spirit,* possessing the Heads of the Modern Saints; And some will have it to be the *Heat* of Zeal, working upon the *Dregs* of Ignorance, as other *Spirits* are produced from *Lees,* by the Force of Fire. Some again think, that when our earthly Tabernacles are disordered and desolate, shaken and out of Repair, the

Spirit delights to dwell within them, as Houses are said to be haunted, when they are forsaken and gone to Decay.

TO set this Matter in as fair a Light as possible; I shall here, very briefly, deduce the History of *Fanaticism,* from the most early Ages to the present. And if we are able to fix upon any one material or fundamental Point, wherein the chief Professors have universally agreed, I think we may reasonably lay hold on That, and assign it for the great Seed or Principle of the *Spirit.*

THE most early Traces we meet with, of *Fanaticks,* in antient Story, are among the *Egyptians,* who instituted those Rites, known in *Greece* by the Names of *Orgya, Panegyres,* and *Dionysia,* whether introduced there by *Orpheus* or *Melampus,* we shall not dispute at present, nor in all likelihood,

Diod. Sic. L. I.
Plut. de Iside
& Osyride

at any time for the future. These Feasts were celebrated to the Honor of *Osyris,* whom the *Grecians* called *Dionysius,* and is the same with *Bacchus:* Which has betray'd some superficial Readers to imagine, that the whole Business was nothing more than a Set of roaring, scouring Companions, over-charg'd with Wine; but this is a scandalous Mistake foisted on the World, by a sort of Modern Authors, who have too litteral an Understanding, and, because Antiquity is to be traced *backwards,* do therefore, like *Jews,* begin their Books at the wrong End, as if Learning were a sort of *Conjuring.* These are the Men, who pretend to understand a Book, by scouting thro' the *Index,* as if a Traveller should go about to describe a *Palace,* when he had seen nothing but the *Privy;* or like certain Fortune-tellers in *Northern America,* who have a Way of reading a Man's Destiny, by peeping in his

* Herod. L. 2.

Breech. For, at the Time of instituting these Mysteries, *there was not one Vine in all *Egypt,* the Natives drinking nothing but *Ale;* which Liquor seems to have been far more antient than Wine, and has the Honor of owing its Invention and Progress, not only to

† Diod. Sic.
L. 1.&3.

the †*Egyptian Osyris,* but to the *Grecian Bacchus,* who in their famous Expedition, carried the Receipt of it along with them, and gave it to the Nations they visited or subdued. Besides, *Bacchus* himself, was very seldom, or never Drunk: For, it is recorded of him that he was the first ¶Inventor of the *Mitre,* which he

¶ *Id. L. 4.*

wore continually on his Head (as the whole Company of *Bacchanals* did) to prevent Vapors and the Head-ake, after hard Drinking. And for this Reason (say some) the *Scarlet Whore,* when she makes the Kings of the Earth drunk with her Cup of Abomination, is always sober herself, tho' she never balks the Glass in her Turn, being, it seems, kept upon her Legs by the Virtue of her *Triple Mitre.* Now, these Feasts were instituted in imitation of the famous Expedition *Osyris* made thro' the World, and of the Company that attended him, whereof the *Bacchanalian* Ceremonies were so many Types and Symbols. From which Account, it is manifest, that the Fanatick Rites of these *Bacchanals,* cannot be *See the Particulars in* Diod. Sic. L. 1.&3. imputed to Intoxications by Wine, but must needs have had a deeper Foundation. What this was, we may gather large Hints from certain Circumstances in the Course of their Mysteries. For, in the first Place, there was in their Processions, an entire *Mixture and Confusion of Sexes;* they affected to ramble about Hills and Desarts: Their Garlands were of *Ivy* and *Vine,* Emblems of Cleaving and Clinging, or of *Fir,* the Parent of *Turpentine.* It is added, that they imitated *Satyrs,* were attended by *Goats,* and rode upon *Asses,* all Companions of great Skill and Practice in Affairs of Gallantry. They bore for their Ensigns, certain curious Figures, perch'd upon long Poles, made into the Shape and Size of the *Virga genitalis,* with its *Appurtenances,* which were so many Shadows and Emblems of the whole Mystery, as well as Trophies set up by the Female * *Dionysia Brauronia.* Conquerors. Lastly, in a certain Town of *Attica,* the whole Solemnity *stript of all its Types, was performed in *puris naturalibus,* the Votaries, not flying in Coveys, but sorted into Couples. The same may be further conjectured from the Death of *Orpheus,* one of the Institutors of these Mysteries †torn in Pieces by Women † *Vid. Photium in excerptis è Conone.* because he refused to *communicate his Orgyes* to them; which others explained, by telling us, he had *castrated* himself upon Grief, for the Loss of his Wife.

OMITTING many others of less Note, the next *Fanaticks* we meet with, of any Eminence, were the numerous Sects of *Hereticks* appearing in the five first Centuries of the *Christian Æra,* from *Simon Magus* and his Followers, to those of *Eutyches.* I have collected their Systems from infinite Reading, and comparing them with those of their Successors in the several Ages since, I find there are certain Bounds set even to the Irregularities of Human Thought, and those a great deal narrower than is commonly apprehended. For, as they all frequently interfere, even in their wildest Ravings; So there is one fundamental Point, wherein they are sure to meet, as Lines in a Center, and that is the *Community of Women:* Great were their Sollicitudes in this Matter, and they never fail'd of certain Articles in their Schemes of Worship, on purpose to establish it.

THE last *Fanaticks* of Note, were those which started up in *Germany,* a little after the *Reformation* of *Luther;* Springing, as *Mushrooms* do at the *End of a Harvest;* Such were *John* of *Leyden, David George, Adam Neuster,* and many others; whose Visions and Revelations, always terminated in *leading about half a dozen Sisters, apiece,* and making That Practice a fundamental Part of their System. For, Human Life is a continual Navigation, and if we expect our *Vessels* to pass with Safety, thro, the Waves and Tempests of this fluctuating World, it is necessary to make a good Provision of the *Flesh,* as Sea-men lay in store of *Beef* for a long Voyage.

NOW from this brief Survey of some Principal Sects, among the *Fanaticks,* in all Ages (having omitted the *Mahometans* and others, who might also help to confirm the Argument I am about) to which I might add several among ourselves, such as the *Family of Love, Sweet Singers of Israel,* and the like: And from reflecting upon that fundamental Point in their Doctrines, about *Women,* wherein they have so unanimously agreed; I am apt to imagine, that the Seed or Principle, which has ever put Men upon *Visions* in Things *Invisible,* is of a Corporeal Nature: For the profounder Chymists inform us, that the Strongest *Spirits* may be extracted from *Human Flesh.* Besides, the Spinal Marrow, being nothing else but a Continuation of the Brain, must needs create a very free Communication between the Superior Faculties and those below: And thus the *Thorn in the Flesh* serves for a *Spur* to the *Spirit.* I think, it is agreed among Physicians, that nothing affects the Head so much, as a tentiginous Humor, repelled and elated to the upper Region, found by daily practice, to run frequently up into Madness. A very eminent Member of the Faculty, assured me, that when the *Quakers* first appeared, he seldom was without some Female Patients among them, for the *Furor Uterinus.* Persons of a visionary Devotion, either Men or Women, are in their Complexion, of all others, the most amorous: For, *Zeal* is frequently kindled from the same Spark with other Fires, and from inflaming Brotherly Love, will proceed to raise That of a Gallant. If we inspect into the usual Process of modern Courtship, we shall find it to consist in a devout Turn of the Eyes, called *Ogling;* an artificial Form of Canting and Whining by rote, every Interval, for want of other Matter, made up with a Shrug, or a Hum, a Sigh or a Groan; The Style compact of insignificant Words, Incoherences and Repetition, These, I take, to be the most accomplish'd Rules of Address to a Mistress; and where are these performed with more Dexterity, than by the *Saints?* Nay, to bring this Argument yet closer, I have been informed by certain Sanguine Brethren of the first Class, that in the Height and *Orgasmus* of their Spiritual Exercise, it has been frequent with them * * * * *; immediately after which, they found the *Spirit* to relax and flag of a sudden with the Nerves, and they were forced to hasten to a Conclusion. This may be further Strengthened, by observing, with Wonder, how unaccountably all Females are attracted by Visionary or Enthusiastick Preachers, tho' never so contemptible in their *outward Men;* which is usually supposed to be done upon Considerations, purely Spiritual, without any carnal Regards at all. But I have Reason to think, the *Sex* hath certain Characteristicks, by which they form a truer Judgment of Human Abilities and Performings, than we our selves can possibly do of each other. Let That be as it will, thus much is certain, that however Spiritual Intrigues begin, they generally conclude like all others; they may branch upwards toward Heaven, but the Root is in the Earth. Too intense a Contemplation is not the Business of Flesh and Blood; it must by the necessary Course of Things, in a little Time, let go its Hold, and fall into *Matter.* Lovers, for the sake of Celestial Converse, are but another sort of *Platonicks,* who pretend to see Stars and Heaven in Ladies Eyes, and to look or think no lower; but the same *Pit* is provided for both; and they seem a perfect Moral to the Story of that Philosopher, who, while his Thoughts and Eyes were fixed upon the *Constellations,* found himself seduced by his *lower Parts* into a *Ditch.*

I had somewhat more to say upon this Part of the Subject; but the Post is just going, which forces me in great Haste to conclude,

SIR,

Yours, &c.

Pray, burn this
Letter as soon
as it comes to
your Hands.

F I N I S.

Appendix:

"An Apology For the &c.", subscribed "June 3, 1709", is not part of the creative act that produced *A Tale of a Tub* in 1697-98 (Elliott 1951, 443-44). It is in fact at two removes from *A Tale of a Tub*. It is Swift's cranky response to the critical reception of the published book in 1704–05. But as Swift's only comment on his most difficult work, it is included here as the appendix it is.

AN

APOLOGY

For the, &c.

IF *good and ill Nature equally operated upon Mankind, I might have saved my self the Trouble of this Apology; for it is manifest by the Reception the following Discourse hath met with, that those who approve it, are a great Majority among the Men of Tast; yet there have been two or three Treatises written expresly against it, besides many others that have flirted at it occasionally, without one Syllable having been ever published in its Defence, or even Quotation to its Advantage, that I can remember, except by the Polite Author of a late Discourse between a Deist and a Socinian.*

Therefore, since the Book seems calculated to live at least as long as our Language, and our Tast admit no great Alterations, I am content to convey some Apology along with it.

The greatest Part of that Book was finished above thirteen Years since, 1696. which is eight Years before it was published. The Author was then young, his Invention at the Height, and his Reading fresh in his Head. By the Assistance of some Thinking, and much Conversation, he had endeavour'd to Strip himself of as many real Prejudices as he could; I say real ones, because under the Notion of Prejudices, he knew to what dangerous Heights some Men have proceeded. Thus prepared, he thought the numerous and gross Corruptions in Religion and Learning might furnish Matter for a Satyr, that would be useful and diverting: He resolved to proceed in a manner, that should be altogether new, the World having been already too long nauseated with endless Repetitions upon every Subject. The Abuses in Religion he proposed to set forth in the Allegory of the Coats, and the three Brothers, which was to make up the Body of the Discourse. Those in Learning he chose to introduce by way of Digressions. He was then a young Gentleman much in the World, and wrote to the Tast of those who were like himself; therefore in order to allure them, he gave a Liberty to his Pen, which might not suit with maturer Years, or graver Characters, and which he could have easily corrected with a very few Blots, had he been Master of his Papers for a Year or two before their Publication.

Not that he would have governed his Judgment by the ill-placed Cavils of the Sour, the Envious, the Stupid, and the Tastless, which he mentions with disdain. He acknowledges there are several youthful Sallies, which from the Grave and the Wise may deserve a Rebuke. But he desires to be answerable no farther than he is guilty, and that his Faults may not be multiply'd by the ignorant, the unnatural, and uncharitable Applications of those who have neither Candor to suppose good Meanings, nor Palate to distinguish true Ones. After which, he will forfeit his Life, if any one Opinion can be fairly deduced from that Book, which is contrary to Religion or Morality.

Why should any Clergyman of our Church be angry to see the Follies of Fanaticism and Superstition exposed, tho' in the most ridiculous Manner? since that is perhaps the most probable way to cure them, or at least to hinder them from farther spreading. Besides, tho' it was not intended for their Perusal; it raillies nothing but what they preach against. It contains nothing to provoke them by the least Scurillity upon their Persons or their Functions. It Celebrates the Church of England as the most perfect of all others in Discipline and Doctrine, it advances no Opinion they reject, nor condemns any they receive. If the Clergy's Resentments lay upon their Hands, in my humble Opinion, they might have found more proper Objects to employ them on: Nondum tibi defuit Hostis: *I mean those heavy, illiterate Scriblers, prostitute in their Reputations, vicious in their Lives, and ruin'd in their Fortunes, who to the shame of good Sense as well as Piety, are greedily read, meerly upon the Strength of bold, false, impious Assertions, mixt with unmannerly Reflections upon the Priesthood, and openly intended against all Religion; in short, full of such Principles as are kindly received, because they are levell'd to remove those Terrors that Religion tells Men will be the Consequence of immoral Lives. Nothing like which is to be met with in this Discourse, tho' some of them are pleased so freely to censure it. And I wish, there were no other Instance of what I have too frequently observed, that many of that Reverend Body are not always very nice in distinguishing between their Enemies and their Friends.*

Had the Author's Intentions met with a more candid Interpretation from some whom out of Respect he forbears to name, he might have been encouraged to an Examination of Books written by some of those Authors above-described, whose Errors, Ignorance, Dullness and Villany, he thinks he could have detected and exposed in such a Manner, that the Persons who are most conceived to be infected by them, would soon lay them aside and be ashamed: But he has now given over those Thoughts, since the weightiest *Men in the* weightiest *Stations are pleased to think it a more dangerous Point to laugh at those Corruptions in Religion, which they themselves must disapprove, than to endeavour pulling up those very Foundations, wherein all Christians have agreed.*

    He thinks it no fair Proceeding, that any Person should offer determinately to fix a name upon the Author of this Discourse, who hath all along concealed himself from most of his nearest Friends: Yet several have gone a farther Step, and pronounced

Letter of
Enthusiasm.

another Book to have been the Work of the same Hand with this; which the Author directly affirms to be a thorough mistake; he having yet never so much as read that Discourse, a plain Instance how little Truth, there often is in general Surmises, or in Conjectures drawn from a Similitude of Style, or way of thinking.

    Had the Author writ a Book to expose the Abuses in Law, or in Physick, he believes the Learned Professors in either Faculty, would have been so far from resenting it, as to have given him Thanks for his Pains, especially if he had made an honourable Reservation for the true Practice of either Science: But Religion they tell us ought not to be ridiculed, and they tell us Truth, yet surely the Corruptions in it may; for we are taught by the tritest Maxim in the World, that Religion being the best of Things, its Corruptions are likely to be the worst.

    There is one Thing which the judicious Reader cannot but have observed, that some of those Passages in this Discourse, which appear most liable to Objection are what they call Parodies, where the Author personates the Style and Manner of other Writers, whom he has a mind to expose. I shall produce one Instance, it is in the 26th Page. Dryden, L'Estrange, *and some others I shall not name, are here levelled at, who having spent their Lives in Faction, and Apostacies, and all manner of Vice, pretended to be Sufferers for Loyalty and Religion. So* Dryden *tells us in one of his Prefaces of his Merits and Suffering, thanks God that he possesses his* Soul in Patience: *In other Places he talks at the same Rate, and* L'Estrange *often uses the like Style, and I believe the Reader may find more Persons to give that Passage an Application: But this is enough to direct those who may have over-look'd the Authors Intention.*

    There are three or four other Passages which prejudiced or ignorant Readers have drawn by great Force to hint at ill Meanings; as if they glanced at some Tenets in Religion, in answer to all which, the Author solemnly protests he is entirely Innocent, and never had it once in his Thoughts that any thing he said would in the least be capable of such Interpretations, which he will engage to deduce full as fairly from the most innocent Book in the World. And it will be obvious to every Reader, that this was not any part of his Scheme or Design, the Abuses he notes being such as all Church of England *Men agree in, nor was it proper for his Subject to meddle with other Points, than such as have been perpetually controverted since the Reformation.*

To instance only in that Passage about the three wooden Machines mentioned in the Introduction: In the Original Manuscript there was a description of a Fourth, which those who had the Papers in their Power, blotted out, as having something in it of Satyr, that I suppose they thought was too particular, and therefore they were forced to change it to the Number Three, *from whence some have endeavour'd to squeeze out dangerous Meaning that was never thought on. And indeed the Conceit was half spoiled by changing the Numbers; that of* Four *being much more Cabalistick, and therefore better exposing the pretended Virtue of Numbers, a Superstition there intended to be ridicul'd.*

Another Thing to be observed is, that there generally runs an Irony through the Thread of the whole Book, which the Men of Tast will observe and distinguish, and which will render some Objections that have been made, very weak and insignificant.

This Apology being chiefly intended for the Satisfaction of future Readers, it may be thought unnecessary to take any notice of such Treatises as have been writ against this ensuing Discourse, which are already sunk into waste Paper and Oblivion; after the usual Fate of common Answerers to Books, which are allowed to have any Merit: They are indeed like Annuals that grow about a young Tree, and seem to vye with it for a Summer, but fall and die with the Leaves in Autumn, and are never heard of any more. When Dr. Eachard *writ his Book about the Contempt of the Clergy, numbers of those Answerers immediately started up, whose Memory if he had not kept alive by his Replies, it would now be utterly unknown that he were ever answered at all. There is indeed an Exception, when any great Genius thinks it worth his while to expose a foolish Piece; so we still read* Marvel's Answer to Parker *with Pleasure, tho' the Book it answers be sunk long ago; so the Earl of* Orrery's *Remarks will be read with Delight, when the Dissertation he exposes will neither be sought nor found; but these are no Enterprises for common Hands, nor to be hoped for above once or twice in an Age. Men would be more cautious of losing their Time in such an Undertaking, if they did but consider, that to answer a Book effectually, requires more Pains and Skill, more Wit, Learning, and Judgment than were employ'd in the Writing it. And the Author assures those Gentlemen who have given themselves that Trouble with him, that his Discourse is the Product of the Study, the Observation, and the Invention of several Years, that he often blotted out much more than he left, and if his Papers had not been a long time out of his Possession, they must have still undergone more severe Corrections; and do they think such a Building is to be battered with Dirt Pellets however envenom'd the Mouths may be that discharge them. He hath seen the Productions but of two Answerers, One of which first appear'd as from an unknown hand, but since avowed by a Person, who upon some Occasions hath discover'd no ill Vein of Humor. 'Tis a Pity any Occasions should put him under a necessity of being so hasty in his Productions, which otherwise might often be entertaining. But there were other Reasons obvious enough for his Miscarriage in this; he writ against the Conviction of his Talent, and enter'd upon one of the wrongest Attempts in Nature, to turn into ridicule by a Weeks Labour, a Work which had cost so much time, and met with so much Success in ridiculing others. The manner how he has handled his* Subject, *I have now forgot, having just look'd it over when it first came out, as others did, meerly for the sake of the Title.*

The other Answer is from a Person of a graver Character, and is made up of half Invective, and half Annotation. In the latter of which he hath generally succeeded well enough. And the Project at that time was not amiss, to draw in Readers to his Pamphlet, several having appear'd desirous that there might be some Explication of the more difficult Passages. Neither can he be altogether blamed for offering at the Invective Part, because it is agreed on all hands that the Author had given him sufficient Provocation. The great Objection is against his manner of treating it, very unsuitable to one of his Function. It was determined by a fair Majority, that this Answerer had in a way not to be pardon'd, drawn his Pen against a certain great Man then alive, and universally reverenced for every good Quality that could possibly enter into the Composition of the most accomplish'd Person; it was observed, how he was pleased and affected to have that noble Writer call'd his Adversary, and it was a Point of Satyr well directed, for I have been told, Sir W.T. *was sufficiently mortify'd at the Term. All the Men of Wit and Politeness were immediately up in Arms, through Indignation, which prevailed over their Contempt, by the Consequences they apprehended from such an Example, and it grew to be* Porsenna's *Case;* Idem trecenti juravimus. *In short, things were ripe for a general Insurrection, till my Lord* Orrery *had a little laid the Spirit, and settled the Ferment. But his Lordship being principally engaged with another Antagonist, it was thought necessary in order to quiet the Minds of Men, that this Opposer should receive a Reprimand, which partly occasioned that Discourse of the Battle of the Books, and the Author was farther at the Pains to insert one or two Remarks on him in the Body of the Book.*

This Answerer has been pleased to find Fault with about a dozen Passages, which the Author will not be at the Trouble of defending, farther than by assuring the Reader, that for the greater Part the Reflecter is entirely mistaken, and forces Interpretations which never once entered into the Writer's Head, nor will he is sure into that of any Reader of Tast and Candor; he allows two or three at most there produced to have been deliver'd unwarily, for which he desires to plead the Excuse offered already, of his Youth, and Franckness of Speech, and his Papers being out of his Power at the Time they were published.

But this Answerer insists, and says, what he chiefly dislikes, is the Design; *what that was I have already told, and I believe there is not a Person in* England *who can understand that Book, that ever imagined it to have been any thing else, but to expose the Abuses and Corruptions in Learning and Religion.*

But it would be good to know what Design *this Reflecter was serving, when he concludes his Pamphlet with a Caution to Readers, to beware of thinking the Authors*

Wit was entirely his own, surely this must have had some Allay of Personal Animosity, at least mixt with the Design of serving the Publick by so useful a Discovery; and it indeed touches the Author in a very tender Point, who insists upon it, that through the whole Book he has not borrowed one single Hint from any Writer in the World; and he thought, of all Criticisms, that would never have been one. He conceived it was never disputed to be an Original, whatever Faults it might have. However this Answerer produces three Instances to prove this Author's Wit is not his own in many Places. *The first is, that the Names of* Peter, Martin *and* Jack *are borrowed from a Letter of the late Duke of* Buckingham. *Whatever Wit is contained in those three Names, the Author is content to give it up, and desires his Readers will substract as much as they placed upon that Account; at the same time protesting solemnly that he never once heard of that Letter, except in this Passage of the Answerer: So that the Names were not borrowed as he affirms, tho' they should happen to be the same which however is odd enough, and what he hardly believes; that of* Jack, *being not quite so obvious as the other two. The second Instance to shew* the Author's Wit is not his own, *is* Peter's Banter (*as he calls it in his* Alsatia *Phrase) upon Transubstantiation, which is taken from the same Duke's Conference with an* Irish *Priest, where a Cork is turned into a Horse. This the Author confesses to have seen, about ten Years after his Book was writ, and a Year or two after it was published. Nay, the Answerer overthrows this himself; for he allows the Tale was writ in 1697; and I think that Pamphlet was not printed in many Years after. It was necessary, that Corruption should have some Allegory as well as the rest; and the Author invented the properest he could, without enquiring what other People had writ, and the commonest Reader will find, there is not the least Resemblance between the two Stories. The third Instance is in these Words:* I have been assured, that the Battle in St. *James's* Library, is *mutatis mutandis,* taken out of a *French* Book, entituled, *Combat des livres,* if I misremember not. *In which Passage there are two Clauses observable:* I have been assured; and, if I misremember not. *I desire first to know, whether if that Conjecture proves an utter falshood, those two Clauses will be a sufficient Excuse for this worthy Critick. The Matter is a Trifle; but, would he venture to pronounce at this Rate upon one of greater Moment? I know nothing more contemptible in a Writer than the Character of a Plagiary; which he here fixes at a venture, and this, not for a Passage, but a whole Discourse, taken out from another Book only* mutatis mutandis. *The Author is as much in the dark about this as the Answerer; and will imitate him by an Affirmation at Random; that if there be a word of Truth in this Reflection, he is a paultry, imitating Pedant, and the Answerer is a Person of Wit, Manners and Truth. He takes his Boldness, from never having seen any such Treatise in his Life nor heard of it before; and he is sure it is impossible for two Writers of different Times and Countries to agree in their Thoughts after such a Manner, that two continued Discourses shall be the same only* mutatis mutandis. *Neither will he insist upon the mistake of the Title, but let the Answerer*

*and his Friend produce any Book they please, he defies them to shew one single
Particular, where the judicious Reader will affirm he has been obliged for the smallest
Hint; giving only Allowance for the accidental encountring of a single Thought,
which he knows may sometimes happen; tho' he has never yet found it in that
Discourse, nor has heard it objected by any body else.*

*So that if ever any design was unfortunately executed, it must be that of this
Answerer; who when he would have it observed that the Author's Wit is not his own,
is able to produce but three Instances, two of them meer Trifles, and all three
manifestly false. If this be the way these Gentlemen deal with the World in those
Criticisms, where we have not Leisure to defeat them, their Readers had need be
cautious how they rely upon their Credit; and whether this Proceeding can be
reconciled to Humanity or Truth, let those who think it worth their while, determine.*

*It is agreed, this Answerer would have succeeded much better, if he had stuck
wholly to his Business as a Commentator upon the* Tale of a Tub, *wherein it cannot
be deny'd that he hath been of some Service to the Publick, and has given very fair
Conjectures towards clearing up some difficult Passages; but, it is the frequent Error
of those Men (otherwise very commendable for their Labors) to make Excursions
beyond their Talent and their Office, by pretending to point out the Beauties and the
Faults; which is no part of their Trade, which they always fail in, which the World
never expected from them, nor gave them any thanks for endeavouring at. The Part of*
Minellius, *or* Farnaby *would have fallen in with his Genius, and might have been
serviceable to many Readers who cannot enter into the abstruser Parts of that
Discourse; but* Optat ephippia bos piger. *The dull unwieldy, ill-shaped Ox would
needs put on the Furniture of a Horse, not considering he was born to Labour, to plow
the Ground for the Sake of superior Beings, and that he has neither the Shape, Mettle
nor Speed of that nobler Animal he would affect to personate.*

*It is another Pattern of this Answerer's fair dealing, to give us Hints that the
Author is dead, and yet to lay the Suspicion upon somebody, I know not who, in the
Country; to which can be only returned, that he is absolutely mistaken in all his
Conjectures; and surely Conjectures are at best too light a Pretence to allow a Man to
assign a Name in Publick. He condemns a Book, and consequently the Author, of
whom he is utterly ignorant, yet at the same time fixes in Print, what he thinks a
disadvantageous Character upon those who never deserved it. A Man who receives a
Buffet in the Dark may be allowed to be vexed; but it is an odd kind of Revenge to go
to Cuffs in broad day with the first he meets with, and lay the last Nights Injury at his
Door. And thus much for this* discreet, candid, pious, *and* ingenious *Answerer.*

*How the Author came to be without his Papers, is a Story not proper to be told, and
of very little use, being a private Fact of which the Reader would believe as little or as
much as he thought good. He had however a blotted Copy by him, which he intended
to have writ over, with many Alterations, and this the Publishers were well aware of,
having put it into the Booksellers Preface, that they* apprehended a surreptitious

Copy, which was to be altered, *&c. This though not regarded by Readers, was a real Truth, only the surreptitious Copy was rather that which was printed, and they made all hast they could, which indeed was needless; the Author not being at all prepared; but he has been told, the Bookseller was in much Pain, having given a good Sum of Money for the Copy.*

In the Authors Original Copy there were not so many Chasms as appear in the Book; and why some of them were left he knows not; had the Publication been trusted to him, he should have made several Corrections of Passages against which nothing hath been ever objected. He should likewise have altered a few of those that seem with any Reason to be excepted against, but to deal freely, the greatest Number he should have left untouch'd, as never suspecting it possible any wrong Interpretations could be made of them.

The Author observes, at the End of the Book there is a Discourse called A Fragment; *which he more wondered to see in Print than all the rest. Having been a most imperfect Sketch with the Addition of a few loose Hints, which he once lent a Gentleman who had designed a Discourse of somewhat the same Subject; he never thought of it afterwards, and it was a sufficient Surprize to see it pieced up together, wholly out of the Method and Scheme he had intended, for it was the Ground-work of a much larger Discourse, and he was sorry to observe the Materials so foolishly employ'd.*

There is one farther Objection made by those who have answered this Book, as well as by some others, that Peter *is frequently made to repeat Oaths and Curses. Every Reader observes it was necessary to know that* Peter *did Swear and Curse. The Oaths are not printed out, but only supposed, and the Idea of an Oath is not immoral, like the Idea of a Prophane or Immodest Speech. A Man may laugh at the Popish Folly of cursing People to Hell, and imagine them swearing, without any crime; but lewd Words, or dangerous Opinions though printed by halves, fill the Readers Mind with ill Idea's; and of these the Author cannot be accused. For the judicious Reader will find that the severest Stroaks of Satyr in his Book are levelled against the modern Custom of Employing Wit upon those Topicks, of which there is a remarkable Instance in the* 65th, *Page, as well as in several others, tho' perhaps once or twice exprest in too free a manner, excusable only for the Reasons already alledged. Some Overtures have been made by a third Hand to the Bookseller for the Author's altering those Passages which he thought might require it. But it seems the Bookseller will not hear of any such Thing, being apprehensive it might spoil the Sale of the Book.*

The Author cannot conclude this Apology, without making this one Reflection; that, as Wit is the noblest and most useful Gift of humane Nature, so Humor is the most agreeable, and where these two enter far into the Composition of any Work, they will render it always acceptable to the World. Now, the great Part of those who have no Share or Tast of either, but by their Pride, Pedantry and Ill Manners, lay themselves bare to the Lashes of Both, think the Blow is weak, because they are insensible, and where Wit hath any mixture of Raillery; 'Tis but calling it Banter, *and the work is done. This Polite Word of theirs was first borrowed from the Bullies in* White-Fryars, *then fell among the Footmen, and at last retired to the Pedants, by whom it is applied as properly to the Productions of Wit, as if I should apply it to Sir* Isaac Newton's *Mathematicks, but, if this* Bantring *as they call it, be so despisable a Thing, whence comes it to pass they have such a perpetual Itch towards it themselves? To instance only in the Answerer already mentioned; it is grievous to see him in some of his Writings at every turn going out of his way to be waggish, to tell us of a* Cow that prickt up her Tail, *and in his answer to this Discourse, he says it is all a Farce and a Ladle: With other Passages equally shining. One may say of these* Impedimenta Literarum, *that Wit ows them a Shame; and they cannot take wiser Counsel than to keep out of harms way, or at least not to come till they are sure they are called.*

To conclude; with those Allowances above-required, this Book should be read, after which the Author conceives, few things will remain which may not be excused in a young Writer. He wrote only to the Men of Wit and Tast, and he thinks he is not mistaken in his Accounts, when he says they have been all of his side, enough to give him the vanity of telling his Name, wherein the World with all its wise Conjectures, is yet very much in the dark, which Circumstance is no disagreeable Amusement either to the Publick or himself.

The Author is informed, that the Bookseller has prevailed on several Gentlemen, to write some explanatory Notes, for the goodness of which he is not to answer, having never seen any of them, nor intends it, till they appear in Print, when it is not unlikely he may have the Pleasure to find twenty Meanings, which never enter'd into his Imagination.

June 3. 1709.

POSTSCRIPT.

S ince the writing of this which was about 4 Year ago; a Prostitute Bookseller hath publish'd a foolish Paper, under the Name of Notes on the Tale of a Tub, *with some Account of the Author, and with an Insolence which I suppose is punishable by Law, hath presumed to assign certain Names. It will be enough for the Author to assure the World, that the Writer of that Paper is utterly wrong in all his Conjectures upon that Affair. The Author farther asserts that the whole Work is entirely of one Hand, which every Reader of Judgment will easily discover. The Gentleman who gave the Copy to the Bookseller, being a Friend of the Author, and using no other Liberties besides that of expunging certain Passages where now the Chasms appear under the Name of* Desiderata. *But if any Person will prove his Claim to three Lines in the whole Book, let him step forth and tell his Name and Titles, upon which the Bookseller shall have Orders to prefix them to the next Edition, and the Claimant shall from henceforward be acknowledged the undisputed Author.*

ABBREVIATIONS
AND SHORT TITLES

The Bible is quoted from *The Holy Bible containing the Old and New Testaments and the Apocrypha* (Greenwich, Connecticut, n.d.). Greek and Latin classics are quoted from the Loeb Classical Library unless stated otherwise and Shakespeare from *The Norton Facsimile. The First Folio of Shakespeare*, ed. Charlton Hinman (New York, 1968). Place of publication is London unless otherwise noted.

Abbadie 1695	Jacques Abbadie, *The Art of Knowing One-self*, tr. T.W. (Oxford, 1695).
Abraham 1948	J. Johnson Abraham, "Some account of the history of the treatment of syphilis", *British Journal of Venereal Diseases* 24 (1948), 153-60.
Addison 1914	Joseph Addison, *The Miscellaneous Works*, ed. A.C. Guthkelch, 2v. (1914).
Anony. 1673	*The Character of a Coffee-House, with the Symptomes of a Town-Wit* (1673).
Anony. 1681	*The Character of an Ill-Court Favourite: Representing the Mischiefs That Flow from Ministers of State When they are More Great than Good* (1681).
Anony. 1691	*The Catch Club, or Merry Companions*, 2v. (1691).
Anony. 1695	*Some Remarks on a Paper, Entituled, The Humble Representation of the Presbyterians, To His Grace, His Majesties High Commissioner. And the Estates of Parliament* (1695).
Anony. 1699	*A Short Account of Dr. Bentley's Humanity and Justice* (1699).
Anony. 1700	*The Character of a Whig, under Several Denominations* (1700).
Anony. 1712	*A Long Ramble, or Several Years Travels, In the much Talk'd of, But never before Discover'd, wandering Island of O-Brazil* (1712).
[Astell] 1696	[Mary Astell], *An Essay in Defence of the Female Sex* (1696).
Arber 1903-06	Edward Arber, *The Term Catalogues, 1668-1709*, 3v. (1903-06).
Aubrey 1898	John Aubrey, *Brief Lives*, ed. Andrew Clark, 2v. (Oxford, 1898).
Bacon 1605	Francis Bacon, *The Twoo Bookes of Francis Bacon. Of the proficience & advancement of Learning* (1605).
Bacon 1620	Francis Bacon, *Instauratio Magna . . . Pars Secunda Operis, quae dicitur Novum Organum* (1620).
Bacon 1640	Francis Bacon, *Of the Advancement and Proficiencie of Learning*, tr. Gilbert Wats (Oxford, 1640).

Barrett 1808	John Barrett, *An Essay on the Earlier Part of the Life of Swift* (1808).
Bateman 1582	Stephen Bateman, *Batman upon Bartholomew* (1582).
Bayle 1710	Pierre Bayle, *An Historical and Critical Dictionary*, tr. Pierre Desmaizeaux, 4v. (1710).
Beatson 1788	Robert Beatson, *A Political Index to the Histories of Great Britain and Ireland*, 2v. (1788).
Beaumont 1961	Charles A. Beaumont, *Swift's Classical Rhetoric* (Athens, Georgia, 1961).
Beeching 1909	H.C. Beeching, *Francis Atterbury* (1909).
Bentley 1697	Richard Bentley, *A Dissertation upon the Epistles of Phalaris . . . And the Fables of Aesop* (1697).
Bentley 1699	Richard Bentley, *A Dissertation upon the Epistles of Phalaris. With an Answer to the Objections of the Honourable Charles Boyle, Esquire* (1699).
Bentley 1713	Richard Bentley, *Remarks upon a late Discourse of Free-Thinking in a Letter of F[rancis] H[are] D.D.*, 2v. in 1 (1713).
Bernier 1671-72	Francis Bernier, *The History of the Late Revolution of the Empire of the Great Mogul*, tr. H.O., 4v. (1671–72).
Beverley 1696	T[homas] B[everley], *Christianity the Great Mystery. In Answer to a late Treatise, Christianity not Mysterious . . .* (1696).
Blackmore 1695	Richard Blackmore, *Prince Arthur. An Heroick Poem* (1695).
Blackmore 1697	Richard Blackmore, *King Arthur. An Heroick Poem* (1697).
Blackmore 1699	[Richard Blackmore,] *A Short History of the Last Parliament* (1699).
Blackmore 1708	Richard Blackmore, *The Kit-Cats. A Poem* (1708).
Blount 1679	Charles Blount, *Anima Mundi: or an Historical Narration of the Opinions of the Ancients Concerning Man's Soul After this Life* [1679].
Blunt 1874	John H. Blunt, *A Dictionary of Sects, Heresies, Ecclesiastical Parties, and Schools of Religious Thought* (1874).
Book of Common Prayer 1704	*The Book of Common Prayer and Administration of the Sacraments, and Other Rites and Ceremonies of the Church, According to the Use Of the Church of England* (1704).
Boswell 1961	James Boswell, *Boswell's Journal of a Tour to the Hebrides*, ed. Frederick A. Pottle and Charles H. Bennett (New York, 1961).
Boyer 1702-03	Abel Boyer, *The History of King William the Third*, 3v. (1702-03)
Boyer 1703-13	Abel Boyer, *The History of the Reign of Queen Anne, Digested into Annals*, 11v. (1703-13).
Boyer 1714	Abel Boyer, *Memoirs of the Life and Negotiations of Sir W. Temple, Bar.* (1714)

Boyle 1698	Charles Boyle, *Dr. Bentley's Dissertations on the Epistles of Phalaris, and the Fables of Aesop, Examin'd* (2nd ed. Oxford, 1698; 1st ed. Oxford, 1698).
Boyle 1718	*Phalaridos . . . Epistolai*, ed. Charles Boyle (Oxford 1718; 1st ed. Oxford, 1695).
Boyle 2000	John Boyle, 5th Earl of Cork and Orrery, *Remarks on the Life and Writings of Dr. Jonathan Swift*, ed. João Fróes (Newark, Delaware, 2000).
Bramhall 1671	John Bramhall, *An Answer to a Letter of Enquiry into The Grounds and Occasions of the Contempt of the Clergy* (1671).
Brink 1986	C.O. Brink, *English Classical Scholarship. Historical Reflections on Bentley, Porson, and Housman* (Cambridge 1986).
Brown 1700	Thomas Brown, *Amusements Serious and Comical, Calculated for the Meridian of London* (1700).
Brown 1720	Thomas Brown, *The Works of Mr. Thomas Brown, Serious and Comical, in Prose and Verse* (5th ed., 4v., 1720; 1st ed., 3v., 1707).
Browne 1646	Sir Thomas Browne, *Pseudodoxia Epidemica; or, Enquiries into Very many received Tenents, and commonly presumed Truths* (1646).
Browne 1650	Sir Thomas Browne, *Pseudodoxia Epidemica*, 2nd ed. (1650; 1st ed. 1646).
Buckingham 1672	George Villiers, 2nd Duke of Buckingham, *The Rehearsal* (1672)
Buckingham 1704-05	George Villiers, 2nd Duke of Buckingham, *The Works of His Grace, George, Late Duke of Buckingham*, ed. Thomas Brown, 2v. (1704-05).
Budgell 1732	Eustace Budgell, *Memoirs of the Life and Character of the Late Earl of Orrery, and the Family of the Boyles* (2nd ed. 1732; 1st ed. 1732).
Buisseret 1984	David Buisseret, *Henry IV* (1984).
Burlingame 1920	Anne E. Burlingame, *The Battle of the Books in its Historical Setting* (New York, 1920).
Burnet 1681-83	Gilbert Burnet, *The History of the Reformation of the Church of England*, 2v. (2nd ed. 1681, 1683; 1st ed. 1679, 1681).
Butler 1967	Samuel Butler, *Hudibras*, ed. John Wilders (Oxford, 1967).
Callières 1705	[François de Callières,] *Characters and Criticisms, upon the Ancient and Modern Orators . . .* , tr. Martin Bladen (1705).
Casaubon 1656	Meric Casaubon, *A Treatise concerning Enthusiasme, as it is an Effect of Nature: but is mistaken by many for either Divine Inspiration, or Diabolicall Possession,* (2nd ed. 1656; 1st ed. 1655).

Cervantes 1612-20	Miguel Cervantes, *The History of the Valorous and Wittie Knight-Errant, Don Quixote*, tr. Thomas Shelton, 2v. (1612-20)
Chasteigner 1657	Henri Louis Chasteigner de la Roche Pozay, *Celebriorum Distinctionum Philosophicarum Synopsis*, (Oxford, 1657; 1ˢᵗ ed. 1617).
CJ	*Journals of the House of Commons*, 1547-1796, 51v. (1803).
Compleat Key 1718	*A Compleat Key to the Eighth Edition of The Dispensary* (1718).
Coppe 1651	Abiezer Coppe, *Coppe's Return to the wayes of Truth* (1651).
Cormick 1972	Jean Ann Cormick, *Humor at the Expense of Shame: Swift, The Athenian Society, and A Tale of a Tub*, Ph.D. Dissertation, University of California, San Diego (1972).
Creech 1682	*T. Lucretius Carus . . . His Six Books De Natura Rerum, Done into English Verse*, tr. Thomas Creech (1682).
Crider 1978	J.R. Crider, 'Dissenting sex: Swift's "History of Fanaticism"', *Studies in English Literature* 18 (1978), 491-508
Crockatt and Monroe 1748	Gilbert Crockatt and John Monroe, *Scotch Presbyterian Eloquence Display'd: or, The Folly of their Teaching Discover'd* (1748; 1ˢᵗ ed. 1692).
CSPD	*Calendar of State Papers, Domestic Series, 1660-1704*, ed. Mary Anne E. Green et al., 44v. (1875-1972).
Cudworth 1678	Ralph Cudworth, *The True Intellectual System of the Universe* (1678)
Curll 1714	Edmund Curll, *A Complete Key to the Tale of a Tub* (3ʳᵈ ed. 1714; 1ˢᵗ ed. 1710).
Davenant 1701	Charles Davenant, *Essays upon I. The Ballance of Power. II. The Right of making War, Peace and Alliances. III. Universal Monarchy* (1701).
Davenant 1702	[Charles Davenant,] *The Old and Modern Whig Truly Represented. Being a Second Part of His Picture and a Real Vindication of His Excellency the Earl of Rochester* (2ⁿᵈ ed. 1702; 1ˢᵗ ed. 1702).
Davenant 1651	Sir William Davenant, *Gondibert. A Heroick Poem* (1651).
Debus 1967	Allen G. Debus, "Renaissance chemistry and the work of Robert Fludd", *Ambix* 14 (1967), 42-59.
Defoe 1697	[Daniel Defoe], *An Enquiry into the Occasional Conformity of Dissenters, in Cases of Preferment. With a Preface to the Lord Mayor, Occasioned by his Carrying the Sword to a Conventicle* (1697).
Delaune 1690	Thomas Delaune, *Angliae Metropolis: Or, The Present State of London* (1690).
Dennis 1939-43	*The Critical Works of John Dennis*, ed. Edward Niles Hooker, 2v. (Baltimore, 1939-43).

Descartes 1680	René Descartes, *Six Metaphysical Meditations; Wherein it is Proved That there is a God*, tr. William Molyneux (1680).
DNB	*The Dictionary of National Biography*, ed. Sir Leslie Stephen and Sir Sidney Lee, 22v. (Oxford, 1959–60).
Donne 1912	*The Poems of John Donne*, ed. H.J.C. Grierson, 2v. (Oxford, 1912).
Dryden 1697	*The Works of Virgil*, tr. John Dryden (1697).
Dryden 1882-93	*The Works of John Dryden*, ed. Sir Walter Scott and George Saintsbury, 18v. (Edinburgh, 1882-93).
Dryden 1956–	*The Works of John Dryden*, ed. H.T. Swedenberg Jr. et al. (Berkeley and Los Angeles, California 1956–).
Dunton 1690-97	John Dunton et al., *The Athenian Gazette/Athenian Mercury*, 20v. (17 March 1690 – 14 June 1697).
Eachard 1671	[John Eachard,] *Some Observations upon the Answer To an Enquiry into the Grounds and Occasions of the Contempt of the Clergy* (4th ed. 1671; 1st ed. 1671).
EB 1910-11	*The Encyclopaedia Britannica*, 11th ed., 29v. (New York, 1910-11).
EHD 1966	*English Historical Documents 1660-1714*, ed. Andrew Browning (1966).
Ehrenpreis 1963	Irvin Ehrenpreis, "Personae," *Restoration and Eighteenth Century Literature; Essays in Honor of Alan Dugald McKillop*, ed. Charles Carroll Camden (Chicago, 1963), 25-37.
Ehrenpreis, Marginalia	Irvin Ehrenpreis' annotated copy of Swift 1958 now in the Ehrenpreis Center for Swift Studies, Westfälische Wilhelms Universität, Münster.
Elias 1982	A. C. Elias Jr., *Swift at Moor Park. Problems in Biography and Criticism* (Philadelphia, 1982).
Elliott 1954	Robert C. Elliott, 'Swift and Dr. Eachard', *PMLA* 69, (1954), 1250-57.
Erasmus 1941	Desiderius Erasmus, *The Praise of Folly*, tr. Hoyt H. Hudson (Princeton, 1941).
Etherege 1974	*Letters of Sir George Etherege*, ed. Frederick Bracher (1974).
Evelyn 1955	John Evelyn, *The Diary*, ed. E.S. de Beer, 6v. (Oxford, 1955).
Ferguson 1906	John Ferguson, *Bibliotheca Chemica*, 2v. (Glasgow, 1906).
Fidge 1691	George Fidge, *Wit for Money* (1691).
Fontenelle 1687	Bernard Le Bovier de Fontenelle, *A Discourse of the Plurality of Worlds*, tr. Sir W.D. (Dublin, 1687).
Fontenelle 1708	Bernard Le Bovier de Fontenelle, *Dialogues of the Dead*, tr. John Hughes (1708).
Forster 1927	E. M. Forster, *Aspects of the Novel*, (New York, 1927).
Forster 1876	John Forster, *The Life of Jonathan Swift*, 2v. (New York, 1876).

Foxe 1570   John Foxe, *Actes and Monumentes*, 1v. in 2 (1570).

French 1963   David P. French, "Swift, Temple and 'A Digression on Madness'", *Texas Studies in Language and Literature* 5 (1963), 42-57.

Garth 1699   Samuel Garth, *The Dispensary: A Poem* (1699).

Gastrell 1726   Francis Gastrell, *The Principles of Deism Truly represented, and set in a clear Light. In Two Dialogues between a Sceptick and a Deist* (4th ed. 1726; 1st ed. 1708).

Gardiner 1998   Anne B. Gardiner, *Ancient Faith and Modern Freedom* (Washington D.C., 1998).

Gildon 1709   Charles Gildon, *The Golden Spy: or a Political Journal* (1709).

Glanvill 1665   Joseph Glanvill, *Scepsis Scientifica: or, Confest Ignorance, the way to Science* (1665).

Glanvill 1670   Joseph Glanvill, *Lógou Threskeía: or, A Seasonable Recommendation, and Defense of Reason, in the Affairs of Religion* (1670).

Goldie 1951   Frederick Goldie, *A Short History of the Episcopal Church in Scotland* (1951).

Gosson 1579   Stephen Gosson, *The School of Abuse* (1579).

Gwagnin 1578   Aleksandr Gwagnin, *Sarmantiae Europeae Descriptio* (Cracow, 1578).

Haight 1955   Anne L. Haight, *Banned Books: Informal Notes on Some Books Banned for Various Reasons at Various Times and in Various Places* (2nd ed. New York, 1955; 1st ed. New York, 1935).

Hall 1609?   Joseph Hall, *The Discovery of a New World* (1609?).

Halliwell 1924   James O. Halliwell, *A Dictionary of Archaic and Provincial Words*, 2v. in 1 (1924; 1st ed. 1847).

Harrington 1656   James Harrington, *The Common-wealth of Oceana* (1656).

Harth 1961   Phillip Harth, *Swift and Anglican Rationalism. The Religious Background of A Tale of a Tub* (Chicago 1961).

Hascard 1683   Gregory Hascard, *A Discourse about the Charge of Novelty Upon the Reformed Church of England* (1683).

Hawes 1996   Clement Hawes, *Mania and Literary Style. The rhetoric of Enthusiasm from the Ranters to Christopher Smart* (Cambridge, 1996).

Heydon 1660   John Heydon, *The Rosie Crucian Infallible Axiomata* (1660).

Heydon 1664   John Heydon, *Theomagia, Or, the Temple of Wisdome* (1664).

Heylyn 1674   Peter Heylyn, *Cosmography in Four Books*, 4v. in 1 (6th ed. 1674; 1st ed. 1652).

Hickes 1681   George Hickes, *The Spirit of Enthusiasm Exorcised* (2nd ed. 1681; 1st ed. 1680),

Higgins 1994   Ian Higgins, *Swift's Politics. A Study in Disaffection* (Cambridge, 1994).

HMC *Lords MSS*	Historical Manuscripts Commission, *The Manuscripts of the House of Lords 1678-1714*, 4v. (1887-94); new series, 10v. (1900-53).
HMC *Portland MSS*	Historical Manuscripts Commission, *The Manuscripts of the Duke of Portland*, 10v. (1891-1913).
Hobbes 1650	Thomas Hobbes, *Elementa Philosophiae de Cive* (Amsterdam, 1650; 1ˢᵗ ed. Amsterdam, 1647).
Hobbes 1935	Thomas Hobbes, *Leviathan or The Matter, Forme and Power of a Commonwealth, Ecclesiasticall and Civill*, ed. A.R. Waller (Cambridge, 1935).
Hodges 1695	[William Hodges,] *Great Britain's Groans: or, An Account of the Oppression, Ruin, and Destruction of the Loyal Seamen of England, in the Fatal Loss of their Pay, Health and Lives, and Dreadful Ruin of their Families* (1695).
Homer 1951	Homer, *The Iliad*, tr. Richard Lattimore (Chicago, 1951).
Hopkins 1966	Robert H. Hopkins, "The personation of Hobbism in Swift's *Tale of a Tub*", *Philological Quarterly* 45 (1966), 372-78.
Irenaeus 1885	Irenaeus, "Against Heresies", *The Ante-Nicene Fathers*, ed. Alexander Roberts and James Donaldson, 10v. (1885).
Johnson 1755	Samuel Johnson, *A Dictionary of the English Language*, 2v. (1755).
Johnson 1779-81	Samuel Johnson, *Prefaces, Biographical and Critical, to the Works of the English Poets*, 10v. (1779-81).
Johnson 1905	Samuel Johnson, *Lives of the English Poets*, ed. George Birkbeck Hill, 3v. (Oxford, 1905).
Johnston 1959	Denis Johnston, *In Search of Swift* (Dublin, 1959).
Stanislaus Joyce 1962	Stanislaus Joyce, *Dublin Diary*, ed. George H. Healey (Ithaca, New York, 1962).
Keith 1682	George Keith, *Truths Defence; Or, the Pretended Examination by John Alexander of Leith . . . Re-Examined and Confuted* (1682).
Kelling and Preston 1984	Harold D. Kelling and Cathy L. Preston, *A KWIC Concordance to Jonathan Swift's A Tale of a Tub* (New York, 1984).
King 1704	[William King,] *Some Remarks on the Tale of a Tub* (1704).
LaCasce 1970	Stewart LaCasce, "Swift on medical extremism", *Journal of the History of Ideas* 31 (October–December 1970), 599-606.
Lee 1689	Nathaniel Lee, *The Princess of Cleve, As it was Acted at Queens Theater in Dorset-Garden* (1689).
Leslie 1698	Charles Leslie, *The Snake in the Grass: Or, Satan transform'd into An Angel of Light* (3ʳᵈ ed. 1698; 1ˢᵗ ed. 1696).
L'Estrange 1684-87	Sir Roger L'Estrange, *The Observator in Dialogue*, 3v. (1684–87).

L'Estrange 1708	Sir Roger L'Estrange, *Fables, of Aesop And other eminent Mythologists: with Morals and Reflexions* (5th ed. 1708; 1st ed. 1692).
La Bruyère 1706	[Jean de La Bruyère,] *The English Theophrastus: Or, The Manners of the Age*, tr. Abel Boyer (2nd ed. 1706; 1st ed. 1702).
Libavius 1619	Andreas Libavius, *Turris Babel sive Judiciorum de Fraternitate Rosaceae Crucis Chaos* (Strassburg, 1619).
Lillywhite 1963	Bryant Lillywhite, *London Coffee Houses* (1963).
Limouze 1948	A. Sanford Limouze, "A note on Vergil and *The Battle of the Books*", *Philological Quarterly* 27 (1948), 85–89.
Livy 1600	*The Romane Historie Written by T. Livius*, tr. Philemon Holland (1600).
Locke 1690	John Locke, *An Essay concerning Humane Understanding* (1690).
Luttrell 1857	Narcissus Luttrell, *A Brief Historical Relation of State Affairs from September 1678 to April 1714*, 6v. (Oxford, 1857).
Mainwaring 1711	Arthur Mainwaring, *Remarks on the Preliminary Articles Offer'd by the French King in Order to Procure a General Peace* (1711).
Marvell 1672-73	[Andrew Marvell,] *The Rehearsal Transprosed*, 2v. (1672–73).
Masson 1856	David Masson, *Essays Biographical and Critical* (Cambridge 1856).
Mather 1685	Samuel Mather, *The Figures or Types of the Old Testament* (Dublin, 1685).
Maybee 1942	John R. Maybee, *Anglicans and Nonconformists 1697-1704. A Study in the Background of Swift's A Tale of a Tub*, Ph.D. Dissertation, Princeton 1942.
Mézeray 1673-74	François de Mézeray, *Abregé chronologique de l'histoire de France*, 6v. (Amsterdam, 1673–74).
Milton 1935	John Milton, *Paradise Lost*, ed. Merritt Y. Hughes (New York, 1935).
Milton 1953-82	John Milton, *The Complete Prose Works*, ed. Don M. Wolfe et al., 8v. in 10 (New Haven, 1953–82).
Misson 1698	Henri Misson de Valbourg, *Memoires et Observations Faites par un Voyageur en Angleterre* (The Hague, 1698).
Montagu 1701	[Charles Montagu, Lord Halifax,] *The Present Disposition of England Considered* (1701).
Montaigne 1700	*Essays of Michael Seigneur de Montaigne*, tr. Charles Cotton, 3v. (3rd ed. 1700; 1st ed. 1685-86).
More 1656	Henry More, *Enthusiasm Triumphatus, Or, A Discourse of the Nature, Causes, Kinds, and Cure, of Enthusiasme* (1656; 2nd ed. 1662).
More 1660	Henry More, *An Explanation of the Grand Mystery of Godliness* (1660).
Moréri 1694	Louis Moréri, *The Great Historical, Geographical and*

Poetical Dictionary, tr. Jean Le Clerc, 2v. (6th ed. 1694; 1st ed. Lyon, 1674).

Morley 1889 — Henry Morley, *The Tale of a Tub and other Works by Jonathan Swift* (1889).

Mueller 1993 — Judith C. Mueller, "Writing under constraint: Swift's 'Apology' for *A Tale of a Tub*", *ELH* 60, (Spring 1993), 101–15

Neville 1681 — [Henry Neville,] *Plato Redivivus: or A Dialogue concerning Government* (1681).

Nichols 1817-58 — John Nichols, *Illustrations of the Literary History of the Eighteenth Century*, 8v. (1817–58).

Nicolas 1842 — Sir Nicholas H. Nicolas, *History of the Orders of Knighthood of the British Empire*, 4v. (1842).

N&Q — *Notes and Queries*, originally anonymous, (1849–2005), 250 v.

Nugel and Freimark 1973 — Bernfried Nugel and Peter Freimark, "Swift's Treatment of Rabbi Jehuda Hannasi in *A Tale of a Tub*", *Notes & Queries* 218 (1973), 3–4.

ODNB — *Oxford Dictionary of National Biography*, ed. H. C. G. Matthew and Brian Harrison, 60v. (Oxford, 2004).

OED — *The Oxford English Dictionary*, ed. James A.H. Murray et al., 2nd ed 20v. (Oxford, 1989).

Ogg 1956-57 — David Ogg, *England in the Reigns of Charles II, James II and William III*, 2nd ed. 3v. (Oxford, 1956–57).

Oldmixon 1709, 1711 — John Oldmixon, *The History of Addresses*, 2v. (1709, 1711).

Olson 1952 — Robert C. Olson, "Swift's Use of the *Philosophical Transactions* in Section V of *A Tale of a Tub*", *Studies in Philology* 49 (1952), 459–67.

Orleans 1690 — Pierre Joseph d'Orleans, *Histoire de M. Constance, première ministre de Roy de Siam* (Tours, 1690).

Orrery 1752 — John Boyle, Earl of Orrery, *Remarks on the Life and Writings of Dr. Jonathan Swift*, 3rd ed. (1752)

Pagitt 1654 — Ephraim Pagitt, *Heresiography Or a description of the Heretickes and Sectaries of these Latter times* (5th ed. 1654; 1st ed. 1645).

Paracelsus 1658 — Paracelsus, *Opera Omnia*, 3v. in 2 (Geneva, 1658).

Parker 1672 — Samuel Parker, *Bishop Bramhall's Vindication of Himself and the Episcopal Clergy from the Presbyterian Charge of Popery . . .* (1672).

Patrizzi 1593 — Francesco Patrizzi, *Nova de Universis Philosophia* (Venice, 1593).

Paulson 1960 — Ronald Paulson, *Theme and Structure in Swift's Tale of a Tub* (New Haven, 1960).

Penkethman 1699 — William Penkethman, *Love without Interest* (1699).

Pepys 1970–83 — *The Diary of Samuel Pepys*, ed. Robert Latham et al., 11v. (Berkeley and Los Angeles, California, 1970–83).

Phil. Trans.	*The Philosophical Transactions of the Royal Society of London,* ed. Henry Oldenburgh et al., 177v. + Supplements (1665–1886)
Phillips 1675	Edward Phillips, *Theatrum Poetarum* (1675).
Philosophie Naturelle 1682	*Philosophie Naturelle de Trois Anciens Philosophes Renommez: Artephius, Flamel, & Synesius* (Paris, 1682).
Photius 1824	Photius, *Bibliotheca,* ed. Immanuelis Bekkeri, 2v. in 1 (Berlin, 1824).
Pilkington 1997	Laetitia Pilkington, *Memoirs,* ed. A.C. Elias, Jr., 2v. (Athens, Georgia, 1997).
Pinkus 1959	Phillip Pinkus, "Swift and the Ancient-Moderns controversy", *University of Toronto Quarterly* 29 (1959), 46–58.
Planché 1876–79	James H. Planché, *A Cyclopaedia of Costume,* 2v. (1876–79).
Plato 1875	*The Dialogues of Plato,* ed. Benjamin Jowett, 5v. (2nd ed., Oxford, 1875; 1st ed., 4v., Oxford, 1871).
POAS 1716	*Poems on Affairs of State,* ed. John Tutchin, 6th ed., 4v. (London, 1716).
POAS Yale	*Poems on Affair of State. Augustan Satirical Verse, 1660–1714,* 7v., ed. George deF. Lord et al. (New Haven, 1963–75).
Polybius 1693	*The History of Polybius,* tr. Sir Henry Sheeres, 2v. (1693).
Prideaux 1697	Humphrey Prideaux, *The True Nature of Imposture Fully Display'd in the Life of Mahomet* (1697).
Prior 1959	Matthew Prior, *The Literary Works,* ed. H. Bunker Wright and Monroe K. Spears, 2v. (Oxford, 1959).
Probyn 1974	Clive Probyn, "Swift's anatomy of the brain: the hexagonal bite of poetry", *Notes & Queries* 219 (July 1974), 250–51.
Quintana 1962	Ricardo Quintana, Review of Harth 1961, *Modern Philology* 60 (1962), 141–43.
Quintana 1965	Ricardo Quintana, *Etudes anglaises* 18 (1965), 5–17
Rochester 1980	*The Letters of John Wilmot, Earl of Rochester,* ed. Jeremy Treglown (Chicago, 1980).
Rochester 1994	John Wilmot, Earl of Rochester, *The Complete Works,* ed. Frank H. Ellis (1994).
Rosenheim 1963	Edward W. Rosenheim, Jr., *Swift and the Satirist's Art* (Chicago, 1963).
Sarpi 1676	Paolo Sarpi, *The History of the Council of Trent,* tr. Nathanael Brent (1676).
Scaliger 1557	Julius Caesar Scaliger, *De Subtilitate* (Paris, 1557).
Scheffer 1674	Johannes Scheffer, *The History of Lapland* (Oxford, 1674).
Scruggs 1973	Charles Scruggs, "Swift's use of Lucretius in *A Tale of a Tub*", *Texas Studies in Language and Literature* 15 (1973), 39–49.

Sedley 1702	*The Miscellaneous Works of the Honourable Sir Charles Sedley*, ed. William Ayloffe (1702).
Settle 1683	Elkanah Settle, *A Narrative of the Popish Plot* (1683).
Shadwell 1683	[Thomas Shadwell,] *Some Reflections upon the Pretended Parallel in the Play called the Duke of Guise* (1683).
Shadwell 1927	*The Complete Works of Thomas Shadwell*, ed. Montague Summers, 5v. (1927).
Shaftesbury 1711	Anthony Ashley Cooper, 3rd Earl of Shaftesbury, *Characteristics of Men, Manners, Opinions, Times*, 3v. (1711).
Sidney 1704	Algernon Sidney, *Discourses concerning Government* (2nd ed. 1704; 1st ed. 1698).
Sleidanus 1644	[Johannes Sleidanus,] *Mock Majesty: Or, The siege of Munster* (1644).
South 1660	Robert South, *A Sermon Preached at S. Mary's Church in Oxon, before the University, on the 29th of July 1660* (1660).
South 1692–94	Robert South, *Twelve Sermons Preached upon Several Occasions*, 2v. (1692–94).
Spence 1966	Joseph Spence, *Observations, Anecdotes, and Characters of Books and Men*, ed. James M. Osborn, 2v. (Oxford, 1966).
Sprat 1958	Thomas Sprat, *History of the Royal Society*, ed. Jackson I. Cope and Harold W. Jones (St. Louis, 1958).
Staley 1979	Robert S. Staley, *Swift's Satirical Commentary in A Tale of a Tub*, Ph.D. Dissertation, University of Colorado, 1979.
Stanley 1656	Thomas Stanley, *The History of Philosophy in Eight Parts* (1656).
Stanley 1687	Thomas Stanley, *The History of Philosophy: Containing the Lives, Opinions, Actions and Discourses of the Philosophers of Every Sect* (2nd ed. 1687; 1st ed. 1655).
Starkman 1950	Miriam K. Starkman, *Swift's Satire on Learning in A Tale of a Tub* (Princeton, 1950).
Statutes of the Realm 1963	*The Statutes of the Realm*, 11v. (1963; 1st printing 1810–28).
Steele 1786	Richard Steele, *The Tatler*, ed. John Nichols, 6v. (1786).
Stephens 1696	[William Stephens,] *An Account of the Growth of Deism in England* (1696).
Stevens 1912	*The Journal of John Stevens, containing a Brief Account of the War in Ireland, 1689–91*, ed. Robert H. Murray (Oxford 1912).
Stevenson 1948	*The Macmillan Book of Proverbs, Maxims, and Famous Phrases*, ed. Burton Stevenson (New York, 1948).

Stillingfleet 1675	Edward Stillingfleet, *Origines Sacrae, Or A Rational Account of the Grounds of Christian Faith* (4th ed. 1675; 1st ed. 1662).
Suidas 1967–71	*Suidas Lexicon*, ed. Ada Adler, 3v. (Stuttgart, 1967–71).
Swift, Deane 1755	Deane Swift, *An Essay upon The Life and Writings of Dr. Jonathan Swift* (2nd ed. 1755; 1st ed. 1755).
Swift 1720	[Jonathan Swift,] *Miscellaneous Works, Comical and Diverting*, By T.R.D.J.S.D.O.P.I.I. . . I. The Tale *of a Tub* . . . with . . . considerable *Additions*, & explanatory *Notes*, never before printed . . . (London, 1720).
Swift 1734	[Jonathan Swift,] *A Tale of a Tub* ... A New Edition ... (London [Holland], 1734).
Swift 1755	*The Works of Jonathan Swift*, D.D., ed. John Hawkesworth, 6v., 4° (1755).
Swift 1808	*The Works of the Rev. Jonathan Swift, D.D., Dean of St. Patrick's, Dublin*, ed. Thomas Sheridan and John Nichols, 19v. (1808).
Swift 1814	*The Works of Jonathan Swift, D.D. Dean of St. Patrick's Dublin . . . With Notes, And A Life of the Author, By Walter Scott, Esq.*, 19v. (Edinburgh, 1814).
Swift 1937	*The Poems of Jonathan Swift*, ed. Harold Williams, 1v. in 3 (Oxford, 1937).
Swift 1939–68	*The Prose Writings of Jonathan Swift*, ed. Herbert Davis et al., 14v. (Oxford, 1939–68).
Swift 1948	Jonathan Swift, *Journal to Stella*, ed. Harold Williams, 1v. in 2 (Oxford, 1948).
Swift 1958	Jonathan Swift, *A Tale of a Tub to which is added The Battle of the Books and the Mechanical Operation of the Spirit*, ed. A.C. Guthkelch and D. Nichol Smith (2nd ed. Oxford 1958, further corrections 1970; 1st ed. Oxford 1920).
Swift 1963	H. Teerink, *A Bibliography of the Writings of Jonathan Swift*, ed. Arthur H. Scouten (Philadelphia, 1963).
Swift 1967	Jonathan Swift, *A Discourse of the Contests and Dissentions between the Nobles and the Commons in Athens and Rome With the Consequences they had upon both those States*, ed. Frank H. Ellis (Oxford, 1967).
Swift 1978	Jonathan Swift, *The Battle of the Books*, ed. Hermann J. Real (Berlin, 1978).
Swift 1985	*Swift vs. Mainwaring: The Examiner and The Medley*, ed. Frank H. Ellis (Oxford, 1985).
Swift 1986	Jonathan Swift, *A Tale of a Tub and Other Works*, ed. Angus Ross and David Woolley (Oxford and New York, 1986).
Swift 1994	Jonathan Swift, *Ein Tonnenmärchen*, tr. Ulrich Horstmann, ed. Hermann J. Real (Stuttgart, 1994).

Swift 1999–2006	*The Correspondence of Jonathan Swift, D.D.*, ed. David Woolley, 4v. (Frankfurt-am-Main, 1999–2006).
Temple 1673	Sir William Temple, *Observations upon the United Provinces of the Netherlands* (1673).
Temple 1690	Sir William Temple, *Miscellanea. The Second Part* (1690).
Temple 1695	Sir William Temple, *An Introduction to the History of England* (1695).
Temple 1701	Sir William Temple, *Miscellanea. The Third Part*, ed. Jonathan Swift (1701).
Temple 1930	Sir William Temple, *The Early Essays*, ed. G.C. Moore Smith (Oxford, 1930).
Thucydides 1634	Thucydides, *The Peloponnesian Warre*, tr. Thomas Hobbes (1634).
Tilley 1950	Morris P. Tilley, *A Dictionary of the Proverbs in England in the Sixteenth and Seventeenth Centuries* (Ann Arbor, Michigan, 1950).
Tindal 1710	Mathew Tindal, *The Merciful Judgments of High–Church Triumphant* (1710).
TLS	*The (London) Times Literary Supplement* (1902–).
Toland 1696	John Toland, *Christianity not Mysterious* (1696).
T.R. 1698	T.R. *An Essay concerning Critical and Curious Learning* (1698).
Traugott 1983	John Traugott, "*A Tale of a Tub*, The Character of Swift's Satire", *A Revised Focus*, ed. Claude Rawson (Newark, Delaware, 1983), 83–126.
Treadwell 1983	Michael Treadwell, "Swift's relations with the London book trade to 1714", *Author/Publisher Relations during the Eighteenth and Nineteenth Centuries*, ed. Robin Myers and Michael Harris (Oxford, 1983), 1–36.
Uphaus 1971	Robert W. Uphaus, "From panegyric to satire: Swift's early odes and *A Tale of a Tub*", *Texas Studies in Literature and Language* 13 (1971), 55–70.
Van Lennep 1965	*The London Stage 1660–1800, Part 1: 1660–1700*, ed. William Van Lennep (Carbondale, Illinois, 1965).
Vaughan 1984	*The Works of Thomas Vaughan*, ed. Alan Rudrum (Oxford, 1984).
Vernon 1841	*Letter Illustrative of the Reign of William III. From 1696 to 1708. Addressed to the Duke of Shrewsbury by James Vernon*, ed. G.P.R. James, 3v. (1841).
Walpole 1758	[Horace Walpole,] *A Catalogue of the Royal and Noble Authors of England*, 2v. (Strawberry Hill, England, 1758).
Ward 1698–1700	Edward Ward, *The London Spy*, 2v. (November 1698–April 1700).
Watts 1720	Isaac Watts, *Divine Songs* (1720; 1st ed. 1715).

Williams 1962	George H. Williams, *The Radical Reformation* (Philadelphia, 1962).
Wood 1818–20	Anthony à Wood, *Athenae Oxoniensis . . . To which are added The Fasti, or Annals of the said University*, ed. Phillip Bliss (3rd ed., 4v., Oxford, 1818–20; 1st ed. Oxford, 1691–92).
Wotton 1694	William Wotton, *Reflections upon Ancient and Modern Learning . . .* (1694).
Wotton 1697	William Wotton, *Reflections upon Ancient and Modern Learning . . . With a Dissertation upon the Epistles of Phalaris . . . and Aesop's Fables.* By Dr. [Richard] Bentley (1697) (2nd ed. of Wotton; 1st ed. of Bentley).
Wotton 1704?	William Wotton's marginalia in the McMaster University copy of Swift 1704[1].
Wotton 1705[1]	William Wotton, *Reflection upon Ancient and Modern Learning. To which is now added, A Defense Thereof, In Answer to the Objections of Sir W. Temple, and others. With Observations upon the Tale of a Tub. Also, A Dissertation upon the Epistles of Phalaris . . . and Aesop's Fables. By Dr. [Richard] Bentley D.D. (1705)* (3rd ed. of Wotton; 2nd ed. of Bentley).
Wotton 1705[2]	William Wotton, *A Defense of the Reflections upon Ancient and Modern Learning. In Answer to the Objections of Sir William Temple, and Others. With Observations upon the Tale of a Tub* (1705).

END NOTES

In the END NOTES titles and salutations ("My Lord") are not
included in the counting of lines.

Commentators upon this elaborate Treatise . . .
will proceed with great Caution (48.13–14).

title-page.7 *Diu multumque desideratum*: "long and eagerly awaited"; since "none of
the Authors" employed by the fictitious bookseller understands Latin (3.25–26), it may
have been Swift who supplied this advertisement for *A Tale of a Tub*.

title-page.14-15 *Basima . . . camelanthi*: "The Citation out of Irenaeus . . . *which seems to
be all Gibberish,* [is] a Form of Initiation used antiently by the *Marcosian* Heretics . . .
Irenaeus thus interprets them: "*I call upon this, which is above all the Power of the Father,
which is called Light, and Spirit, and Life, because thou hast reigned in the Body*" (Wotton
1705[1], 532; Irenaeus 1885, i.346).

title-page.16–18 *Juvatque novos decerpere flores,/Insignemque meo capiti petere inde
coronam,/Unde prius nulli velarunt tempora Musae* Lucret.: "I love to pick fresh flowers
and to seek a glorious chaplet from fields where the Muses have not yet crowned
anyone" (Lucretius, *De rerum natura*, i.928–30).

2.6 *A Panegyrical Essay upon the Number T H R E E*: "which Word is the only one that
is put in Capitals in that whole *Page*" (Curll 1714, 30).

3. title, line 4 *Sommers*: John Somers, Baron Somers of Evesham, was a Whig
magnate, President of the Royal Society (1699–1704), and "general patron of the
literati" (Swift 1967, 134). Swift defended him in *A Discourse of the Contests and
Dissentions between the Nobles and Commons in Athens and Rome* (October 1701) and when
he dedicated *A Tale of a Tub* to him (c. 1704), he was still expecting employment or
preferment in the Church. But the epistle dedicatory was immediately recognized as
deeply sarcastic. It was a "Pretence of a Dedication" (King 1704, 6) and Edmund Curll
called it "jocose" (Curll 1714, 6). In January 1711 Swift privately dismissed Somers as "a
false deceitful rascal" (Swift 1948, 173) and publicly excoriated him in *The Examiner* (1
February 1711). It has been observed that the dedication to Somers is "couched in the
very rhetoric which Swift is attacking" in *A Tale of a Tub* (Beaumont 1961, 2).

3.2 *Prince*: Prince Posterity (7.title, line 5).

3.23 *DETUR DIGNISSIMO*: "Let it be given to the most worthy', the superlative of
the commonplace, "Detur digniori', "Let it be given to the worthier'.

3.29 *the sublimest Genius of the Age*: Addison inscribed a presentation copy of his
Remarks on Several Parts of Italy (1705) "To Dr. Jonathan Swift . . . the greatest genius of
the age" (Masson 1856, 148). In 1712 Swift mocks "Lord *Sommers*, that great Genius,
who is the Life and Soul . . . of our [atheist] Party" (Swift 1939–68, vi.152).

4.10–11 *those, to whom every Body allows the second Place, have an undoubted Title to the
First*: "each of [the Greek admirals] voted for himself, but most of them gave second
place to Themistocles" (Herodotus, viii.123).

4.18 *Aristides*: In *A Discourse of the Contests and Dissentions* (1701) Swift represents
Somers, Lord Chancellor (1697–1700), as Aristides, "a Person of the strictest Justice,
and best acquainted with the Laws" (Swift 1967, 94).

4.32 *mounting a Breach, or scaling a Wall*: mocking Addison's panegyric *To the King*

(1695), dedicated "To the Right Honourable Sir John Lord Somers" in which "Our *British* Youth [are said to be] . . . Ambitious . . . /Who first shall storm the Breach, or mount the Wall" (Addison 1914, i.19, 42–43; Higgins 1994, 124). Somers however was "something of a Libertine" (Macky 1733, 50), and his "mounting" was exclusively sexual. In one of his exploits he kept "*Bl—t* in Jayle, while he lay with his Wife" (*POAS* Yale, vi.16).

4.39 *Readiness in Favouring deserving Men*: as Lord Chancellor, Somers had the power to confer all ecclesiastical benefices under £20 a year that were in the King's gift (Beatson 1788, i.228).

4.41 *Virtue*: "I allow him to have possessed all excellent Qualifications except Virtue" (Swift 1939–68, v.258).

5.4 *Enemies*: In April 1701 a Tory majority in the House of Commons impeached Somers for his role in the Partition Treaties (1698–1700), William III's secret negotiations with Louis XIV to put Louis' grandson on the Spanish throne. Somers was acquitted and Swift wrote *A Discourse of the Contests and Dissentions* justifying the acquittal (Swift 1967, 48–49, 62–63).

5.5 *they*: all editions read "they" although the antecedent is "the Bright Example".

5.7–8 *adorn the History of a late Reign*: e.g. "[Somers is] a Person of great Parts, Deep Learning, manly Eloquence, easy Address, and a bold Stickler for the Liberties of *England*" (Boyer 1702–03, ii.323); *late Reign*: that of William III (1688–1702).

5.9–11 *as Dedications have run . . . a good Historian will not be apt to have Recourse thither, in search of Characters*: Swift repudiates his panegyric of Somers; *Characters*: the moral and mental qualities that distinguish an individual (*OED*).

title.2 *Bookseller*: the bookseller who bought the manuscript of *A Tale of a Tub* and published it and whom Swift is "personating" is Benjamin Tooke Jr. John Nutt, the trade publisher whose name appears on the title page, undertook to distribute the work (Treadwell 1983, 9, 14).

6.1 *Six Years*: presumably 1699–1704.

6.4 *the second*: *The Battle of the Books*, the occasion for which was the publication of Richard Bentley's *A Dissertation upon the Epistles of Phalaris* in the second edition of William Wotton's *Reflections upon Ancient and Modern Learning* (June 1697; Arber 1903–06, iii.28).

6.8 *a Person, since dead*: Sir William Temple?

6.18 *a surreptitious Copy*: "It is neither to satisfie the importunity of friends, nor to prevent false copies (which and such like excuses I know are expected in usual Prefaces) that I have adventured abroad this following Treatise" (Stillingfleet 1675, sig. b2r).

6.18 *a certain great Wit*: cousin Thomas Swift (Curll 1714, 4n.).

6.19–20 *fitted to the Humor of the Age*: Miguel Cervantes, *The Historie of the most Renowned Don Quixote . . . Now made English according to the Humour of our Modern Language*, tr. John Philips (1687); Troiano Boccalini, *Advertisements from Parnassus . . . Newly Done into English and adapted to the Present Times*, tr. N. N. 3v. (1704); Jean de La Bruyère, *The Characters, or The Manners of the Age*, 3d ed. (1702; Swift 1958, 29.n1).

6.22 *in its Naturals*: "not altered or improved in any way" (*OED*), not "fitted to the Humor of the Age" (6.19–20).

6.22 *a Key*: Edmund Curll published *A Complete Key to the Tale of a Tub* in 1710.

title.3–5 *To . . . Posterity*: the preface to the third volume of Sir Roger L'Estrange's *The Observator* is addressed "To Posterity" (L'Estrange 1684–87, iii.1).

7.1–2 *the Fruits of a very few Leisure Hours, stollen from the short Intervals of a World of Business*: mocking Dr. Richard Blackmore's apology for the first of his five epic poems, "*the Entertainment of my idle hours . . . and* Intervals *that . . . I have had from the* Business *of my* Profession" (Blackmore 1695, sig. c2r).

7n* *The Citation out of Irenaeus*: title-page. Plate 4.

7.18 *our Studies*: Grubstreet publications; *our vast flourishing Body*: "the Writers of and for GRUB-STREET" (23.6).

7.19 *this Person*: Time, the tutor of Posterity.

8.16 *the Center*: of the earth (*OED*).

8.17 *Pipes*: clyster pipes for administering enemas (*OED*).

8.26 *Maire du Palais*: Lord Chamberlain of the Household.

8.27 *hors de Page*: "out of Guardianship" (Sidney 1704, 211n.)

8.36 *Numbers are offered to Moloch*: "they . . . cause their sons and their daughters to pass through the fire to Moloch" (Jeremiah 32.35).

9.3 *Appellant for the Laurel*: candidate to succeed Nahum Tate as poet laureate of England upon the death of William III (March 1702).

9.14–15 *uncontroulable Demonstration*: incontrovertible reasoning.

9.20 *posted fresh upon all Gates and Corners*: new publications were advertized by "pasting up the Title-Pages at the Corners of the Streets" (King 1704, 5).

9.23 *the Memorial of them was lost among Men, their Place was no more to be found*: "the remembrance of them to cease from among men . . . and there was found no place for them" (Deuteronomy 32.26, Revelation 20.11).

9.30–34 *a huge Cloud . . . in the Form of a Bear, another . . . with the Head of an Ass, a third . . . with Claws like a Dragon: and Your Highness should in a Minutes think fit to examine the Truth; 'tis certain, they would all be changed in Figure and Position*: "*Antony*. Sometime we see a clowd thats Dragonish,/A vapour sometime, like a Bear, or Lyon . . . That which is now a Horse, even with a thoght/the Racke dislimes [the cloud wipes out]" (*Antony and Cleopatra*, IV.xiii.12–20; Swift 1958, 35.n4).

10.11 *Translation of Virgil . . . printed in large Folio*: Dryden's *Virgil* (July 1697) was commissioned by the publisher, Jacob Tonson, and sold by subscription in a very pretentious and expensive format, including dedications, prefaces, commendatory verses, notes, postscripts, &c. that Swift parodies in *A Tale of a Tub*; *well bound*: the sheets were delivered to the subscribers *un*bound (Dryden 1956– , vi.846).

10.13 *Tate*: Nahum Tate (1652–1715) graduated B.A. from Trinity College Dublin in 1672 and published his first volume of verse five years later in London. His version of *The Tragedy of King Lear* (1681) ends happily with the marriage of Edgar and Cordelia. He collaborated with Dryden in *The Second Part of Absalom and Achitophel. A Poem* (1682). As poet-laureate he presented William III with "a curious ode" on his forty-ninth birthday (Luttrell 1857, iv.579).

10.17 *Durfey*: Thomas Durfey (1653–1723), who stuttered, was called "Sing-Song *Durfey*." He made up for his diminutive size by a prodigious output of verse: "Some 7953 Songs, 2250 Ballads, and 1956 Catches," not to mention twenty-five comedies that he wrote or adapted for the London stage (Brown 1700, 51; Fidge 1691, 20). To someone who could not believe how badly Durfey wrote, Dryden replied, "*You don't know my Friend* Tom *so well as I do; I'll answer for him, he shall write worse yet*" (Swift 1985, 173).

10.19 *Rymer*: Thomas Rymer (1641–1713), critic and antiquarian, attributed the shortcomings of Elizabethan tragedy to the fact that Aristotle was "so little studied." In his major critical work *A Short View of Tragedy* (1692), he dismissed *Othello* as "a Bloody Farce, without salt or savour" (Rymer 1956, 76, 164); *Dennis*: John Dennis (1657–1716), "A stiff Politish Critick," wrote a reply to Jeremy Collier's *A Short View of the Immorality and Profaneness of the English Stage* (1698) in which he argued that "there is no People on the Face of the Earth, so prone to Rebellion as the *English*" if they are not diverted by plays (Dennis 1939–43, i.167).

10.20 *B—tl–y*: Richard Bentley D.D. (1662–1742), was a Fellow of the Royal Society, and chaplain in ordinary to William III. His "immense Erudition" is no longer in question: he discovered "a new world in the realm of mind" and became the one classical scholar of the late Renaissance whose textual criticism and commentary retain interest today (Brink 1986, 49, 60). The "Squable" with the "Bookseller" came about as the result of Sir William Temple's pronouncement in his essay "Upon Ancient and Modern Learning" that "the oldest Books we have, are still . . . the best" and "the Epistles of *Phalaris* . . . have more Race, more Spirit, more Force of Wit and Genius, than any others I have seen" (Temple 1690, 58–59). Temple's essay unfortunately rekindled the silly Ancient/Modern controversy in England just as it was dying out in France.

The Royal Society in Gresham College, the corporate headquarters of the New Science, which Temple had disparaged in his essay, recruited William Wotton (10.25) to answer Temple. Wotton's *Reflections upon Ancient and Modern Learning* (1694) is more respectful of Temple, a baronet, retired ambassador, and belletrist, than it needed to have been. But for the second edition of *Reflections upon Ancient and Modern Learning* (1697) Wotton recruited his friend, Richard Bentley, to add "A Dissertation upon the Epistles of Phalaris" and Bentley was not respectful of Temple at all. He proved for all time that the epistles of Phalaris, a bloodthirsty Sicilian tyrant of the sixth century B.C., are a forgery of the second century A.D. and that Temple "could neither discover the true Time, nor the true Value of his Authors" (Wotton 1697, ²6).

The so-called Christ Church wits at Oxford somehow found it necessary to defend Temple (who left Cambridge without a degree) by publishing a new edition of Phalaris. This chore was assigned to a seventeen-year-old undergraduate, the Honourable Charles Boyle (who succeeded as the fourth Earl of Orrery in 1703), with the collaboration of his tutors and others. Boyle charged a London bookseller, Thomas Bennet, to procure a collation of the manuscript of Phalaris in the King's Library in St. James's Palace of which Richard Bentley was the Keeper. In his preface to the published edition (1695) Boyle, with all the arrogance of a sciolist, sarcastically referred to Bentley's characteristic courtesy ("pro singulari sua humanitate") in recalling the manuscript of Phalaris before one Gibson had finished the collation (Boyle 1695, sig. a4v). Bentley replied that the manuscript was duly "used and return'd" without "the least suspicion . . . that [Gibson] had not finished the collation" (Bentley 1697, ²67).

10.25 *W–tt–n*: William Wotton, B.D. and F.R.S. (1666–1727), was a child prodigy who read the gospel of St. John in Greek at the age of five. His *Reflections upon Ancient and Modern Learning* (1694) is an important progress report on the New Science at the end of the seventeenth century. He entered the Ancient/Modern controversy because he knew that Temple's "Hypothesis" that "the Learning of the present Age, is only a faint, imperfect Copy from the Knowledge of former Times" (Wotton 1694, 6–7, 9) is wrong. And because Temple's "Hypothesis" is indefensible, Swift turns it into a joke in

The Battle of the Books. Since Wotton really flatters Temple by taking him seriously—his claim that he has "all along taken care not to speak too positively" (Wotton 1697, 374) is just — he cannot understand the violence of Swift's animus against him.

10.25–26 *a good sizeable volume*: Wotton's *Reflections on Ancient and Modern Learning* (1694) runs to 359 pages.

10.26–27 *a Friend*: Temple the Ancient is a friend of Father Time.

10.27–28 *gentlemanly Stile*: 120.28–29.

10.30 *Discoveries equally valuable for their Novelty and Use*: "*sublime Discoveries upon the Subject of Flies and Spittle*" (55.17–18).

10.30 *Yokemate*: half of a married couple (119.3), anticipating the climactic shish kebab, "this pair of Friends transfixed" (121.30).

10.32 *Elogies*: characterizations (*OED*), not elegies or eulogies.

10.32 *cotemporary*: "cotemporary" and "contemporary" were both current at this time (*OED*), but Swift may have chosen "cotemporary" because Bentley had called it "*a downright Barbarism*" (Bentley 1699, lxxxvi).

10.33 *a larger Work*: i.e. "*A Character of the present Set of Wits in this Island*" (2.4).

10.37 *the Universal Body of all Arts and Sciences*: mocking the aim of the Royal Society "to make faithful *Records*, of all the Works of *Nature*, or *Art*" (Sprat 1958, 61).

10.40 *Princes*: schoolboys. Classical texts bowdlerized for classroom use were designated "Ad usum Delphi" ("for the use of the dauphins"; Swift 1994, 203).

12.1 *The Wits of the present Age*: "the Nation was now over run with the Works of the boldest and most learned Advocates for a Republick, such as *Hobbs, Milton, Ludlow, Harrington*, and *Algernon Sidney* . . . whose Title Pages, as it were in Defiance of Monarchy, were publickly affixed to the Gate of the Royal Palace of *Whitehall*" (Boyer 1702–3, iii.290).

12.3 *a long Peace*: if he is writing in "this present Month of *August* 1697" (14.9–10), Swift anticipates the September 1697 signing of the Treaty of Ryswick that ended a nine-year war with France (Luttrell 1857, iv.258, 275). Swift also makes an ironical reflection on the *short* "Intervals of Peace" (Swift 1967, 103) between the "almost . . . perpetual Course . . . either of Civil or of Foreign Wars" (Temple 1690, 64) in England during the past 100 years. The phrase in Juvenal, "We are now suffering the evils of a long peace," is not ironical (*Satires*, vi.292–93).

12.8 *one*: "that great Work," a center for advanced studies with more than eleven schools (12.35–13.11).

12.14–15 *a Grand Committee*: either a committee of the whole House of Lords or Commons, or one of the four standing committees (for religion, grievances, courts of justice, trade) appointed annually by the House of Commons (*OED*, s.v. **Grand**).

12.16–17 *when they meet a Whale, to fling him out an empty Tub*: "to throw out a tub to the whale" is proverbial (Tilley 1950, 688); "if the great Leviathan will be amused by an empty barrel, it is a composition easily made" (Vernon 1841, i.405).

12.20 *all other Schemes of Religion and Government*: the reference is to Chapter 19 of the *Leviathan* (1651), "*Of the severall Kinds of* Common-wealth *by Institution, and of Succession to the Soveraigne Power*" in which Hobbes analyzes the "inconvenience" of every form of government (including the limited monarchy of Britain) except absolute monarchy.

12.22 *Rotation*: James Harrington (1611–1677) disseminated his utopian ideas both in *The Common-Wealth of Oceana* (1656), dedicated to Oliver Cromwell, and in the Rota Club that from November 1659 to February 1660 met at the Turks Head tavern,

Westminster (Lillywhite 1963, 603–4). Upon the Restoration of Charles II he was committed to the Tower but never tried. One of Harrington's radical ideas, "Rotation," or term limits for legislators, has been enacted into law in twenty-two of the fifty United States.

12.23 *The Ship in danger*: "O Navis, referent in mare te novi/fluctus" ("O ship of state, innovations threaten to blow thee out to sea again"; Horace, *Odes*, I.xiv.1–2).

12.28 *apt to fluctuate*: until January 1649 England was a monarchy; until 1654 it was a military dictatorship; until 1658 it was a republic (protectorate); until 1660 it was a military dictatorship; after May 1660 it was a monarchy.

12.32–33 *to employ those unquiet Spirits*: "to fix and settle piercing and volatile Wits" (Montaigne 1700, i.64).

12.35 *a large Academy*: "The Academy set up by Cardinal *Richlieu* [1635], to amuse the Wits of that Age and Country, and divert them from raking into his Politicks and Ministery [sic]" (Temple 1690, 354–55).

12.36 *nine thousand seven hundred forty and three Persons*: "9324 Prelates, *viz.* in every Parish one" (Pagitt 1654, 73).

13.7 *a large Pederastick School*: the "penetrating Reader" (26.2) will observe that Swift is saying that a "large" number of Anglican clergymen are pederasts.

13.8 *the Spelling School*: it is "a difficult Matter to read modern Books and Pamphlets; where the Words are so . . . varied from their original Spelling, that whoever hath been used to plain *English*, will hardly know them by Sight" (Swift 1939–68, iv.12).

13.9 *The School of Swearing*: Richard Bentley's "ill Words" were infamous (Boyle 1698, 11, 289).

13.10 *Salivation*: drooling is symptomatic of the highly toxic mercury treatment for syphilis.

13.11 *Tops*: cf. "Rotation" (12.22); *Spleen*: melancholy or depression; "the spleen," Swift said, "is a disease I was not born to" (Swift 1948, 303).

13.11 *Gaming*: gambling.

13.22–24 *a most ingenious Poet . . . compared himself to the Hangman, and his Patron to the Patient*: the "ingenious Poet" is Dryden, whose alleged "Patron" is George Villiers, 2d Duke of Buckingham; "the Hangman" is Jack Ketch, the alleged executioner of Charles I, whose imagined "Patient" is Buckingham. Dryden wished he could apply to himself what Mrs. Ketch said: "to make a malefactor die sweetly, was only belonging to her husband" (Dryden 1882–93, xiii.98–99).

13.23 *something new*: Buckingham, the character of Zimri in Dryden's *Absalom and Achitophel* (1681) "coud every hour employ,/With something New to wish, or to enjoy!" (Dryden 1956– , ii.21).

13.24–25 *Insigne, recens, [ad huc] indictum ore alio*: "Something extraordinary, new, and as yet unuttered by other lips" (Horace, *Odes*, III.xxv.7–8).

13.35 *fixed*: solidified; "When . . . stupid alchymists . . . try/To fix . . . /This volatile mercury,/The subtil spirit all flies up in fume" (Swift 1937, 49).

14.2 *towardly*: seasonable (*OED*).

14.6 *former*: mentioned before, aforesaid. *Obs.* (*OED*).

14.7–8 *Refiners*: "He that makes a thing too fine breaks it" (Tilley 1950, 636) is a proverb quoted by Sir William Temple: "Few things in the world or none, will bear too much refining, a Thred too fine spun will easily break" (Temple 1690, 304).

14.10–11 *should descend to the very bottom of all the Sublime*: an oxymoron; i.e. should get to the bottom of the highest, the transcendent, which is beyond comprehension.

14.11 *hold*: think, consider (*OED*).

14.19–22 *in Bed... Hunger... a long Course of Physick*: bed rest and a strict diet were prescribed for patients undergoing mercury therapy for a venereal disease.

14.19–20 *a Reason best known to my self*: i.e. "Poxes ill cured" (26.16).

14.30 *Prefaces*: Richard Bentley was attacked for "having so large an Acquaintance . . . with . . . *Prefaces, Prolegomena, Apparatus's, Introductions*, &c." (Boyle 1698, 193).

14.37 *For a Man to set up for a Writer, when the Press swarms with, &c.*: "those intolerable Crowds of Pamphlets, which are every Day obtruded upon us; such a Glut of Verse and Prose, that . . . If a Man sets up for a Poet . . . Destruction is the Word" (Sedley 1702, sig. A3).

14.39 *The Tax upon Paper*: imposed 8 March 1697 (Luttrell 1857, iv.193).

14.39 *the Number of Scriblers, who daily pester, &c.*: "a multitude of Scriblers, who daily pester the World with their insufferable Stuff" (Dryden 1956– , iv.8).

15.4 *SIR, It is meerly in Obedience to your Commands that I venture into the Publick*: "*My motive . . . was principally to comply with the injunctions of a Great Man*" (Polybius 1693, i.sig. a1v).

15.14 *A Mountebank*: a quack selling his medicines on a raised platform (Plate 5).

15.15 *fit*: short period of time (*OED*, Obs).

15.29–30 *Printed in a different Character . . . something extraordinary*: "printed in a distinct Character . . . a certain sign of a Flower" (Marvell 1672–73, i.192).

15.36 *Fee-Simple*: absolute possession (*OED*); *Presentation*: bestowal (*OED*).

15.38 *Elogy*: characterization (10.32).

15.39 *I speak without Vanity*: "without vanity I may own . . ." (Dryden 1956– , xi.322); "I abhorr Vanity" (Boyle 1698, 202).

16.4 *without one grain of Satyr*: Temple deplored satire: "I wish, the Vein of Ridiculing all that is serious and good . . . may have no worse effects"; "Another Vein which has . . . helpt to corrupt our Modern Poesy, is that of Ridicule, as if nothing pleased but what made one Laugh" (Temple 1690, 71, 351).

16.7 *Hors'd*: mounted on someone's back to be flogged (*OED*).

16.17 *Weeds*: "ev'ry stinking weed [dissenting sect] so lofty grows,/As if 'twould overshade the Royal Rose [Church of England]" (Swift 1937, 37) is Swift's justifiably bitter response to the Act of the Scottish Parliament for abolishing Episcopacy (July 1689). Toleration was not granted to Anglicans in Scotland as it had been to Presbyterians in England by the Act of Toleration (May 1689). Episcopal curates in Scotland who did not leave voluntarily were "rabbled" out of their churches and manses (Goldie 1951, 27) and the Presbyterian Kirk became the established Church of Scotland.

16.17–18 *Weeds have the Preeminence*: proverbial: "Weeds overgrow the corn" (Tilley 1950, 716).

16.18–19 *the first Monarch of this Island*: James VI of Scotland (1566–1625) succeeded as James I of England in 1603 and became the self-styled monarch of Britain, although not so recognized by the English Parliament.

16.20 *root out the Roses . . . and plant the Thistles*: James V of Scotland (1512–1542) is credited with instituting a collar for the Order of the Thistle, "and as the Rose was the principal ornament of the Collar of [the Order of] the Garter, a Thistle was made that of the Scottish Collar" (Nicolas 1842, iii.10). The Order of the Thistle was revived by James II in 1687 and again by Queen Anne in 1703.

16.22 *Itch*: cf. 148.5.

16.22–24 *the Satyrical Itch . . . was first brought to us from beyond the Tweed*: Swift mocks Temple, who calls satire "the Itch of our Age" (Temple 1690, 71): it was a xenophobic commonplace that Scottish immigrants brought scabies, or the itch, into England (*POAS* Yale, vi.273).

16.26 *their*: "Satyrists" (16.6).

16.37 *Penyworth*: bargain.

16.39–40 *an ancient Author*: John Dryden?

17.3 *Lethargy*: apoplectic stroke; "This State Lethargy is such an Apoplectic Symptom, as is commonly the Forerunner of Death to the Body Politick" (Davenant 1701, 1).

17.4 *the former*: i.e. satire; cf. 14.6n.

17.11 *Follies and Vices are innumerable*: "The Species of Folly and Vice are infinite" (Swift 1967, 121).

17.13 *the Cardinal Virtues*: justice, prudence, temperance, and fortitude (*OED*).

17.16 *it is all *Pork*: the commonplace is not in Plutarch, but it is in Livy: "a feast of good tame swine . . . and . . . serving it up with divers sauces, hath made all this faire shew" (Livy 1600, 916); "All the variety of his Treat is Pork" (Marvell 1672–73, i.320).

17.29–36 *In the Attick Commonwealth . . . however considerable for their Quality or their Merits*: On the Polity of the Athenians, ii.18, once attributed to Xenophon (Swift 1958, 51.n3).

17.32–33 *Creon . . . Hyperbolus*: "Creon" is a mistake for "Cleon." Cleon and Hyperbolus are giants, mentioned together in Aristophanes, *The Clouds*, 549–51 (Swift 1958, 51.n4).

17.38 *all are gone astray*: "They are all gone aside" (Psalms 14.3).

17.38–39 *there is none that doth good*: "there is none good" (Matthew 19.17).

17.39 *the very Dregs of Time*: the Latin form of the commonplace is *in Romuli faece* ("in the dregs of Romulus") that Swift quotes in *A Discourse of the Contests and Dissentions* (1701; Swift 1967, 126).

17.40–41 *Honesty is fled with Astraea*: Juvenal, *Satires*, vi.19–20.

18.1 *Splendida bilis*: shiny black bile, an imaginary bodily fluid believed to cause manic behaviour, such as that of Orestes when he kills his mother (Horace, *Satires*, II.iii.141).

18.4 *Covent-Garden*: the theatre and red light district of Stuart London.

18.6 *White Hall*: Whitehall Palace was the London residence of English monarchs until it was destroyed by fire in January 1698.

18.6 *Inns of Court*: law schools and lawyers' lodgings.

18.11–12 *starved half the Fleet*: "Sixty or Seventy Thousands [were] Run out [cheated] of their Pay" (Hodges 1695, 3).

18.14 *such a one*: probably Thomas Wharton, 1st Marquis of Wharton (1648–1715). "the greatest rake in England" (*DNB*, xx.1329), author of *Lilli-burlero*, and a Whig magnate.

18.6 *such an Orator*: probably Daniel Finch, Earl of Nottingham (1647–1730), a Tory magnate who defected to the Whigs: "When once he begins, he never will flinch, / But repeats the same Note a whole Day, like a *Finch*" (*POAS* Yale, vii.527).

18.18–19 *Scandalum Magnatum*: slandering magnates; "the Law makes even *Truth* a *Scandal* when publisht for the Defamation of any of our *Peers*" (Davenant 1702, 1).

18.24–25 *A Panegyrick upon the World*: advertized above (2.7).

18.25 *a Second Part*: "a pernicious Kind of Writings, called *Second Parts*" (83.13).

18.26 *A Modest Defence . . . of the Rabble in all Ages*: advertized above (2.10); an ironic surrogate for *A Discourse of the Contests and Dissentions* (1701; Swift 1967, 163).

18.27 *Appendix*: Bentley's *A Dissertation upon the Epistles of Phalaris* is published as an appendix to the second edition of Wotton's *Reflections upon the Ancient and Modern Learning* (1697).

18.30–31 *a certain Domestic Misfortune*: contracting the pox (14.19–22n.).

19.9 *exalted . . . above them*: "For Chiarlatans [quack doctors] can do no good,/Until th'are Mounted in a Crowd" (Plate 5) (Butler 1967, 259).

19.12 *get quit of Number*: to get free of "the multitude, the common herd" (*OED* s.v. **Quit**, a).

19.14 *Evadere . . . labor est*: *Aeneid*, vi.128–29. The translation (55.12–13) is Dryden's (Dryden 1956– , v.532).

19.15–16 *the Philosopher's Way . . . erecting Edifices in the Air*: "To build castles in the air" is proverbial (Tilley 1950, 84); "*Philosophers* build . . . Edifices they call Systems. . . . They lay their Foundations in the Air" (Brown 1720, iii.94).

19.18–19 *Socrates . . . suspended in a Basket to help Contemplation*: "*Strepsiades*. Why in a basket dost thou view the gods? *Socrates*. I could not elevate / My thoughts to contemplation of these mysteries, / Unlesse my Intellect were thus suspended" (Stanley 1656, ³72).

19.23 *North-West Regions*: Britain (47.27).

19.24 *this great Work*: "to be heard in a Crowd" (19.7).

19.29 *Ladder*: which criminals mounted to be hanged and from which they delivered their last words (Plate 8).

19.29 *Stage-Itinerant*: on which touring theatrical companies and quack doctors performed (Plate 5).

20.11 *Senes ut in otia tuta recedant*: "When old they may retire into perfect ease" (Horace, *Satires*, I.i.31).

20.24 *the profound Number THREE*: the literary marketplace was sensitized to the number three by the Trinitarian controversy of 1690–1696, undertaken to determine whether belief in the Holy Trinity, the first of the thirty-nine Articles of Religion of the Church of England, entails "three Minds or Modes, or Properties, or internal Relations, or Oeconomies, or Manifestations, or external Denominations, or else no more than a Holy Three, or Three Somewhats" (Stephens 1696, 20). "The Publick were of Opinion, That the First [Robert South] proved there is but One *God*; and the other [William Sherlock], That there are Three" (*POAS* Yale, vi.105n.). The controversy grew so heated that William III intervened to stop it.

20.26–27 *There is now in the Press . . . a Panegyrical Essay of mine upon this Number*: the Narrator, not Swift, is the author of this notional essay (2.4). But this is one of the "Handles" (Wotton 1705¹, 525) that enabled Swift's political enemies to represent him as "A Man who to please the very worst Men among us, the *Deists, Socinians* [Unitarians], and *Free-Thinkers* . . . has ridicul'd Christianity" ([Mainwaring] 1711, 23).

20.32 *Sylva Caledonia*: literally "Scottish forest"; metaphorically "Presbyterian Kirk."

20.34 *for . . . Reasons to be mentioned*: 22.22–23.

20.37 *uncovered Vessel*: a pun on 1) pulpit (many English pulpits have richly ornamented canopies or baldaquins; those in Scotland are "uncovered," "with little Ornament" (20.36) and 2) head (Quakers did not remove the hat during Meeting; Plate 30), with side glances at 3) phallus (134.32).

20.39 *Influence on human Ears*: phalluses; hanging causes an erection.

21.3 *Publication*: the *early* 1755[H] their *early* 1704–1705. Samuel Smith (1620–1698), chaplain of Newgate prison, monopolized publication of the last dying words of prisoners about to be hanged (Plate 8).

21.5 *John Dunton*: an eccentric and resourceful bookseller (1659–1733) who commissioned Sir William Temple to write a history of England that was never undertaken (Elias 1982, 55–59). Swift's first published work, his "Ode to the Athenian Society" (1692), appeared in a supplement to volume five of *The Athenian Gazette*, a Grubstreet production that Dunton published from 1690 to 1696. It was this poem that provided the occasion for Dryden's apocryphal remark, "Cousin Swift, you will never be a poet" (Johnson 1779–81, viii.12).

21.11 *preferred*: promoted, advanced in status or rank (*OED*).

21.17 *Philosophers*: natural philosophers, scientists; adepts in occult science (*OED*).

21.19 *Air being a heavy Body*: "The notion of the *Air's* weight and spring, hath been so well settled by innumerable Experiments of this present Age [by Galileo, Torricelli, etal.] that hardly any considering Person doth now doubt of it" (*Phil. Trans.* xv (20 May 1685), 1002); "the Atmosphere is a heavy Body" (Boyle 1669, 2).

21.20 *the System of Epicurus*: Epicurus (342–270 B.C.) is a Greek philosopher who established a school in his garden at Athens that became wildly popular. He discarded the ethic and logic of Plato and Aristotle and based his philosophy upon "unreasoning" sensation and ideas (which he imagined as second-hand sensations stored in the memory). His ethic involved withdrawal from business and pursuit of pleasure. His anti-intellectualism and antagonism to experimental science may have appealed strongly to Swift. But Swift ridiculed the Epicurean cosmology – falling atoms collide at random to create everything that exists – which is the subject of Lucretius's *De rerum natura* (1st c. B.C.), a work that Swift read three times in 1697 (Swift 1958, lvi). Sir William Temple withdrew from government business in 1680, laid out his garden at Moor Park, Surrey, and wrote an essay "Upon the Gardens of Epicurus." He gathered about him a coterie that included Swift, his cousin Thomas Swift (Temple's chaplain), and a poet, John Pomfret. Despite Temple's protestations to the contrary, relations between the sexes in his garden "were not entirely what is termed Platonic" (*EB* 1910–11, ix.683; *Modern Philology* 81 (1982), 75).

21.27 *Lucr. Lib. 4*: Lucretius, *De rerum natura*, iv.526–27. The translation is that of Thomas Creech (1682, 118; Swift 1958, 60.n1).

21.31 *parallel to the Horizon, so*: "parallel to the Horizon, [so] that a line through their navel will passe through the Zenith and centre of the earth" (Browne 1646, 179).

22.7 *much upon a Line, and ever in a Circle*: "To raise a spirit in his Mistresse circle" (*Romeo and Juliet*, II.i.24).

22.16 *Type*: "a person, object, or event of Old Testament history, prefiguring some person or thing revealed in the New Testament" (*OED*), as Jonah's delivery from the belly of the whale is a type of Christ's resurrection.

22.20 *Modern Saints in Great Britain*: "them that are sanctified in Christ Jesus, called to be saints" (1 Corinthians 1.2), "the elect under the New Covenant" (Swift 1986, 207).

22.21–22 *as we have said*: 22.22–23.

22.23 *it is the Quality of rotten Wood to give Light in the Dark*: Robert Boyle's experiments in "shining Wood" are reported in *Phil. Trans.* ii (6 January 1668), 581–93; "rotten Wood . . . give[s] light without the help of Reflexions" (Dunton, *The Athenian Gazette* 5 (5 December 1691), Question 7).

22.23 *perorare [conclude] with a Song*: a clergyman arraigned for a felony could claim exemption from trial in the secular courts (and a possible hanging), if he could "sing" his neck verse, the Latin of Psalm 51.

22n.* *Head full of Maggots*: while still an undergraduate at Oxford Samuel Wesley published *Maggots: or, Poems on Several Subjects, never before handled* (1685).

22n.* *burnt*: in September 1697 John Toland's *Christianity not Mysterious* (1696) was cited as blasphemous by a grand jury in Dublin and ordered to be burnt by the common hangman.

22.34 *turn . . . off*: kick the ladder (Plate 8) away, with the hangman's noose already around the culprit's neck (*OED*, s.v. **Turn**, 73).

23.1 *transferring of Propriety*: stealing; plagiarizing.

23.4 *Six-peny-worth of Wit*: perhaps an early version of *Six Pennyworth of Wit; or Little Stories for Little Folks of all Denominations* (1780?) which is an anthology of flat jokes and doggerel verse.

23.4–5 *Westminster Drolleries*: an anthology of popular songs and play songs without music (1671).

23.6 *the Writers of and for GRUB-STREET have . . . triumph'd over Time*: contradicted by 9.16–17.

23.6 *GRUB-STREET*: a street near Bethlem Hospital for the Insane (Bedlam) "much inhabited by writers of small histories, dictionaries, and temporary poems" (Johnson 1755).

23.18 *Gresham*: from its incorporation in 1662 the Royal Society of London held its meetings in Gresham College, an endowed educational institution (84.14–16) founded in 1597 (Plate 9). In March 1665 the Royal Society began publication of *Philosophical Transactions* which, with brief interruptions, continues today; *Will's*: the "Beaux-Esprits" met at Will's Coffee-house in Covent Garden. It was here, at the corner of Russell and Bow streets, that young Alexander Pope thrust himself in to see "the most celebrated wits of that time" presided over by "Mr. Dryden" (Spence 1966, i.29); *edify*: build up (*OED*).

23.29 *Archimedes . . . upon a smaller Affair*: a Greek born in Sicily (c. 287–212 B.C.), Archimedes was the greatest mathematician and engineer of antiquity. His remark about "a *smaller* Affair" is "give me a place to stand and I will move the earth."

24.4 *Briguing*: intriguing, plotting.

24.13–14 *Husks and . . . Harlots*: A reminiscence of the parable of the Prodigal Son [Luke 15.11–32]: "'husks' because Swift thought experimental research useless, and 'harlots' because of the immorality of the stage". Jeremy Collier's *Short View of the Immorality and Profaneness of the Stage* appeared in 1698 (Swift 1958, 65.n2).

24 side note **Virtuoso Experiments, and Modern Comedies*: in Thomas Shadwell's comedy, *The Virtuoso* (1676), Sir Nicholas Gimcrack, the experimental virtuoso, transfuses 64 ounces of sheep's blood into a man who "from being . . . raging mad, became wholly Ovine . . . [and] bleated perpetually" (Shadwell 1927, iii.130).

24.22–23 *Wisdom is a Fox, who after long hunting, will at last cost you the Pains to dig out*: it is suggested that Swift parodies the homiletic style of Scots Presbyterian preachers: "But for thy own bairns, Lord, feed them with the plumdanes [*prunes*] and raisins of thy promises; and e'en give them the spurs of confidence, and boots of hope, that like new spean'd [*weaned*] fillies they may loup [*jump*] over the fold-dikes of grace" (Maybee 1942, 369; Crockatt and Munroe 1748, 117).

24.25 *Sack-Posset*: a restorative made of hot milk, sherry, sugar and spices.

24.28 *'tis a Nut . . . may cost you a Tooth, and pay you with nothing but a Worm*: "[John

Cleveland, the poet] gives us many times a hard Nut to break our Teeth, without a Kernel for our Pains" (Dryden 1956– , xvii.30).

24.31 *Types*: 22.16; *Fables*: "the auncient sages wrapt up the sciences in poeticall fables and misterious allegories" (Temple 1930, 144).

24.34 *Coaches over-finely painted and gilt*: Plate 10.

24.38 *Pythagoras, AEsop, Socrates*: traditionally ugly men.

25.1 *travel in*: to work hard at (*OED*, s.v. **Travail**. v.).

25.6 *Exantlation*: drawing out, as water from a well (*OED*).

25n† *a Latin Edition . . . above an hundred Years old*: the Narrator is "mistaken", *The History of Reynard the Fox* is not a Grubstreet chapbook; Hartmann Schopper's *Opus Poeticum de admirabili fallacia et astutia Vulpeculae Reinekes* (A Poetic Work on the Amazing Deceptiveness and Slyness of Reynard the Fox; Frankfurt, 1567) is anti-Catholic satire (Swift 1958, 67.n2; Plate 11).

25,13–14 *the Apocalyps of all State-Arcana*: Grubstreet cant for "disclosure of all state secrets."

25.15 *several Dozens*: of Grubstreet "Productions" (25.2).

25.18–36 *Tom Thumb . . . The Wise Men of Gotham*: with the exception of Dryden's *The Hind and the Panther* (1687), Roman Catholic apologetics in the form of an expanded beast fable, these are the titles of chapbooks, cheaply printed, crudely illustrated stories, ballads, religious tracts sold by vagrant chapmen (pedlars).

25.20 *Metampsycosis*: transmigration of the soul into a new body after death (*OED*), a tenet of the Pythagorean philosophy. Tom Thumb, one inch tall, is frequently swallowed and vomited up in a parody of metempsychosis.

25.21 *Artephius*: a legendary figure sometimes identified with the 12th century alchemist, Al Toghrâi (Ferguson 1906, i.51). According to Roger Bacon, Artephius's discovery of the Grand Elixir enabled him to live more than 1000 years. He is alleged to have been an ironist, an earlier incarnation of Jonathan Swift perhaps: "he has some-what concealed the main object of the art . . . frequently seeming to say the opposite of what he had said before, wishing to leave to the judgment of the reader, the right way as well as the wrong way [le bon chemin, aussi bien que le mauvais]" (*Philosophie Naturelle* 1682, sig. A2v).

25.22 *an Adeptus*: an alchemist who has discovered the great secret of transmuting base metal into gold (*OED*, s.v. **Adept**).

25.24 *Reincrudation*: "the retrogradation of a substance . . . to a degree of a lower order" (Paracelsus 1894, ii.378).

25.24–25 *the Marriage between Faustus and Helen*: the Faust of folklore, who sells his soul for forbidden knowledge, and the unattainable Helen of Troy first appeared together in print in the Frankfurt *Faustbuch* (1587). *The Judgment of God shewed upon one J. Faustus, Dr. in Divinity*, the English chapbook (from which Helen is expurgated), was published in 1670.

25.25 *dilucidate*; clean up, clarify, explicate; *fermenting*: exciting, inflaming (*OED*); *Male and Female Dragon*: the alchemical figure of two serpents in a circle biting each other's tail "represent the two principles mercury and sulphur, the former winged, as being female and volatile, the latter without wings, as being male and fixed" (James C. Brown, *A History of Chemistry* (Philadelphia, 1913, 161–62).

25.27 *WHITTINGTON and his Cat*: Richard Whittington (d. 1423), third son of William Whittington, was a successful merchant and thrice Lord Mayor of London. It is only in legend that he is a poor scullery boy who invests his cat in a merchant adventure that returns him £300,000.

25.27–28 *Rabbi: Jehuda Hannasi*: Judah Ha-nasi (fl. 200 A.D.) figures in the long process of committing to writing the heretofore orally transmitted Mishnah. Both the Jerusalem and the Babylonian Talmud came to include a Mishnah (civil and ceremonial laws supplementary to the Pentateuch) and a Gemara (interpretation of the Mishnah). Judah Ha-nasi's redaction of the Babylonian Mishnah became canonical, but he was not "Mysterious," i.e. a Rosicrucian. The Babylonian Gemara (c. 600 A.D.) became more popular because it is more detailed than the Jerusalem Gemara (c. 450 A.D.) (Nugel and Freimark 1973, 3). Swift "personates the Style and Manner" (142.23) of Richard Bentley.

25.32 *Scotus to Bellarmin*: John Duns Scotus (c.1266–1308), a scholastic philosopher; Robert Cardinal Bellarmine (1542–1621), a Catholic apologist, like Dryden.

25.33 *TOMMY POTTS*: a chapbook version of the Fair Rosamund legend. The grain of sense amid the nonsense is the invidious attribution of the chapbook to Dryden as a "Supplement" to *The Hind and the Panther* (1687). The "Supplement" may be Dryden's epilogue to John Bancroft's *Henry the Second, King of England; with the Death of Rosamund* (1692).

25.35 *The Wise Men of Gotham*: a joke book attributed without evidence to Dr. Andrew Boorde (c. 1490–1544). "Wise" is ironical; "the Mad Men" of the usual title do stupid things in the manner of Struwwelpeter; *cum Appendice*: if Wotton's *Reflections upon Ancient and Modern Learning* (1694) is "An Abstract" (26.3) of *The Wise Men of Gotham*, then Bentley's *A Dissertation upon the Epistles of Phalaris*, &c., appended to the second edition of Wotton's *Reflections upon Ancient and Modern Learning* (1697), becomes the "Appendix" to a joke book.

26.6 *the whole Work*: 25.1–2.

26.10–11 *Pro's and Con's upon Popish Plots*: a plot in 1679 to assassinate Charles II, burn London, restore Catholicism to England and James II to the throne, was largely a fabrication of Titus Oates (1649–1705). Having first defended the reality of the Plot in *The Character of a Popish Successour* (1681), Elkanah Settle turned around and exposed it as "some deform'd Hagg . . . [who] having danced too long . . . is forced to withdraw; where after laying by her false Curls, her false Teeth, and her Glass Eye . . . ee'n goes to Bed, and is just now falling asleep" (Settle 1683; 25; cf. Swift 1937, 580–83; Cormick 1972, 157).

26.11 *Meal-Tubs*: another Catholic plot (1679) to assassinate Charles II and Anthony Ashley Cooper, Earl of Shaftesbury, was largely the fabrication of Thomas Dangerfield (c.1650–1685). Evidence of the plot was found in the meal tub of Elizabeth Cellier, "the Popish midwife"; *Exclusion Bills*: the reference may be to three bills in Parliament (1679–81) to exclude Catholic James, Duke of York, from succeeding his brother, Charles II, or to the Test Act of 1673, which excluded dissenters from places in the government or military: "Have they [Anglican clergy] not long since got their Bill of Exclusion to be passed into a Law whereby no Man can enjoy a Place of Profit or Trust in the State, but whom they qualify at their Altars?" (Stephens 1696, 22).

26.11–12 *Passive Obedience*: in the last years of the reign of Charles II, high-flying Anglican clergymen revived the principles of *jure divino* and non-resistance: if the authority of the king derives from God (*jure divino*), he is answerable only to God and it is sinful to resist him in any way.

26.12 *Addresses of Lives and Fortunes*: addresses to the throne, whether signed by local grand juries, justices of the peace, or territorial magnates, were attempts to exert popular pressure on the royal prerogative. After 27 May 1679 when Charles II prorogued Parliament to prevent passage of the first Exclusion Bill, the *London Gazette* was flooded with "loyal" addresses urging the King to convene Parliament. They were opposed by addresses of abhorrence, deploring interference in the royal prerogative and offering to stand by the King with their lives and fortunes. "'Tis a poor Address," John Oldmixon observes, "that has not *Lives* and *Fortunes* in it" (Oldmixon 1709–11, i.8).

26.18–19 *my Nose and Shins*: the Narrator's saddle nose and ulcerated shins are symptoms of mercury therapy, not of venereal disease (Abraham 1948, 155–56).

26n[†] *L'Estrange, Dryden*: 142.25.

26.23 *a Conscience void of Offence*: "I [Paul] exercise myself, to have a conscience void of offence toward God, and toward men" (Acts 24.16; Swift 1720, 45).

26.31 *this Treatise*: *A Dissertation upon the Principal Productions of Grub-street* (2.5; 25.1–2).

27.2–3 *Titles . . . that Humor of multiplying them*: Thomas Fuller's *The Church-History of Britain* (1655) has thirteen title-pages (Swift 1958, 72.n1). Dryden's *Virgil* (1697) was published by subscription. There were 101 subscribers who paid five guineas to have a full-page engraving emblazoned with their coat of arms; the names of 240 "second subscribers" were simply printed.

28.2 *Once upon a Time*: "*the common old Wives introduction*" (Swift 1720, 47).

28.1* *a Man who had Three Sons . . . upon his Death-Bed . . . spoke . . . of . . . Legacies to bequeath*: "a Lord and his Three Sons . . . his . . . Legacy to them upon his death-bed" (Plate 12).

28.10 *fresh and sound*: "Thy raiment [in the Wilderness] waxed not old upon thee" (Deuteronomy 8.4; Wotton 1705[2], 49).

28.13 *wear them clean*: "be clean, and change your garments" (Genesis 35.2).

28n* *Martyn*: Martin represents Martin Luther (58n*) and "*the* Church *of* England" (28n*).

28n[†] *An Error . . . of the learned Commentator. Lambin*: "evidently written by Swift" (Swift 1958, 73.n2); the "Commentator" is Wotton; Denis Lambin (Dionysius Lambinus; 1516–72), the great classical scholar of his age, is a type of Richard Bentley. The verb *lambiner*, to dawdle, or trifle, was coined to describe Lambinus's scholarship.

28n[¶] *The New Testament*: implicit is the Protestant belief that "*the Doctrine and Faith of* Christianity" (28n[†]) is contained only in the New Testament, the Christian writers of the first five centuries being supererogatory (Swift 1994, 217).

28n[†] *by the Coats are meant the Doctrine and Faith of Christianity*: "Religion . . . *you have brought to be no more than an* Old Coat" (Gildon 1709, sig. A7r).

28.20 *the Story says*: the first indication that *A Tale of a Tub* is assumed to be pre-written and that the Narrator is retelling an old story, or plagiarizing from "Authors of that Age" (29.23) and padding it out with digressions.

28.26 *Gyants . . . Dragons*: "The enemys of Christianity, & Hereticks" (Swift 1734, 50n).

28.27 *producing themselves*: cf. "young stagers in Divinity, upon their first producing themselves into the World" (Swift 1939–68, ii.46–47).

29.5 *the Watch*: every ward in London appointed old men to patrol the streets and call out the hours of the night. Armed only with a pole and a bell, they were subject to attack by "scowrers" (89.6) and drunks; *Bulks*: low wooden sheds projecting from the front of shops, on which prostitutes occasionally conducted their business.

29.7 *Bayliffs*: officers of justice who served arrest warrants (*OED*).

29.8 *Locket's*: Adam Locket was proprietor of a fashionable "ordinary" (dining place) in Spring Garden, Whitehall (Lillywhite 1963, 337).

29,12 *sub dio*: in broad daylight, out of doors. If the fashionable brothers think that levees are held out of doors, they have not attended a levee; *a Goose*: a pun on 1) the proverbial silly goose (Tilley 1950, 270), and 2) the gooseneck handle of the tailor's smoothing iron.

29,24 *Tenents*: obsolete form of "tenets," beliefs held by a political party or religious sect (*OED*).

29.32 *Jupiter Capitolinus*: cackling of the geese in the temple of Jupiter at Rome enabled Marcus Manlius to put to rout a surprise attack by the Gauls in 390 B.C. Thereafter a gorgeously arrayed goose was annually borne in procession as "a subaltern Divinity" (29.37).

29.33 *Hell*: Hudibras's squire, Ralpho, "by Birth a Taylor," had "seen hell" (Butler 1967, 14–15), a place under the tailor's cutting table where scraps of cloth are thrown.

29.37–38 *Deus minorum Gentium*: "a god of the Gentiles."

29.38 *that Creature*: "to prick a louse" is to be a tailor (*OED* s.v. **Louse**, sb.).

30.2 *Cercopithecus*: a long-tailed, lice-eating monkey, worshipped in Thebes (Juvenal, xv.4).

30.5 *Yard*: 1) a wooden spar (yard-arm) on which square sails are furled; 2) the tailor's measuring rod, 3) its "mystical Attribute" (30.6); the phallus, supporting a further pun on "Seamen" (30.5)/semen.

30.8–9 *the Universe . . . a large Suit of Cloaths, which invests every Thing*: "The World is . . . compassed about with a coat" (Stanley 1687, 764).

30.11 *Primum Mobile*: in the Ptolemaic universe, the outermost celestial sphere whose turning turns everything else (*OED*).

30.12–17 *What is that which some call Land, but a fine Coat faced with Green . . . and what a fine Doublet of white Satin is worn by the Birch*: "What is the *Heart*, but a *Spring* . . . and the *Joynts*, but so many *Wheeles*" (Hobbes 1935, xviii).

30.13 *Water-Tabby*: watered (iridescent) silk (*OED* s.v. **Tabby**).

30.17–18 *what is Man himself but a Micro-Coat*: "Man is the Microcosme" (*Phil. Trans.* xi (25 March 1676), 553; Starkman 1950, 68n).

30.21–22 *Religion a Cloak*: "no Man is esteemed . . . who wears Religion otherwise than as a *Cloak*" (South 1692–94, i.439).

30.22 *Surtout*: an overcoat (*OED*).

30.23 *Conscience a Pair of Breeches*: "Linnen Breeches signifie Chastity" (Mather 1685, 651).

30.25 *Postulata*: premises.

30n* *Microcosm . . . as Man hath been called by Philosophers*: "PHILOSOPHERS say, that Man is a Microcosm" (Swift 1939–68, i.246).

31.1 *Lawn*: a kind of fine linen of which the sleeves of bishops' robes are made (*OED*).

31.3 *These Professors*: "The Worshippers of this [tailor] Deity" (30.7).

31.6 *the Soul was the outward*: "the soule of this man is his cloathes" (*All's Well that Ends Well*, II.v.49).

31.7 *ex traduce*: the traditional view held that a new soul is created *ab utero* at birth; traducianists maintained that the soul was transmitted from the parents *ex traduce* at the moment of conception (*OED* s.v. **Traduction**); the traditional view creates a problem: "if every man hath a new Soul infus'd into him at birth by God, and not lineally descended to him from Adam . . . how then can they [sic] be guilty of, or suffer for Original Sin?" (Blount 1679, 25).

31.8 *daily . . . Circumfusion*: the body is encompassed about or circumfused with clothing in the daily act of dressing (*OED*).

31.8–9 *in Them we . . . have our Being*: "in him [God] we live, and move, and have our being" (Acts 17.28).

31.10 *All in All, and All in every Part*: proverbial (Tilley 1950, 8); "it is a plain *contradiction* in natural discourse, to say of the soul of man, that it is *tota in toto, et tota in qualibet parte corporis*, grounded neither upon Reason nor Revelation" (Hobbes 1650, sig. E8r).

31.16 *Sheer wit*: "This Scene will make you die with laughing . . . it is a Scene of sheer Wit, without any mixture" (Buckingham 1672, 21).

31.18 *Delicatesse*: delicacy (*OED*).

31.23 *Race*: "This is like Sr W. Temple" (Wotton 1704?, 62); Temple introduced this meaningless oenological term into literary criticism: "I think the Epistles of *Phalaris*, to have more Race . . . than any others I have ever seen, either ancient or modern" (Temple 1690, 59).

31.39 *not to add to, or diminish*: "ye shall not add unto the word which I command you, neither shall ye diminish ought from it" (Deuteronomy 4.2; Swift 1994, 219).

32.1 *all of a Piece*: F. *tout d'une pièce*; after 28.29–30 the style is Frenchified, mocking Sir William Temple, who "affects the use of *French* words, as well as some Turns of Expression peculiar to that Language" (Boyer 1714, 422).

32.3 *Shoulder-knots*: large knots of ribbon or lace, worn on one shoulder, were introduced from France c.1670 (Planché 1876–79, i.462).

32.4 *Ruelles*: literally the space between the bed and the wall; boudoirs where ladies of fashion held morning receptions (*OED*).

32.8–9 *the Twelve-peny Gallery*: 22.13.

32.9 *first Sculler*: scullers, plying only one oar on the Thames, cost only half of what a pair of oars cost; the *first* sculler was the next in line to receive a passenger; *the Rose*: a tavern next door to the Theatre Royal in Covent Garden (Lillywhite 1963, 487).

32.14 *Temper*: middle course, compromise (*OED*).

32.18 *totidem verbis*: in just so many words.

32.19–20 *inclusivè, or totidem syllabis*: included in the whole will, or in just so many syllables.

32.25–26 *tertio modo, or totidem literis*: by a third way, or in just so many letters.

32.43 *in Terminis*: according to the terms (of the Will).

33.8 *in Q.V.C. . . . K*: "in certain old manuscripts sometimes spelled with a 'K,'" mocking Bentley's scholarship.

33.13 *Jure Paterno*: "by paternal right"; recalling *jure divino*, "by divine right," and mocking the high-flying Anglican priests who claimed that the Stuarts' right to the throne derived, not from English law, but from God alone, whereas William III was only a "Parliamentary" king.

33.25 *altum silentium* [recte: *alta silentia*]: "deep silence" (*Aeneid*, x.63).

33.25–26 *circumstantial*: unimportant (*OED*).

33.27 *aliquo modo essentiae adhaerere*: somehow adheres in the essence.

33.29 *Aristotelis Dialectica . . . de Interpretatione*: there is no work of Aristotle entitled *Dialectica*. Swift may refer to a Latin anthology of Aristotle's works on logic. *De interpretatione*, probably by Aristotle, is about language and thinking.

33.33–34 *duo sunt genera, Nuncupatory and scriptory*: there are two kinds: oral and written.

33.34–36 *that in the Scriptory Will . . . there is no . . . Mention about Gold Lace, conceditur: But, si idem affirmetur de nuncupatorio, negatur*: "that there is no mention of gold lace in the New Testament is conceded. But if the same is affirmed of the oral tradition, it is denied"—a parody of the style of scholastic debate in Latin practised in schools and colleges.

33.36 *we heard a Fellow say . . . that he heard my Father's Man say, that he heard my Father say*: "Tradition" (Wotton 1704?, 67).

34.6–7 *Flame-Coloured Satin*: "the *Fire of Purgatory*, and that Custom which hath arisen from it of praying for *the Dead*" (Curll 1714, 10). Curll also cites the relevant passage in the Apocrypha: "if he had not hoped that they that were slain should have risen again, it had been superfluous and vain to pray for the dead" (2 Maccabees 12.44).

34.8–9 *My Lord C——*: Sir John Conway, 2d Bart. (c. 1663–1721; Wotton 1704?, 68), was a Tory M.P. for Flintshire and a "scowrer" (89.6): with "some others, rambling in the night, [they] fell upon the watch and beat them severely" (Luttrell 1857, ii.238). In 1696 he refused to sign the Association to defend William III after the assassination attempt; *Sir J. W.*: Sir John Walter, 3d Bart. (c.1673–1722; Wotton 1704?, 68), was "an honest drunken fellow" (Swift 1948, 374) and a Tory M.P. for Appleby and Oxford city.

34.20 *a Codicil annexed*: "Apocriphal writings" (Wotton 1704?, 69).

34.24 *written by a Dog-keeper*: the apocryphal Book of Tobit purports to be "the words of Tobit," but the "Dog-keeper" is his son, Tobias: Raphael the angel and Tobias "went forth both and the young man's dog with them" (Tobit 5.16).

35.2 *Fringe*: Charles II wore a waistcoat [vest] with gold fringe (Planché 1876–79, i.193).

35.8 *the Brother*: Peter, the brother so "well Skill'd in Criticisms," personates the pedantic "Style and Manner" of Richard Bentley (Wotton 1705[2], 53).

35.10–11 *Fringe, does also signify a Broom-stick*: mocking "the *Romanists* frivolous Distinction of *latría* and *douleía*" (Curll 1714, 10); *latría* is worship due to God alone (*OED*); the distinction is introduced by Augustine (*City of God*, 10.1).

35.15 *understood in a Mythological, and Allegorical Sense*: "Transubstantiation" (Wotton 1704?, 70).

35.18 *one that spoke irreverently of a Mystery*: the grand jury of Middlesex presented John Toland's *Christianity not Mysterious* (1696) as scandalous, "tending to prove that the Trinity, &c. may be comprehended by reason" (Luttrell 1857, iv.226–27). "The Author [whom Wotton assumed to be Sir William Temple] . . . copies from Mr. *Toland*, who always raises a Laugh at the Word *Mystery*, the Word and Thing whereof he is known to believe to be no more than a *Tale of a Tub*" (Wotton 1705[2], 53).

35.18–20 *a Mystery . . . ought not to be over-curiously pryed into*: "If you explain them, they are Mysteries no longer" (Swift 1939–68, ix.77).

35.24 *Indian Figures*: "Image worship" (Wotton 1704?, 71).

35n* *The Allegory here is direct, W. Wotton*: Wotton 1705[2], 53.

35.40 *W. Wotton*: Wotton 1705[2], 53–54.

36.5 *Will*: "The Bible" (Wotton 1704?, 72). Wotton is wrong. Swift's note reads "The New Testament" (28n[1]).

36.8–9 *Points . . . tagg'd with Silver*: *literally*: laces tipped with metal for attaching hose to doublet; *allegorically*: "Doctrines that promote the . . . Wealth of the [Catholic] Church" (59n*).

36.9–10 *ex Cathedrâ*: in canon law the Pope is infallible when speaking *ex cathedra* (from the papal throne).

36.14 *totidem verbis*: 32.18.

36.15 *Multa absurda sequerentur*: "many logical absurdities result."

36.22 *Practice*: scheming in an underhand way and for an evil purpose (*OED*).

36.23 *contriving a Deed of Conveyance*: "Thus the Pope, upon the decease of the duke of Ferrara without lawful issue, seized the dutchy, as falling to the holy see, *jure divino*" (Swift 1808, ii.258n.).

37.4–5 *Rules . . . laid down by . . . Moderns*: "pedantry of rules" (Swift 1937, 46).

37.19–21 *Persons as invented or drew up Rules . . . by observing which, a careful Reader might be able to pronounce upon the productions of the Learned*: "formerly [critics] . . . were Defenders of Poets, and Commentators on their Works: to Illustrate obscure Beauties; to place some passages in a better light, to redeem others from malicious Interpretations" (Dryden 1956– , iv.364).

37.26 *Edenborough Streets*: chamberpots in Edinburgh were emptied into the streets at night with the warning "Gardyloo," for, as Boswell observes, there were "no covered sewers" in Edinburgh (Boswell 1961, 11).

37.34 *Judge*: recalling the homicidal George Jeffreys, 1st Baron Jeffreys of Wem (1644–1689), who presided over the Bloody Assizes after the Duke of Monmouth's defeat at Sedgmoor (July 1685).

37.36–37 *Restorers of Antient Learning*: "to [the first critics] we owe the Editions of all the antient Authors . . . [and] the restoring of the old Copies, maimed with Time or Negligence" (Temple 1701, 257).

38.3 *Momus*: the son of Night by parthenogenesis, Momus criticizes the other gods: Venus's feet make too much noise when she walks, and thus becomes the progenitor of Modern critics.

38.3–4 *Hybris . . . Zoilus . . . Tigellius*: Hybris is pride, "Sufficiency" (Temple 1690, 53); Zoilus was the scourge of Homer; Tigellius attacked Horace.

38.5 *B—tl-y . . . Dennis*: Bentley (10.20) demonstrated that Sir William Temple's much-admired and "most Ancient" Epistles of Phalaris were in fact "Supposititious, and of no very long Standing" (Bentley 1697, 6); *Rymer* (10.19); *Wotton* (10.25); *Perrault*: Charles Perrault (1628–1703) was a lawyer, bureaucrat, poet, architect, and writer of fairy tales. To flatter Louis XIV he wrote *Le Siècle de Louis le Grand* (1687), arguing the superiority of modern French notables to their ancient counterparts, which precipitated the Ancient/Modern controversy. Boileau and Racine laughed at Perrault's poem, but Bernard Le Bovier de Fontenelle (1647–1757) defended him in "Une Digression sur les anciens et les modernes" (1688), which in turn precipitated Sir William Temple's "An Essay upon Ancient and Modern Learning" (1696); *Dennis* (10.19).

38.10 *Heroick Virtue*: heroic virtue got a bad press in Milton's *Paradise Lost* (1674), xi.690–97, and in Jeremy Collier's *Essays upon Several Moral Subjects* (1697), [2]5–6.

38.13 *Giants and Dragons*: 28.26; is the Narrator, who has a "peculiar Honour" for Aeolists (71.33), saying that the three Christian brothers were "a greater Nuisance to Mankind, than any of those Monsters they subdued" (38.13–14)?

38.17 *Hercules*: "The image of William III as Hercules was . . . ubiquitous in . . . [the] iconography of the period" (Higgins 1994, 68). Swift may be suggesting that William should immolate himself as Hercules did on Mt. Oeta in Thessaly.

38.27–28 *the proper Employment of a True Antient Genuin Critick*: "truly great Criticks

... have taken as much Pains ... to expose Authors ... as ever others did to praise them" (Wotton 1694, 318–19).

38.29 *hunt those Monstrous Faults*: "A Modern CRITICK ... Reads an Author in search of his *Faults*" (Ward 1698–1700, X.4).

38.29–32 *Cacus ... Hydra's Heads ... Augeas's Dung ... Stymphalian Birds*: subduing the Hydra, a monster with nine heads, mucking out the stables of King Augeas, and exterminating the man-eating birds in the swamp of Stymphalus in Arcadia, are three of the twelve labours of Hercules. Disposing of Cacus, a monster with only three heads, is non-canonical (Virgil, *Aeneid*, viii.194).

38.34–35 *a True Critick ... is a Discoverer and Collector of Writers Faults*: "By a *Critick*, was originally understood a *good Judge*; with us now-a-days, it signifies no more than a *Fault-finder*" (La Bruyère 1706, 5).

38.37 *Sect*: class; profession (*OED, Obs.*).

39.19–20 *turn ... over Night and Day*: "exemplaria Graeca / nocturna versate manu, versate diurna" (turn over Greek models night and day) (Horace, *Ars poetica*, 268–69; Swift 1958, 96.n1).

40.4 *Mythology*: a narrative having a hidden meaning, like Aesop's fables; *Hieroglyphick*: having a hidden meaning, like Egyptian hieroglyphics. The Rosetta Stone that made it possible to decipher hieroglyphics was discovered in 1790.

40.11–41.12 *It well deserves ... taetro consueta necare*: in his genealogy of "the True Critick" (40.2) Swift "personates the Style and Manner" (142.23) of Richard Bentley.

40.22–24 *the Nauplians ... fairer Fruit*: "the ass ... by nibbling ... the shoots of a vine ... caused a more plenteous crop of grapes" (Pausanias, *Description of Greece*, ii.38; Swift 1958, 98.n2).

40.22 *Argos* 1755[H] *Argia* Σ.

40.24 *Herodotus*: "*in the Western Part of* Libya, *there were* ASSES *with* HORNS" (Herodotus, *History*, iv.191) which Swift converts into a pun on 1) critics armed with quill pens and inkhorns, and 2) cuckolds.

40.25 *in terminis*: in clear text, not in hieroglyphics.

40.29 *Ctesias*: a 5th c. B.C. Greek historian whose *Persica*, a history of Assyria and Persia in 23 books, survives mainly in extracts by Photius and Diodorus Siculus.

40.30–32 *whereas all ... extream Bitterness*: Photius 1824, i.48–49; Swift 1958, 98.n4.

40.33–34 *those Antient Writers treated this Subject only by Types and Figures*: "*the Wisdom of the Ancients has been still* [always] *Wrapt up in* Veils *and* Figures" (L'Estrange 1708, sig. A4r; Rosenheim 1963, 80).

40.38–39 *a vast army ... put to flight ... by the Braying of an ASS*: Herodotus, *History*, iv.129; Swift 1958, 99.n1).

40.40 *Philologers*: scholars, humanists (*OED*).

41.1 *Scythian Ancestors*: from the linguistic coincidence, L. *Skythia*, Gk. *Skothia* (69.11), Sir William Temple concluded that the original Scots were Scythians. These Asiatic tribes (usually called "hordes") drove out the Cimmerians from the steppes north of the Black Sea and established an empire that lasted from the 7th to the 2d century B.C.: "*Scyths* ... [by] an easie Change of the word, were called *Scots*" (Temple 1695, 22).

41.6 *Diodorus*: "may be a slip for Dicaearchus" (Swift 1958, 99.n3). But Dicaearchus of Messenia does not say that a weed on Mt. Helicon is fatal to those who smell it. He says that a shrub on Mt. Pelion is fatal to snakes that smell it (*Fragmenta historicorum Graecorum* (c.1841–70, ii.261–62; Swift 1958, 100.n1).

41.12 *Floris odore hominem taetro consueta necare*: "[Trees] whose *Blossoms* with their *Odor* kill." The translator (Creech 1682, 20) omits "tetro," foul (odours); both authoritative editions of the text, accidentally (Swift 1958, 100.n1) or deliberately (Paulson 1960, 118–19), read "retro," backside (odours), flatulence.

41.13–14 *Ctesias . . . used with much severity*: "*Ctesias*, whom *Aristotle . . .* branded for a Lyar" (Wotton 1705², 42–43).

41.14–20 *Among the rest . . . Brains flie out of his Nostrils*: Photius 1824, i.47; Swift 1958, 100.n4.

41.20 *Serpent that wants Teeth*: "Salamander Ld Cutts" (Wotton 1704?, 85). John Cutts (1661–1707), created Baron Cutts of Gowran, Ireland in 1690, was a poet, an authentic hero of William's wars, and a Whig M.P. "Swift's scurrilous invective against a brave man [in "The Description of a Salamander" (1705)] is inexcusable" (Swift 1937, 82).

41.26-27 *in specie*: in kind.

41.39–42 *Hemp . . . is bad for Suffocations*: both the hangman's noose and marijuana derive from *Cannabis sativa*; "Let not Hempe his Wind-pipe suffocate" (*Henry V*, III.vi.45). The Scythians burned hemp in censers in religious ceremonies.

42.1 *taken but in the seed*: "a young hemp" is destined to be hanged (*OED*).

42.4 *Malevoli*: Terence (c. 195–159 B.C.) refers to his critics as *malevoli* [enemies]; Terence, i.6, 118; Swift 1958, 101.n1).

42.7 *Themistocles*: when taunted by media types, Themistocles admitted that "He could not tune a lyre or play the harp, but he could make a small town [Athens] into a great and glorious city" (Plutarch, *Themistocles*, ii.3; Swift 1958, 101.n2).

42.14 *Hell*: 29.33–37; *Goose*: 29.31.

42.17 *the Composition of a Man*: "Nine tailors make a man" (Tilley 1950, 649); *Valour*: the tailor pressed by Falstaff is Francis Feeble (*2 Henry IV*, III.ii.150).

42.18 *Weapons*: the tailor's goose (29.31) and the critic's goose quill pen.

42.19 *the first*: "a *True Critick* is . . . set up . . . at as little Expence as a Taylor" (42.11–13).

42.20 *Layings out*: expenditures; *free*: admitted to the privileges of a corporation or guild (*OED*).

42.29–30 *Works . . . entirely lost*: "*Pedant's* Character . . . Quoting Books . . . not extant . . . As* Aristotle *says in his lost Treatise of the* Sicilian *Government*" (Boyle 1698, 98).

42.36 *sine Mercurio*: without mercury, punning on 1) mercury amalgam as a backing for mirrors, 2) mercury as wit (13.35), and 3) mercury therapy for syphilis.

44.6–7 *to take mightily upon him*: the Pope "taking to himself the Title of . . . *Dominus Dominorum*" (Curll 1714, 12).

44.16 *a Better Fonde*: a larger supply; "This *Fond* being not sufficient in times of Wars" (Temple 1673, 106).

44.17 *Projector*: inventor, promoter, "operator."

44.17 *virtuoso*: a gentleman scientist (Starkman 1950, 72).

44.19 *Lord Peter's Invention*: "The Romish Doctrine concerning Purgatory, Pardons, Worshipping and Adoration, as well of Images, as of Reliques, and also Invocation of Saints, is a fond [foolish] thing, vainly invented, and grounded upon no warranty of Scripture, but rather repugnant to the word of God" (*Book of Common Prayer* 1704, sig. P12v).

44.24 *without Vanity*: 15.39.

44.27 *Academies abroad*: the Académie Française was founded in 1634 in Paris; the Accademia del Cimento in 1657 in Florence.

44.34–35 *a Large Continent*: "Purgatory" (Wotton 1704?, 94); "the fear of Hell was abated by the invention of Purgatory" (Hascard 1683, 3).

44.35 *Terra Australis incognita*: although the west coast of Australia had been charted by Dutch sailors, the whole subcontinent was still unexplored at the end of the 17th century. William Dampier, Lemuel Gulliver's "Cousin," surveyed the west coast in 1688 and published *A New Voyage round the World* in 1697.

44.36 *Penny-worth*: bargain.

45.3–4 *again, and again, and again, and again*: as long as they could pay for masses for the dead, Papists could be sure that their dead loved ones were in Purgatory, not in Hell.

45.5–6 *Sovereign Remedy for the Worms*: satirizing 1) the ease with which relief for the gnawing of the "Worm" of conscience is secured in the confessional booth, and 2) the false claims of quack medicines, with the further implication that the "remedies" of the confessional booth are quack remedies.

45.6 *the Spleen*: 1) clinical depression; 2) a fashionable psychosomatic disease that "only seizeth on the *Lazy*, the *Luxurious*, and the *Rich*" (Swift 1939–68, xi.248).

45.13 *Whispering Office*: "Auricular Confession" (Wotton 1705[2], 55).

45.14 *Hypochondriacal*: melancholia, thought to be caused by vapours arising from the spleen.

45.16 *Repeating Poets*: who recite their own verses.

45.18 *An Ass's Head*: a priest hearing confession.

45.22 *Eructation or Expiration, or Evomition*: belching, exhaling, or vomiting (*OED*).

45.23–24 *Office of Ensurance*: indulgence slips by which sins could be remitted, as sold by Chaucer's Pardoner, are transmogrified into insurance policies. The discovery by Pope Sixtus (1476) that indulgence slips were equally effective for the dead, greatly increased sales. It was Martin Luther's opposition to the sale of an indulgence proclaimed by Pope Leo X that precipitated the 95 theses, nailed to the church door at Wittenberg in November 1517, from which the Protestant Reformation traditionally takes its origin.

45.26 *Friendly Societies*: (in the singular) the name of a particular fire insurance company founded in 1684; otherwise the generic name for various fire-, health-, or burial-insurance societies.

45.29–30 *Puppets and Raree-Shows; the great Usefulness whereof*: Swift to his cousin Deane Swift in Portugal, June 1694: "your [religious] Processions . . . have good Effects, to quiet common Heads, and infuse a gaping Devotion among the Rabble" (Swift 1963–65, i.15).

46.2 *Common Pickle*: 1) two parts vinegar and one part salt brine, 2) holy water.

46.11 *Pimperlim pimp*: 1) consecrated salt, an ingredient in holy water. "Holy-water differs only in Consecration from Common Water" (Wotton 1705[2], 55); 2) a magical powder of great potency: "Here are the Rarities of [Bartholemew] Fair, /Pimperle-Pimp and the wise Dancing Mare" (Anony. 1691, ii.39).

46n* *W. Wotton*: the "penetrating Reader" (26.2) will observe that Wotton's footnote merely repeats the text and explains nothing (Staley 1979, 167).

46.12 *Spargefaction*: sprinkling (*OED*).

46.16 *scall'd Heads*: ringworm.

46.17 *never hindring . . . at Bed or Board*: "*Dr. Kirleus* . . . hindring no business, undertakes to cure all Ulcers, Sores, Scabs, Itch, Scurf, Leprosies, and *Venereal Disease*" (*The Flying Post*, No. 281 (27 February–2 March 1697), verso). Jonathan Swift Sr. had the itch (Pilkingon 1997, i.31).

46.18 *Bulls*: a papal bull or edict, has a leaden seal or *bulla* (L. bubble) attached to it by a ribbon. Elizabeth I was excommunicated by a papal bull in 1571.

46.23–24 *Bulls of Colchos*: Jason's impossible tasks to win the golden fleece were to hitch up King Aeëtes' fire-breathing bulls with solid brass hooves, plow the fields of Ares, the war god, and sow dragon's teeth.

46.25 *Running*: allowed to run instead of being stabled.

46.25 *Allay*: exhausting the breed.

46.27 *Decline*: "the word is frequent with Sr W.T." (Wotton 1704?, 98).

46.31 *Lead*: 46.31; *roaring*: threatening excommunication.

47.2 *Art*: artifice, trickery (*OED*).

47.7 *Varias inducere plumas, and Atrum desinit* [recte *desinat*] *in piscem*: "to spread many-coloured feathers," and "ends in a black fish" (Horace, *Ars poetica*, 2–4).

47.10 *Fishes Tails*: less ceremonious than papal edicts, papal briefs are sealed with wax, impressed with the pope's private seal: St. Peter fishing and the words "*Sub annulo piscatoris*" (under the ring of the fisherman; Swift 1958, 111.n6).

47.15 *Appetitus sensibilis*: Thomas Aquinas distinguishes animal appetites (*appetitus sensibilis*) from intellectual appetites (*appetitus intellectivus*; Swift 1958, 112.n1). Swift failed philosophy during one term at Trinity College Dublin (Forster 1876, i.52).

47.19 *Coyl*: noisy disturbance (*OED*).

47.20 *Pulveris exigui jactu*: "by the tossing of a little dust (These storms of passion . . . are quelled and laid to rest)" (Virgil, *Georgics*, iv.87). In the same term Swift was *bene* in Greek and Latin (Forster 1876, i.52).

47.26 *Bullbeggars*: 1) "the visionary Tribe of . . . *Goblins* . . . and of *Bulbeggars*, that serve . . . to fright Children into whatever their Nurses please" (Temple 1690, 344), 2) papal bulls (46.18).

47.27 *North-west*: 19.23.

47.28 *baited . . . so terribly*: fights to the death between dogs and chained bulls were daily entertainment at the Bear Garden in Southwark. Pepys found it "good sport . . . But . . . very rude and nasty" (Pepys 1970–83, vii.245–46).

47.32–33 *a certain Sum of Money*: "one may see the Fees to be paid . . . for expedition of those Pardons, in the *Taxa Cancellariæ Romanæ*" (Swift 1720, 84).

48.9 *Man's Man*: 1) a manservant, a valet (*OED* s.v. **Man**. 10.a.), 2) St. Gregory the Great (c. 540–604), the first pope to wield political power, subscribed his letters "*Servus Servorum Deï*" (Servant of the Servants of God; Swift 1958, 113.n3).

47n[†] *in Articulo Mortis*: under sentence of death; *the Tax Cameræ Apostolicæ*: the charge for engrossing a pardon levied by the Papal Treasury (Camera Apostolica; Swift 1958, 113.n4).

48.14 *Verè adepti*: Rosicrucians capable of turning base metal into gold; Sir Hudibras's squire, Ralpho, was "In *Rosy-Crucian Lore* . . . / *Verè adeptus*" (Butler 1967, 17).

48.16 *Arcana*: secrets.

48.17 *the Operation*: the performance of something, a scientific experiment (*OED*).

48.19 *Innuendo*: a law Latin term introducing an interpolated explanation, equivalent to "that is to say" (*OED*).

48.31 *call himself God*: "the School-men and Canonists . . . giving divine proprieties [characteristics] to the Pope, even to call him God" (Sarpi 1676, 176).

48.32 *says my Author*: 28.20; *three old high-crown'd Hats*: the papal tiara (Plate 14).

48.33–34 *a huge Bunch of Keys*: "I will give unto thee [Peter] the keys of the kingdom of heaven" (Matthew 16.19).

48.34 *an Angling Rod*: "I [Jesus] will make you fishers of men" (Matthew 4.19).

49.7 *Boutade*: "Any Body but Sr W. Temple [whom Wotton believed to have written *A Tale of a Tub*] would have said *Sally*" (Wotton 1704?, 103).

49.10–11 *would not allow his Brothers a Drop of Drink*: "Refusing the [Communion] cup to the Laity" (Wotton 1704?, 104); "The Cup of the Lord is not to be denied to the Lay people: . . . both the parts of the Lords Sacrament [bread and wine] . . . ought to be ministred to all Christian men" (*Book of Common Prayer* 1704, sig. Qlv).

49.17–18 *Bread . . . is the Staff of Life*: "Transubstantiation" (Wotton 1704?, 104); the belief that the consecrated bread and wine of the eucharist literally change into the body and blood of Christ, was formalized by Pope Innocent III (1198–1216) who "may boast of the two most signal triumphs over sense and humanity, the establishment of transubstantiation, and the origin of the Inquisition" (*TLS*, 14 July 1995, 5). "Transubstantiation . . . is repugnant to the plain words of Scripture . . . and hath given occasion to many Superstititions" (*Book of Common Prayer* 1704, sig. Qlr).

49.21 *Barm*: froth that forms on the top of fermenting malt liquors, which is used to leaven bread (*OED*).

49.28 *The Elder*: Martin (the Church of England).

50.2 *the younger*: Jack (the dissenting sects).

50.4 *take me along with you*: "Falstaff: . . . take me with you: whom meanes your Grace?" (1 Henry IV, II.iv.512; Swift 1958, 117.n2).

49n* *Concomitants*: concomitance, 1) existing together, 2) the coexistence of the body and blood of Christ in *both* elements of the eucharist, especially in the bread (*OED*). This doctrine justified denying wine to the laity (Plate 15).

50.17–18 *G— confound you . . . if you offer to believe otherwise*: "*Infalability*"(sic) (Wotton 1704?, 106).

50.28–29 *Vintners*: wine sellers notoriously mix and adulterate wines.

50.38 *Rupture*: "Reformation" (Wotton 1704?, 108).

51.3 *lucid Intervals*: periods of temporary sanity (*OED*).

51.7 *not only swearing* 1755^H Swearing, not only Σ.

51.9 *a Cow at home*: "Relicks" (Wotton 1704?, 108).

51.14 *Chinese Waggons*: "they have *Carts* and *Coaches* driven with *sails*" (Heylyn 1674, iii.184; Plate 16); "Sails [drive] thir Cany Waggons" (Milton, *Paradise Lost* [1667], iii.439); Dirk F. Passmann, *N&Q*, 231 (December 1986), 482–84.

51.17 *to bait*: to rest.

51.29–30 *the Will . . . by which they presently saw how grossly they had been abused*: "Taught by the Will produc'd . . . /How long they had been cheated" (Dryden 1956– , ii.121).

51.29 *took a Copia vera*: literally, made a fair copy, *metaphorically*, translated the Latin Bible into the vernacular languages.

52.12 *Dragoons*: after the revocation of the Edict of Nantes (1685) Louis XIV ordered mounted infantry armed with muskets to be quartered in the houses of Protestants to enforce his decrees.

53.7 *O Universe . . . me thy Secretary*: the Narrator's version of "Secretary of Nature," which Suidas calls Aristotle (Suidas 1967–71, i.358), which Joseph Glanvill calls "the miraculous *Des-Cartes*" (Glanvill 1665, 155), and which John Heydon calls himself (Heydon 1664, t.p.).

53.8–9 *Quemvis perferre* [recte *sufferre*] *laborem / Suadet, & inducit noctes vigilare serenas*: "that induces me to suffer any hardship you please and to invigilate the quiet nights" (Lucretius, *De rerum natura*, i.141–42).

53.12 *Containing and Contained*: Swift mocks Wotton: "By *Anatomy*, there is seldom any thing understood [by the Ancients] but the Art of laying open the several Parts of the Body with a Knife, that so the Relation which they severally bear each to other may be clearly discerned. This is generally understood of the *containing* Parts, Skin, Flesh, Bones, Membranes, Veins, Arteries, Muscles, Tendons, Ligaments, Cartilages, Glands, Bowels . . . As for the Examination of the Nature and particular Texture of the *contained* Parts, Blood, Chyle, Urine, Bile, Serum, Fat, Juices of the Pancreas, Spleen and Nerves, Lympha, Spittle, Marrow of the Bones, Mucilages of the Joints, and the like; [the Ancients] made very few Experiments" (Wotton 1694, 193).

53.15 *Anatomy*: skeleton (*OED*; Plate 18).

53.20–21 *Instruction and Diversion*: "Poets aim either to instruct or to amuse" (Horace, *Ars poetica*, 333).

53.21 *Readings*: reading notes.

53.26 *Fastidiosity, Amorphy, and Oscitation*: fussiness, shapelessness, and drowsiness; the first two are Swift's mock-pedantic coinages; the third mocks Bentley specifically: "'Tis a mere oscitation of our Scholiast" (Bentley 1697, 119).

53.31 *Utile and . . . Dulce*: "miscuit utile dulci,/lectorem delectando pariterque monendo" (he mixes profit and pleasure, delighting and instructing the reader at the same time; Horace, *Ars poetica*, 343–44).

53n* *The Learned Person . . . endeavouring to annihilate so many Antient Writers*: Bentley 1697, passim.

54.1–2 *whether there have been ever any Antients or no*: "And to speake truly, *Antiquita seculi Iuventus Mundi* [antiquity is the youth of the world]. These times are the ancient times, when the world is ancient, & not those which we account ancient *Ordine retrogrado*, by a computacion backward from our selves" (Bacon 1605, i.23v).

54.9 *O-Brazile*: a notional island west of Ireland (Plate 19) "seldome appears twice in a posture [in the same location]" (Anony. 1673, 6); "the Stress of the *O-Brazilian* Philosophy consists in puzzling and confounding the Truth, that it may never be found" (Anony. 1712, 38).

54n* *Painters Wives Island*: included so the map-maker's wife *"might have an Island of her own"* (Heylyn 1674, Appendix, 161).

54.12 *Undertaker*: one who engages in the serious study of a science (*OED*).

54.15 *balneo Mariae*: "our secret fire, our sulphur water, called *Bain Marie*" (*Philosophie Naturelle* 1682, 28).

54.15 *Q.S.*: *Quantum Sufficit* (as much as necessary); *Lethe*: a river in the classical underworld whose water induced total forgetfulness of the past [one of the Narrator's symptoms] (Virgil, *Aeneid*, vi.703–18).

54.17 *Sordes and Caput mortuum*: sediment remaining after the distillation or sublimation of any substance marked by skull and cross-bones in alchemical texts.

54.19 *two Drams*: 1/4 ounce in apothecaries' weight.

54.20 *Catholick*: of universal use or application (*OED*).

54.24 *Abstracts . . . reduceable upon paper*: this was Swift's practice: "Books . . . read . . . From Jan: 7. 1696/7 / *Sleidan*'s Coment: abstracted . . . / Council of *Trent* abstr: . . . / *Diodorus Siculus*, abstr: . . . / *Cyprian* & *Irenaeus*: abstr:" (Swift 1958, lvi).

54.25 *Medulla's, Excerpta quaedam's, Florilegia's*: the best parts, selected extracts, anthologies.

54.29 *Arcanum*: an alchemical secret, a "curious *Receipt*" (54.9–10).

54.29–35 *Homer . . . design'd his Work for a compleat Body of all Knowledge Human*,

Divine, Political, and Mechanick: "there was no Secret in Divinity, natural and moral Philosophy, and the Mathematicks to boot, but was fairly imply'd in [Homer's] Writings" (Fontenelle 1708, 19–20).

54.34–35 *all Knowledge*: "*Homer* was without Dispute the most Universal *Genius* that has been known in the World . . . in his Works [are] the best and truest Principles of all . . . Sciences or Arts" (Temple 1690, 320–21).

54. side note *Xenophon*: *Convivium*, iv.6 (Swift 1958, 127.n2).

54.37 *Cabalist*: a student of the cabbalah, an unwritten mystical interpretation of the Torah (the first five books of the Old Testament) revealed by God to Moses. It derives "profound meaning from acrostics; letters and numbers can be added and the total has philosophical value" (*TLS*, 3 November 1995, 27); cf. "the Number of O's multiplied by *Seven*, and divided by *Nine*" (85.7).

54.38 *Opus magnum*: the conversion of base metal into gold.

55.2 *Sendivogius*: Michal Sdziwoj (L. Sendivogius) may or may not have been a Pole born near Cracow in 1556 or 1566, who died at Gravarna in 1636 or 1646 and may or may not have possessed a red powder that transmuted lead into gold. His *Dialogus Mercurii, Alchymistae et Naturae* (Cologne: 1607) was translated by John French as *A New Light of Alchymie* (1650, rptd. 1674; Ferguson 1906, ii.365–69); *Behmen*: Jacob Behmen (1575–1624), a German mystical Protestant theologian, 13 of whose books were translated into English between 1645 and 1662. He "was not an alchemist. But he employed alchemical phraseology and imagery to illustrate his religious views" (Ferguson 1906, i.111).

55.2 *Anthroposophia Theomagica*: Thomas Vaughan (1622–1666), twin brother of Henry Vaughan, the poet, was an alchemist and disciple of Cornelius Agrippa. He published *Anthroposophia Theomagica: or, A Discourse of the Nature of Man and his state after death; Grounded on his Creator's Proto-Chimistry, and verifi'd by a practicall Examination of Principles in the Great World* (1650) and other mystical works under the pseudonym Eugenius Philalethes.

55.3 *Sphaera Pyroplastica*: the phrase occurs in Vaughan's receipt for "The Grand Elixir" (126.35–36): "Rx ten parts of celestial slime. Separate the male from the female, and then each from its earth, naturally, however, and without violence. Conjoin after separation in due, harmonic, vital proportion. The soul, descending straightway from the pyroplastic sphere, shall restore its dead and deserted body by a wonderful embrace" (Vaughan 1984, 69, 605; Swift 1994, 234).

55.4–5 *Vix crederem Autorem hunc unquam audivisse ignis vocem*: "I can scarcely believe that [Homer] ever heard the voice of fire," as Zoroaster claimed to have done (Patrizzi 1593, sig. F6r). Thomas Vaughan put Zoroaster's motto, "*Audi ignis vocem*," on the title-page of *Anthroposophia Theomagica* (1650) and Henry More provides a helpful translation: "in plain English, Hear the voice . . . of fire" (More 1650, 70; Swift 1958, 358).

55.8 *Save-all*: a device for allowing candles to be wholly burned (*OED*; Plate 20).

55.11 *gross Ignorance*: "in many material and very curious Parts of Learning, the Ancients were . . . grossly ignorant" (Wotton, 1697, iv).

55.16–17 *the happy Turns and Flowings*: in "Mr. *Wotton*'s Book . . . There is indeed a *Flowingness of fine Language, and Rapidity of Smooth Numbers and Periods*" (T.R. 1698, 50).

55.17–18 *sublime Discoveries upon the Subject of . . . Spittle*: Wotton reports the recent discovery of the four different sources of spittle in the mouth (Wotton 1694, 204–5). Temple refers sarcastically to "The admirable Virtues of the noble and necessary Juice" (Temple 1701, 282).

55.26 *within these last three Years*: since the publication of Wotton's *Reflections upon Ancient and Modern Learning* (1694).

55.28–29 *the Inventor of the Compass, of Gun-Powder, and the Circulation of the Blood*: "the *Compass, Printing,* the *Circulation of the Blood* . . . are fundamentally all in *Homer*" (Eachard 1671, 44; Elliott 1954, 1252).

55.30–31 *a compleat Account of the Spleen*: a review of the second edition of Sir George Ent's *Apologia* (1683; for Harvey's discovery of the circulation of the blood) adds "some account of the *Spleen*" (*Phil. Trans.* xv (22 July 1685), 1105–06; Olson 1952, 460–61).

55.31–32 *Political Wagering*: "Several wage[r]s were this day laid . . . that the French king is dead . . . a wager of 10,000 duccatoons to one that a . . . general peace would be [proclaimed] before the 20th instant" (Luttrell 1857, iv.108, 261).

55.33 *Dissertation upon Tea*: Johannis Nicolai Pechlini, *Theophilus Bibaculus, sive de Potu Theae Dialogus* (The Lover of Tea-drinking, or, a Dialogue on the Drinking of Tea; Frankfurt: 1684) is reviewed in *Phil. Trans.* xv (28 January 1685, 870; Olson 1952, 462).

55.33 *Method of Salivation without Mercury*: David Abercromby, *Tuta, ac efficax Luis Venereae, saepe absque Mercurio, ac semper sine Salivatione mercuriale, Curandae methodus* (A sure and effective method of curing venereal disease without mercurial salivation; 1684) is reviewed in *Phil. Trans.* xiv (20 June 1684), 620; Olson 1952, 463–64.

55.33 *Mercury*: "*Mercury* in Venereal Distempers, is . . . a Specifical Remedy" (Wotton 1694, 189), but it is also highly toxic. Swift told Letitia Pilkington that Jonathan Swift Sr. died of mercury poisoning (Pilkington 1997, i.31).

55.34 *my own . . . Experience*: 14.19–22.

56.9 *Mouse-Traps*: hawked in the streets in 17th century London like brassières in 21st century Dakar.

56.9–10 *Every Man his own Carver*: proverbial (Tilley 1950, 83); equivalent to Sir William Temple's "Sufficiency" (Temple 1690, 3, 53). "In latter days . . . Every-one chuses *to carve* for himself . . . *Ragouts* and *Fricassees* are the reigning Dishes, in which every thing is . . . dismembered and thrown out of all Order" (Shaftesbury 1711, iii.112–13).

56.36 *we are just going to begin*: "The Epilogue of merry *Andrew*'s Farce was . . . '*we are just a going to begin*'" (Ward 1698–1700, X (August), 12).

56.37 *Prefaces . . . Introductions, Prolegomena's, Apparatus's*: "*Prefaces, Prolegomena, Apparatus's, Introductions*" (Boyle 1698, 193).

56.39 *as far as it would go*: the Dedication of Dryden's translation of *The Satires of Juvenal* (1693) runs to 53 folio pages and the Dedication of *The Works of Virgil* (1697) to 47 pages (Swift 1958, 131.n2).

57.13–14 *a very considerable Addition to the Bulk*: "the *Prefaces* of *Dryden,* / . . . Tho' meerly writ at first for filling / To raise the Volume's Price a Shilling" (Swift 1937, 648; Swift 1958, 131.n3).

57.17–18 *a long Digression unsought for, and an universal Censure unprovoked*: presumably Bentley's 152-page "unsought for" appendix to the 2d edition of Wotton's *Reflections upon Ancient and Modern Learning* (1697) with its "unprovoked" censure of Sir William Temple's *Essay upon Ancient and Modern Learning* (1690).

58.22–23 *their Father's Will*: *The New Testament* (28 n[1]).

58.34 *reducing*: "reducyng thyngs to the foundation . . . of the Scripture" (Foxe 1570, 1005; Higgins 1994, 130).

58.36–59.1 *MARTIN . . . JACK*: "Luther . . . Calvin" (Wotton 1704?, 125).

59.3–4 *Men in the Dark, to whom all Colours are the Same*: "all Colours will agree in the Darke" (Bacon 1625, 16).

59.6 *Complexions*: mixtures of hot/cold, wet/dry humours that determine an individual's temperament according to 17th century physiology. Jack's complexion is splenetic (60.22), Martin's is phlegmatic (61.18).

59.9 *Memory*: the mother of the Muses.

59.12 *deal entirely with Invention*: Jonson and Beaumont "borrow'd all they writ from Nature: I [Bayes] am for fetching it purely out of my own fancie" (Buckingham 1672, 13).

59.15 *in Method*: according to the rules and practice of history writing (37.2).

59.23 *Points*: 36.8, tagged laces for fastening clothing.

59.28 *this great Work*: "Reformation" (Wotton 1704?, 127).

59.31 *Fringe*: "Alluding to the commencement of the Reformation in England, by seizing on the abbey lands" (Swift 1814, xi.132).

59.31 *He*: the grammatical antecedent is "Martin Luther," but it was Henry VIII not Martin Luther who "stript away ten dozen Yards of Fringe", i.e. seized the abbey lands (1535–1539).

59.34 *proceed more moderately*: "Martin Luther, *having abolished the gainfull doctrine of Indulgences, proceeds with more caution in reforming other abuses*" (Swift 1720, 105).

59.38 *falling*: falling off.

60.3 *Indian Figures*: "The abolition of the worship of saints was the second grand step in [the] English reformation" (Swift 1814, xi.132).

60.4 *as you have heard in its due place*: 36.8–9.

60.23 *Zeal*: excessive affect; "The north, where the idol of zele was set" (Coverdale Bible, Ezekiel 8.3; *OED*).

60.25–26 *Analytical Discourse upon . . . Zeal*: 2.8.

60.28 *tangible Substance*: "The first [*terra Elementaris*] is a visible, *Tangible* substance, pure, *fixed*, and Incorruptible" (Vaughan 1984, 67).

60.30 *Subscription*: Jacob Tonson published the 4th edition of *Paradise Lost* (1688) and Dryden's *Virgil* (1697) by subscription (payment in advance with subscribers' names listed in front matter).

60.36 *A Rogue that lock'd up his Drink*: "Denied the cup to the laity" (Swift 1808, 300; Swift 1958, 138.n1; Plate 15).

60.41 *set about the Work immediately*: "John Calvin *sets about reforming with more violence & fury than* Luther" (Swift 1720, 107; Plate 21).

61.3 *a Parcel of Gold Lace*: "Church Government under Bishops" (Wotton 1704?, 131).

61.5–6 *rent the main Body of his Coat from Top to Bottom*: "Removing Episcopacy, and setting up Presbytery in its Room" (Swift 1808, 301; Swift 1958, 138.n2).

61.5–6 *tore off the whole Piece, Cloth and all, and flung it into the Kennel*: "The presbyterians, in discarding forms of prayer [as in *The Book of Common Prayer*], and unnecessary Church ceremonies [such as bowing to the altar], disused even those founded in scripture" (Swift 1814, xi.135); *Kennel*: a gutter in the middle of the street.

61.18 *Martin . . . extremely flegmatick and sedate*: Lord Orrery read this as "a satir against . . . the slow and incomplete reformation of the Lutherans" (Orrery 1752, 191–92). Martin stands both for Luther and for the Church of England.

61.25–27 *the Testament of their good Father . . . prescrib[ed] Agreement, and Friendship, and Affection between them*: "As to Rites and Ceremonies, and Forms of Prayer, he ["a Church-of-England Man"] allows there might be some useful Alterations; and more, which in the Prospect of uniting Christians might be very supportable" (Swift 1939–68, ii.5).

61.28 *dispensable*: permissible in some circumstances (*OED*).

61.39–40 *fly out and spurn against*: burst out in open hostility.

62.3 *still in Peter's Livery*: "Calvinistical *Zeal . . . look*[s] *very like the* Superstition *of the* Roman Catholicks" (Curll 1714, 18).

62.5 *Garnish*: money extorted from a new prisoner by the jailer or other prisoners (*OED*).

62.6 *Exchange-Women*: shopkeepers in the Royal Exchange in Cornhill or in the New Exchange (1609–1737) in the Strand, a kind of bazaar for women's clothing (Swift 1958, 140.n4).

62.8 *Lace . . . and Fringes*: as features of Scottish Presbyterianism "Lace" may stand for "new Methods of forcing and perverting Scripture" (33n**1**) and "Fringes" may stand for confiscated abbey lands, many of which, as Dryburgh and Melrose, are in Scotland.

62.13 *to dress up Necessity into a Virtue*: proverbial (Tilley 1950, 699).

62.13–14 *the Fox's Arguments*: to prove that it is better *not* to have a tail (L'Estrange 1708, 116).

62.15 *bobtail'd*: with his cloak cut short like a Presbyterian preacher (Swift 1808, ii.303).

62.25 *Lanthorns*: "the new Lights of the *Quakers* came first out of the dark Lanthorns of the *Papists*" (Bramhall 1671, 14) (Plate 32).

62.26 *Beggar*: F. *Gueux*, a contemptuous term for Protestant in the 16th c. (*OED*).

62.29 *Sect of Aeolists*: "Holders forth" (Wotton 1704?, 135).

62.31 *Original*: derivation (*OED*).

62.32 *—Mellæo contingens cuncta Lepore*: *recte* "Musæo . . .," "touching all with the grace of the Muses" (Lucretius, *De rerum natura*, i.934); deliberately or inadvertently Swift substitutes "Mellæo" for "Musæo": "touching everything with honey-sweet pleasure" (Scruggs 1973, 42).

63.3 *an Iliad in a Nut-Shell*: Cicero's anecdote, "in nuce inclusam Iliadem Homeri carmen in membrana scriptum tradit Cicero" (Cicero tells of a parchment copy of Homer's *Iliad* enclosed in a nutshell; Pliny, *Natural History*, vii.21), became proverbial (Stevenson 1948, 1704): "*Homers Iliades in a nutte shell . . .* Little Chestes may holde greate Treasure" (Gosson, 1579, sig. F4r).

63.12 *Ollio's, Fricassées and Ragousts*: an olio is a Spanish stew. *A Tale of a Tub*, with its disparate parts of *A Tale of a Tub* and its digressions, *The Battle of the Books*, and *A Discourse concerning the Mechanical Operation of the Spirit*, is itself a very Spanish stew.

63.22 *Forein Troops in a State*: upon conclusion of the war with France (September 1697) Robert Harley, leader of the opposition, proposed a bill to send William's Dutch troops back to the Netherlands (*POAS* Yale, vi.45–46).

63.32 *exspatiating*: digressing (*OED*).

64.8 *Index*: Bentley's "index learning" is repeatedly under attack (Boyle 1698, 68, 145, 197, 286).

64.15–16 *catch . . . Sparrows with flinging Salt on their Tails*: proverbial (Tilley 1950, 51).

64.17 *Regarding the End*: "If . . . a man . . . shall also end his life well, then he is . . . worthy to be called blest; but we must wait till he is dead" (Herodotus, 1.32).

64.18 *Hercules's Oxen . . . Backwards*: Cacus, a three-headed monster, stole Hercules's oxen by pulling them backwards into his cave. When Hercules discovered the loss, he strangled him (Virgil, *Aeneid*, viii.193–261).

64.20-21 *the Army of the Sciences . . . drawn up into its close Order*: in the table of contents to Wotton's *Reflections upon Ancient and Modern Learning* (1694).

64.23 *Systems*: "The most ingenious way of becoming foolish is *by a system*" (Shaftesbury 1711, i.290).

64.25 *Labor is the Seed of Idleness*: proverbial: "From labor there shall come forth rest" (Stevenson 1948, 1330, ¶8).

64.26 *gather the Fruit*: "*Behold the rip'ned Fruit* [of the Royal Society], *come gather now your Fill*" (Sprat 1958, sig. B2r). It was on "a Surfeit of Fruit" (Swift 1939–68, v.193) that Swift blamed his illness during his first visit to Sir William Temple.

64.27 *sublime*: deep; *literally*, raised up (*OED*).

64.28 *not . . . a sufficient Quantity of new Matter*: Swift is mocking Wotton, "a very skillful *Computer*" (64.33–34), who worries that "the next Age will not find very much Work [in physics and mathematics] . . . to do" (Wotton 1694, 348).

64.36–37 *those, who maintain the Infinity of Matter*. Democritus: "There are infinite Worlds in the infinite space" (Stanley 1687, 764); "that the sum of matter be finite . . . I have proved not to be so" (Lucretius, *De rerum natura*, ii.527–28).

64.37 *it*: wit (65.19–20).

65.4–6 *that highly celebrated Talent . . . of deducing Similitudes . . . very surprizing . . . from the Genitals of either Sex, together with their proper Uses*: e.g. "If thou wouldst have me true, be wise / And take to cleanly sinning; / None but fresh lovers' pricks can rise / At Phillis in foul linen" (Rochester 1994, 200).

65.10 *typical*: distinctive, characteristic (*OED*).

65.11–12 *Pygmies . . . quorum pudenda crassa, & ad talos pertingentia*: "Pygmies . . . whose privy members were thick and knocked against their ankles" (Photius 1824–25, i.46; Swift 1958, 147.n2).

65.17–18 *Custom . . . to blow up the Privities of their Mares, that they might yield the more Milk*: (Herodotus, iv.2; Swift 1958, 147.n3).

65.19 *Fonde*: (44.14).

65.29 *Boulters*: fishing lines with many hooks (*OED*); the context indicates that Swift thought boulters were some kind of strainer.

66.1 *Chains . . . in a Library*: Plate 22.

66.1–2 *when the Fulness of Time is come*: "when the fulness of time was come, God sent forth his Son, made of a woman" (Galatians 4.4); *haply*: perhaps (*OED*).

66.7 *Delight . . . Instruction*: 53.28–29

66.11 *Yield*: harvest "of *bright Parts*, and *Flowers*" (65.28).

66.15–16 *far to the North, it was hardly possible . . . to travel, the very Air was so replete with Feathers*: "the Scythians say that the air is [so] full [of feathers] that none can . . . traverse the land" (Herodotus, iv.31). Swift converts Herodotus's feathery snow into showers of goose-quill pens.

67.3 *Æolists*: Æolus is the god of wind, which he keeps in a cave (Virgil, *Aeneid*, i.50).

67.4–5 *Æolists, maintain the Original Cause of all Things to be Wind, from which Principle this whole Universe was at first produced, and into which it must at last be resolved*: "Air is the Principle of the Universe, and of which all things are engendred, and into which they resolve" (Stanley 1687, 63; Harth 1961, 66–67).

67.5 *Breath*: "God formed man of the dust of the ground, and breathed into his nostrils the breath of life" (Genesis ii.7).

67.7 *Quod procul a nobis flectat Fortuna gubernans*: "may ruling Fortune turn away from us [the end of the world]" (Lucretius, *De rerum natura*, v.107).

67.8 *Anima Mundi*: "To be plaine then, this Principle is *Anima Mundi*, or the universall *spirit* of Nature" (Vaughan 1984, 109).

67.9 *the Spirit . . . or Wind of the World*: "The *Spirit* then . . . is nothing else but that *Flatulency* . . . as *Winde* out of [a bellows] applied to the fire" (More 1662, 12).

67.11 *the Forma informans*: "*FORMA Abstracta*, seu *separata à materia*, seu *forma per se subsistens*, seu *immaterialis*, ut Deus & Intelligentiae. *Informans*, seu *forma perficiens materiam*, seu *forma intra rem*, ut forma substantialis ignis*" (the abstract form, or form separated from matter, or form existing by itself, or immaterial form, such as God and the Intelligences. The form that informs [matter], or the form that completes matter, or the form within matter, such as the substantial form of fire) (Chasteigner 1657, 73–74; Swift 1958, 151.n2).

67.14–15 *what is Life it self, but . . . the Breath of our Nostrils? Whence it is very justly observed by Naturalists, that Wind still continues of great Emolument in certain Mysteries*: "INSPIRATION . . . is nothing but the blowing into a man some thin and subtile aire, or wind" (Hobbes 1935, 295; Hopkins 1966, 375); "All this is like Mr Hobb's banter upon in-blowing" (Wotton 1704?, 147).

67.15 *the Breath of our Nostrils*: Genesis 2.7; Lamentations 4.20.

67.16–17 *Wind . . . in certain Mysteries*: "As *wind* i'th' *Hypocondries* [small intestine] pent / Is but a blast if downward sent; / But if it upwards chance to fly / Becomes new *Light* and *Prophecy*" (Butler 1967, 174) and madness (76.30–31).

67.18–19 *the Emittent, or Recipient Organs*: "the Genitals of either Sex" (65.6).

67.21 *two and thirty Points*: of the mariner's compass, an "Ancient" discovery, the development of which seems to have been long neglected by the "Moderns" (Temple 1690, 48); "my Lord Mayor's going to *Pin-maker's-Hall* [94.n†], to hear a Sniveling Non-Con Separatist Divide and Subdivide [his sermon] into the Two and Thirty Points of the Compass" (Penkethman 1699, 13).

67.25 *Operation*: power to operate (*OED*).

67.26 *Primordium*: wind as raw material; "wind was not only soul and spirit to the Aeolists, but . . . matter too, *primordium*, or prima materia" (Starkman 1950, 49).

67.29 *three . . . Animas*: "If we take heed to the soule in comparison to [its] working, wee finde three manner of vertues, *Vegetabilis*, that giveth lyfe, *Sensibilis*, that giveth feeling, *Racionalis*, that giveth reason" (Bateman 1582, sig. D2r).

67.29–30 *three distinct Anima's or Winds . . . a fourth*: "*The three* Anima's *bestow'd on Man by* [the scholastic] *Philosophers are the* Vegetativa, *the* Sensitiva, *&* Rationalis, *& the fourth bestow'd by the* Aeolists *is the* Spiritualis" (Swift 1720, 120; Swift 1958, 152.n1).

67.31 *Bumbastus*: Philipp Aureol Theophrast Bombast von Hohenheim (c. 1490–1541), styled Paracelsus [greater than Celsus], a Roman physician of the 1st century B.C., was a mineralogist, epidemiologist, chemist, pharmacologist, physician, and cabbalist. As his pseudonym implies, Paracelsus rejected the traditional therapy based on the humours, publicly burnt the works of Galen, and experimented with chemotherapy. His involvement with magic however obscured his real advances (LaCasce 1970, 600); *Cabalist*: 67.31.

67.31–32 *placing the Body of Man, in due position to the four Cardinal Points*: "Paracelsus, who according to the cardinall points of the world divideth the body of man; and therefore working upon humane ordure and by long preparation rendring it od[or]iferous [fragrant], he terms it *Zibeta Occidentalis* [civet, a heavy oil secreted from the anus of the civet cat, is used in making perfume], Western *Civet*, making the face the East, but the posteriors the *America* or Western part of his microcosme" (Browne 1650, 54).

68.3 *Quinta essentia*: "Quatuor enim Elementa universus mundus sunt: Et ex illis homo constitutus est. In numero ergo Quintus est, hoc est, Quinta Essentia, extra Elementa quatuor ceu nucleus extractus est" (the four elements [air, earth, fire, and water] are the cosmos as a whole, and out of them Man has been constituted. He is fifth in succession therefore, that is, the fifth essence besides the four elements from which he has been extracted as a catalyst (Paracelsus 1658, ii.664a; Swift 1958, 359); "*This they call the* Divine Spirit *or inward light, which they cherish & use on all occasions, & improve frequently into Enthousiasm, Inspiration, & other Spiritual gifts*" (Swift 1720, 120).

68.7 *hid under a Bushel*: "Neither do men light a candle, and put it under a bushel, but on a candlestick; and it giveth light unto all that are in the house" (Matthew 5.15).

68.9 *BELCHING*: extemporaneous prayer or sermon.

68.14 *several Hundreds link'd together*: at a Presbyterian synod.

68.16 *Tun*: a wine barrel holding 252 gallons (*OED*).

68.17 *Vessels*: "the Lord said . . . he [Ananias] is a chosen vessel unto me" (Acts 9.15).

68.23 *Learning puffeth Men up*: "knowledge puffeth up" (1 Corinthians 8.1).

68.24 *Words are but Wind*: "words are wind" (Heydon 1664, 36); *Ergo, Learning is nothing but Wind*: a valid syllogism; "Words . . . are, the signs of our *Ideas* only, and not [of] Things themselves" (Locke 1690, 245).

68.27 *Eructation*: 1) belching or throwing up; 2) improvisatory prayer or utterance (*OED*).

68.32 *Vapors*: "*Religion* by the disparagement of *Reason* [hath] been . . . *spiritualized* into an *heap* of *vapours*" (Glanvill 1670, 32).

68.35–36 *Vapors issuing forth . . . distorted the Mouth, bloated the Cheeks, and gave the Eyes a terrible kind of Relievo. At which Junctures, all their Belches were received for sacred*: "the snuffling and twang of the nose, passes for the gospel-sound; and the throwings [contortions] of the face for the motions of the spirit" (Crockatt and Monroe 1748, 14); *Relievo*: the part of a work of art projecting from a plane surface (*OED*); *Belches*: "a *Conforming Dissenter* . . . is very Devout and Deliberate in his own Extempore *Belchings*" as opposed to reading from the Book of Common Prayer (Anony. 1700, 75).

68.37 *Devotes*: "*devote* and *devotee* were used indifferently from *c.* 1675 to 1725" (*OED*).

69.1–3 *Their Gods were the four Winds, whom they worshipped, as the Spirits that pervade and enliven the Universe, and as those from whom alone all Inspiration can properly be said to proceed*: "O ye winds of God" (*The Book of Common Prayer* 1683, sig. B3r); "the Spirit comes from the *Foure Winds*" (Vaughan 1984, 88).

69.4 *Latria*: the highest degree of worship (*OED*); *the Almighty-North*: 1) the head-quarters of Satan's rebellion (*Paradise Lost*, v.689); 2) Scotland and northern Ireland, whence Calvinist theology reached England.

69.5 *Megalopolis*, the capital of Arcadia.

69.6 *Omnium Deorum Boream maxime celebrant*: "Of all the gods, they honour Boreas [the north wind] the most" (Pausanias, VIII.xxxvi.6).

69.9 *Coelum Empyræum*: the heaven of heavens.

69.11 *Skotia*: 1) *"Skotías*, which is a temple of Hecate" (Diodorus Siculus, i.96; Swift 1958, 155.n1); 2) Greek *skotos*, darkness.

69.13 *a Region of the like Denomination*: Scotland: *"Our Dissenters in England, who pretend to a much larger share of the Spirit, than those of the establisht Church, own the Kirk of Scotland for their Mother Church, where the Gospel shines in its greatest purity & lustre"* (Swift 1720, 123).

69.21 *preserving Winds in Casks or Barrels*: "a bag . . . wherein he bound . . . the blustering winds" (*Odyssey*, x.19); "an Art as vain, as *Bottling up of Wind*" (Swift 1937, 21).

69.21 *Barrels*: *"Many Dissenters, affecting extraordinary plainness & simplicity, have their Pulpits of a figure not unlike a barrel or tub"* (Swift 1720, 124; Plate 6).

69.30 *Funnel*: *"Such funnels were formerly used in the Temple of Delphos, as it is further explained in the following paragraph"* (Swift 1720, 124).

69.33 *disembogues whole Tempests*: "dissenting . . . Preachers fill the Peoples Heads with Wind" (Parker 1672, sig. dlv).

69.33–34 *as the Spirit from beneath gives him Utterance*: "they . . . began to speak with other tongues, as the Spirit gave them utterance" (Acts 2.4).

69.34–35 *issuing ex adytis, and penetrabilis*: "æternumque adytis effert penetrabilis" (from the inner recesses brings undying fire; *Aeneid*, ii.297), which Swift elaborates into a pun on 1) farting, and 2) providing spiritual enlightenment, with a glance perhaps at contracting the pox.

69.34–70.1 *issuing ex adytis and penetralibus . . . the Wind . . . breaking forth . . . [the Presbyterian preacher] delivers his oracular Belches to his panting Disciples*: "Flatulency . . . mounting to the Head . . . makes the *Enthusiast* to admiration fluent and eloquent" (More 1662, 12).

70.8–13 *antient Oracles, whose Inspirations were owing to certain subterraneous Effluviums of Wind . . . It is true indeed that these were frequently managed . . . by Female Officers, whose Organs were understood to be better disposed for the Admission of those Oracular Gusts*: in the Temple of Apollo at Delphi questions [in writing, please] were answered by the Pythian sibyl seated on the sacred tripod. The mephitic vapors, or "subterraneous *Effluviums*" by which the priestess was traditionally inspired, are fictional.

70.11 *managed and directed by Female Officers*: "Holy Women and Sisters in the Faith, Elder Widdows . . . and Deaconesses, did many Religious and Charitable Services in the Primitive Christian Churches" (Maybee 1942, 118).

70.20–26 *And, whereas the mind of Man, when he gives the Spur and Bridle to his Thoughts, doth never stop, but naturally sallies out . . . With the same Course and Wing, he falls down plum into the lower Bottom of Things*: these lines have been read as autobiographical, recalling Swift's failed experiments in panegyric in Pindaric stanzas (Uphaus 1971, 67–68), but there is no real evidence and the soaring-crashing-into-*bathos* image recurs frequently in impossibly autobiographical contexts (70.22–34).

70.21–22 *a strait Line drawn by its own Length into a Circle*: "a streight line continued grows a Circle" (Marvell 1672–73, i.206); a sexual pun (22.6–7).

70.33 *over-shot*: over-extended (*OED*).

70.34 *dead Bird of Paradise*: "It was an ancient belief that Birds of Paradise had no feet, but always continued on the wing, until their death" (Swift 1814, xi.151).

70.35 *Metaphysical Conjectures*: Swift parodies "the metaphysick stile" on which "it may be doubted whether absurdity or ingenuity has the better claim" (Johnson 1779–81, i.¹49, 87).

71.8 *in Act*: in fact, in reality (*OED*).

71.12–14 *Camelion . . . Moulinavent*: "The worshippers of wind or air found their evil spirits in the chameleon by which it was eaten, and the windmill, Moulin-à-vent, by whose four hands it was beaten" (Morley 1889, 123); "by CAMELION and MOULINAVENT, are understood Church and State; that is, the Episcopal Church of England by law established, and the Monarchy" (Barrett 1808, 34).

71.13 *Eruction*: belching (*OED*).

71.19 *that polite Nation of Laplanders*: "they are rude, barbarous, and without the knowledge of Arts or Letters . . . Idolaters . . . great Sorcerers" (Heylyn 1674, ii.428).

71.23 *buy their Winds . . . from the same Merchants*: the Finnish Laplanders are authentic Aeolists because they "sell winds to those Merchants that trafic with them" (Scheffer 1674, 58).

72.8 *Madness or Frenzy*: "Credite mihi, anathymiasis si in cerebrum [it], in toto corpore fluctum facit. *Trimalchio apud Petronnius*. Anathymiasis vapor est & exhalatio, quae hic de ventris flatibus intelligenda" (Believe me, if an anathymiasis gets into the brain, it makes a disturbance in the whole body. Anathymiasis, air and exhalation, is to be understood here as abdominal flatulence; Swift 1808, ii.320).

72.9 *the greatest Actions*: "Our greatest Agitations have ridiculous Motives and Causes" (Montaigne 1700, iii.386).

72.11–12 *New Schemes in Philosophy . . . New Religions:* "new religions: new philosophie" (Casaubon 1656, 185; Ehrenpreis, Marginalia, 162).

72.19–20 *great Turns are not always given by strong Hands*: a commonplace; "Great Events are not always produced by *great Causes*" (Anony. 1681, 14).

72.20 *Adaption*: accommodation (*OED*).

72.22 *the upper Region of Man*: "vapours and exhalations rising from the lower regions of the brain become condensed in the same way that clouds and rain form on the earth" (Debus 1967, 48–49).

72.30–32 *Human Understanding, seated in the Brain, must be troubled and overspread by Vapours, ascending from the lower Faculties*: the "*Heart*, which evaporates and sends up to the Seat of the superior Faculties of the Soul, continual Fumes and Clouds, which obnubilate and darken the *Understanding*" (Abbadie 1695, 99); "*Enthusiasts* for the most part are intoxicated with vapours from the lowest region of their Body" (More 1662, 28); "But if it upwards chance to fly / Becomes new *Light* and *Prophecy*" (Butler 1967, II.iii.775–76).

72.37–73.18 *A certain Great Prince . . . a certain State-Surgeon . . . An absent Female*: Henri IV (1553–1610) was educated a Protestant and promulgated the Edict of Nantes (1598). He married Maria de 'Medici in October 1600, but in January 1609 he conceived a violent passion for Henriette Charlotte de Montmorency, Princesse de Condé, a nymphet of fourteen. When the Prince de Condé removed her to Brussels in the Habsburg empire (August 1609), the king "maddened by the 'loss' . . . became quite irrational" (Buisseret 1984, 174) and prepared to attack Brussels with 30,000 soldiers to retrieve her. The "Protuberancy" (73.18–19) however was deflated when Henri was fatally stabbed by a lunatic named François Ravaillac in May 1610 (Mézeray 1673–74, vi.371–74, 385–89).

73.21–22 *the Poet's never-failing Receipt of Corpora quaeque*: "somebody else" (Lucretius, *De rerum natura*, iv.1065).

73.23–24 *Idque petit corpus mens unde est saucia amore;/Unde feritur, eo tendit, gestio coire*: "the body seeks that which wounded the mind with love . . . it is drawn to the source of the blow and yearns to copulate" (Lucretius, *De rerum natura*, iv.1047, 1055).

73.26 *adust*: scorched (*OED*); *Choler*: yellow bile; one of the four humours of mediaeval physiology: blood, yellow bile, black bile (melancholy), and phlegm; *turned head*: to turn and face the enemy (*OED*), the opposite of "to turn tail"; the heat of his passion for Henriette Charlotte, whom he called Dulcinée, converted Henri's semen into bile and overset his brain. Swift mocks contemporary Galenic medicine.

73.31–32 *Cunnus teterrima belli / Causa*: "Cunt is the most frightful cause of war" (Horace, *Satires*, I.iii.107).

74.6 *the Human* 1755[H] Human Σ.

74n[†] *Paracelsus*: 358.20–27.

74.11 *Fistula*: Louis XIV was cut for an anal fistula (festering ulcer) in 1687.

74.24 *Bedlam*: Bethlem Hospital for the Insane (Plate 23), where the Narrator has been a patient (79.31–32).

74.28 *Diogenes*: Diogenes the Cynic (404–323 B.C.), a crank who lived on the streets of Athens until he took up residence in a tub, was the mirror image of Epicurus. He based his philosophy on 1) virtue (which he defined as avoidance of pleasure), teaching that pain and hunger, although intrinsic evils, can reinforce virtue, and 2) self-reliance: when he saw a boy drinking water from his hand, he threw away his drinking cup. He called Plato's lectures a waste of time and Plato in turn called him "A Socrates gone mad" (Diogenes Laertius, vi. 24, 54).

74.26 *Apollonius*: Apollonius of Tyana in modern Turkey (born c.4 B.C.), was a Pythagorean philosopher who travelled into India and became a miracle-worker contemporary with Jesus; *Paracelsus*: 67n[†]; *Descartes*: René Descartes (1596–1650), the French philosopher, mathematician, musicologist, physicist, physiologist, meteorologist, and Rosicrucian, received his early education in a Jesuit school but attended no university. He wrote his *Discours de la Méthode* in 1619 while on active duty in the Bavarian army at Neuburg. On 11 November 1619 he had a mystical experience (assisted by sleeping in a tile oven) in which he was "filled with enthusiasm [i.e. vapours] and discovered the foundation of a marvelous science" (*EB* 1910–11, viii.80). Finishing his education on the Grand Tour in 1622–25, he settled permanently in Holland in 1629 and died at Stockholm in 1650.

74.29 *Phlebotomy*: opening a vein, a popular medical procedure of no therapeutic value.

74.34–35 *a certain Fortuitous Concourse*: "the fortuitous Concourse of Atoms" (Temple 1690, 82).

74.37 *Clinamina*: in the Epicurean cosmology *clinamen* is the bias or deviation that enables falling atoms to collide and thus to create everything that exists (Lucretius, *De rerum natura*, ii.242–92).

75.1–3 *Cartesius reckoned to see . . . the Sentiments of all Philosophers, like so many lesser Stars . . . rapt and drawn within his own Vortex*: "If in that little *Vortex* a Planet less than that which rules there, do incroach, it is carried on by the greater, and forc'd indispensibly to turn about it" (Fontenelle 1687, 59).

75.7 *the Narrowness of our Mother Tongue*: a sarcastic allusion to the complaint that language is inadequate to praise sufficiently god-like Epicurus (Lucretius, v.1–5).

75.12 *peculiar*: particular (*OED*).

75.12–17 *a peculiar String . . . if you . . . strike gently upon it . . . those of the same Pitch . . . will . . . strike exactly at the same time*: "if a Viol String . . . be touched . . . another string . . . will at the same time tremble of its own accord" (*Phil. Trans.* xii (April 1677), 839–40).

75.23–24 *a Caution . . . to beware of being cheated by our Hackney-Coachmen*: Swift plays fast and loose with Cicero's friend C. Trebatius Testa, who is stationed not in England but in Gaul. What Cicero said was: "You are more cautious as a soldier than you were as a lawyer, for you showed no desire . . . to see a parade of British charioteers [*essedarios*]" (Cicero, *Epistulae ad Familiares*, VII.x.2).

75.26–27 *Est quod gaudeas te in ista loca venisse, ubi aliquid sapere viderere*: "You may well congratulate yourself on having reached a place where you may pass as an expert" (Cicero, *Epistulae ad Familiares*, VII.x.1).

75.33 *W–tt–n*: 10.25–30.

75.33–34 *in appearance ordain'd for great . . . Performances*: with a pun on "ordain'd" (Plate 28).

76.3 *Enthusiasm*: religious hysteria; "*if ever* Christianity *be exterminated, it will be by* Enthusiasme" (More 1660, vi).

76.10 *Postulatum*: assumption, hypothesis (*OED*).

76.11 *Angles*: "[atoms] have small angles a little projecting so that they can tickle our senses" (Lucretius, *De rerum natura*, ii.428–29).

76.13 *to cut the Feather*: to make fine distinctions, to split hairs; proverbial (Tilley 1950, 208).

76.14–15 *how this numerical Difference in the Brain, can produce Effects of so vast a Difference*: "How the same Nerves are fashion'd to sustain / The greatest Pleasure, and the greatest Pain" (Garth 1699, 3; *POAS* Yale, vi.64).

76.16 *Jack of Leyden*: Johann Bockholdt/Jan Bockleszoon/Jan Beukelszoon (1509–1536), an Anabaptist tailor from Leiden, took to running through the streets "in enthusiastic Raptures, [crying] out, Repent and be Baptized." When the Anabaptists seized Münster in 1532 Bockholdt pretended a divine commission to succeed the Biblical David as king of the new Zion. He decreed a total community of goods, including women, and took many wives himself, one of whom he publicly beheaded. When the Prince Bishop of Münster retook the city in June 1535, Bockholdt and two of his lieutenants were tortured to death in the marketplace and their carcasses exposed in iron cages hung from the Gothic spire of St. Lambertskirche (height 312'; Sleidanus 1644, 3, 5–6, 9, 16, 24; Moréri 1694, i.sig. 2E2v–2E3r).

76.19 *Perpensity*: attention (*OED*).

76.33–36 *the Brain in its natural Position and State of Serenity, disposeth its Owner to pass his Life in the common Forms, without any Thought of subduing Multitudes to his own Power, his Reasons, or his Visions*: e.g. "'Tis indifferent to me whether there be another in the world who thinks as I do" (Etherege 1974, 168).

77.4 *Cant*: the peculiar phraseology and intonation of dissenting preachers; "Really to understand the Quaker-*Cant* is learning a new *Language*" (Leslie 1698, sig. c4v); *Vision*: "VISION is the Art of seeing Things invisible" (Swift 1939–68, iv.252).

77.9–10 *Happiness . . . is a perpetual Possession of being well Deceived*: "The perfect Joy of being well deceived" (Rochester 1994, 52); "The really sad thing is not to be deceived . . . Not to be deceived is to be lonely" (Erasmus 1941, 136).

77.23 *adapt*: apt, appropriate.

77.23 *fade and insipid*: flat and dull, "a fade insipid mixture" (Swift 1937, 50); "Doth any man doubt, that if there were taken out of Mens Mindes, vaine Opinions, flattering Hopes, false Valuations, Imaginations as one would, and the like; but it would leave the Mindes of a Number of Men poore shrunken Things; full of Melancholy, and Indisposition, and unpleasing to themselves" (Bacon 1625, 2–3).

77.32–33 *Unmasking . . . never . . . fair Usage*: "stripping the disguises from actors . . . would . . . spoil the whole play" (Erasmus 1941, 37; Paulson 1960, 80).

77.38–78.1 *The two Senses, to which all Objects first address themselves, are the Sight and the Touch; These never examine farther than the Colour, the Shape, the Size, and whatever other Qualities dwell, or are drawn by Art upon the Outward of Bodies*: "*Sense* is not *Knowledge* . . . reaching not to the *Essence* or *Absolute Nature* of [things] . . . but only taking notice of their *Outside*" (Cudworth 1678, 635).

78.8 *Wrong*: this is a textual crux, if it is not a deliberate error. Although the authorial editions, 1704[1] and 1755[H] read "Right," "Wrong" seems to be right (Starkman 1950, 42n.).

78.9 *the Outside hath been infinitely preferable to the In*: "these are only *Outsides* to Amuse the Ignorant, these stately *Scutcheons* [in a funeral procession] serve but to hide a *dead Corpse*" (Anony. 1681, 4).

78.11 *a Woman flay'd*: convicted whores were drawn through the streets "at Cart's Arse ty'd" (Brown 1720, iv.323) and followed by the public hangman wielding a bull-whip.

78.21–22 *[he] who held Anatomy to be the ultimate End of Physick* [medicine]: probably William Wotton: "*Anatomy* is one of the most necessary Arts to open to us Natural Knowledge of any that was ever thought of" (Wotton 1694, 190; Probyn 1974, 251).

78.24–25 *Films and Images that fly off upon his Senses from the Superficies of Things*: "[what makes vision possible are] what we call images of things [*simulacra*]; which, like films that peel off from the outermost surface of objects, fly about at random through the air" (Lucretius, *De rerum natura*, iv.30–32).

78.28 *the Possession of being well deceived*: 77.7–10; "to be deceived is base" (Plato 1875, iv.349).

78.28–29 *a Fool among Knaves*: "the clearest candidate . . . was Temple himself" (French 1963, 50), who was fooled to the top of his bent by Charles II (Ogg 1956–57, i.332–34, 355; ii.557, 577, 585); "Better be a Fool than a Knave" is proverbial (Tilley 1950, 227).

79.5 *one Man*: when an ugly crevasse opened in the Roman Forum (362 B.C.), the soothsayers declared that it would not close until Rome's most valuable possession was thrown into it. When Marcus Curtius rode fully armed into the crevasse, it promptly closed (Livy, vii.6).

79.7 *Another*: Empedocles (c. 500–475), born in Sicily, was a Pythagorean philosopher, a poet, and a scientist: air is a material substance; mind is dependent upon matter; different proportions of air, earth, fire, and water produce everything that exists. According to one legend he died when he jumped or fell into the crater of Mt. Etna, of which a subsequent eruption refunded his sandal (Diogenes Laertius, viii.51–77).

79.11 *Brutus*: Lucius Junius Brutus (fl. 509 B.C.) saved his life by feigning insanity (L. *brutus* means "stupid"). He played a leading role in expelling the Tarquins from Rome (Dionysius of Halicarnassus, iv.67, 77ff.).

79.14 *Ingenium par negotiis*: in Tacitus the phrase means "equal to the job" (Boyer 1703–13, vi.39).

79.19–20 *Sir E——d S——r, Sir C——r M——ve, Sir J—n B—ls, J—n H-w, Esq;*: one consequence of the abortive plot to assassinate William III on 15 February 1696 was an

Act for the better Security of His Majesty's Person (27 April 1696) which required all government office-holders and Members of Parliament to join an Association "to assist each other . . . in the Support and Defence of his Majesty's most Sacred Person and Government" (*CJ*, xi.470). These four Tory Members refused to sign the Association. Swift further implies that they were candidates for admission to Bedlam. Sir John Bolles, 4th Bart. of Scampton, Lincs. (1669–1714), was certified as a lunatic in 1709 (HMC *Lords MSS*, n.s. viii.273–74). Sir Edward Seymour (1633–1708) and John Grubham Howe (c. 1657–1722) were highly excitable, to say the least (*POAS* Yale, vi.22n., 424n., 494n.). The behavior toward William III of Sir Christopher Musgrave, 4th Bart. of Edenhall (1632?–1704) was said to be inexcusable (*CSPD 1691–1692*, 333).

79.21–23 *a Bill for appointing Commissioners to Inspect into Bedlam . . . who shall be empowered to send for Persons, Papers, and Records*: on 4 May 1699 William III reluctantly gave his royal assent to a money bill to which had been tacked a chapter appointing commissioners to inspect into William's prodigal grants of forfeited estates of Jacobites in Ireland, who were empowered to "send . . . for . . . Persons . . . Papers . . . and Records" anywhere "in the said Realme of Ireland" (*Statutes of the Realm* 1963, vii. 547). William's grants were within his prerogative but highly impolitic: 135,820 acres to Willem Bentinck, Earl of Portland; 108,633 acres to Arnold Joost van Keppel, Earl of Albemarle; 36,148 acres to Henri de Massue de Ruvigny, Earl of Galway; 26,480 acres to Godard van Reede, Baron de Ginkel; 95,649 acres, "all of the Private Estate of the late King James," to Elizabeth Villiers, William's cast mistress, &c., &c. The last four paragraphs of A Digression on Madness were written *after* 4 May 1699. The carefully concealed equation of Ireland and madness is also remarkable.

79.22 *the Parts adjacent*: including Grub Street (23.6) and Gresham College. (23.18).

79.27 ——————: *"Ecclesiastical"* (Swift 1755, i.[1]103).

79.33 *Student*: a visit to see the patients in the new Hospital of St. Mary of Bethlem (Plate 23), "vulgarly called *Bedlam*" (Delaune 1690, 91), was like a visit to the Bronx zoo today.

79.36 *into Flanders among the Rest*: new officers and recruits embarked on 4 April 1696 to join the British army in Flanders with William III following in May (Luttrell 1857, iv.40, 54), to open the last inconclusive campaign of an inconclusive war with France over succession to the throne of Spain.

79.39 *a green Bag*: for carrying a lawyer's briefs.

79.41 *Westminster Hall*: the law courts; *a Third*: a merchant with a shop in the City, the mercantile part of London within the old city wall.

80.2 *Ecce cornuta erat ejus facies*: "[when Moses came down from Mount Sinai] his face shone" (Exodus 34.29).

80.4 *the Whore of Babylon*: there was cause for panic when it was revealed that the Catholic plot to assassinate William III included a French army of 15,000 men at Calais ready to descend on the English coast and James Fitzjames, Duke of Berwick, the illegitimate son of James II already in London to lead a popular insurrection to restore his father to the English throne (Luttrell 1857, iv.21).

80.6 *Priviledg'd Places*: government appointments, usually sinecures, providing privileges such as board wages (free meals) in addition to salaries.

80.8 *a Fourth*: a courtier (80.16–22).

80.21 *parting with Money for a Song*: to buy/sell something for a song is proverbial (Tilley 1950, 617–18).

80.24 *a . . . slovenly Mortal*: a physician (80.34).

80.25 *dabling in his Urine*: Antonio Eygel's *Apologema pro Urinis Humanis* (Amsterdam: 1672), which appraises "the *Taste* of Urine," is reviewed in *Phil. Trans.* viii (22 December 1675), 6173–77).

80.26 *Reversion of his own Ordure*: into the original food.

80.27 *reinfunds*: pours in again (*OED*).

80.29 *Declination*: an astrological, not an alchemical, term; Swift may have meant "descension," a method of distillation.

80.34 *Warwick-Lane*: The Royal College of Physicians was in Warwick Lane from 1674 to 1825 (*POAS* Yale, 1963–75, vi. opp. p. 63).

81.3 *the Orator of the Place*: the receptionist at Bedlam; in Ned Ward's account he is "leaning upon a Money-box" (Ward 1698–1700, i.11).

81.6 *Heark in your Ear*: "*Lear*. See how yond Iustice railes upon yond simple theefe: Hearke in thine eare: Change places, and handy-dandy which is the Iustice, which is the theefe" (*King Lear*, IV.v.156–60).

82.12 *Moorfields*: both Grub Street and Bedlam were in Moorfields parish.

82.12 *Scotland-Yard*: an adjunct of Whitehall Palace converted to government offices and the site of Mrs. Wells' coffee house (Lillywhite 1963, 635), is now the headquarters of the metropolitan police.

82.12 *Guild-Hall*: the city hall of London, rebuilt in 1411, was destroyed in the Great Fire of 1666 and again rebuilt.

82.23 *writ it in a Week at Bits and Starts, when he could steal an Hour from his urgent Affairs*: Richard Blackmore M.D. boasted that he wrote *Prince Arthur. An Heroick Poem. In X Books* (1695) in "the Vacancies and Intervals . . . from the Business of my Profession" (30.6–9).

83.3 *Neglect of taking Brimstone*: brimstone, or sulphur, was applied externally as a salve for *Sarcoptes scabiei*, the itch. Swift told Laetitia Pilkington that his father died of mercury treatment for the itch (Pilkington 1997, i.31).

83.6 *Troglodyte*: original inhabitant; cave dweller. The "Troglodyte Philosopher" may be Francis Bacon: "The *Idols of the Cave* take their rise in the peculiar constitution . . . of each individual . . .. Men become attached to certain particular sciences and speculations, either because they fancy themselves the authors and inventors thereof [folly embossed], or because they have bestowed the greatest pains upon them and become most habituated to them [folly inlaid]" (Bacon 1620, 58; Swift 1986, 216–17).

83.8 *Embossed*: standing out in relief (*OED*).

83.10 *the lightest will be ever at the Top*: "the *Dregs* fly up to the Top" (Swift 1985, 180).

83.13–14 *Second Parts . . . [by] The Author of the First*: John Eachard wrote 160 pages on *The Grounds and Occasions of the Contempt of the Clergy and Religion Enquired into in a Letter Written to R.L.* (1670) and then wrote 220 pages of *Some Observations upon the Answer to an Enquiry into the Grounds and Occasions of the Contempt of the Clergy: with Some Additions. In a Second Letter to R.L. By the Same Author* [1672].

83.16 *Bl——re*: Richard Blackmore M.D. (1654–1729), "England's Arch-Poet" (Swift 1732, ²69), published the first of his five epics, *Prince Arthur. An Heroick Poem. In X Books*, in March 1695, adumbrating the exploits of Prince William of Orange. Although Blackmore complained that "the Muses . . . Had of the Royal Favour little Share" in William's reign (Blackmore 1708, 4), William responded magnanimously by appointing Blackmore a physician-in-ordinary, a place worth £200 a year, and conferring upon him the honor of knighthood on 18 March 1697. A few days later out came *King*

Arthur. An Heroick Poem. In Twelve Books, two more than before, its title-page advertizing both of Blackmore's new honors.

83.16 *L——ge*: Sir Roger L'Estrange (1616–1704), Charles II's surveyor of the imprimery and *chef de propagande*, was chiefly responsible for enforcing the Licensing Act of 1662. He was famous for his printing-house raids with his dog Towser and *"his little Pack of inferiour Crape-gown-Men* [clergymen] *yelping after him"* (Shadwell 1683, 8). His most effective propaganda appeared in *The Observator* in which he kept up a relentless attack on dissenters and the first Whigs from April 1681 to March 1687.

83.18 *Rectifier of Saddles, and Lover of Mankind*: to put the saddle on the right horse is proverbial (Tilley 1950, 580). Here it refers to Richard Bentley's insistence that he did not, *"pro singulari sua humanitate"* (with his wonted love of humanity) (Boyle 1718, sig. b1v), withhold the King's Library manuscript of Phalaris from the Hon. Charles Boyle's collator, as Boyle claimed.

83.20 *the Furniture of an Ass*: Boyle complained that Bentley in quoting "the old *Greek* Proverb, *That* Leucon *carries one thing, and his Ass quite another"* (Bentley 1697, 74), was distinguishing between the text of Phalaris and the ass who edited it (Boyle 1698, 219, 220), thereby calling Boyle an ass, an act of *scandalum magnatum*, providing grounds for a lawsuit.

83.31 *to set up the Leavings in the Cupboard*: to save a "Second Part" for later publication.

83.32–33 *the Dogs under the Table may gnaw the Bones*: "the dogs eat of the crumbs which fall from their Master's table" (Matthew 15.27).

84.9–10 *Perspiration*: the Narrator's nonsense is a satire on current medical practice: the sweat-box and salivation (induced by mercury therapy) were recommended procedures in treating syphilis (Abraham 1948, 154, 155).

84.10–11 *I wake, when others sleep*: "spend the tranquil nights in wakefulness" (Lucretius, *De rerum natura*, i.142).

84.14 *seven of the deepest Scholars*: the "Scholars" are the seven endowed professors at Gresham College who lectured once a week (successively) on seven topics: astronomy, geometry, medicine, law, divinity, rhetoric, and music; according to a spurious letter of Aristeas to Philocrates, the Septuagint text was the work of seventy-two scholars who were shut up in seventy-two cells, and in seventy-two days produced identical versions (Swift 1958, 185.n1).

84.20 *their Majesties*: "every Prince in *Christendom*" (Swift 1958, 185.n2).

84.31–32 *Night . . . the universal Mother*: "In the beginning . . . darkness was upon the face of the deep" (Genesis 1.12).

85.1–2 *far beyond . . . the Hopes . . . of the Sower*: "Elegancies . . . beyond the Intention . . . of the Artist" (Montaigne 1700, i.180).

84.side note *Rosycrucians*: Rosicrucianism is a "Gnostic" mystery cult and a "hoax" that began in Germany with the publication of an anonymous pamphlet, *Fama Fraternitatis, dess Löblichen Ordens des Rosenkreutzes* (An Account of the Brotherhood of the Meritorious Order of the Rosy Cross; Kassel: 1614). The pamphlet was translated into English by "Eugenius Philalethes" (Thomas Vaughan) in 1652 (as *The Fame and Confession of the Fraternity, of the Rosie Cross*.

85.4 *glance a few Innuendo's*: interject a few "that is to say's" (Swift 1958, 114.n2).

85.7 *the Number of O's multiplied by Seven, and divided by Nine*: for the student of the Kabbala "letters and numbers can be added and the total has philosophical value" (*TLS*, 3 November 1995, 27).

85.7 *Opus Magnum*: 85.11.

85.16 *Bythus and Sige*: figures in Irenaeus's creation myth: "At last this Bythus [profundity] determined to send forth from himself the beginning of all things, and deposited this production . . . in his contemporary Sige [silence], even as seed is deposited in the womb. She then, having received this seed, and becoming pregnant, gave birth to Nous [the beginning of all things]" (Irenaeus 1885, i.316); cf. Proverbs 8.12–30.

85.16 *Acamoth*: Hebrew, *hokma*, "wisdom," a figure in another creation myth: "from [Achamoth's desire of] returning [to him who gave her life], every soul belonging to this world, and that of the Demiurge [creator of physical existence] himself, derived its origin. All other things owed their beginning to her terror and sorrow. For "*A cujus lacrymis humecta prodit Substantia, à risu lucida à tristiti solida, & à timore mobilis*" (from her tears all that is liquid is formed, from her smile all that is shining, from her sadness all that is substantial, and from her fear all that is unstable; Irenaeus 1885, i.321).

85.18–19 *Eugenius Philalethes hath committed an unpardonable Mistake*: presumably the chemical experiment in which Thomas Vaughan inhaled mercury vapor and died (*DNB*, xx.181).

86.3–6 *I . . . shall henceforth hold on with . . . an even Pace to the End of my Journey, except some beautiful Prospect appears within sight of my Way*: "yet will I not deny my self the satisfaction of going a mile or two out of the way, to gratifie my senses with some new and diverting prospect" (Blount 1679, sig. A3r). Swift mocks Charles Blount, a deist, and a writer "whom he had a mind to expose" (142.24; Hopkins 1966, 378).

87.3 *a new and strange Variety of Conceptions*: "Whosoever through his private judgment, willingly and purposely doth openly break the Traditions of the Church . . . ought to be rebuked openly" (*Book of Common Prayer* 1704, sig. Q1v).

86n* *The True Criticks*: Swift 1958, 93.n4.

87.13 *Types*: Old Testament "Shadows" of New Testament "Substances" (22.16); the Old Testament "having [only] a shadow of good things to come, and not the very image of the things" (Hebrews 10.1).

87.23–24 *the Matter was deeper and darker, and therefore must have . . . more of Mystery at the Bottom*: "au fonds du vaisseau & de l'eau demeure le gros & l'espois, car . . . apres le vaisseau refroidi tu trouveras au bas le feces noires, arses, & bruslées" (the liquid in the bottom of the test-tube will remain thick and clotted; for after it cools, you will find a sediment, black, desiccated, and adust; *Philosophie Naturelle* 1682, 36).

87.24–26 *I will prove this very Skin of Parchment . . . to be the Philosopher's Stone, and the Universal Medicine*: "*a just banter on the superstitious veneration for the Bible, that most Dissenters shew on all occasions*" (Swift 1720, 157).

87.27–28 *he resolved to make use of it [the Bible] in the most necessary, as well as the most paltry Occasions of Life*: "*Nothing can be Lawfully done or used, even in the affairs of common life . . . unless there be either Command or Example in Scripture for it*" (Anony. 1695, 6; Maybee 1942, 242).

88.4 *Authentick Phrase for demanding the Way to the Backside*: "Can anything be prophaner than this?" (Wotton 1705[2], 61). "Presbyterians . . . affected to call every thing by a Scripture-name" (Walpole 1758, ii.38).

88.8–9 *a Passage near the Bottom*: "The Passage" is in Revelation 22.11: "He which is filthy, let him be filthy still." This clause may have been "foisted in by the Transcriber" (88.9) for it is "omitted by the Codex Alexandrinus and six cursive MSS." (Swift 1958, 191.n1), mocking Bentley's style.

88.14 *a strange kind of Appetite*: for combustibles to feed his inner light, the "perpetual Flame in his Belly" (88.16–17); *Snap-Dragon*: "A game . . . (usually held at Christmas) consisting of snatching raisins out of a bowl . . . of burning brandy . . . and eating them whilst alight" (*OED*).

88.14–15 *livid Snuffs of a burning Candle*: extinguishing a candle by putting it in the mouth.

88.24 *bounce his Head against a Post*: "his *Face* Broke against the Posts of a *Tavern Door*" (Anony. 1700, 67).

88.26–27 *a Blow of Fate*: "Prædestination" (Wotton 1704?, 199).

88.31 *It was ordain'd*: "To ridicule Prædestination Jack walks blindfold through the Streets . . . This is a direct Prophanation of the Majesty of God" (Wotton 1705², 61).

88.31–32 *some few Days before the Creation*: "i.e. by God himself" (Wotton 1704?, 199).

89.6 *scower*: "To roam about at night uproariously breaking windows, beating the watch, and molesting wayfarers" (*OED*).

89.8 *Lights*: eyes (slang).

89.14 *blind Guides*: "*Herodians* with thir blind guides are in the Ditch already" (Milton 1953–82, iii.499).

89.13–22 *For, O ye Eyes . . . a noisome Bog*: Jack describes an encounter with a prostitute whereupon he is clapped; cf. 134.22–37.

89.19–20 *Lauralco . . . Lord of the Silver Bridge*: "That Knight which thou seest there with the yellow armour, who beares in his shield a Lyon crownd, crouching at a Damzels feete, is the valorous *Lauralco*, Lord of the *Silver Bridge*" (Cervantes 1612–20, i.146) with a pun on a prosthetic silver bridge to reconstruct a nose destroyed by syphilis.

89.21 *foolish Lights*; *ignis fatuus* (foolish fire); Will-o'-the-Wisp (swamp gas) traditionally misleads travellers into the mire.

89.26–27 *a new Deity . . . by some called Babel, by others Chaos*: Andreas Libavius, *Turris Babel sive Judiciorum de Fraternitate Rosaceae Crucis Chaos* (The Tower of Babel, or the Chaos of Opinions about the Brotherhood of the Rosy Cross) (Strassburg 1619; Swift 1958, 194.n2).

89.28 *Temple*: Stonehenge.

89.36–38 *IN Winter he went always loose and unbuttoned, and clad as thin as possible, to let* in *the ambient Heat; and in Summer, lapt himself close and thick to keep it out*: "The inhabitants [of Fooliana] are of a hard constitution, going bare-brested, & thin attired in the depth of winter, to take ayre the better: marry in the heate of summer, they were [sic] rugge [coarse wool] gownes, and cloakes above that, to keep out heate the better" (Hall 1609?, 125–26; Morley 1889, 147.n2).

90.3 *Vizard*: the hangman's black mask (*OED*).

90.5 *a strange Kind of Speech*: 77.4–5.

90.6–7 *the Spanish Accomplishment of Braying*: two Spanish aldermen try to locate a lost burro by loud braying: "Gossip," says one, "betweene you and an Asse there is no difference, touching your braying . . . These praises and extollings (sayd the other) doe more properly belong to you . . . your sound is lofty, you keepe very good time, and your cadences [are] thicke and sudden" (Cervantes 1612–20, ii.164).

90.7 *arrect*: pricked up like an ass's ears, erect; with a sexual pun.

90.11–12 *a Disease, reverse to that called the Stinging of the Tarantula*: tarantism was a hysterical malady of Italian peasants attributed to the "sting" of a tarantula; dancing the tarantella to music in 6–8 time with whirling triplets was supposed to be the sovereign remedy (*OED*). In the "reverse" of the disease, the music *causes* Jack's madness, which is a circuitous way of saying that "Calvin was against church musick" (Swift 1808, ii.353).

90.12 *run Dog-mad, at the Noise of Musick*: "Against Organs" (Wotton 1704?, 203).

90.14–15 *Westminster-Hall . . . Billingsgate . . . a Boarding School . . . the Royal Exchange . . . a State Coffee-house*: respectively: "litigation, scurrilous pamphlets, dissenters' academies, commercial frauds or usury, political plotting" (Ehrenpreis Marginalia, 196).

90.16 *Colours*: a pun on 1) battle flags of a regiment or ship (*OED*); to fear no colours, to have no fear, is proverbial (Tilley 1950, 110) and 2) rhetorical figures, stylistic embellishment (*OED*).

90.17 *Aversion to Painters:* "Against Pictures" in church windows (Wotton 1704?, 203).

90.21 *over Head and Ears into the Water*: "[total] Immersion in baptism" (Swift 1808, ii.353). The articles of faith of the first Baptist Church in England (1661) relating to baptism states "That baptism or washing with water . . . in no wise appertaineth to infants" (*EB*, iii.372).

90.25 *Medicine . . . convey'd in at the Ears*: "*Nothing conduceth more powerfully to sleep than long insipid Sermons*" (Swift 1720, 163; Swift 1939–68, ix.210–18).

90.26 *Balm of Gilead*: "Is there no balm in Gilead" (Jeremiah 8.22).

90.26 *Pilgrim's Salve*: "pork fat and isinglass [a gelatin made from the air bladders of fish]" (Halliwell 1924, 624).

90.28 *the famous Board*: Nichols quotes an advertizement of 1682: "At the sign of the Woolsack in Newgate-market, is to be seen, a strange and wonderful thing, which is, an *elm*-BOARD, being touched with a hot iron, it doth express itself, as if it were a man dying with *groans* and trembling" (Steele 1786, v.379).

90.31–32 *a good Slap in the Chaps*: "whosoever shall smite thee on thy right cheek, turn to him the other also" (Matthew 5.39).

91.2 *Lend a reasonable Thwack*: "Mortification" (Wotton 1704?, 205).

91.7 *Janisary*: a member of the Turkish sultan's body guard (*OED*).

91.12 *the Great Mogul*: the Emperor of Hindustan (*OED*).

91.24–25 *the Phrenzy and the Spleen of both having the same Foundation*: the "Foundation" is infallibility, papal infallibility of the Romanists and the Quakers' infallibility of the inner light: "the Dictates and Leadings of Gods Spirit in us are infallible" (Keith 1682, 65; Maybee 1942, 114).

91.26–27 *Pair of Compasses . . . fixed Foot . . . Center . . . Circumference*: Swift recycles the famous "twin compasses" metaphor to imply that Peter and Jack are lovers (Donne 1912, i.50).

92.1 *Medicines for the Worms*: "Penance *and* Absolution" (45n*).

92.5–6 *the poor Remainders of his Coat*: "A medley of Principles" (Wotton 1704?, 207).

92.19 *Flanting*: flaunting, displaying oneself in an unbecomingly splendid or gaudy attire (*OED*).

92.24–25 *Desunt nonnulla*: "several [lines] are missing."

92.31 *Effugiet tamen hæc sceleratus vincula Proteus*: "But slippery Proteus will still escape" (Horace, *Satires*, II.iii.71).

92.39 *Tenure*: effort "to catch and keep" attention (92.35–36).

92.40–93.1 *slitting of one Ear . . . sufficient to propagate the Defect thro' a whole Forest*: "Thus as Aristotle observeth [*Historia Animalium*, vi.29], the Deers of Arginusa had their ears divided; occasioned at first by slitting the ears of [a] Deer" (Browne 1650, 278; Swift 1958, 201.n1).

93.2 *Loppings and Mutilations*: the most celebrated lopping was that of the Presbyterian William Prynne (1600–1669) on 30 June 1637 "for writing seditious schismatical Books against the Hierarchy of the Church." "The High-Church Executioner . . . not only seared *Prynn*'s Cheeks with an exceeding hot Iron, but in taking away what was left of one of his Ears, par'd off a piece of his Cheek, and left a piece of his other Ear hanging on for some time, after he had barbarously hack'd it" (Tindal 1710, 6).

93.3 *Ears . . . of late so much exposed*: 1) by publishing "seditious schismatical Books," and 2) by not wearing wigs.

93.4–5 *under the Dominion of Grace*: the period between the execution of Charles I (January 1649) and the Restoration of Charles II (May 1660).

93.12 *exposing their ears*: during the Civil Wars Royalists wore wigs; the Parliamentary party cut the hair short, hence Roundheads.

93.13–14 *when the Vein behind the Ear happens to be cut, a Man becomes a Eunuch*: "[Scythians] cut the vein behind each ear . . . by this treatment the seed is destroyed" (Hippocrates, *De aere, aquis, locis*, xxii.10).

93.15 *edifying by them*: sizing up the "Type of Grace in the *Inward*" man (93.7).

93.23 *Cloven Tongues*: "And when the day of Pentecost was fully come, they were all with one accord in one place. And suddenly there came a sound from heaven as of a rushing mighty wind, and it filled all the house where they were sitting. And there appeared unto them cloven tongues like as of fire, and it sat upon each of them" (Acts 2.1–3).

93.29 *Holding forth*: preaching; "Holding forth the word of life" (Philippians 2.16); "The phrase . . . was taken up by the Non-Conformists about the year 1642" (*OED*); "the *Rooters* and *Th[o]rough Reformers* . . . being . . . busied, some in Pulpits, and some in Tubs, in the grand Work of Preaching and holding forth" (South 1660, 28).

93.34 *black Border*: a decorative edging or ruffle around a clerical cap; suggesting opportunistic conformity to the Church of England(?).

93.36–37 *my General History of Ears*: "See the Catalogue, before the Title [2.9]" (Swift 1720, 169).

94.side note *Including Scaliger's*: as the leading exponent of Aristotelian physics and metaphysics, Julius Caesar Scaliger (1484–1558) enjoyed the most distinguished scientific and literary reputation of his age. In *De Subtilitate* (1557), 856–57, he added a sixth sense, tickling, to the traditional five.

94.18 *Oscitancy*: drowsiness (53.24).

94.25–26 *Peter got a Protection*: by a letter of protection the monarch grants immunity from arrest to anyone engaged in his service (*OED*). This "Protection" is a metaphor for James II's Declaration of Indulgence (April 1687) by which he granted immunity from arrest under the penal laws for Roman Catholic officers, military and civil.

94.27–28 *Jack and [Peter] . . . Design . . . to trepan Brother Martin into a Spunging-house, and there strip him to the Skin*: entrapping Martin into a place of temporary confinement for arrested debtors and stripping him to the skin as if by his creditors is a metaphor for stripping away academic offices from Anglican clergymen during the reign of James II (1685–88; Ogg 1956–57, iii.180–86).

94.30–31 *Jack . . . stole [Peter's] Protection*: by the Act of Toleration, to which William III gave his assent in May 1689, "their Majesties Protestant subjects" were granted immunity from the penal laws and Catholic subjects were expressly excluded (Ogg 1956–57, iii.232–34).

94.31 *Jack's Tatters came into Fashion*: Sir Humphrey Edwin (1642–1707) was an immensely rich merchant and a rigid Independent (Congregationalist). He attracted the notice of James II who was anxious to conciliate dissenters in order to obtain their help in relaxing the penal laws against Roman Catholics. "On 11 October 1687 he was sworn in as alderman of Tower ward, on the direct appointment of the king . . . On the 18th of the following month the king knighted him, at Whitehall, and a few weeks later appointed him sheriff of Glamorganshire" (*DNB*, vi.554). But Sir Humphrey was also an occasional conformist who took communion in the Church of England to qualify himself for public office, a practice that Daniel Defoe called "*playing Bo-peep* with God Almighty" (Defoe 1697, 17). Sir Humphrey was elected Lord Mayor on 30 September 1697 and shocked London by attending Independent services in Pinner Hall on Sunday 7 November 1697 in full mayoral regalia, mounted on the City horse and attended (against his will) by the City Sword-bearer (Luttrell 1857, iv.303, 309).

94.32 *Custard*: an open pie made with meat, eggs, and milk, like a quiche; it was served at "a most sumptuous Dinner" on 29 October 1697 in the Guild Hall, installing the new Lord Mayor (Luttrell 1857, iv.299).

96.1–2 *The Conclusion*: the conclusion has been reached because Swift has brought the mock-history of Christianity down to a crashing anticlimax on Sunday 7 November 1697 (94n[†]).

96.6–7 *Books must be suited to their several Seasons*: "Books like fruits have their season, out of which, without ceasing to be useful or pretty, they are no longer sought after. As long as people talk about an issue or an event in the world, a current news item that they bring up in company, every book about it, however feeble it may be, is favorably received" (Orleans 1690, sig. éii).

96.11–12 *the Bookseller who bought the Copy of this Work*: Benjamin Tooke Jr. (xx.14–15).

96.22–23 *a small Treatise upon the* ——: clap; *if it hold up*: i.e. the good weather.

96.23 *Author*: *Dr. Bentley's Dissertation on the Epistles of Phalaris, and the Fables of AEsop Examin'd by the Honourable Charles Boyle, Esq*; was published, not by Benjamin Tooke Jr., but by Thomas Bennet.

96.26 *Durfy's last Play*: as of November 1697 the last play of Thomas D'Urfey (10.17) was *The Intrigues of Versailles*, which opened in May 1697 and was not revived (Van Lennep 1965, 477).

96.29 *Congreve*: Swift and William Congreve (1670–1729) were at Kilkenny grammar school together and at Trinity College Dublin they had the same tutor, St. George Ashe. In November 1693 when Congreve's first two plays had been successfully produced, Swift wrote "To Mr. Congreve" to "be printed before" one of his published plays, but apparently never sent it (Swift 1937, 43).

97.1–3 *pass . . . for wondrous Deep . . . because it is wondrous dark*: "conclude the depth by the obscuritie of my Sense" (Montaigne 1700, iii.352).

97.5 *upon Nothing*: "Upon Nothing" by John Wilmot, Lord Rochester, was published in 1680 (Rochester 1994, 201).

97.15 *ut plenus vitae conviva*: "like a banqueter surfeited with life" (Lucretius, *De rerum natura*, iii.938).

97.18 *Repose*: "the true ultimate End of *Ethicks*" (61.32–33), mocking the Stoic ideal of *ataraxia*; "The Serene Peaceful State of being a Fool among Knaves" (78.28–29).

97.19 *Times so turbulent and unquiet*: when the second Parliament of William III convened in October 1696, eight campaigns in Ireland, the Continent, the Channel, and the Caribbean had brought Britain close to bankruptcy. "This decay of Publick Credit created the greatest Confusion and Disorder in the World; our Affairs seem'd reduc'd to Extremity, and the Government was look'd on to be at a stand. All Men were at a Gaze, and stood wondering what the Parliament would do" (Blackmore 1699, 45).

97n[†] *the Peace of Riswick*: signed 10 September 1697 (Luttrell 1857, iv.275).

97.21–22 *among a very Polite Nation in Greece*: in the marketplace of Troezen in Corinth is "a sanctuary of the Muses . . . Upon [an old altar not far off] they sacrifice to the Muses and to Sleep, saying that Sleep is the god . . . dearest to the Muses" (Pausanias, III.xxxi.3).

97.27 *the Author's Spleen*: the Narrator's spleen; Swift was not subject to the spleen: "no man is thoroughly miserable unless he is condemnd to live in Ireland, and yet I have not the Spleen; for I was not born to it" (Swift 1963–65, i.154); Swift's motto was "Vive la bagatelle" (Swift 1963–65, iii.382).

97.32–34 *I have thought fit to make Invention the Master, and to give Method and Reason, the Office of its Lacquays*: "I my self, the Author of these momentous Truths, am a Person, whose Imaginations are hard-mouth'd, and exceedingly disposed to run away with his *Reason*" (81.18–20).

98.2 *my Book of Common-places*: "Dr. [Charles] *Dav*[enan]*t* . . . hath a Political Common-place-Book, filled with glittering Passages from *Tacitus, Livy*, and *Salust*" (Anony. 1704, 4).

98.6 *Ambages*: beating about the bush (*OED*).

98.14 *Liberty . . . of the Press*: a bill to renew the Licensing Act of 1662 was defeated in the House of Commons in 1695, not in order to promote "Liberty . . . of the Press," but to break the monopoly "whereby both Houses of Parliament are disabled to order any thing to be printed" without entering it in the Registry of the Company of Stationers. Accordingly, on 3 May 1694 was ended "the Discipline of the last Reigns when *Scribere* was *Agere*, and Thinking was Treason" (*CJ*, xi.305–06; Montagu 1701, 7).

101.6–7 *written . . . 1697*: since a serious defense of Sir William Temple was impossible, Swift undertook to turn the Ancient/Modern controversy into a mock epic joke. "Nothing," Wotton said, "wounds so much as a Jest" (Wotton 1697, 419). Swift began writing after publication of Bentley's *A Dissertation upon the Epistles of Phalaris* in the second edition of Wotton's *Reflections upon Ancient and Modern Learning* (July 1697). Swift could not have finished *The Battle of the Books* until after publication of Charles Boyle's *Dr. Bentley's Dissertation upon the Epistles of Phalaris, and the Fables of Aesop, Examin'd*, which was "In the Press" in February 1698 (Arber 1903–06, iii.60) and is mentioned on pp. 233, 240, 252, 254, and 258 below.

101.10–11 *Aesop*: the legendary composer of animal fables is said by Herodotus (ii.134) to have been a freed Greek slave of the 6th century B.C. Sir Roger L'Estrange's edition, *The Fables of Aesop* (1692), was "both the Last and the Worst" (Bentley 1697, 135); *Phalaris*: the tyrant of Acragas in Sicily (c.570–554 B.C.), and the antitype of Saddam Hussein, the tyrant of Iraq, is most famous for the brazen bull in which his political enemies were roasted alive, their screams "modulated by a small Pipe" (Budgell 1732, 163) representing the bellowing of the bull. The letters attributed to Phalaris, recognized by Erasmus and others to be forgeries, were said by Sir William Temple to "have more Race, more Spirit, more Force of Wit and Genius, than any others I have ever seen" (Temple 1690, 59).

101.12–15 *the Doctor falls hard upon a new Edition of Phalaris, put out by the Honourable*

Charles Boyle . . . to which, Mr. Boyle replyed at large, with great Learning and Wit; and the Doctor, voluminously, rejoyned: the Christ Church wits followed up the edition of Phalaris (1695) with *Dr. Bentley's Dissertation on the Epistles of Phalaris . . . Examin'd* (1698). Francis Atterbury, the future Bishop of Rochester, complained that "In laying out the design of the book, in writing above half of it and . . . attending the press, half of my life went away" (Beeching 1909, 19), but he put Boyle's name on the title-page. In "Boyle on Bentley" Bentley's scholarship is dismissed as index-learning and Sir William Temple is celebrated as "the most Accomplish'd Writer of the Age" (Boyle 1698, sig. A4r). But "You will not think the Character of Sir William Temple too great," George Smalridge says, "when you find Mr. Boyle preferred to a good post by Sir William's interest for the compliments he has paid him; which is not unlikely he may" (Nichols 1817–58, iii.271). Temple however died in January 1699 before he could prefer Boyle (or Swift) "to a good post." Bentley replied "voluminously" (560 pages) in *A Dissertation upon the Epistles of Phalaris. With an Answer to the Objections of the Honourable Charles Boyle, Esquire* (1699).

    101.19 *St. James's Library*: the Royal Library in St. James's Palace, of which Richard Bentley was appointed Keeper in December 1693 (Swift 1958, 214.n1).

    101.21 *a decisive Battel; But . . .*: the account ends indecisively in a textual hiatus (121.35).

    102.9 *Understandings*: minds, intellects (*OED*).

    103.1–2 *A Full and True Account*: Wing (ii.103–05) records 66 titles beginning with these words.

    103.side note *Riches produceth Pride;/Pride is War's Ground, &c. Vid. Ephem. de Mary Clarke; opt. Edit.*: Vincent Wing's *Almanack* (Ephmerides) was printed by Mary Clarke from 1680 to 1693. The epigraph in the upper left hand corner (Plate 26) reads, "War begets Poverty,/Poverty Peace:/Peace maketh Riches flow,/(Fate ne'er doth cease:)/ Riches produceth Pride,/Pride is War's ground,/War begets Poverty, &c../(The World) goes round." "Opt. Edit." [best edition] mocks Bentley's pedantry.

    103.13–14 *Invasions usually travelling from North to South*: "Conquest having proceeded from the North to the South" (Temple 1690, 293).

    103.18 *the Politicks*: "that branch of moral philosophy dealing with the . . . social organism as a whole (*obs.*)" (*OED*).

    103.18 *the Republick of Dogs*: Hobbes's state of nature: "no Arts, no Letters, no Society" (Hobbes 1935, 84).

    103.28–29 *State of War, of every Citizen against every Citizen*: "this Warre of every man against every man" (Hobbes 1935, 85).

    104.13–14 *the two Tops of the Hill Parnassus*: "the *Ancients* and *Moderns* . . . each possess'd a different summit of Parnassus" (Callières 1705, 4), sacred to the Muses. Like Moor Park "the top of Parnassus [was] a place of safety and of quiet, from the reach of all noises and disturbances of the Region below" (Temple 1690, 64).

    104.19 *the East*: "There is nothing more agreed, than, That all the Learning of the *Greeks* was deduced Originally from *Egypt* or *Phoenicia*" (Temple 1690, 12).

    105.1 *by Resolution and by . . . Courage*: "Victory has generally followed the smaller numbers, because . . . those who have the smaller Forces, endeavour most to supply that Defect by . . . Discipline, and Bravery" (Temple 1690, 295).

    105.2 *by the greatness of their Number*: "For the Scribblers are infinite, that like Mushrooms or Flies, are born and dye in small circles of time" (Temple 1690, 4).

    105.10 *Gall and Copperas*: inks were made of oak galls and copperas (ferrous sulphate, or green vitriol) or oak galls and lamp-black (soot); double meanings of "gall" and "vitriol" are evident.

105.13 *Trophies on both sides*: "the victory [at Actium] was thus challenged on both sides . . . The *Corinthians* did set up a Trophie, because in the Battell they had the better all day . . . And the *Corcyræans* set up a Trophie, because they had sunke 30. Gallies of the *Corinthians* . . . Thus each side claimed victory" (Thucydides 1634, 30). For the Greeks, trophies were "Monuments, in remembrance of having made the Enemy turne their backes" (ib., 18); for Swift, trophies were title-pages "fixed up in all Publick Places" (Swift 1958, 222.4–5).

105.15 *A laudable . . . Custom, happily reviv'd of late*: Swift implies that the Moderns are "the beaten Party" (105.13–15).

105.29 *there*: "IN these Books" (105.28); *inform them*: give these books their essential quality or character (*OED*).

105.32 *Brutum hominis*: "that part of man which *Paracelsus* calls *Homo Sydereus*, and more appositly *Brutum hominis*: but Agrippa *Idolum*, and Virgil *Ethereum, sensum atque Aurai Simplicis Ignem*; This part I say, which is the *Astral Man* hovers sometimes about the *Dormitories* of the Dead, and that because of the *Magnetism, or Sympathie* which is between him and the Radical, vital moysture" (Vaughan 1984, 89).

103.34–35 *a restless Spirit haunts over every Book*: "In that deep Grave a Book/ . . . And . . . her troubled Ghost still haunts there" (Swift 1937, 27).

105.39–40 *to bind them to keep the Peace*: playing on the legal formula, to bind them over to keep the peace (*OED*; Swift 1986, 219); *Chains*: Plate 22.

105.41 *the Works of Scotus*: John Duns Scotus (c.1266–1308), the eponym of "dunce," was born in Scotland and, as a Franciscan monk, became professor of theology, "Doctor Subtilis," at the University of Paris. "The Works" are his *Opera Omnia*, 12 vols. 2° (Leiden, 1639) that Swift could have seen in chains in "a certain great Library" (106.1) when he took his M.A. degree in July 1691 at Oxford.

106.3–4 *Plato . . . among the Divines*: "Plato, *the greatest* Philosopher . . . (*I had almost said the greatest Divine too) that ever lived*" (Neville 1681, sig. A6v); "Christianity . . . hath very much suffered by being blended up with Gentile philosophy" (Swift 1939–68, ix.249).

106.7 *Polemicks of the larger Size*: folio volumes.

106.10 *a new Species*: octavo volumes.

106.11 *instinct*: inspired, motivated.

106.22 *the King's Library*: the Royal Library in St. James's Palace of which Richard Bentley was appointed librarian in December 1693..

106.25 *an Historian . . . retained by neither Party*: "*an* Historian . . . *is of neither Party*" (Burnet 1681–83, ii.sig. a2v; Swift 1978, 39).

106.28 *Guardian*: Keeper, Richard Bentley (10.20–24).

106.31 *the Antient Chiefs*: Phalaris and Aesop.

106.33–37 *tendency towards his Center; a Quality, to which those of the Modern Party, are extreme subject . . . a mighty Pressure about their Posteriors and their Heels*: "tied Weights so heavy to their Heels, as to depress them to the Center" (8.6–16). The "penetrating Reader" will notice that Swift is saying that the Moderns are obese.

107.6–7 *a strange Confusion of Place among all the Books*: Bentley's complaint that "the Library was not fit to be seen" (Boyle 1698, 14) is confirmed by a French tourist who found it "en pitoyable état" (Misson 1698, 32).

107.16 *the Seven Wise Masters*: *The History of the Seven Wise Masters of Rome* (14 London editions in black letter from 1653 to 1697) is a Grubstreet version in prose of *The Seven Sages of Rome* (c. 1275), a metrical romance in the form of a frame story.

107.16–17 *Virgil . . . with Dryden on one side, and Withers on the other*: Swift abandoned a translation of the *Aeneid* in 1692 because so much of it was "confounded silly nonsense in English" (Swift 1963–65, i.10).

107.17 *Withers*: George Wither (1588–1667), a lyric poet and satirist of the school of Spenser, raised a troop of horse for the Parliament in 1642. Captured by the Royalists, his life was spared when Sir John Denham declared that so long as Wither lived he could not be the worst poet in England. After the Civil Wars Wither devoted himself to non-conformist inspirational, controversial, and prophetic works in verse and prose and became Dryden's standard for bad verse (Dryden 1956– , xvii.12).

107.18–19 *Advocates for the Moderns, chose out one*: William Wotton, who "examine[d] the Number and Strength" (107.20) of the Moderns in *Reflections upon Ancient and Modern Learning* (1694).

107.25 *Case*: physical condition (*OED*).

107.30 *manifest*: obvious (*OED*).

107.35–36 *the Moderns . . . more Antient*: "Dispute, whether there have been ever any *Antients* or no" (54.1–2).

108.10 *Temple*: the Ancient/Modern controversy was introduced into England from France by Sir William Temple's "An Essay upon Ancient and Modern Learning" (Temple 1690, 1–72).

108.15 *conversed*: conversant (*OED*).

108.18 *a certain Spider*: "if [the Wit and Mind of Man] worketh upon it selfe, as the *spider workes his webbe*, then it is endlesse, and brings forth *Cob-webs of Learning*, indeed admirable for finenesse of thred and worke, but of no Substance and Profit" (Bacon 1640, 30).

108.21 *some Giant*: Cacus (38.30).

108.22 *Turn-pikes*: spiked barriers fixed across a road as a defense against sudden attack (*OED*; Swift 1939–68, v.189.23–24); *Palissadoes*: pointed stakes fixed in the ground (*OED*).

108.22 *the Modern way of Fortification*: Swift's pacificism encourages him to sneer at Louis XIV's Commissaire-Général de Fortifications, Sébastien de Vauban (1633–1707), who revolutionized the science of fortification and siegecraft. He was a Protestant who had the courage in 1689 to petition Louis XIV to republish the Edict of Nantes.

108.33 *Thrice he endeavoured . . . and Thrice the Center shook*: an epic commonplace: "Thrice he leapt at him . . . and thrice did Apollo beat back his shining shield" (Homer 1951, v.436–37); "thrice he lifted high the Birth-day brand,/And thrice he dropt it" (Pope 1939–67, i.245–46).

108.36 *Beelzebub*: "Baal-zebub the god of Ekron" (2 Kings 1.2) is Satan's "Companion dear" in the revolt of the angels (Milton 1935, v.673); *his Subjects*: flies (*Muscae domesticae*).

108.39 *acquitted himself from the Toils*: heroic diction for "freed himself from the cobweb."

109.9 *pruned*: preened (*OED*).

109.16 *your Betters*: "One's superior . . .. from 16th to 18th c. often applied to a single person" (*OED*).

109.22 *Opposite*: adversary, opponent (*OED*).

109.26 *Drone-Pipe*: the bass pipe of a bagpipe plays only one continuous note (*OED*).

109.30 *Improvements in the Mathematicks*: chapter xiv of *Reflections upon Ancient and Modern Learning* shows "how far the Modern Mathematicians [Descartes, Newton, Leibniz, et al.] have out-done the Ancients" (Wotton 1694, 162).

109.35–36 *visit . . . all the Flowers and Blossoms of the Fields and the Garden*: "range through Fields, as well as Gardens" (Temple 1690, 323).

110.2 *spinning out all from yourself*: "like spiders, to spin out of themselves" (Plutarch, *Isis and Osiris*. 359F).

110.10–13 *engendering on it self . . . produces nothing at last, but Fly-bane and a Cobweb: Or That, which . . . brings home Honey and Wax*: "spiders . . . make cobwebs out of their own substance. But the bee . . . gathers its material from the flowers of the garden and the fields, and transforms and digests it by a power of its own" (Bacon 1620, 115); "How doth the little busy Bee/Improve each shining Hour" (Watts 1720, 23).

110.11 *Fly-bane*: the venom of spiders (*OED*).

110.12 *long Search, much Study, true Judgment*: the facts blow up in Swift's face; this describes Bentley's accomplishment.

110.17 *so much loss of Time*: singled out as Swift's final judgment of the Ancient/Modern controversy (Pinkus 1959, 51).

110.21–22 *the Regent's Humanity*: 106.28–29.

110.22–23 *tore off his Title-page, sorely defaced one half of his Leaves*: "AEsop did not write a Book of his Fables . . . one Half of the Fables now extant . . . [are] above a Thousand Years more recent than He" (Bentley 1697, 142, 146).

110.24-26 *He . . . turned himself to . . . an Ass*: Aesop "recalls his arts," like Proteus, "turns himself into all kinds of extravagant shapes" (Virgil, *Georgics*, iv.440–41) and at last into an ass, so Bentley can mistake him for "a *Modern.*"

110.30 *adapt*: fit, suited 77.23.

111.9–10 *a large Vein of . . . Satyr*: 16.3–4; "the Vein of Ridiculing all that is serious and good . . . has over-run both the Court and the Stage" (Temple 1690, 71).

111.24 *Consults*: deliberations; "the great consult [in Hell]" (Milton 1935, i.798).

111.27 *the Horse*: epic *poems*; the "grunting Reader" (94.10) is reminded that the combatants are not authors, but "Creatures, call'd *Books*" (112.17–18) (Plate 25).

111.28 *Tasso*: the epic poem of Torquato Tasso (1544–95), *Gerusalemme Liberata* (1576, 1581), is based on Christian and romance material. Davenant called him "the first of the Moderns," but Temple opined that he lacked "Wings for so high Flights" (Davenant 1651, ¹6; Temple 1690, 348).

111.29 *Milton*: "After these three [Ariosto, Tasso, Spenser], I know none of the Moderns that have made any Atchievements in *Heroick* Poetry worth Recording" (Temple 1690, 349).

111.29 *Withers*: 107.16–17; *The Light Horse*: lyric poems: *Abraham Cowley* (1618–677) was the favorite English poet of Rochester and Milton (Rochester 1980, 15–16; Johnson 1779–81, i.¹145). His second volume of verse, *The Mistress, or Several Copies of Love Poems* (1647), were love poems written by a poet "who had only heard of another sex" (ibid., i.¹106). His next volume, *Poems* (1656), includes Cowley's "Pindarique Odes," which introduced into England "the Pindarick folly" (ibid., viii.⁷4).

111.29 *The Light Horse were Commanded . . .*: the catalogue of commanding officers is an epic convention (Homer 1951, ii.494–877; *Aeneid*, vii, 641–817).

111.30 *Despreaux*: Nicolas Boileau-Despréaux (1637–1711), the self-styled "legislateur du Parnasse," wrote his *Ode sur la prise du Namur* (1693) in Pindaric stanzas, but his appearance here wants explanation. Boileau was not a lyric poet but a "*True Modern Critick*," publishing his *Art poétique* in 1674, *and* a noted Ancient, attacking Perrault (115.33) in a series of *Réflexions critiques* (1694–1713); *the Bowmen*: philosophical treatises: René Descartes, *Meditationes de prima philosophia* (Amsterdam: 1642), Pierre

Gassendi, *Syntagma philosophiae Epicuri* (Lyons: 1649), Thomas Hobbes, *Leviathan* (1651); "I do not . . . reckon the several *Hypotheses* of *Descartes,* Gassendi, or Hobbes, as Acquisitions to real Knowledge, since they may only be Chimæra's" (Wotton 1697, 262).

111.33 *Evander:* "A lapse of memory. Swift is referring to the arrow . . . of Acestes" (*Aeneid,* v.525–28; Swift 1958, 236.n1).

111.33 *like the Canon-ball into Stars:* "that Cannon-Ball,/That, shot in th'aire, point blank . . ./. . . ne'r came backwards, down again;/But . . ./Hangs like. . ./. . . a Star" (Butler 1967, 164–65).

111.33–34 *Paracelsus:* 67n†.

111.34 *Stink-Pot Flingers:* chemistry treatises; a stink-pot is 1) a hand-missile emitting a suffocating smoke (*OED*); 2) a chamber-pot.

111.35 *Rhœtia:* Rhœtia, or Rhætia, was the Roman province between the Swiss Alps and the Danube; Paracelsus was born in Einsiedeln in the canton of Schwyz.

111.35 *Dragoons:* medical treatises: William Harvey (1578-1657) reported his discovery of the circulation of the blood to the Royal College of Physicians in a lecture on 17 April 1616 and published it in *Exercitatio Anatomica de Motu Cordisi et Sanguinis in Animalibus* (Frankfurt: 1628). Sir William Temple, who was "unwilling to believe the *Circulation of the Blood,* because he could not see it," was set straight by Wotton (Wotton, 1694, 217-18).

111.36 *Aga:* a title of honour, originally in the Ottoman Empire (*OED*). It is suggested that by calling Harvey an aga Swift is calling him a non-Christian (Swift 1978, 55).

111.38–39 *white Powder . . . killed without Report:* "White Powder, does Execution but makes no noise" (Lee 1689, 23).

111.39–40 *heavy-armed Foot, all Mercenaries:* history books are relegated to the bottom of the military hierarchy, pikemen fighting for pay: Francesco Guicciardini, *L'historia d'Italia* (Firenze: 1561); Enrico Caterino Davila, *Historia delle guerre civili di Francia* (Venetia: 1630); Polydor Virgil, *Anglicae Historiae libri XXVI* (Basel: 1534); George Buchanan, *Rerum Scoticarum Historia* (Edinburgh; 1582); Juan de Mariana, *Historiae de rebus Hispaniae* (Toledo: 1592, 1605); William Camden, *Rerum Anglicarum et Hibernicarum Annales Regnante Elisabetha* (Leiden: 1639).

111.40 *Guicciardine* 1755[H] *Guiccardine* Σ.

111.41 *Engineers:* mathematicians; Johann Müller of Königsberg (Regiomontanus; 1436–76), *De triangulis* (Nürnberg: 1533); John Wilkins, *Mathematical Magick, or the Wonders that may be performed by Mechanical Geometry* (1648); Wilkins (1614–1672), Warden of Wadham College, was one of the founders of the Royal Society.

112.1 *a confused Multitude:* Catholic theological treatises: John Duns Scotus (105.41–106.8); Thomas Aquinas, "*Aristotle Sainted*" (Glanvill 1665, 117), *Summa Theologica* (Mainz: 1467); Roberto Francesco Romolo Bellarmine, *Disputationes de controversiis Christianae fidei, adversus huius temporis Hæreticos* (Ingolstadt, 1556).

112.4 *Calones:* officers' servants; pamphlet writers: "By calling this disorderly rout *calones* the author points both his satyr and contempt against all sorts of mercenary scriblers, who write as they are commanded by the leaders and patrons of sedition, faction, corruption, and every evil work: they are stiled *calones* because they are the meanest and most despicable of all writers, as the *calones* . . . were the meanest of all slaves or servants whatsoever" (Swift 1755, i.[1]146n.; *L'Estrange.* 176.26n†).

112.7 *Army of the Ancients . . . much fewer:* "a long and obstinate War . . . maintained on the [Moderns'] Part . . . by the greatness of their Number" (104.41–105.2).

112.10 *Vossius and Temple*: Isaak Vos (Vossius; 1618–89), a classical scholar, was born in Leiden. He taught Greek to Queen Christina of Sweden and lived in England after 1670. He was created D.C.L. at Oxford in September 1670 and presented with a prebend in the royal chapel at Windsor in May 1673, although he was to refuse the last rites of the Church on his deathbed. He is bracketed with Temple as admirers of Chinese medicine (Wotton 1694, 147). In February 1697 Temple gave Swift a copy of Vossius's *De Sibyllinis* (1679). Swift inscribed it "Donum Illus^{mi} D[octi] D[omini] G[ulielmi] Temple" (A gift of the illustrious and learned Sir William Temple) but later obliterated the inscription (Elias 1982, 109).

112.19 *Momus*: the son of Nox (Night) was expelled from heaven for his criticism of the gods and goddesses.

112.23–24 *all Things past, present, and to come*: "Kalchas . . . who knew all things that were, the things to come, and the things past" (Homer 1951, i.69–70).

112.29–32 *Servants to Jupiter . . . fastened to each other . . . [and] to Jupiter's great Toe*: "Let down out of the sky a cord of gold . . ./all you who are gods and . . . goddesses" (Homer 1951, viii.19–20; Swift 1958, 239.n3); the germ of the Great Chain of Being concept in scholastic philosophy; "the transcendentals of *NATURE, or Universall Ideas* doe in some sort reach things Divine. Wherefore *Homers famous Chaine of Naturall Causes, tyed to the foot of Iupiters Chaire* was celebrated" (Bacon 1640, 113), of which fastened "to Jupiter's great Toe" (112.32) is the mock-epic equivalent.

112.30 *Caravan*: group (*OED*).

112.34 *a long hollow Trunk*: a megaphone or "*Tuba Stentoro-Phonica*, an Instrument of Excellent Use, as well at Sea, as at Land," invented by Sir Samuel Moreland, Bart. (*Phil. Trans.* vi [22 January 1672], 3056).

112.36 *Second Causes*: what appear to be "*Accidents* or *Events*" to "mortal Men," in scholastic philosophy are "*Second Causes*," the first or efficient cause being God: "Nature is but the chain of second causes; and to suppose second causes without a first, is beneath the Logick of *Gotham*" (Glanvill 1665, 183).

113.1–36 *Momus, fearing the worst: "Momus . . . bent his Flight to . . . Criticism. She dwells on the Top of a snowy Mountain . . . Ignorance, her Father . . . [her] Teats, at which a Crew of ugly Monsters were greedily sucking . . . Goddess, said Momus . . . Haste . . . to the British Isle . . . the Goddess . . . began a Soliloquy. 'Tis I . . . who give Wisdom to Infants and Idiots . . . Come . . . let us ascend my Chariot*: Swift mocks Blackmore conspicuously and Milton (Milton 1935, ii.745ff.) dimly: "the Prince of Darkness flew away/To . . . fierce Discord/ . . . On this sharp Rock (Blackmore 1697, 61) . . . Her Parent Ignorance/ . . . from her Breast squeez'd Juice like blackish blood,/Her hateful Offspring's most delicious food (ib.62) . . . Hell's proud Monarch . . . thus bespoke . . . Go haste to *Albion* (ib.63) . . . [Discord] Reply'd . . . I first in Heav'n did Strife and Uproar move (ib.64) . . . And strait she mounted in the Air (ib.68)."

113.6 *Ignorance, her Father and Husband*: as Satan is the father and husband of Sin (Milton 1935, ii.747–67).

113.7 *Pride her Mother*: Sufficiency; "Not that we are sufficient of ourselves . . . but our sufficiency is of God" (2 Corinthians 3.5); "the worst composition out of the pride and ignorance of mankind" (Temple 1690, 3).

113.20 *who . . . will ever sacrifice, or build Altars*: "will any still . . . lay sacrifice upon her [Juno's] altars?" (*Aeneid*, i.48–49; Swift 1958, 241.n1).

113.24 *staid not for an answer*: jesting Pilate "would not stay for an Answer" (Bacon 1625, 1; Swift 1958, 241.n2).

113.38 *Sophister:* an undergraduate; Charles Boyle was an undergraduate at Christ Church, Oxford, when he was assigned to make a new edition of the letters of Phalaris.

113.29 *instinct:* inspired, motivated.

113.37 *Hecatomb:* 100 oxen.

113.39–40 *Chariot . . . drawn by tame Geese:* the mock-epic equivalent of the chariot of Venus, drawn by doves.

114.5 *Shelves, now desart . . . once inhabited by a Colony of Virtuoso's:* presumably because enlisted in the Modern army (Swift 1958, 242.n2).

114.11 *W–tt–n . . . begot by . . . this Goddess:* "the mother who bore you [Achilles] was immortal" (Homer 1951, i.280).

114.13–14 *But first . . . she cast about to change her Shape:* "But first he [Satan] casts to change his proper shape" (Milton 1935, iii.634).

114.16 *Octavo:* 106.10–11. Wotton's *Reflections upon Ancient and Modern Learning . . . With a Dissertation . . . By Dr. Bentley* (1697) is an octavo volume.

114.19 *Decoction of Gall and Soot:* ink.

114.19–20 *Head . . . Voice . . . Spleen:* 113.12–14.

114.30 *Dulness and Ill-Manners:* Bentley, "a . . . Dull, Unmannerly PEDANT" (Anony. 1699, 140).

114.31 *she vanish'd in a Mist:* "Apollo . . . vanished into thin air" (*Aeneid,* ix.656–58).

114.35–36 *a hundred Tongues and Mouths:* "Nay, had I [the Sibyl] a hundred tongues, a hundred mouths" (*Aeneid,* vi.625; Swift 1958, 243.n3).

114.37–38 *Say, Goddess . . . who was it that first advanced:* "Tell me . . . you Muses . . . who was the first . . . to win" (Homer 1951, xiv.508–09).

114.38–40 *Paracelsus . . . observing Galen . . . darted his Javelin:* "Paracelsus . . . introduced . . . new Methods of [medical] Practice, in opposition to the Galenical" (Temple 1701, 206).

115.3 *bore the wounded Aga . . . on their Shields to his Chariot:* William Harvey M.D. (111.36): "others bore him [Satan] on their Shields/Back to his Chariot" (Milton 1935, vi.337–38).

115.8 *Bacon:* Sir William Temple's approval of Bacon, "The great Wits [intellectuals] among the moderns have been . . . *Sir Philip Sidney,* [and] *Bacon*" (Temple 1690, 61), is here dramatized: "Aristotle . . . miss'd the valiant Modern."

115.11 *Defect in his Head-piece:* Descartes' theory of vortices?

115.12–14 *whirled the valiant Bow-man round; till Death . . . drew him into his own Vortex:* "Atreides killed him [Hippolochos] . . . and sent him spinning" (Homer 1951, xi.145–47).

115.13–14 *Death, like a Star of superior Influence, drew him into his own Vortex:* "*Jupiter.* . . had we been his Neighbors . . . would doubtless with ease have swallow'd us up in his *Vortex*" (Fontenelle 1687, 59).

115.18–19 *Homer . . . on a furious Horse:* "*Homer* had more fire and rapture" (Temple 1690, 320).

115.21 *Say Goddess, whom he slew first, and whom he slew last:* "who then was the first and who the last that they slaughtered" (Homer 1951, v.703).

115.22 *Gondibert:* Sir William Davenant's *Gondibert: An Heroick Poem* (1651) based on Christian and romance material mercifully breaks off in the middle, but Hobbes calls it the "equal . . . of *Homer*" (Davenant 1651, [¹82, misnumbered 84]).

115.23 *not so famed for his Speed:* "during my journey in this worke [I, Davenant] have mov'd with a slow pace" (Davenant 1651, ¹32).

115.23–24 *Docility in kneeling, whenever his Rider would mount*: "that Beast [Hudibras's mount] would kneel . . ./. . . to take his rider up" (Butler 1967, 14).

115.25–26 *spoiled Homer of his Armour*: "if I take his life . . ./I will strip his armour and carry it to sacred Ilion" (Homer 1951, vii.81–82).

115.30 *bit the Earth*: "bit the vast earth" (Homer 1951, xxiv.738).

115n† *Denham . . . not the real Author of Coopers-Hill*: "*Cooper*'s-Hill . . ./Was writ by a Vicar, who had forty pound for't" (*POAS* 1716, i.210).

115.32 *W–sl–y*: Samuel Wesley (1662–1735) was a classmate of Daniel Defoe in the nonconformist academy at Newington Green, but conformed and graduated B.A. from Exeter College, Oxford. He became a brother-in-law and collaborator in *The Athenian Gazette* of John Dunton, and father of John Wesley, the Methodist evangelist. He wrote much "Holy-Doggerel" (*POAS* Yale, vi.107n.) including *The Life of Our Blessed Lord and Saviour Jesus Christ. An Heroic Poem* (1693) in ten books embellished with 60 copper plates. He made the first edition of *The Dunciad* (1728), but did not survive the cut.

115.32–34 *Homer . . . took Perrault . . . hurl'd him at Fontenelle*: *Le Siecle de Louis le Grand* (1687) by Charles Perrault and "Une Digression sur les anciens et les modernes" (1688) of Bernard Le Bovier de Fontenelle (1657–1757) are major texts in the Ancient/Modern controversy.

115.34 *dashing out both their Brains*: a comic *doublage* of a conventional epic conclusion to hand-to-hand combat, "spattered brains" (Homer 1951, xi.98; *Aeneid*, v.413).

115.35–37 *Virgil . . . was mounted on a dapple grey Steed, the slowness of whose Pace, was an Effect of the highest Mettle*: this delightful oxymoron may reflect Swift's limited admiration of Virgil: "Folijs tantum ne carmina manda &c [trust not thy verses to leaves] . . . 'tis confounded silly nonsense in English" (Swift 1999–2006, i.111).

116.1–2 *sorrel*: reddish brown (*OED*); in Jacobite mythology the horse that stepped in a molehill and threw William III was named Sorrel. The King never recovered and Sorrel was canonized (*POAS* Yale, vi.364–66); *a Foe*: Dryden.

116.11–12 *the Lady in a Lobster*: the chalky part of the stomach of a lobster, fancifully supposed to resemble the outline of a seated woman (*OED*); in Shadwell's *The Sullen Lovers* (1668) Sir Positive At-all (a caricature of Sir Robert Howard, Dryden's brother-in-law and collaborator) has written a play called *The Lady in the Lobster* (Shadwell 1927, i.53).

116.14–16 *Dryden in a long Harangue . . . called him Father*: in a 47-page "Dedication" of his translation of the *Aeneid* Dryden boasts "that *Virgil* in Latine, and *Spencer* in English, have been my Masters" (Dryden 1697, sig. (e)2r; Swift, 1958, 247.n2).

116.14–20 *Dryden . . . proposed an Exchange of Armor . . . Virgil consented (for the Goddess . . . cast a Mist before his Eyes) tho' his was of Gold, and cost a hundred Beeves, the others but of rusty Iron*: "Zeus . . . stole away the wits of Glaukos/who exchanged with Diomedes . . . armour/of gold for bronze, for nine oxen's worth the worth of an hundred" (Homer 1951, vi.234–36; Swift 1958, 247.n3).

116.26–27 *Lucan . . . upon a fiery Horse*: *De Bello Civile*, known as *Pharsalia*, was the epic poem of Marcus Annaneus Lucanus (39–65 A.D.). He "made some very high flights" (Temple 1690, 324).

116.29–30 *Bl–ckm–re . . . one of the Mercenaries*: *Prince Arthur. An Heroick Poem. In X Books* (1695) and *King Arthur. An Heroick Poem. In Twelve Books* (1697) might be expected to qualify as epic poems and cavalry troopers, but Swift demotes them to the bottom of the military hierarchy: historians armed with a spear and fighting for pay. Despite his success as a physician, Sir Richard Blackmore M.D. (83.16) could not ride as a dragoon (111.35) because he had not yet published a medical treatise.

116.32–33 *AEsculapius . . . turn'd off the Point*: the Greek god of medicine intervenes because Blackmore's "skill as a physician attoned for his dullness as a poet" (Swift 1755, [1]i.153n.).

116.39 *Creech*: Thomas Creech (1659–1700) published *T. Lucretius Carus . . . his six books de Natura rerum, done into English verse* (Oxford: 1682) and *The Odes, Satyrs, and Epistles of Horace. Done into English* (Oxford: 1684) and hanged himself.

116.39–117.2 *the Goddess Dulness . . . Father Ogleby*: as Turnus pursues the phantom of Aeneas fashioned by Juno, Aeneas's tutelary deity, and is borne home to his father, Daunus (*Aeneid*, x.635–80), so Creech pursues the phantom of Horace fashioned by Dulness, Creech's tutelary deity, and is borne home to his father, Ogilby.

117.2 *Ogleby*: John Ogilby (1600–76), "one of the prodigies" of one age (Phillips 1675, [2]114), became a generic term for bad poetry in the next. Ogilby was a successful and sometimes brilliant dancing master, theatrical producer, translator, publisher, book designer, and cartographer. But when he died—perhaps in the very month of his death—he was translated into a commodity: "Much *Heywood, Shirly, Ogleby* there lay,/ But loads of *Sh*—— almost choakt the way" (Dryden 1956– , ii.56–57). "Mr. *Ogilby* would have perhaps got some Reputation, if he had aspired no higher than *Reynard the Fox*: But having ventur'd to translate in Verse the sublimest *Latin* Poets, his Name will, as long as the *English* Tongue lives, signify a *Poetaster*" (*Compleat Key* 1718, 19).

117.3–5 *Pindar . . . Never advancing in a direct Line, but wheeling with incredible Agility and Force*: Swift's first literary ambition was to write mock-Pindaric stanzas in the manner of Cowley; but the only features that Swift imitated successfully were Pindar's obscurity and digressiveness (Swift 1978, 88).

117.3 *Oldham . . . and Afra*: Pindar slays John Oldham (1653–83) and Aphra Behn (1640–89) for their mock-Pindaric stanzas.

117.12 *scarce a dozen Cavaliers*: "twice six chosen men" (*Aeneid*, xii.899–900); *as Cavaliers are in our degenerate Days*: "as men are now," an epic commonplace (Homer 1951, v.304, xii.383, 449, xx.286).

117.16 *the Shield . . . given Him by Venus*: for writing *The Mistress, or Several Copies of Love Poems* (1647), "infinitely below his Pindariques" (Dryden 1956– , iv.7).

117.18–19 *thrice . . . thrice*: 108.33.

117.21–22 *spare my Life, and possess . . . the Ransom which my Friends will give, when they hear that I am alive*: "Take me alive . . ./and my father would make you glad with abundant ransom,/were he to hear that I am alive" (Homer 1951, x.378–81).

117.23–24 *your Carcass shall be left for the Fowls of the Air, and the Beasts of the Field*: "on you the dogs and the vultures shall feed" (Homer 1951, xxii.335–36; Swift 1958, 249.n4).

117.22–25 *Pindar . . . raised his sword, and . . . cleft the wretched Modern in twain*: Turnus "brandishes his uplifted sword;/ the steel cleaves the head in twain" (*Aeneid*, ix.749–50).

117.26 *one half*: Cowley's *Poems* (1656) that includes the "Pindarick Odes."

117.27 *the other half*: Cowley's *The Mistress, or Several Copies of Love Poems* (1647).

117.27–28 *This Venus took, and wash'd it seven times in Ambrosia . . . so it became a Dove*: "Venus . . . by her harnessed doves . . . came to . . . the river Numicius . . .She bade the river-god wash away from Aeneas all his mortal part . . . [She] touched his lips with ambrosia . . . and so made him a god" (Ovid, *Metamorphoses*, xiv.596–607; Swift 1978, 90–91).

117.36–37 *from a Squadron of. . . heavy armed Foot, a Captain, whose Name was B–ntl–y* (Plate 27): as historian Richard Bentley (10.20–24) trails a pike for pay with the rank of captain. As a principal in the Ancient/Modern controversy he had expected to be a general (118.24–26).

117.side note *Hiatus valdè deflendus in MS.*: a most regrettable hiatus in manuscript.

117.38–118.1 *Tall, but without Shape or Comeliness; Large, but without Strength or Proportion*: Swift deflates Denham's famous pentameter couplet in *Cooper's Hill* (1655), "Though deep, yet clear, though gentle, yet not dull, / Strong without rage, without ore-flowing full," into an unrhymed tetrameter couplet.

118.1 *patch'd up of a thousand incoherent Pieces*: Bentley's *A Dissertation upon the Epistles of Phalaris* (1697) is "patch'd up" of innumerable quotations, 239 marginal notes, and at least five "*ibids.*"

118.3 *an Etesian [Gk. annual] Wind*: a northwest wind that blows every summer in the Mediterranean (*OED*), serving here to mock Wotton (Wotton 1694, 102, 133).

118.5 *his Breath, corrupted into Copperas . . . [and] Gall*: Bentley *breathes* ink (105.10).

118.7 *atramentous*: inky (*OED*).

118.7 *Flail*: during the panic induced by Titus Oates's Popish Plot (1679–80), Londoners armed themselves with "Protestant Flails" (*POAS* Yale, ii.opp. p. 12), a kind of hinged blackjack.

118.12–13 *his crooked Leg, and hump Shoulder*: "Thersites . . ./ . . . was the ugliest man who came beneath Ilion. He was/bandy-legged . . . with shoulders/stooped" (Homer 1951, ii.212–18).

118.21–24 *he conceived . . . they were all a Pack of Rogues . . . Sons of Whores . . . d-mn'd Cowards . . . and nonsensical Scoundrels*: an exaggerated sample of Bentley's style occurs above (109.5–8), an actual sample is this: "That Idiot of a Monk [Planudes] has given us a Book . . . that, perhaps, cannot be match'd in any Language, for Ignorance and Nonsense" (Bentley 1697, 147).

118.26–29 *You, said he, sit here idle, but, when I, or any other valiant Modern, kill an Enemy, you are sure to seize the Spoil. But I will not march one Foot against the Foe, till you all swear to me, that, whomever I take or kill, his Arms I shall quietly possess.* Bentley's speech is based on Thersites' complaint to Agamemnon that when "I, or some other Achaian take a prisoner, Agamemnon gets the lion's share of the ransom" (Homer 1951, ii.225–31), which in turn mocks Achilles' petulant complaint to Agamemnon about Achilles' share in captured slave girls (Homer 1951, i.121–29, 148–71).

118.30 *Scaliger*: Joseph Justus Scaliger (1540–1609), the son of Julius Caesar Scaliger (94.side note), "excell'd in Critical Learning" (Moréri 1694, i.sig. 5F1r). His editions of Ausonius, Catullus, Theocritus, Lycophron, Seneca, Varro, Manilius, and Juvenal qualify him for single combat with Bentley.

118.33 *thy Study of Humanity*: a pun on 1) Bentley's study of the Greek and Latin classics, *litterae humaniores*, and 2) Bentley's alleged discourtesy to the Hon. Charles Boyle (106.28–29).

119.1–3 *B–NTL–Y . . . took his beloved W-tt-n*: the Bentley-Wotton sally parodies the fatal night patrol of Nisus and Euryalus (*Aeneid*, ix.176–449).

119.3 *his beloved W-tt-n*: (Plate 28); the "careful Reader" (37.18) will recall that the first school to be established in the "Academy" for Modern Studies is "a large

Pederastick School" (13.7); the innuendo here and at 119.19–20, 119.36, 121.6 seems dragged in.

119.3–4 *by Policy or Surprise*: "by fraud or guile/What force effected not" (Milton 1935, i.646–47).

119.5–7 *March . . . to the Right of their own Forces; then wheeled Northward . . . Aldrovandus's Tomb, which they pass'd on the side of the declining sun*: Bentley's and Wotton's march vaguely recalls Satan's assault on Eden: "the right hand coast . . . wheel the North . . . the Sun's decline" (Milton 1935, ii.633; iv.783, 792).

119.7 *Aldrovandus's Tomb*: the "Tomb" of Ulisse Aldrovandi (1522–1605), an "infinitely better" naturalist than Pliny (Wotton 1697, 317), may be the 13 folio volumes of his *Opera Omnia* (Bologna: 1599–1668; Swift 1958, 253.n2).

119.14 *conscious*: witnessing.

119.31–32 *Phalaris was just that Minute dreaming, how a most vile Poetaster had lampoon'd him, and how he had got him roaring in his Bull*: in the last paragraph of *Dr. Bentley's Dissertations on the Epistles of Phalaris . . . Examin'd* (1698) Charles Boyle consigns Bentley to Phalaris's brazen bull (Plate 29): "'twill be too late to repent when he begins to bellow" (Boyle 1698, 290). Bentley then reminded Boyle that Phalaris "*at last* bellow'd *in his own Bull*" (Bentley 1699, xliii).

119.33–34 *a Wild Ass*: Bentley.

119.35 *Faces*: 1755[H] Faces 1704[1]–1704[3] Faces, 1705[4]–1710[5]. Faces. 1755[H].

119.39 *in the Language of Mortal Men*: "river . . . called Xanthos by the gods, but by mortals Skamandros" (Homer 1951, xx.73–74; *Helicon*: a mountain in Greece sacred to the Muses; Swift may have meant Hippocrene, a spring on Mt. Helicon which is the source of poetic inspiration.

120.5 *nothing but Mud*: "the man who wants only as much as he needs, neither drinks muddy water nor drowns in a flood" (Horace, *Satires*, I.i.59–60; Swift 1958, 255.n1).

120.10 *The one he could not distinguish*: Charles Boyle (Plate 24).

120.17–18 *Man for Man, Shield against Shield, and Launce against Launce*: "spear by spear, shield against shield . . . man against man" (Homer 1951, xiii.130–31).

120.19 *fights like a God, and Pallas or Apollo are ever at his Elbow*: as in the case of Lord Somers (4.31–32), the epic heightening of Temple's non-existent military prowess is reduced to mock epic bathos by the homely phrase "at his Elbow."

120.19 *Mother*: Criticism (114.9, 114.31–32).

120.19–21 *Oh, Mother! . . . grant me to Hit Temple with this Launce, that the Stroak may send him to Hell*: an epic convention: "Athene; grant me that I may kill this man" (Homer 1951, v.117–18).

120.22–24 *The first Part of his Prayer the Gods granted . . . but the rest, by a perverse Wind sent from Fate, was scattered in the Air*: an epic convention: "Zeus . . . granted him one prayer, and denied him the other" (Homer 1951, xvi.249–50); "Phoebus . . . vouchsafed that half his prayer should prosper; half he scattered to the ambient breezes" (*Aeneid*, xi.74–95).

120.26–27 *the Goddess, his Mother . . . adding Strength to his Arm*: "Athene . . . put strength into the man's shoulders" (Homer 1951, xvii.567–69).

120.28–29 *Temple neither felt the Weapon touch him, nor heard it fall*: Sir William Temple, Bart. was "*mortify'd*" to be called Wotton's "Adversary" (144.16–18); for Wotton, as a country parson, like Swift, was "very low . . . low low very low" (marginalia in the Yale copy of Wotton's *Reflections* 1694 (Yale 1742 Library 9-6-16, pp. 101, 144).

120.31–32 *Apollo . . . his Fountain*: Helicon (119.39).

120.33 ————: Henry Aldrich (1647–1710), Dean of Christ Church, Oxford "desired [Charles Boyle] (Plate 24) to put out a new Edition of the *Epistles of Phalaris*" (Budgell 1732, 157).

120.36 *all the Gods*: besides the Dean, Henry Aldrich, the Christ Church wits included Charles Boyle's two tutors, Francis Atterbury the future Bishop of Rochester (1713–1723) and John Freind who became a distinguished London physician and Tory Member of Parliament, and George Smalridge the future Bishop of Bristol (1714–1719) who is credited with writing "the designedly humorous part" of "Boyle against Bentley," i.e. Boyle 1698 (*DNB*, xviii.383).

120.40 *a Wild Ass*: "Is there any thing so assur'd, resolute, disdainful, contemplative, serious, and grave as an Ass?" (Montaigne 1700, iii.254).

121.3 *Philomela*: the nightingale.

121.9 *new polish'd and gilded*: Boyle's edition of Phalaris (1695) was bound in polished calf with gold lettering on the spine.

121.12–13 *a woman in a little House, that gets a painful Livelihood by Spinning*: "a careful widow/. . . working to win a pitiful wage" (Homer 1951, xii.433–35); Swift converts epic pathos into mock epic comedy: Boyle hunting down Bentley and Wotton becomes a farm woman rounding up her runaway geese.

121.18 *in Phalanx*: mock epic exaggeration; two warriors cannot form a phalanx; *a Spear*: Bentley's *A Dissertation upon the Epistles of Phalaris* (1697).

121.19–20 *Pallas . . . took off the Point*: "Pallas . . . would not let the point penetrate" (Homer 1951, xi.437–38).

121.20–21 *a dead Bang against the Enemy's Shield*: "the shield gave out a hollow clang" (Homer 1951, xiii.409).

121.24 *the Weapon*: Boyle's *Dr. Bentley's Dissertation on the Epistle's of Phalaris . . . Examin'd* (1698); presumed publication of this work in February 1698, "In the Press, and will be publish'd in a few days" (Arber 1903–06, iii.60), sets a *terminus a quo* for the writing of *The Battle of the Books* (Plate 3).

121.25 *flanking down*: bringing the arms down upon the flanks (*OED*).

121.28–29 *Woodcocks*: "As wise as a woodcock" is proverbial (Tilley 1950, 750).

121.30 *Friends transfix'd*: the poetic justice is exact: as Bentley skewered the epistles of Phalaris and the fables of Aesop in one volume, so Boyle in one volume (1698) skewers Wotton's *Reflections upon Ancient and Modern Learning* and Bentley's *A Dissertation upon the Epistles of Phalaris . . . and the Fables of Aesop*, which were published in one volume (1697).

121.32 *Charon*: ferries souls over the river Styx to the underworld for one *obolus* (one-sixth of a *drachma*), a very cheap trip.

121.33 *beloved, loving Pair . . . immortal shall you be*: "Happy pair [Nisus and Euryalus]! If aught my verse avail, no day shall ever blot you from the memory of time" (*Aeneid*, ix.446–47; Limouze 1948, 88).

131.37 *Desunt caetera*: "the rest is missing"; "in so doubtfull a taking the delightfull History stopped and remained dismembred" (Cervantes 1612–20), i.63).

122.1–12 *The Bookseller's Advertisement*: like "The Bookseller to the Reader" (28–29) this advertisement is (without evidence) traditionally attributed to Swift.

122.5–6 *kept it . . . some Years*: presumably 1697–1704 (6.3).

124.4 *Mechanical Operation*: "Beads, Pictures, Rosaries and Pixes:/The Tools of working out Salvation,/By meer Mechanick Operation" (Butler 1967, 231).

124.8 *Beaux Esprits*: "*The* Beaux-Esprits, *The Men of* Ayr, *and* Wit, *are pleased with Meeting the Sacred, and Awful* Mysteries *of* Christian Religion *under* Burlesque, *and* Raillery" (Beverley 1696, 4).

124.8 *New England* 1755[H] New Holland Σ.

124.14–15 *Westminster-Hall* . . . *St. Paul's Church yard, and Fleet-street*: "bookselling centres" (Swift 1958, 262.n1).

125.8 *the Iroquois Virtuosi*: a virtuoso "has his Correspondents in e'ry part of the World" ([Astell], 1696, 97); among the "*Virtuoso Experiments*" (24.side note) of the Iroquois is "eating alive some Prisoners of War" (Fontenelle 1687, 18).

125.12 *the literati of Tobinambou*: the literati are said to be illiterate; the Tupinamba, on the east coast of Brazil, "is a Nation wherein there is . . . no Knowledge of Letters" (Montaigne 1700, i.324).

125.13 *Ordinaries*: mail deliveries (*OED*).

125.19 *a Visit*: Mahomet's "famous Night-journey from *Mecca* to *Jerusalem*, and from thence to *Heaven*, of which he tells us in the 17*th* Chapter of his *Alcoran*" (Prideaux 1697, 41).

125.20 *several Vehicles*: neither the Koran nor Prideaux mention "fiery Chariots, wing'd Horses, and celestial Sedans" (125.21).

125.22 *Mahomet . . . would be born to Heaven upon nothing but his Ass*: Trygaeus prefers a dung beetle (Aristophanes, *The Peace*, 73–77). Muhammad describes his mount as "a Beast as white as Milk, and of a mixt Nature between an *Ass* and a *Mule*" (Prideaux 1697, 42). Jesus enters Jerusalem mounted upon an ass "that it might be fulfilled which was spoken by the prophet [Zechariah 9.9] saying . . . thy King cometh . . . sitting upon an ass" (Matthew 21.4–5).

125.34–36 *whatever in my small Reading, occurs, concerning . . . our Fellow-Creature* [the ass], *I do never fail to set it down*: on 19 occasions (Kelling and Preston 1984, 110–11).

126.22–23 *not to suit and apply them to particular Occasions*: 13.28–34.

126.30–31 *Revolutions of the greatest Figure in History*: "mighty Revolutions . . . in Empire" (76.32–33).

126.35 *the Philosopher's Stone*: something supposed by alchemists to turn base metal into gold (*OED*); *the Grand Elixir*: a medicine supposed to heal all wounds and cure all diseases (*OED*); "as useless a search, as that of the Universal Medicine, or the Philosophers Stone" (Temple 1701, 20).

126.36 *The Planetary Worlds*: "Discoveries of new Worlds in the Planets" (Temple 1701, 283).

126.36 *Squaring of the Circle*: converting a circle into a square of the same area; Swift's tutor at Trinity College Dublin, St. George Ashe, published a paper demonstrating (unsuccessfully) that it was possible (*Phil. Trans.* xiv (20 August 1684), 672–76).

126.36–37 *The Summun Bonum*: the thing mostly to be desired (*OED*).

126.41 *Holy Ground*: "the Lord said . . . put off thy shoes from off thy feet, for the place whereon thou standest is holy ground" (Exodus 3.5; Swift 1958, 266.n3).

127.3–4 *often mistaken for each other*: "*Jack* . . . *Peter* . . . *often mistaken for each other* . . . W. Wotton" (91n[1]).

127.12 *Authors*: Casaubon 1656, More 1656.

127.21 *British Workmen*: anachronistic "class overtones" are noted by *marxisant* critics (Hawes 1996, 107).

127.31–35 *Hippocrates tells us . . . the Heads of Infants*: "I will begin with the Longheads

. . . Originally custom was chiefly responsible for the length of the head, but now custom is reinforced by nature . . . As soon as a child is born they remodel its head with their hands . . . and force it to increase in length . . . Custom originally so acted that through force such a nature came into being; but as time went on the process became natural" (Hippocrates, *Airs, Waters and Places*, xiv). "Our Ancestors, the *Scythians*" is Swift's embellishment.

127.36–37 *in the Form of a Sugar-Loaf*: "their [the inhabitants of Fooliana] heads like sugar lo[a]ves" (Hall 1609?, 124).

128.1 *that refined People*: the Scythians were nomadic barbarians (Herodotus, iv.passim).

128.2 *Round-heads*: adherents of the Parliamentary party in the Civil Wars (1642–48), so called because they cut their hair short; "if a man have long hair, it is a shame unto him" (1 Corinthians 11.14).

128.4 *a black Cap*: worn by dissenting preachers.

127.14 *launching out the Soul*: i.e. above matter; "there are three general ways of ejaculating the Soul, or transporting it beyond the Sphere of Matter" (127.6–7).

128.19–20 *Corruption of the Senses is the Generation of the Spirit*: a commonplace witticism: "The corruption of a Poet is the Generation of a Statesman" (Dryden 1956– , ix.10); "The Corruption of *Reason* was the Generation of his Wits" (Anony. 1700, 3).

128.30 *the Profane*: the uninitiated (*OED*).

128.35 *the Primitive Way of Inspiration*: "the immediate Act of God . . . called, *Prophecy* or *Inspiration*" (127.8–9).

128.37 *the Apostles . . . in one place*: "The apostles . . . were all with one accord in one place" (Acts 2.1).

128.41–129.1 *the Spirit instructed the Apostles in the Gift of speaking several Languages*: "The apostles . . . began to speak with other tongues, as the Spirit gave them utterance" (Acts 2.4).

129.7–8 *the Cloven Tongues never sat upon the Apostles Heads while their Hats were on*: (Plate 30). "when the day of Pentecost was fully come . . . there appeared unto [the apostles] cloven tongues like as of fire, and it sat upon each of them" (Acts 2.1–3); "The *Descent of the H. Ghost* . . . in the Shape of Cloven Tongues, at the first Pentecost . . . is one of the Subjects of his Mirth: And because in our Dissenting Congregations the Auditory used formerly with great Indecency to keep on their Hats in Sermon Time, therefore . . . the Cloven Tongues never sat upon the Apostles Heads, while their Hats were on" (Wotton 1705², 64).

129.10 *the Word, Spirit . . . understood for a supernatural Assistance, approaching from without*: 130.9–20; "but the Gifts of which the Apostle speaks ["there are diversities of gifts, but the same Spirit" (1 Corinthians 12.4)] . . . are wholly Supernatural, and immediately proceed from the Spirit of God" (Hickes 1681, 3).

129.16–17 *prevent Perspiration . . . as we may, perhaps, farther shew*: 132.15–21.

129.side note *Bernier*: "there are such that are believed to be true Saints, illuminated and perfect *Jauguis* [yogis], entirely united to God . . . [in] *these* raptures . . . they spend many hours together in being insensible, and beholding in that time, as they give out, God himself, like a very bright and ineffable Light . . . after they have fasted many days . . . 'tis requisite first to keep themselves alone retired from all company, directing the Eyes steadily towards Heaven for a while, then gently casting them down again, and then fixing them both so as to look at one and the same time upon the tip of their Nose . . . and remaining firm and intent in that posture, until such a Light do come" (Bernier 1671–72, iii.136–38).

129.30–31 *the Art of See-saw on a Beam, and swinging by Session upon a Cord*: the women of Moscow "occupying the ends of a kind of board, take turns moving up and down, or more often hang a rope in a semicircle between two posts and as they sit on the rope are pushed and borne back and forth" (Gwagnin 1578, f. 24r); *by Session*: while seated.

129.32 *Scythian Ancestors*: Herodotus (iv.21.117) locates the Sarmatae on the eastern boundary of Scythia and mentions that they allowed much freedom to their women: "Woman-ruled Sarmatae" was conflated with the nation of the Amazons on the Black Sea (*EB*, xxiv.220). At a later date the Sarmatae became the ruling clan of the Scyths (*EB*, xxiv.527).

129.38–40 *a Knot of Irish, Men and Women . . . a short Pipe of Tobacco [is] handed round the Company; each preserving the Smoak in his Mouth, till it comes again to his Turn to take in fresh*: the people of Carrigogunnell "all smoke, women as well as men, and a pipe an inch long serves the whole family . . . Seven or eight will gather . . . each taking two or three whiffs gives it to his neighbour, commonly holding his mouth full of smoke till the pipe comes about to him again" (Stevens 1912, 139; Swift 1958, 272.n3). *Qu.* where did Swift see the ms. journal of John Stevens, now B.M. Ms. Add. 36296?

130.1 *Consort*: musicians playing together (*OED*).

130.3 *Heads and Points*: head to head and foot to foot (*OED*, s.v. **Head**, 46).

130.9–20 *the Spirit approaches . . . the Spirit would soon faint*: tumescence . . . detumescence.

130.12–20 *moving your Body up and down . . . grow languid*: underneath this pile of verbiage couples are rutting.

130.18 *Interstitia*: intervals between actions (*OED*, s.v. **Interstice**).

131.10 *Cœlum Empyræum*: in ancient cosmology the sphere of fire; in Christian cosmology the abode of God and the angels.

131.21–22 *Dum fas atque nefas exiguo fine libidum/Discernunt avidi*: "mad with desire, they distinguish right and wrong only by the fine line their passions draw" (Horace, *Odes*, I.xviii.10–11; Swift 1958, 275.n3).

131.24 *cloven Tongues*: 129.7–8; *cloven Feet*: the Devil in Christian mythology (*OED*).

131.26–27 *the Cant of our English Enthusiastick Preachers*: 77.4–6.

131.30–31 *to interpose . . . preternatural Power without an absolute . . . Necessity*: "let no god intervene, unless the problem is worthy of such a solution" (Horace, *Ars poetica*, 191–92; Swift 1808, 438).

131.34–35 *if he hath knockt his Head against a Post*: "if he happened to bounce his Head against a Post" (88.23–24).

131.40–132.1 *this Mystery of venting spiritual Gifts is nothing but a Trade*: "*Godliness is now not only a* Gain *but a* Trade" (Gildon 1709, sig. A6v).

132.16 *quilted Caps*: "he [William Prynne (93.2n)] wore a long quilt cap, which . . . served him as an umbrella to defend his eies from the light" (Aubrey 1898, ii.174).

132.24 *the Picture of Hobbes's Leviathan*: Plate 31.

132.34 *hamated*: furnished with hooks or "crooked Prickles" (*Phil. Trans.* xix (September 1697), 685); some of Epicurus's atoms are "magis hamatis" (more hooked) than others (Lucretius, *De rerum natura*, ii.394, 405).

133.14 *Musical Instruments . . . made from the Bones of an Ass*: "Aesop said . . . that the modern flute-makers . . . use bones from asses" (Plutarch, *Septem Sapientem Convivium*, 151A).

133.17 *Os sacrum*: a triangular bone that forms the back of the pelvis (*OED*), the "Rump-bone" (Butler 1967, 277).

133.24 *The Bearers of this Light, resembling Lanthorns, compact of Leaves from old Geneva Bibles; Which Invention, Sir H-mphry Edw-n, during his Mayoralty, of happy Memory, highly approved and advanced; affirming the Scripture to be now fulfilled, where it says, Thy Word is a Lanthorn to my Feet, and a Light to my Paths*: "Sir *Humphrey Edwin* [94n†] is made to apply the Words of the Psalmist . . . [Psalms 119.105], to a whimsical Dark Lanthorn of our Authors own Contrivance; wherein he poorly alludes to *Hudibras*'s *Dark-Lanthorn of the Spirit* [Butler 1967, 16], which none can see by but those that bear it" (Plate 32) (Wotton 1705[2], 59–60). Wotton fails to recognize a simile: the Quakers' inner light is like a dark lantern with a slide by which the light can be concealed (*OED*, s.v. **Dark-lantern**); *Geneva Bibles*: the Geneva Bible (aka the Breeches Bible) was translated by English refugees in Geneva during the murderous reign of Catholic Mary I: the New Testament was published in 1557 and both Testaments in 1560. "At least 140 editions" of the latter were published between 1560 and 1644 (*EB*, iii.901).

133.34 *it is frequent for a single Vowel to draw Sighs from a Multitude*: "from a Monasillable . . . can *Raise* many Points of Doctrine" (Anony. 1700, 77); "to make people sigh and cry by meer repetition of *Scripture words*" (Eachard 1672, 138).

133.36 *Liquid*: the sounds denoted by the letters *l, m, n, r* (*OED*).

133.41 *Hawking, Spitting*: "a stock of *Scripture phrases* . . . with helpful *ahs, hems, coughs, spittings, wipings*" (Eachard 1672, 166).

134.2–3 *it is of no Import through what Vehicle it is conveyed*: "it is of no Import from what Originals this *Vapour* proceeds" (76.10–11).

134.6–7 *my Critical Essay upon the Art of Canting*: 2.14–15.

134.22 *AS yet*: 2 Kings 13.25, 2 Chronicles 20.33.

134.23 *Banbury*: a town in Oxfordshire noted for the zeal of its Puritan inhabitants (*OED*).

133.20–21 *The first Ingredient, towards the Art of Canting, is a competent Share of Inward Light*: "The Two Principal Qualifications of a Phanatick Preacher are, his Inward Light . . ." (22n*).

134.28–29 *a perpetual Game at Leap-Frog . . . sometimes the Flesh is uppermost, and sometimes the Spirit*: "can any thing be more blasphemous" (Wotton 1705[2], 64); "I [Paul] delight in the law of God . . . But I see another law in my members, warring against the law of my mind, and bringing me into captivity to the law of sin which is in my members . . . So then with the mind I myself serve the law of God, but with the flesh the law of sin" (Romans 7.22–25).

134.28–29 *sometimes, the Flesh is uppermost, and sometimes the Spirit*: "the flesh lusteth always contrary to the Spirit" (*Book of Common Prayer* 1704, sig. P12r).

134n* *W. Wotton*: the source of the reference is Wotton 1705[2], 65.

134.30 *Rippon*: spurs made in Ripon, Yorkshire, are proverbially superior.

134.35 *Repetition*: recitation of something learned by heart (*OED*); *Lecture*: in the Church of Scotland, a prolonged exposition of a passage of Scripture (*OED*).

134.37 *honourable Wounds, all before*: "bloudy wounds, but all before" (Butler 1967, 66).

135.4 *the Rod of Hermes*: mercury therapy for venereal disease.

135.6 *broke down the Bridge*: skeletal deformation of the nose in the late stages of syphilis; 89.19–20.

135.10–11 *Snuffle of a Bag-pipe*: "This Light inspires, and playes upon/The nose of Saint, like Bag-pipe-drone" (Butler 1967, 16.509-510).

135.13–15 *no Doctrine pass'd for Sound and Orthodox, unless it were delivered thro' the Nose*: "The Snuffling and Twang of the Nose, passes for the Gospel sound" (Crockatt and Munroe 1748, 14; Maybee 1942, 239).

135.17 *the same Experiment*: 135.18–21.

135.18 *Darius*: "concerning the making of a king, they resolved that he should be elected whose horse . . . should first be heard to neigh at sunrise. Now Darius had a clever groom . . . he brought a mare that was especially favored by Darius' horse . . . and let the stallion have his way with the mare. At dawn of day . . . [when] they came to the place where the mare had been picketed . . . Darius' horse trotted up to it and whinnied" (Herodotus, iii.84–86; Swift 1958, 282.n1).

135.32 *fuliginous*: sooty (*OED*).

135.39–40 *Spirits are produced from Lees, by the Force of Fire*: as brandy is distilled from fermented wine.

136.10–12 *Rites known in Greece by the Names of Orgya, Panegyres and Dionysia, whether introduced there by Orpheus or Melampus*: "Melampus . . . they say, brought from Egypt the rites, which the Greeks celebrate in the name of Dionysus" (Diodorus Siculus, i.97; Swift 1958, 283.side note).

136.20 *Antiquity is to be traced backwards*: 107.35–36.

136.21 *Conjuring*: causing something to happen by magic, e.g. by saying the Lord's Prayer backwards.

136.22–23 *pretend to understand a Book, by scouting thro' the Index*: "get a thorough Insight into the *Index*" (64.8).

136.27–28 *not one Vine in all Egypt . . . nothing but Ale*: "For wine they use a drink made of barley [whisky]; for they have no vines in their country" (Herodotus, ii.77; Swift 1958, 284.n2).

136.30–32 *Osyris . . . Bacchus . . . in their famous Expedition, carried the Receipt of it [ale] along with them, and gave it to the Nations they visited*: Swift certainly knew that it was wine, not ale, that Osiris/Dionysus/Bacchus introduced everywhere in this "famous Expedition" into east Africa. But the evocation of Bacchus crowned with vine leaves and lolling in his chariot drawn by a lion and a tiger, attended by Pan, Silenus, goats, satyrs riding on asses, orgiasts of all sexes bearing thyrsi, cymbals, drums, pipes, flutes, and giant wooden phalluses, to advertize the merit of right English ale is a notable mock-epic image (Diodorus Siculus, i.15; iii.62–64; Swift 1958, 284.n3).

136.33–37 *Bacchus . . . was the first Inventor of the Mitre, which he wore continually on his Head . . . to prevent Vapors and the Head-ach after hard Drinking*: "in order to ward off the headaches which every man gets from drinking too much wine he bound about his head" the *mitra*, a wreath of vine leaves (Diodorus Siculus, iv.4; Swift 1958, 284.n4).

136.37–38 *the Scarlet Whore . . . makes the Kings of the Earth drunk with her Cup of Abomination*: "the great whore . . . With whom the kings of the earth . . . have been made drunk with the wine of her fornication . . . was arrayed in . . . scarlet" (Revelation 17.1–4); popularly identified with the Church of Rome (*OED*).

136.39 *always sober herself*: Swift's invention(?); "the great whore" is "drunken with the blood of saints, and . . . martyrs of Jesus" (Revelation 17.6).

136.40 *Triple Mitre*: Plate 14.

137.10 *Fir, the Parent of Turpentine*: crowns of fir are worn by celebrants in the Dionysia; Scotch fir was the source of turpentine in England as *"Knocking Jack of the North"* John Knox (62.26) was the source of Presbyterianism in England.

137.13–15 *curious Figures . . . the Shape and Size of the Virga genitalis, with its Appurtenances*: the penis and testicles.

137.side note *Dionysia Brauronia*: "the nocturnal rites performed every year in honour of Dionysus [at Brauron, Attica] I must not divulge to the world at large" (Pausanias, ii.37).

137.20–22 *Orpheus, one of the Institutors of these Mysteries . . . was torn in Pieces by Women, because he refused to communicate his Orgyes to them*: "Orpheus died at the hands of Thracian . . . Women who tore him to pieces because he would not attend their orgies" (Photius 1824–25, i.140; Swift 1958, 285.n2).

137.20–24 *Orpheus . . . castrated himself upon Grief, for the Loss of his Wife*: Swift's invention (?); Photius says simply "grieving for his wife he came to hate the whole sex" (ibid.).

137.20 *Simon Magus*: a sorcerer from Samaria and one of the earliest converts to Christianity tried to buy the power of the Holy Ghost (Acts 8.9–24). In Christian legend he is a false Messiah, a rival Messiah, the founder of Gnosticism, and a mock-St. Paul. Swift read the account of him in Irenaeus, *Contra Haereses*, I.xxiii, where he identifies himself as God, and Helena, a prostitute (Helen of Troy in a previous incarnation), as Sophia, the first conception of God's mind (Proverbs 8.22–30; Ecclesiasticus 24.1–4).

137.28 *Eutyches*: Eutyches (378–454 A.D.), archimandrite of a monastery near Constantinople, denied that Jesus was two natures (God and man) joined in one person, the monophysite heresy, which is still upheld by churches in Armenia, Egypt, and Ethiopia (*EB*, ix.958). Why Swift includes the ascetic Eutyches in the "System" (137.28) of sexual license remains unexplained.

137.33–34 *one Fundamental Point, wherein they are sure to meet . . . is the Community of Women*: "The . . . Goods of Christians are not common . . . as certain Anabaptists do falsely boast" (*Book of Common Prayer* 1704, sig. Q2r).

137.33 *sure to meet, as Lines in a Center*: 21.31–32.

137.34 *Community of Women*: "Anabaptists . . . [have] many wives . . . being provided for out of the common stock" (Pagitt 1654, 30).

137.39 *John of Leyden*: 76.16; *David George*: Jan Joriszoon/David Joris/David George (c. 1501–1566) of Delft, was a poet and painter on glass. Rebaptized as an Anabaptist in 1533 he identified himself as Christus David, "greater than Christ himself" and enjoyed mystical visions, the gift of prophecy, and (allegedly) "plures uxores." In 1544 he resettled in Basel under the name of Jan van Brugge. He is said (mistakenly) to have taught that "no man . . . is confined to one woman; but that procreation of children shall be promiscuous or in common" (More 1656, 33). Posthumously convicted of heresy by the University of Basel, his body was exhumed and burnt (along with his portrait and published works of which there were more than 200), thereby fulfilling one of his prophecies (*EB*, xv.512).

137.39 *Neuster*: Adam Neuser/Neuster (?–1576), born into a Lutheran family in Gunzenhausen, Ansbach, was dismissed from Calvinist St. Peters in Heidelberg (c. 1570) for preaching Arianism. He traveled first to London and finally to Constantinople. There he was converted to Islam, which commends polygamy: "Marry women of your choice, Two or three, or four" (*The Holy Qu-ran*, iv.3; Crider 1978, 503n.).

138.8 *the Family of Love*: an Anabaptist sect "of the Melchiorite-Mennonite strain, [close] to Schwenckfeldian Spiritualism" (Williams 1962, 479–80), founded by David Joris (137.39), who was succeeded by Henrick Niclaes (c. 1502–80). They preached the deification of man and denied the existence of sin (Blunt 1874, 158–60); cf. "Article XV . . . if we say we have no sin . . . the truth is not in us" (*Book of Common Prayer* 1704, sig. P12r).

138.8 *Sweet Singers of Israel*: Abiezer Coppe (1619–1672), an apostate Sweet Singer, records the creed of "that religion I have passed through": "there is no sin . . . Man is very God . . . Adultery and Fornication is no sin . . . Community of wives is lawful" (Coppe 1651, sig. A2r).

138.11–12 *the Seed . . . is of a Corporeal Nature*: "an absent *Female*" (73.18).

138.18 *the Thorn in the Flesh*: "there was given to me a thorn in the flesh, the messenger of Satan to buffet me lest I should be exalted above measure" (2 Corinthians 12.7); "Is not this to ridicule St. *Paul's* own Description of his own Temptation" (Wotton 1705[2], 65).

138.18 *tentiginous*: provocative of lust (*OED*).

138.18–20 *a tentiginous Humour, repelled and elated to the upper Region, found by daily Practice, to run frequently up into Madness*: "the *Moderns* mean by *Madness*, only a Disturbance or Transposition of the Brain, by Force of certain *Vapours* issuing up from the lower Faculties" (76.29–31).

138.20 *the Faculty*: the members of the Royal College of Physicians.

138.22 *Furor Uterinus*; nymphomania, morbid sexual desire in women (*OED*); this is the reading of 1704[2]; 1704[1] and 1755[H] read *furor* ————.

138.24 *the same Spark*: "the *Spirit* being the same in all" (134.2).

138.36 *the Spirit to relax and flag*: "the *Spirit* would soon faint and grow languid" (130.19–20); the "careful Reader" (37.18) will note a double metaphor: a Modern seduction is a fanatic sermon and *vice versa*.

138.40 *Men*: a 16th–17th century spelling of *mien*, "The air, bearing, carriage or manner of a person, and expressive of character or mood" (*OED*, s.v. **Mien**).

139.1–2 *the Sex hath certain Characteristics, by which they form a truer Judgment of Human Abilities and Performings*: "The Proportion of Largeness [of ears], was not only lookt upon as an Ornament of the *Outward* Man, but as a Type of Grace in the *Inward*" (93.6–7).

139.11–13 *the Story of that Philosopher, who, while his Thoughts and Eyes were fixed upon the Constellations, found himself seduced by his Lower Parts into a Ditch*: "To look at the stars and fall into a ditch" is proverbial (Tilley 1950, 630); "Thales . . . fell into a well as he was looking up at the stars" (Plato, 1875, iv.324); "a whore is a deep ditch" (Proverbs, 23.27).

140.13 *two or three Treatises written expresly against it*: William King, *Remarks on the Tale of a Tub* (1704); William Wotton's *Observations upon the Tale of a Tub* was published in two forms: 1) as an appendix to the third edition of his *Reflections upon Ancient and modern Learning* (1705[1]) and 2) as a separate publication (1705[2]). Both editions were announced in February and published in June 1705 (Arber 1903–06, iii.446, 473).

140.14 *many others that have flirted at it*: The *Tale of a Tub, Revers'd* (1705); sigs. A3r, A5r; Daniel Defoe, *The Consolidator: or, Memoirs of Sundry Transactions from the World in the Moon* (1705), 33; Thomas Durfey, *An Essay towards the Theory of the Intelligible World. Intuitively Considered. Designed for Forty-nine Parts. Part III. Consisting of a Preface, a Postscript, and a little Something between. By Gabriel John, Enriched with a Faithful Account of his Ideal Voyage, and Illustrated with Poems by several Hands, as likewise with other strange Things not insufferably Clever, nor furiously to the Purpose. The Archetypally Second Edition . . .* (17—), 148–49, 195; Charles Gildon, *The Golden Spy* (1709), sig. A3r–A8r.

140.16–17 *the Polite Author of a late Discourse between a Deist and a Socinian*: "Obscenity does pretty well; but, as an Ingenious Author [marginal note: *Tale of a Tub*] has lately observ'd . . . unless the Scene be now and then relieved with Prophaneness, it goes but heavily off" (Gastrell 1726, 36–37; Swift 1958, 3.n3).

140.22 *eight Years before it was published*: "keep your work beside you for nine years" (Horace, *Ars poetica*, 388).

140.22 *The Author was then young*: Swift became 29 in November 1696; he may be mocking the Hon. Charles Boyle: "I was very Young when I appear'd on that occasion" [publication of the epistles of Phalaris in 1695] (Boyle 1698, sig. A3v); Boyle became 19 in August 1695.

140.26 *to what dangerous Heights some Men have proceeded*: "Some Men, under the Notions of weeding out Prejudices; eradicate Religion, Virtue, and common Honesty" (Swift 1939–68, i.243); the reference may be to Descartes: "(if I had a designe to establish any thing that should prove *firme* and *permanent* in sciences) . . . I should clearly cast aside all my former opinions" (Descartes 1680, 1).

140.29–30 *the World having been already too long nauseated with endless Repetitions upon every Subject*: "the World is surfeited with the same Things over and over" (Temple 1701, 260).

141.2 *a young Gentleman much in the World*: as Swift remembers it, but in fact he was a non-resident prebendary of Kilroot living "much out of Company" at Moor Park, near Farnham in Surrey (Swift 1937, 15).

141.5–6 *he could have easily corrected . . . had he been Master of his Papers for a Year or two before their Publication*: a common complaint: "*I have not been yet two years about it, nor ever saw all or halfe my Papers together*" (Harrington 1656, sig. air).

141.21 *Celebrates the Church of England*: "patently absurd" (Traugott 1983, 100), but see xiii.22–27 above.

141.23 *lay upon their Hands*: as a thing to be dealt with or attended to (*OED*, s.v. **Hand**, 32g).

141.25 *Nondum tibi defuit Hostis*: "You have never lacked enemies" (Lucan, *De bello civili*, i.23; Swift 1958, 5.n1).

142.2 *the weightiest Men in the weightiest Stations*: John Sharpe, Archbishop of York (1645–1714) "by showing [*A Tale of a Tub*] to the Queen, debarred [Swift] from a bishoprick" (Johnson 1905, iii.10.15–16).

142.9 *another Book*: Anthony Ashley Cooper, 3d Earl of Shaftesbury, *A Letter concerning Enthusiasm to my Lord [Somers]*(1708); "All my Friends will have me to be the Author . . . But mine it is not" (Swift 1963–65, i.100).

142.14–16 *Had the Author writ a Book to expose the Abuses in Law, or in Physick, he believes the Learned Professors in either Faculty, would have been so far from resenting it, as to have given him Thanks for his Pains*: "*a Man may not only make new Discoveries and Improvements in Law or Physick . . . but also for so doing be deservedly encourag'd and rewarded*" (Toland 1696, v; Mueller 1993, 103).

142.17 *Religion . . . ought not to be ridiculed*: "there be certaine Things, which ought to be priviledged . . .: Namely Religion" (Bacon 1625, 195).

142.19–20 *Religion being the best of Things, its Corruptions are likely to be the worst*: proverbial (Tilley 1950, 120).

142.24 *the 26ᵗʰ Page*: 26 n†.

142.26 *Faction, and Apostacies*: "Faction" refers to Sir Roger L'Estrange, the indefatigable Tory propagandist (83.16); apostasy to John Dryden, who was raised a Puritan, converted to the Church of England (c. 1660) and finally to Roman

Catholicism (1685), in the company of Nell Gwyn, at "no greate losse to the Church" (Evelyn 1955, iv.497).

142.27–29 *Dryden . . . thanks God that he possesses his Soul in Patience*: "Then said [Jesus] unto them . . . In your patience possess ye your souls" (Luke 21.10–19); "I have seldom answered any scurrilous lampoon . . . [but] suffer'd in silence and possess'd my Soul in quiet" (Dryden 1956– , iv.59–60).

142.29–30 *'Estrange . . . uses the like Style*: "I have been *Baited* with *Thousands* upon *Thousands* of *Libells.* I have Created *Enemies* . . . [but] Their *Scandals* are *Blown-over.* Their *Malice, Defeated,* And whenever *my Hour comes,* I am ready to Deliver up my *Soul,* with the *Conscience* of an *Honest Man*" (L'Estrange 1684–87, i.sig.3r).

143.2 *a Fourth*: presumably the throne.

143.7 *Four being much more Cabalistick*: "the number 4 is the Fountain and Head of the whole Divinity, and the *Pythagorians* call it the perpetual Fountain[,] nature" (Heydon 1660, 31).

143.19 *Dr. Eachard . . . his Book*: six "Answerers . . . started up" to John Eachard's *The Grounds and Occasions of the Contempt of the Clergy and Religion Enquired into* (Eachard 1671; Swift 1958, 9.n1).

143.23 *Marvel's Answer to Parker*: Samuel Parker's *A Discourse of Ecclesiastical Politie: wherein The Authoritie of the Civil Magistrate over the Conscience of Subjects in Matters of Religion is Asserted; The Mischiefs and Inconveniences of Toleration are Represented, and all Pretences pleaded in behalf of Liberty of Conscience are fully Answered* (1670) was answered by Andrew Marvell's *The Rehearsal Transpros'd* (1672). Parker responded with *A Reproof to the Rehearsal Transpros'd* (1673), but did not reply to Marvell's counterattack, *The Rehearsal: The Second Part* (1673) for "the odds and victory lay on Marvell's side" (Wood 1818–20, iv.231).

143.24 *the Earl of Orrery's Remarks*: Charles Boyle succeeded as 4th Earl of Orrery in 1703; his edition of the epistles of Phalaris (1695) was attacked by Richard Bentley in *A Dissertation upon the Epistles of Phalaris* (1697); Boyle responded with *Dr. Bentley's Dissertation on the Epistles of Phalaris . . . Examin'd* (1698), but he did not respond to Bentley's *A Dissertation upon the Epistles of Phalaris. With an Answer to the Objections of the Honourable Charles Boyle, Esquire* (1699).

143.36 *One*: Dr. William King's *Some Remarks on the Tale of a Tub* (1704) was written hurriedly to deny authorship of the anonymous work and to distance himself as far as possible from "a Tincture of such Filthiness, as renders it unfit for the worst of Uses" (King 1704, 10), which is the worst of stale jokes.

144.5 *The other*: William Wotton's *Observations upon the Tale of a Tub* (1705[1]).

144.13–14 *a certain great Man*: Wotton's work (Wotton 1705[2]) was an *Answer to the Objections of Sir W. Temple,* Swift's first employer. Temple was a retired diplomat and belletrist whose "gran rifiuto" was a four-fold refusal of the secretaryship of state (*DNB,* xix.526–28).

144.20–21 *Porsenna's Case*: Porsenna, an Etruscan king, retreated from Rome after being told by C. Mucius Scaevola that "Three hundred of us have sworn" to assassinate him (Florus, *Epitoma,* I.4.10).

144.31 *Interpretations which never once entered into the Writers' Head*: "Homer. I always suspected . . . People wou'd spy out Mysteries in my Works, that I never apprehended my self" (Fontenelle 1708, 20).

145.4–5 *through the whole Book he has not borrowed one single Hint from any Writer in the World*: a conventional boast; Epicurus bragged that "his writings . . . contain not a single citation from other authors" (Diogenes Laertius, *Life of Epicurus,* x.26), but *A Tale of a Tub* is a *pasticcio* of phrases from other writers (xxii; cf. Johnson 1905, iii.66).

145.9 *a Letter of the late Duke of Buckingham*: "Father *Peter . . .* Father *Martin,* and Father *John*" ("To Mr. Clifford, on his Humane-Reason" (Buckingham 1704–05, ii.67; Swift 1958, 13.n2).

145.16 *Banter*: nonsense; raillery (*OED*), a neologism of which Swift failed "to stop the Progress" (Swift 1939–68, ii.176).

145.16–17 *Peter's Banter . . . upon Transubstantiation*: 49.17–22.

145.16 *Alsatia*: a precinct in the parish of Whitefriars (London) which until 1697 was a sanctuary for debtors and criminals (*OED*).

145.17–18 *the . . . Duke's Conference with an Irish Priest*: Buckingham is waited on by a Catholic priest intent to convert him. Buckingham pretends that a cork is a horse, "a fine Gelding"; Father Fitzgerald objects: "I see no Horse . . . 'tis a Cork, and nothing but a Cork" (Buckingham 1704–05, ii.35–36). Peter pretends that a crust of bread is "good, natural Mutton"; Jack objects; "it seems to be nothing but a Crust of Bread" (50.12). The parallel is indeed close but Swift "confesses" that he had seen Buckingham's jeu d'esprit *"about ten Years after his Book was writ"* (145.18–19).

145.25–27 *I have been assured, that the Battle in St. James's Library, is mutatis mutandis, taken out of a French Book, entituled, Combat des livres, if I misremember not*: Wotton 1705², 68.

145.26 *a French Book*: François de Callières, *Histoire Poetique de la Guerre nouvellement declarée entre les Anciens et les Modernes* (Paris: 1688); "Aside from the title the *Histoire Poetique* and *The Battle of the Books* have nothing in common" (Swift 1994, 197).

146.1 *his Friend*: in a pregnant sense; Richard Bentley (119.3).

146.21 *Minellius*: Jean Minell (1625–1683), a Dutch scholar who edited Latin texts for grammar schools; *Farnaby*: Thomas Farnaby (1575?–1647), a leading schoolmaster of his day and a classics scholar of international reputation, was commissioned by Charles I to write a new Latin grammar for the schools (*DNB*, vi.1082); "His Notes . . . have done Youth a great . . . service; being short . . . and principally calculated for the Understanding of the Text" (Bayle 1710, ii.1286).

146.23 *Optat ephippia bos piger*: "the lumbering ox dreams of a saddle" (Horace, *Epistles*, I.xiv.43).

146.27–28 *the Author is dead*: Wotton 1705², 67; Wotton thought that Sir William Temple, who died in 1699, wrote *A Tale of a Tub.*

147.23 *the Idea of an Oath*: "this refined Way of Speaking was introduced by Mr. Locke . . . instead of desiring a Philosopher to describe or define a Mouse-trap . . . I must gravely ask, what is contained in the Idea of a Mouse-trap? (Swift 1939–68, ii.80).

147.30 *the 65ᵗʰ Page*: 65.4–6.

147.31 *Raillery*: "Raillery is the finest Part of Conversation . . . some Turn of Wit" (Swift 1939–68, iv. 91).

148.7–8 *a Cow that prickt up her Tail*: Virgil observes that rain never comes unannounced: "the heifer looks up to heaven, and with open nostrils snuffs the breeze" (*Georgics*, i.373–76). Wotton turns Virgil's observation into a labored witticism at Virgil's expense: the "English Farmer's . . . *Red Cow that prick'd up her Tail,* an Infallible Presage of a coming Shower" (Wotton 1694, 101).

148.8–9 *all a Farce and a Ladle*: "our *Tale-teller* strikes at the very Root ['of the Doctrines of the Church of *England*']. *'Tis all* with him *a Farce, and all a Ladle,* as a very facetious Poet says upon another occasion" (Wotton 1705², 57). The "facetious Poet" is Matthew Prior. In "The Ladle" (1704) Prior tacks a Sancho Pançan crudity onto the end of Ovid's sentimental Baucis and Philemon story (*Metamorphoses*, viii.629–724).

When Philemon gives to his wife one of the three wishes that Fortune had bestowed upon him, Baucis wishes for a common wooden ladle. Philemon wishes it was in her arse:

> A Ladle! cries the Man, a Ladle! . . .
> What should be Great, You turn to Farce:
> I wish the Ladle in your A—.

The last wish has to be used to "get the Ladle out again" (Prior 1959, i.206, ii.889).

148.9–10 *Impedimenta Literarum*: literary padding, filler.

148.13–14 *a young Writer*: 140.19.

148.14 *He wrote only to . . . Men of Wit and Tast*: a common claim, "'tis enough for me/If Sedley, Shadwell, Sheppard, Wycherley,/Godolphin, Butler, Buckhurst, Buckingham,/. . . Approve my sense" (Rochester 1994, 101).

148.19–20 *the Bookseller has prevailed on several Gentlemen, to write some Explanatory Notes*: the title-page of the 1710 edition of *A Tale of a Tub* advertizes "Explanatory Notes by W. W–tt–n, B.D. and others" (Swift 1958, 1). There are 199 of these of which 29 are extracted from the 3d edition of Wotton's *Reflections upon Ancient and Modern Learning . . . With Observations upon the Tale of a Tub* (1705[1]), thereby promoting Wotton, the critic of *A Tale of a Tub*, into "*the learned Commentator*" (44 n[†]) on *A Tale of a Tub*.

148.24–27 *a Prostitute Bookseller . . . hath presumed to assign certain Names*: the abominable Edmund Curll, in *A Complete Key to the Tale of a Tub* (1710), assigned *A Tale of a Tub* proper, "the General History of Christianity," and "*A Mechanical Account of the Operation of the Spirit*" to Swift's "little Parson-cousin," Thomas Swift B.D., who did not, however, "step forth" to "prove his Claim to three Lines in the whole Book" (148.33–36).

INDEX